SIR GAWAIN AND THE GREEN KNIGHT

PEARL

CLEANNESS

PATIENCE

Edited by
J. J. ANDERSON
University of Manchester

Based on the former Everyman edition by
A. C. CAWLEY and J. J. ANDERSON

EVERYMAN
J. M. DENT · LONDON
CHARLES E. TUTTLE
VERMONT

Introduction, notes and critical apparatus
© J. M. Dent 1996

Sir Gawain and the Green Knight, Pearl, Cleanness, Patience
first published in Everyman's Library in 1976

This edition first published in 1996
All rights reserved

J. M. Dent
Orion Publishing Group
Orion House, 5 Upper St Martin's Lane,
London WC2H 9EA
and
Charles E. Tuttle Co., Inc.
28 South Main Street,
Rutland, Vermont 05701, USA

Typeset in Sabon by CentraCet Ltd, Cambridge
Printed in Great Britain by
The Guernsey Press Co. Ltd, Guernsey, C. I.

British Library Cataloguing-in-Publication Data
is available upon request

ISBN 0 460 87510 8   821.1 AND

CONTENTS

NOTE ON THE EDITOR

J. J. ANDERSON is Senior Lecturer in English Language in the University of Manchester. He is a graduate of the University of Otago and has taught in the University of Adelaide and the University of Sydney. His interests and publications are chiefly in the fields of medieval literature and early English drama. His scholarly editions of *Patience* and *Cleanness* were published by Manchester University Press in 1969 and 1977, respectively. He is involved in the Records of Early English Drama project in various capacities, and his edition of the records of Newcastle upon Tyne was published in the Records of Early English drama series in 1982. He has published scholarly articles on a range of subjects, including Chaucer, *Piers Plowman* and Shakespeare.

PREFACE

This edition is based on the former Everyman edition of *Sir Gawain and the Green Knight, Pearl, Cleanness and Patience* by the late A. C. Cawley and myself. With the aim of helping readers coming to the poems for the first time and perhaps not very familiar with Middle English it offers the Middle English texts with some modernisation of spelling and full on-the-page glossing of difficult words and sentences, together with notes (in a separate section) which explain allusions and discuss points of interest.

In the former Everyman edition Professor Cawley was responsible for the texts of and introductions to *Gawain* and *Pearl*, and I was responsible for *Cleanness* and *Patience*, which he had invited me to add to his original edition of *Gawain* and *Pearl* only. Ours was a friendly collaboration, and some years ago Professor Cawley asked me to consider writing new introductions to *Gawain* and *Pearl*. When I eventually came to investigate what might be done it seemed to me and to the publishers that a more thoroughgoing revision of the *Gawain* and *Pearl* sections of the edition was desirable, to take account of the great amount of new work on these two poems (particularly *Gawain*) which has been done in the thirty-five years or so since Professor Cawley edited them. Accordingly I have not only written new introductions for *Gawain* and *Pearl* but have entirely re-edited the texts and re-done the translations, consulting other editions and the Early English Text Society facsimile of the manuscript, and have rewritten the notes on language and metre. I have also supplied an explanatory notes section covering all four poems, and a list of manuscript emendations. Apart from the new notes I have left *Cleanness* and *Patience* as they were in the former edition, except for some minor changes to the translations.

In my editing of *Gawain* and *Pearl* I have made particular use of the editions of Andrew and Waldron, Barron, Gordon, Tolkien-Gordon-Davis, and Vantuono. Some of the explanatory notes to *Cleanness* and *Patience* are based on notes in my Manchester University Press editions of these poems. I have made constant use of the great fund of information about Middle English words provided by the Middle English Dictionary.

I am delighted to acknowledge the help of my wife Joy, who has supported me at every stage of the editing; her careful reading of my manuscript has resulted in many improvements. My colleague Gale Owen-Crocker helped me with the texts of *Cleanness* and *Patience* many years ago, and my former PhD student Susan Rastetter has enriched my understanding of *Pearl* through her study of the liturgical background to the poem. Mrs Winifred Cawley has generously given her consent to my undertaking the new edition. I owe a special debt to Arthur Cawley himself, mentor and friend; time passes, but the experience of preparing this new edition has only served to deepen the respect I have always had for his work.

JJA

INTRODUCTION

The four poems *Pearl, Cleanness, Patience* and *Sir Gawain and the Green Knight* are found in that order in a single manuscript (British Library MS Cotton Nero A.x., Art. 3) belonging to the end of the fourteenth century or the beginning of the fifteenth, and they are thought to have been written during the latter half of the fourteenth century. The manuscript itself is unremarkable except for the fact that there are coloured illustrations to the poems, rather crudely drawn and often careless of detail, which appear to have been done to fill up blank pages and spaces before and after the texts.

In their own day, despite their excellence, the poems never achieved the popularity and wide publication of *The Canterbury Tales* and *Piers Plowman*. Subsequently they sank into obscurity and remained to all intents and purposes unknown until the nineteenth century. Like *Piers Plowman* they belong to a native tradition of alliterative writing which goes back to Old English, and are part of the final flowering of that tradition. As sophisticated poems reflecting the aristocratic culture of the day, they are comparable with the work of Chaucer. They are, however, un-Chaucerian in their subject-matter and in their religious and moral emphasis, which links them rather to other alliterative poems. Though there is no external evidence, most readers think that they are by the one author (whose name is not known), as there are several similarities of subject matter, theme, and style between them, and the same powerful imagination seems to be at work in all four. The language which they have in common is rich, brilliant and distinctive, a fusion of a north-western dialect of Middle English with an alliterative vocabulary much of which is traditional and archaic.

Pearl

Pearl is one of the world's great poems on the theme of human pain and Christian hope. It is essentially a dream dialogue between father and daughter. At the beginning the Dreamer is distressed by his loss of a precious pearl in a garden; the reader gathers as the poem proceeds that the pearl is his daughter who died in infancy and who is buried there. He falls asleep and dreams, and in his dream a beautiful woman, whom he recognises but does not identify, appears to him on the far side of a stream in an otherworldly landscape. They talk: he wants to be with her, and she says this cannot be. Driven by a complex mixture of emotions, including love, envy, and above all the desire to be with her, he questions her persistently. She answers his every argument with the cool authority of Christian doctrine, urging him not to want to possess her but to understand her new status: she is in Heaven, and is part of a different order which transcends earthly values and relationships. At last she allows him to see the Heavenly City, with herself as one of the virgins who follow Christ the Lamb in procession through the City. The sight of 'my lyttel quene' moves the Dreamer more than all the glory of Heaven; futilely he attempts to cross the stream to join her, and in doing so loses her again, for the effort wakes him. He is left reflecting on his dream experience and on his loss. He is in a better state than before his dream, for his initial anguish has gone, and he accepts what has happened and the comfort offered by his faith. But the comfort does not come easily; his acceptance is born largely of resignation, and his positive statements have a tinge of uncertainty and sadness about them.

The Dreamer's behaviour in his dream demonstrates the intractability of basic human attitudes. Despite giving the appearance of responding to the Maiden's teaching, his dream-self remains the same from beginning to end, unable to give up earthly notions of possession, justice, and hierarchy: he cannot understand how one who died so young might merit the reward of being made a queen in Heaven. He remains incorrigibly literal-minded, worrying (perhaps with a sarcastic edge to his tone of voice) that the Maiden has no roof over her head; you tell me of Jerusalem, he says, but Jerusalem is not here where you are but in Judea. When he sees the wounded Christ at the end of the vision, his response is one of shocked wonder: 'Alas, thoght I, who did that spyt?' Naive and impulsive, he is forever at the mercy of his emotions, whatever assurances he may give the Maiden that he has learned wisdom from her. The poem does not hold him up to ridicule; on the contrary, he is a most sympathetic figure. It is the Maiden whom the reader, like the Dreamer, finds it hard to come to terms with as she tries to help him to an understanding of the heavenly perspective. She states great doctrines memorably and movingly, but although there are daughterly moments she does not respond to the Dreamer as he wants her to, remaining intractably apart, like the Heaven she speaks for. The poem drives home the point that the Christian view of things is at bottom alien to and contradictory of common human experience. The poem is the record of an attempt to bridge the gap between human and divine (an attempt no doubt inspired by the poet's loss of a beloved daughter), and a statement of the impossibility of doing so in any convincing way.

The poem works allusively and indirectly. In the first stanza the poet makes no mention of a daughter but says that he has lost a precious pearl. The identification of pearl with female loved one emerges gradually, through hints and suggestions, and it is not until the last stanza that the father–daughter relationship is confirmed, still indirectly. The pearl is the loved one in both earthly and heavenly manifestations, and more generally a symbol in which earthly and heavenly values converge, both a precious possession and an image of permanence and perfection. The multiple meanings of the pearl symbol define the boundaries of the Dreamer's experience. It is an experience which, as he constantly indicates, he grasps only imperfectly. With its shadowy images of regeneration in the first section and the dazzling confirmation of these in the dream, the poem enacts the famous verse of St Paul: 'For now we see through a glass, darkly; but then face to face.' But though he sees Heaven face to face the Dreamer is unable to apprehend it. The Dreamer's report of his dream is full of expressions which convey the inexpressibility of what he sees. The allusive and indirect method itself conveys the bafflement of the ordinary Christian trying to make the promises of Christian doctrine work for him.

The poem achieves a considerable intensity by its conjunction of the simple and the sublime. Human speech is pitched against the organ tones of great passages from the Bible and echoes of the liturgy. In stylistic terms this conjunction is expressed by the use of simple words in unusual ways, and in particular by giving the words a metrical setting of great complexity, so that the poem itself, in its ornateness and its flowing, circular movement, suggests a gorgeous pearl. Its length is significant; it is long enough to build up intensity by its slow, steady advance, but not so long that the intensity becomes difficult to sustain. Steeped in the Christian Middle Ages as it is, *Pearl* is a poem which, in its moving but unsentimental consideration of love, grief and the longing for a transcendental resolution, speaks directly to audiences beyond its times.

Cleanness

At the end of the poem, the narrator refers to the 'three ways' in which he has dealt with his theme, and these 'three ways' must refer to the three main stories which the poem contains, those of the Flood, Sodom and Gomorrah, and Belshazzar's Feast.[1] But the poem begins with a general discussion of the virtue of cleanness, with reference to the sixth beatitude: 'Blessed are the pure in heart, for they shall see God' (Matt. 5:8), and to the parable of the wedding feast (Matt. 22:1–14 and Luke 14:16–24), which is given an extended retelling. Then come brief accounts of the Fall of the Angels and the Fall of Man, leading into the first major narrative, that of the Flood. In between the three main stories are two passages of comment, each of which looks backward to the preceding story and forward to the next. It is difficult to pinpoint exactly where one story or section ends and another begins; the poet refuses to allow us to chop the poem up into neat compartments.

The structure is handled fluidly and so is the theme. To summarize what the poet means by cleanness is difficult as the whole poem is a working out of the concept. From the outset, the poet insists on the negative side of his subject. We are told that God rewards cleanness (line 12), but there is rather more emphasis on the fact that He is angry with uncleanness (lines 4–5, 16, 21), and the positive statement of the beatitude, with its promise of the beatific vision, is immediately recast in negative terms:

---

[1] The main biblical sources for these narratives are: the Flood, Gen. vi. 1–ix. 2; Sodom and Gomorrah, Gen. xviii. 1–xix. 29; Belshazzar's Feast, Jer. lii. 1–27, conflated with 2 Chron. xxxvi. 11–20 (for the siege and destruction of Jerusalem), and Dan. iv. 25–v.31 (for the feast).

As so says, to that syght seche schal he never
That any unclannesse has on, auwhere abowte. (29–30)

The main argument of the poem is that cleanness is an essential
virtue because God cannot tolerate uncleanness. Fundamental to
this argument is a distinction between a more general and a more
specific kind of uncleanness. The former kind alienates man from
God, depriving him of the heavenly reward for the pure in heart,
but it is redeemable through penance. Uncleanness in this sense
is part of all sin, or, we may say, it is sin itself in one of its
aspects; hence the long miscellaneous list of sins in lines 177–92.
But the more specific kind of uncleanness is irredeemable,
producing a violent reaction in God so that He is moved to take
drastic vengeance, like a man in the grip of a passion he cannot
control. The poet goes to great lengths to make the distinction
when he contrasts God's 'moderate' punishment of Lucifer and
Adam with the violent destruction of the whole world in the
Flood. God's violence here, as in the destruction of Sodom and
Gomorrah, is occasioned by man's 'filth of the flesh', his
indulgence in perverted sexual practices. In the story of Belshaz-
zar's Feast, the occasions are Zedekiah's idolatry and Belshaz-
zar's profanation of the sacred vessels of the Temple. The poet
seems to be saying that it is the uncleanness of sin which God
finds hardest to tolerate, to the extent that, when a sin is unclean
in an extreme way, He forgets His own nature. Cleanness is part
of God's very being, as the poet insists constantly (e.g. lines
17–22), but, more than this, God's cleanness, as 'cortaysye', is
that aspect of the divine nature which is of most benefit to man,
the channel of God's grace; Christ, the ultimate expression of
God's charity to man, is presented in the poem as the epitome of
cleanness and courtesy. What God cannot abide is the wilful
rejection of His best gifts, the refusal of men to respect Him in
His charity. Thus sodomy is a perversion of God's greatest
physical gift to man, which enables him to experience on earth
something of the bliss of Paradise (line 704). Zedekiah and
Belshazzar indulge in a kind of spiritual sodomy,[1] abusing the

---

[1] Or sodomy may be regarded as physical sacrilege; cf. Margaret Williams,
The Pearl-Poet (New York, 1967), p. 43: 'The defilement of the sacred vessels is
a sacrilege; impurity in a member of Christ is also a sacrilege, in the light of St
Paul's words: "If any man defile the temple of God, him shall God destroy, for
the temple of God is holy, which temple you are." (1 Cor. iii. 17).'

gift of worship whereby God has established channels of spiritual communication with man; so Zedekiah turns his back on the Covenant in which God bestows His grace on the Jewish people, and Belshazzar perverts the instruments of God's worship to the use of Satan (line 1449), in spite of the example of his father before him. We are warned that to accept the gift of the sacrament of penance, and then to turn to sin again, is an act of disrespect which will rouse God to the anger He reserves for extreme uncleanness (lines 1133–44). Such wanton refusal of God's grace is profoundly unnatural; hence the Dead Sea, which 'overturns all of the laws of nature' (line 1024), turning everything to corruption, is an image of the sin of Sodom and Gomorrah. It is set against the ministry of Christ, 'king of nature', whose cleanness makes all corruption whole. It is appropriate that such unnatural sin evokes an 'unnatural' response from God, driving Him out of His divine reasonableness. In hindsight, one can see some of these matters adumbrated in the wedding feast parable. As the poet explains, the feast is an allegory of the kingdom of Heaven, to which, by God's grace, all Christians are invited. In His charity, God accepts people of all kinds at His feast, the worse as well as the better, so long as they are prepared to make the effort to come and to present themselves decently. But twice He is made angry, first by those who make excuses not to come, secondly by the man who comes in foul clothes. In both instances, it is the flouting not only of God, but of God's grace, which gives intolerable offence.

Though the emphasis in the three main stories is on uncleanness and its punishment, there is a positive side to each, embodied chiefly in Noah, Abraham and Nebuchadnezzar. The cleanness of all three is seen to consist in the respect they show to God, manifested for instance in Noah's sacrifice to the Lord after the departure from the Ark, Abraham's hospitality under the oaks of Mamre, and Nebuchadnezzar's respectful treatment of the Temple vessels. And if God reacts to extreme uncleanness with violent hostility, cleanness in man is seen to move him in an opposite way, activating His mercy; so God establishes His covenant with Noah 'In comly comfort ful clos and cortays wordes' (512). God responds both to Abraham's hospitality and to his plea that He should show mercy to Sodom and Gomorrah; the point of the poet's retention of the long biblical dialogue in which Abraham makes his plea is to show the extent of God's response, and, to sharpen the point, the poet greatly develops the biblical hint (Gen. 19:29) that Lot's salvation later is to be ascribed to Abraham's intervention with God on his behalf. Nebuchadnezzar's cleanness carries more weight with God than does his pagan background, and it is on this that his great power is shown to depend.

Although the poem has a main theme and a main line of development, it is by no means entirely linear in either theme or structure. The main theme generates others which are related to it in various ways, for instance, the theme of external beauty and inner uncleanness, and the theme of the fall of pride which is prominent in the last section of the poem. From a structural point of view, the poem's meaning depends to a considerable extent on implied parallels and contrasts between one passage and another, the passages often being widely separated. Thus the fall of Lucifer functions chiefly as an example of sin punished in moderation, in contrast to 'filth of the flesh', and the main relation is a contrastive one with the episode of the Flood. But Lucifer is also an example of the sin of pride, and here there is a parallel, made obvious by parallelisms of language, with Nebuchadnezzar's fall later; this relation is also contrastive, however, in that whereas Nebuchadnezzar repents and regains his former position, Lucifer does not. Again, Lucifer's sin is like Adam's in that it does not attract God's anger, but unlike Adam's in that it is never expiated. Adam sins through disobedience, failure in 'trawthe', and he therefore relates not only to the Flood and to Lucifer but also to Lot's wife, whose sin is likewise 'mistrauthe', though the relation is contrastive in that the 'mistrauthe' of Lot's wife involves contempt for God as well as disobedience, while Adam's does not. One may go on to compare and contrast Lot's wife with Sarah and with the good wife of Belshazzar. One relation leads to another, and the number of possible relations is very large, indeed hardly definable. Such thematic and structural fluidity makes for a rich texture, enabling the poet to impose complex meaning on pre-existing material in an economical fashion.

The complexity of the poem's theme and structure is matched by a wide range of poetic effect. There is the cheerful freshness of Abraham's open-air meal with God, the splendour of the decorations of the Temple vessels, the superlative celebration of the birth of Jesus, tender but with an intellectual content which gives the passage strength. But the poem is dominated by images of violence and horror, such as the panic-stricken flight of men and animals as they try to escape the rising flood-waters, moving to us, but, horrifyingly, not to God; the cataclysmic destruction of Sodom and Gomorrah; the savage treatment of the Jews by Nebuchadnezzar and Nebuzaridan; the ruthlessly efficient killing of Belshazzar. The detail is explicit to the point of disgust – flesh rotting in the mud after the Flood, the stomachs of the women of Jerusalem ripped open so that their bowels burst out over the ditches, Belshazzar's brains a bloody mess on the bedclothes. Poetry and argument together insist on God's abhorrence of the most loathsome of sins.

Patience

Most of *Patience* is taken up with a retelling of the story of Jonah as it is found in the Book of Jonah in the Bible. The poet holds Jonah up to us as an example of impatience, to be contrasted unfavourably with the patience of God – a view of the Jonah story which appears to be very much the poet's own, standing apart from the traditional interpretations. There is a preface to the story in which the poet speaks in his own voice, offering a pragmatic argument in favour of patience; it may be a displeasing virtue, but if one does not have it in times of trouble, one's troubles will only become worse. He refers to the Beatitudes, taking the eighth as embodying the virtue of patience; Matt. 5:10 has 'Blessed are they which are persecuted for righteousness' sake', which the poet interprets as 'Thay ar happen also that con her hert stere' (27). The poet quotes all eight of the Beatitudes, mainly to establish a connection between poverty and patience; poverty is first in the series of Beatitudes, patience last, and they receive the same reward. Moreover, we are told, they are of the same kind, as the only valid response to poverty is patience. Poverty does not feature in the story of Jonah (unless we are to take it that Jonah, deprived of his comforts in the belly of the whale and on the plain outside Nineveh, endures a kind of poverty), and it seems likely, particularly in view of the slightly rueful, whimsical tone of the prologue, that poverty is introduced because it is something the poet knows about in his own life; it is an example of a 'destyné due' requiring patience which is of immediate concern to him. The connection between his 'destyné due' and Jonah's is rather elaborately made in lines 49–60.

Jonah in the poem is a splendid example of one who cannot 'steer his heart', as he is unable to accept either good or bad fortune with equanimity – he reacts impulsively both to God's command that he should go to Nineveh and to God's gift of the woodbine. The whale teaches Jonah the need for obedience to God's will, but the lesson is not properly learned, for when God changes His mind about destroying Nineveh Jonah cannot accept the situation, seeing only that God has made him a liar. God uses the woodbine to demonstrate to Jonah his new error – his selfish insistence on justice – and to show that true patience involves not only acceptance of compelling circumstance, but active charity. The poet convinces us that patience is indeed a highly desirable virtue, and we are made aware of possible serious consequences of impatience. But the story is managed with a light touch and an awareness of its comic possibilities. Jonah is a prophet of God and he is capable of an appropriate dignity, as in his prayer from the whale's belly, but he is also a wilful old man ludicrously pitting himself against the power of God, and being constantly slapped down for his pains. He is so human in his failings, and the cards are so heavily stacked against him, that he wins some sympathy from the reader. We at least see what he means when he accuses God: 'With alle meschef that thou may, never thou me spares' (484). At the same time we recognize that Jonah is in the wrong in putting his own honour before the salvation of a city. Amusement, sympathy and criticism are kept nicely in balance. God too is attractive, dignified but approachable, though we are not allowed to forget the terrible possibilities of His absolute power. In this poem, however, the power is always tempered by patience, so that God teaches by example as well as by correction. God has a real relationship with Nineveh, and still more with Jonah, whom He treats like an erring child. The pervading tone of the poem, established already in the prologue, is one of light irony, appropriate for exposing the absurdity of Jonah's conduct.

It is natural to consider *Cleanness* and *Patience* together. Each poem takes as its subject one of the virtues of the Beatitudes, which is then applied to stories from the Bible. The stories as the poet tells them are based firmly on the biblical text, in its Latin Vulgate version, which the poet must have had before him as he composed. The poet uses a variety of means to adapt his original to his own purposes, the most obvious of these being imaginative elaboration, as with the storm and the whale in *Patience*, the Temple vessels and the flight from the Flood in *Cleanness*. In both poems the major elaborations are showpieces of an outstanding poetic talent. But, in spite of such basic similarities, the two poems read very differently. *Cleanness* has an epic sweep, a formidable complexity, and an uncompromising morality; in the passage on the birth of Christ it rises to sublimity. By comparison *Patience* is small-scale in every sense, not only much shorter but more accessible and personal. We enter into Jonah's thoughts and feelings in a way that we cannot with any of the characters in *Cleanness*, and the message of *Patience* is softened by a play of irony and humour which is absent in the longer poem. Singly and together the poems amount to an impressive achievement, contributing to the status of MS. Cotton Nero A.x as the most important collection of Middle English poems outside the work of Chaucer.

Sir Gawain and the Green Knight

Of the four poems in the manuscript, *Sir Gawain and the Green Knight* is the one which fits most obviously into a well-defined medieval genre – that of Arthurian romance. Stories based on the exploits of the knights of King Arthur's Round Table were the dominant mode of fiction in western Europe in the later Middle Ages. The poem's storyline conforms to the norms of the genre. One of Arthur's knights is singled out as hero and sent on a quest which challenges his knightly qualities through trials of his physical and mental courage and of his courtly skills. The poem inhabits a typical romance landscape between fantasy and medieval reality. The story is a good one with high entertainment value, exciting, intriguing, amusing, and full of insights into human behaviour. It is remarkable compared with other Arthurian romances for the tightness of its construction, in particular the way in which the three major plot-elements – the beheading, the exchange of winnings, and the temptation – are intricately linked together. The motifs of the beheading and the temptation are found separately in several other romances (there are particularly striking parallels between the beheading game in *Sir Gawain* and the French romance *Caradoc*), but the combination of the motifs, whereby the beheading game frames the exchange of winnings and the temptation, is undoubtedly the work of the poet. When Gawain strikes off the Green Knight's head in exchange for a promise that he will stand a return blow in a year's time, it seems that his courage and capacity to keep a promise are being tested. When he stays with Bercilak in his castle and agrees with him that they will exchange their daily winnings, and then subsequently finds himself sexually tempted by Bercilak's wife, he seems to be subject to a new and entirely separate test. But in the second beheading episode, in which Gawain does not lose his head but merely receives a minor cut from the Green Knight's axe, it emerges that the outcome of the beheading game has depended on Gawain's behaviour in the exchange of winnings.

The poem is notable for its evocation of the wider medieval ideal of chivalric life, manifested most strikingly in the descriptions of clothes, armour, castles, feasts, hunting, and other appurtenances of aristocratic chivalric civilisation. It is not only the long set-pieces such as the cutting up of the deer which are memorable, but also many shorter and less prominent descriptions, such as that of the axe the Green Knight carries when he rides into Arthur's court, closely observed down to the green buttons which attach the tassels to the lace looped along the handle.

This civilisation is presented in a somewhat ambiguous way, and there is a constant subterranean suggestion, never articulated, that it may not be as well-founded as it seems. The poem begins by hinting at the darker side of the founding of Britain and the 'blysse and blunder' mixed together which have characterised Britain's later history, and the concluding lines return to the same distancing and ambiguous perspective. The suggestion of a hostile natural world is carried by descriptions of harsh landscapes in the cold of winter which, though briefer, are as memorable as the descriptions of courtly life. The worlds of nature and civilisation are linked by the threatening figure of the Green Knight, whose appearance suggests both a wild man of the woods and a great medieval lord; when he rides into Arthur's court he carries a sprig of winter holly in the one hand and a battle-axe in the other. The hostility of nature is linked to the threat of the passing of time in a long passage on the succession of the seasons, which are described as merging seamlessly into each other from one winter to another in a timeless cycle that casts a long shadow over the ultimate validity of any purely human enterprise.

From the first Gawain takes a more serious view of the virtues of chivalry than his fellow knights. Arthur's court in this poem is in the first flush of its youth, full of high spirits. Gawain too is young, but his youth shows in his idealism more than in high spirits. It seems that he aspires not only to perfect courtesy (for which he was famed in Arthurian tradition) but to perfect 'trawthe', knightly honour in all its aspects, as his elaborate speech when he offers to take up the Green Knight's challenge hints at, and as the poet's lengthy elucidation of the meaning of the pentangle figure on his shield makes clear. But events show that the seriousness with which he takes himself, which means that he must act with perfect chivalry in every situation, brings with it a heavy penalty. In Bercilak's castle the daily attempts of his host's beautiful wife to seduce him make it hard for him not to abandon one or more of his pentangle virtues. No doubt because he is weakened by his long struggle to hold the line with her he eventually makes a mistake when she comes at him from another angle, appealing to his fear for his life by offering him her girdle, which she claims will magically protect him against being killed. With his coming encounter in mind, Gawain takes the girdle and breaks his agreement with Bercilak by failing to hand it over to him as part of his day's winnings. In the reciprocal beheading match the Green Knight explains that the nick in the neck which he inflicts on Gawain is for this minor failing. To Gawain, however, who has given no sign that he is aware of having done anything wrong at all, the Green Knight's revelations are devastating; he has been exposed as imperfect, and for him this means that all his knighthood is in ruins. He is still devastated at the end of the poem, despite being welcomed back by the Arthurian court in a way which indicates that they see his exploit as a triumph rather than a failure.

There is perhaps the implicit suggestion that had Gawain centred himself on his faith instead of on his pentangle he might have been better able to resist the lady's blandishments and to accept his own failures. There may also be an implicit suggestion that Gawain's judges are themselves wanting. Of the two great courts in the poem, Camelot and Hautdesert, the former is subject to the whims of an immature Arthur, the latter controlled by the malicious Morgan la Fee, whose agents, Bercilak and his wife, may seem after the revelations at the end of the poem to be coldly manipulative. The poem however does not take any line or lead readers to any simple value judgments. Rather, like much of Chaucer's work, it draws readers into active response to the story and prompts them to attempt to weigh up the issues for themselves.

NOTE ON LANGUAGE AND METRE

Vocabulary

The language of the four poems is a sophisticated literary language based on a North-West Midlands variety of Middle English, with a number of features which set it apart from the East Midlands language of Chaucer, such as the high proportion of words of Scandinavian origin, and in particular a special poetic vocabulary which has its roots in the poetic vocabulary of Old English and which it shares to a greater or lesser extent with other Middle English alliterative poems. The most important feature of this poetic vocabulary is the large group of synonyms for 'man', such as *burne, freke, gome, hathel, lede, renk, segge, wyy*, which are Middle English forms of Old English poetic words. The poetic vocabulary has several words of Scandinavian origin (e.g. *tulk* is added to the English synonyms for 'man'). In addition, ordinary prose words may be used regularly in poetic senses, usually specialised or generalised, such as the verb *bowe* which usually means not 'bow' but 'go'. In general the *Pearl*-poet is linguistically resourceful, using words across their normal range of meaning and beyond it, and alert to possibilities of multiple meaning, ambiguity, and word-play.

Spellings

Only spellings which may give difficulty to a reader unfamiliar with Middle English are noticed.

Many words occur with or without final *-e*, which is used unsystematically for the most part: *honest, honeste*. Sometimes *-e* is used instead of final *i* or *y* (here printed as *é*): *Maré*, 'Mary'; *cortaysé*, 'courtesy'.

an, on are alternative spellings in words with a short vowel: *man, mon*.

Short *u* may be written as *o, u, ou*: *lofly, luflych, louflych*.

y is used interchangeably with *i* as a vowel symbol: *prince*, *prynce*.

qu varies with *wh* and *w* (*quyle, while, wyle; whene, quene*), and with *c, k* (*quoynt, coynt, koynt*).

w varies with *u* (*trwe, true*), and with *v*: *vyf, wyf*. In *Wawan* (beside *Gawan*) and *Wenore* (beside *Gwenore*), *w* is a northern French and Anglo-Norman sound and spelling.

Grammatical forms

Only forms which may give difficulty to a reader unfamiliar with Middle English are noticed.

In nouns, the genitive singular is frequently uninflected in genitive combinations: *Israel Dryghtyn*, 'God of Israel'; *segge fotes*, 'man's feet'.

Uninflected plurals occur sometimes, e.g. *lyght*, 'light(s)' is invariably uninflected in the plural, and *bonk* occurs beside the more usual *bonkes*.

In adjectives, the demonstrative *that* has plural *tho* 'those'.

In third person personal pronouns, the feminine forms are *ho, scho* 'she', the neuter forms *hit, hyt* 'it'. The possessive case of the neuter is *hit* 'its'. *hit arn* occurs frequently with the sense 'they are, there are'. Plural forms are *her, hor* 'their', *hem, hom* 'them'.

In verbs, the second and third person singular present indicative ending is *-(e)s*; the plural ending is *-e(n)*, less frequently *-es*, *-e*, or no ending. The imperative plural ending is *-(e)s*. The regular present participle ending is *-ande*. The past participle sometimes ends in *-e*. The word *con* (meaning 'did') is often used as an auxiliary together with an infinitive to form the past tense, and, in *Pearl*, the present tense (meaning 'does').

Metre

Cleanness, Patience, and *Gawain*, like other Middle English alliterative poems, are written in alliterative long lines which follow the basic metrical principles of Old English verse, i.e. the long line is divided into two half-lines each containing two stressed syllables and a varying number of unstressed syllables, the two halves of the line being linked by alliteration on at least two, usually three, of the stressed syllables. The long lines do

not rhyme. The usual but by no means invariable alliterative
pattern for the line is aa // ax, as in the following example:

/   /   /   /

The gome upon Gryngolet // glydes hem under (*Gawain* 748)

   a   a   a   x

As in other Middle English alliterative verse, extended first half-
lines with three stressed syllables instead of two are common:

/   /   /   /   /

Highe hilles on uche a halve // and holtwodes under (*Gawain* 742)

a   a   a   x   x

A vowel may alliterate with any other vowel, *h* with itself or a
vowel. A number of consonant groups may be regarded by the
poet as single consonants for purposes of alliteration, notably
sc, sm, sp, st.

In *Cleanness* and *Patience*, marginal marks in the manuscript
indicate that the lines are grouped together in fours. The poet
does seem to shape his thought accordingly, though he does not
allow this grouping to become a straitjacket.

In *Gawain*, stanzas are defined by the 'bob and wheel', a
group of five short rhyming lines (rhyming *ababa*, and often
with alliteration as well) which comes at the end of the stanza
after a varying number of long lines (mostly between fifteen and
twenty-five). The bob line has just one stress and usually two
syllables; the wheel lines have three stresses and a brisk accentual
rhythm. The meaning of the bob line is often reinforcing and
emphatic, while that of the wheel tends both to sum up the
stanza which it concludes and anticipate the next stanza.

Pearl is written in stanzas of twelve lines, rhyming *ababa-
babbcbc*. The lines have four stresses and they make consider-
able though not regular use of alliteration, but their rhythm is
best thought of as accentual, a kind of iambic tetrameter, rather
than as a development of the stress-based rhythm of alliterative
poetry. An even more striking feature of the metre than the
complexity of the stanza form is the intricate system used to link
one stanza to another. The last line of the first stanza is a refrain
line which runs for five stanzas, to be replaced by a new refrain
line for the next five stanzas, and so to the end of the poem; the

refrain line for the last section contains the phrase *prynces paye*, so that the last line of the poem echoes the first, as it does also in *Patience* and (in effect) in *Gawain*. In addition each stanza is linked to the next by the repetition of its last word or a variant of it at the beginning of the next; this device (called concatenation) also links the groups of five stanzas to each other. There is one grouping of six stanzas instead of five, in section XV; the point of this may be numerological, to bring the total number of stanzas to 101, as *Gawain* also has 101 stanzas. The *Pearl*-stanza is found elsewhere in Middle English, but none of the other poems which use it match the metrical elaborateness of *Pearl*.

NOTE ON THE EDITED TEXT

The Middle English text keeps the spellings of words as they are in the manuscript with the exception of the following modernisations: *i* and *j*, and *u* and *v*, are regularly differentiated as vowel and consonant; the archaic letter *þ* ('thorn') is transcribed as *th*, and the archaic letter *ȝ* ('yogh') as *y*, *gh*, or *w*, as appropriate; final *(t)ȝ* is transcribed as *s*. The manuscript is conservatively edited, i.e. the original manuscript readings are retained wherever reasonably possible. However, some emendation of the original is necessary because of scribal error and because the manuscript is illegible in places; such emendations are not noticed in the text, but a list of the more important or problematic of them follows the text.

In *Pearl* a large illuminated initial capital marks the beginning of each new section of the poem, and the twenty sections are confirmed by metrical criteria. In *Cleanness* the text is divided into three sections, and in *Gawain* into four (the sections in *Gawain* are traditionally known as 'fitts') on the basis of the extra large illuminated initials in the manuscript, and the fivefold division of the text of *Patience* is similarly based on the occurrence of five large illuminated initials. In the texts of *Cleanness* and *Patience* the lines are grouped in fours in accordance with the marginal marks found beside every fourth line in the manuscript (the same marks are used to mark off the stanzas in *Pearl* and *Gawain*), though some other editions of these poems print the texts continuously. The titles are editorial.

The on-the-page glossing is intended as an aid to understanding the original text, not as a substitute for it. It is comprehensive, on the principle that too much help is better than too little, given the difficulty of the language of these poems. The renderings are prosaic and literal, respecting as far as possible the Middle English sense, though sometimes that is uncertain, and often no translation could possibly do justice to the density of meaning of the original. Some instances of particular difficulty with the manuscript text or its interpretation are discussed in the Notes.

PEARL

I

Perle, plesaunte to prynces paye
To clanly clos in golde so clere;
Oute of oryent, I hardyly saye,
Ne proved I never her precios pere.
5 So rounde, so reken in uche araye,   *beautiful; every setting*
So smal, so smothe her sydes were,
Quere-so-ever I jugged gemmes   *wherever; judged*
　　gaye,   *bright*
I sette hyr sengeley in synglere.
Allas! I leste hyr in on erbere;   *lost; a garden*
10 Thurgh gresse to grounde hit fro me yot.   *grass; went*
I dewyne, fordolked of luf-daungere
Of that pryvy perle wythouten spot.

Sythen in that spote hit fro me sprange,   *since; place*
Ofte haf I wayted, wyschande that wele
15 That wont was whyle devoyde my wrange,
And heven my happe and al my hele.
That dos bot thrych my hert thrange,
My breste in bale bot bolne and bele.
Yet thoght me never so swete a sange
20 As stylle stounde let to me stele.
For sothe ther fleten to me fele,

1-4 Pearl, pleasing to a prince's taste, (fit) to be finely set in brightest
　　gold; from out of the east, I say with certainty, I never found her
　　precious equal.

8 I set her apart as unique.

11-12 I pine away, grievously wounded by the power of (my) love for
　　that pearl of mine without spot.

14-23 Often have I watched, longing for that precious thing that once
　　was accustomed to drive away my sorrow and increase my happiness
　　and all my well-being. That (watching) does nothing but grievously
　　weigh down my heart, swell and burn my breast in torment. Yet it
　　seemed to me there was never so sweet a song as (the one) a quiet hour
　　let steal to me. Indeed many (songs) came to me there, to think of her

To thenke hir color so clad in clot.
O moul, thou marres a myry juele,
My privy perle wythouten spotte.   *own*

25 That spot of spyses mot nedes sprede,
Ther such ryches to rot is runne.
Blomes blayke and blwe and rede   *yellow*
Ther schynes ful schyr agayn the sunne.   *will shine; brightly*
Flor and fryte may not be fede   *flower; fruit; faded*
30 Ther hit doun drof in moldes dunne;
For uch gresse mot grow of graynes dede –
No whete were elles to wones   *otherwise; barn*
    wonne.   *brought*
Of goud uche goude is ay bygonne;
So semly a sede moght fayly not,
35 That spryngande spyces up ne sponne
Of that precios perle wythouten spotte.   *from*

To that spot that I in speche expoun   *describe*
I entred in that erber grene,   *garden*
In Auguste in a hygh seysoun,   *festival time*
40 Quen corne is corven wyth crokes kene.   *cut; sharp sickles*
On huyle ther perle hit trendeled doun
Schadowed this wortes ful schyr and schene –
Gilofre, gyngure and gromylyoun,   *gillyflower; gromwell*
And pyonys powdered ay bytwene.
45 Yif hit was semly on to sene,   *good to look upon*
A fayr reflayr yet fro hit flot.

---

colour so clad in clay. O earth (of the grave), you spoil a beautiful jewel.
25–6 That place is bound to be covered with spice plants, where such richness is run to decay.
30–1 Where it (i.e. the pearl) fell down into the dark earth; for each plant must grow from dead seeds.
33–5 From what is good every good thing is always begun; so lovely a seed might not fail to produce flourishing spice plants (lit. so that flourishing spice plants did not spring up).
41–2 On the mound where the pearl had rolled down these most bright and beautiful plants cast a shadow.
44 And peonies scattered everywhere amongst (them).

Ther wonys that worthyly, I wot and wene,
My precious perle wythouten spot.

Bifore that spot my honde I spenned   *clasped*
50 For care ful colde that to me caght;   *because of; came*
A devely dele in my hert denned,
Thagh resoun sette myselven saght.
I playned my perle that ther was   *mourned*
   spenned   *imprisoned*
Wyth fyrce skylles that faste faght;
55 Thagh kynde of Kryst me comfort kenned,
My wreched wylle in wo ay wraghte.
I felle upon that floury flaght,   *turf*
Suche odour to my hernes schot;   *brain*
I slode upon a slepyng-slaghte
60 On that precios perle wythouten spot.   *above*

II

Fro spot my spyryt ther sprang in space;
My body on balke ther bod in sweven.
My goste is gon in Godes grace   *spirit; through*
In aventure ther mervayles meven.
65 I ne wyste in this worlde quere that hit wace,   *knew; was*
Bot I knew me keste ther klyfes cleven.
Towarde a foreste I bere the face,   *turned my face*
Where rych rokkes wer to dyscreven.   *splendid; to be seen*
The lyght of hem myght no mon leven,   *believe*
70 The glemande glory that of hem glent;   *gleaming; shone*

46-7 No less sweet a fragrance floated from it. There dwells that precious one, I know and believe.

51-2 A heavy grief lay deep in my heart, though reason reconciled me (to my loss).

54-6 With fierce arguments that fought hard (against each other). Though the nature of Christ offered me comfort, my wretched will laboured on in sorrow.

59 I slid into a deep sleep.

61-2 From that place there my spirit sprang out in space; my body stayed there asleep on the mound.

64 On a quest to where marvellous things take place.

66 But I knew myself transported to where cliffs cleave (the sky).

For wern never webbes that wyyes weven
Of half so dere adubbement.   *glorious splendour*

Dubbed wern alle tho downes sydes   *adorned; hillsides*
Wyth crystal klyffes so cler of kynde.   *clear by (their) nature*
75 Holtewodes bryght aboute hem bydes   *woods; lie*
Of bolles as blwe as ble of Ynde.
As bornyst sylver the lef on slydes,
That thike con trylle on uch a tynde.
Quen glem of glodes agayns hem glydes,
80 Wyth schymeryng schene ful schrylle thay schynde.
The gravayl that on grounde con grynde   *gravel; crunched*
Wern precious perles of oryente;
The sunnebemes bot blo and blynde   *were only dark and dim*
In respecte of that adubbement.

85 The adubbemente of tho downes dere   *glorious hills*
Garten my goste al greffe foryete.
So frech flavores of frytes were,
As fode hit con me fayre refete.
Fowles ther flowen in fryth in fere,
90 Of flaumbande hwes, bothe smale and grete. *flaming colours*
Bot sytole-stryng and gyternere
Her reken myrthe moght not retrete;
For quen those bryddes her wynges bete,
Thay songen wyth a swete asent.   *sang; harmony*
95 So gracios gle couthe no mon gete   *exquisite pleasure; get*
As here and se her adubbement.

---

71 For never were fabrics woven by men.
76–80 With tree-trunks as blue as indigo (lit. as blue as colour of India).
   Like burnished silver the leaves slide over each other, quivering close
   together on every branch. When the light falls on them from clear
   patches of sky, they shone most dazzlingly with shimmering brightness.
86–9 Made my spirit forget all grief. There were such sweet fragrances
   of fruits (that) they refreshed me well, as (though they were) food.
   Birds flew together in the woods there.
91–2 But neither citole-string nor player on the cithern might reproduce
   their beautiful music. (The citole and cithern are guitar-like
   instruments.)

So al was dubbet on dere asyse
That fryth ther fortwne forth me feres.
The derthe therof for to devyse   *glory; describe*
100 Nis no wyy worthé that tonge beres.   *man; worthy*
I welke ay forth in wely wyse;   *walked; joyful*
No bonk so byg that did me deres.   *hindrance*
The fyrre in the fryth, the feier con ryse
The playn, the plonttes, the spyse, the peres,
105 And rawes and randes and rych reveres –
As fyldor fyn her bonkes brent.
I wan to a water by schore that scheres;
Lorde, dere was hit adubbement!   *its*

The dubbemente of tho derworth depe
110 Wern bonkes bene of beryl bryght.
Swangeande swete the water con swepe,
Wyth a rownande rourde raykande aryght.
In the founce ther stonden stones stepe,
As glente thurgh glas that glowed and glyght,
115 As stremande sternes, quen strothe-men slepe,
Staren in welkyn in wynter nyght.   *shine; sky*
For uche a pobbel in pole ther pyght   *pebble; pool; set*
Was emerad, saffer, other gemme gente,   *sapphire; or; noble*
That alle the loghe lemed of lyght,
120 So dere was hit adubbement.

97–8 So all adorned in glorious fashion was that wood where fortune
    leads me forth.
103–7 The further (I went) into the wood the more beautiful grew the
    meadow, the plants, the spices, the pear-trees, and hedgerows and river
    lands and rich river meadows – their steep slopes like pure gold thread.
    I came to a stream flowing along by the shore.
109–15 The splendour of those beautiful deeps were lovely banks of
    bright beryl. Swirling sweetly the water swept along, flowing straight
    on with a murmuring sound. Bright stones were set in the bottom there,
    that glowed and gleamed like a beam of light through glass, as
    streaming stars, when men of this world are asleep.
119 So that all the pool gleamed with light.

III

The dubbement dere of doun and dales,   *hill*
Of wod and water and wlonk playnes,   *lovely meadows*
Bylde in me blys, abated my bales,   *increased; torments*
Fordidden my stresse, dystryed my paynes.
125 Doun after a strem that dryyly hales
I bowed in blys, bredful my braynes.
The fyrre I folwed those floty vales,
The more strenghthe of joye myn herte straynes.
As fortune fares, ther as ho fraynes,
130 Whether solace ho sende other elles sore;
The wyy to wham her wylle ho waynes
Hyttes to have ay more and more.

More of wele was in that wyse   *joy; of that kind*
Then I cowthe telle thagh I tom hade,   *could; leisure*
135 For urthely herte myght not suffyse   *earthly*
To the tenthe dole of tho gladnes glade.   *part; pleasures*
Forthy I thoght that Paradyse   *and so*
Was ther over gayn tho bonkes brade.   *against; broad*
I hoped the water were a devyse
140 Bytwene myrthes by meres made.
Byyonde the broke, by slente other slade,   *by slope or valley*
I hoped that mote merked wore.
Bot the water was depe, I dorst not wade,
And ever me longed ay more and more.   *I longed*

145 More and more, and yet wel mare,   *still more*
Me lyste to se the broke byyonde;

124–32 Took away my distress, destroyed my sorrows. Down along a
ceaselessly flowing stream I went in bliss, my mind brimful. The further
I followed those well-watered valleys the stronger the joy that fills my
heart. (Just) so Fortune behaves, wherever she puts (men) to the test,
whether she sends pleasure or pain; the man on whom she bestows her
favour comes to have ever more and more.

139–40 I thought the water was a division made between delights (i.e.
between Paradise and where the Dreamer was standing) along their
boundaries.

142 I thought that walled city (of Paradise) would be situated.

146 I wished to see beyond the brook.

For if hit was fayr ther I con fare,   *where I went*
Wel loveloker was the fyrre londe.   *lovelier; farther*
Abowte me con I stote and stare,   *I stopped and stared*
150 To fynde a forthe faste con I fonde;   *ford; eagerly; tried*
Bot wothes mo iwysse ther ware,   *perils; more; indeed*
The fyrre I stalked by the stronde.
And ever me thoght I schulde not wonde   *hesitate*
For wo ther weles so wynne wore.
155 Thenne nwe note me com on honde
That meved my mynde ay more and more.

More mervayle con my dom adaunt.
I sey byyonde that myry mere   *saw; pleasant water*
A crystal clyffe ful relusaunt;   *all gleaming*
160 Mony ryal ray con fro hit rere.
At the fote therof ther sete a faunt,   *sat; child*
A mayden of menske, ful debonere;   *noble maiden; gracious*
Blysnande whyt was hyr bleaunt;   *shining; robe*
I knew hyr wel, I hade sen hyr ere.   *seen; before*
165 As glysnande golde that man con schere,
So schon that schene anunder schore.
On lenghe I loked to hyr there;   *for a long time; at her*
The lenger, I knew hyr more and more.

The more I frayste hyr fayre face,
170 Her fygure fyn quen I had fonte,
Suche gladande glory con to me glace
As lyttel byfore therto was wonte.
To calle hyr lyste con me enchace,
Bot baysment gef myn hert a brunt;

---

152 The further I walked (cautiously) along the bank.
154–5 For (fear of) harm, (in a place) where there were such pleasing
    delights. Then a new matter came to my notice.
157 A greater marvel overtook my reason.
160 Many glorious rays (of light) shone from it.
165–6 Like gleaming cut gold, so shone that beautiful maiden under the
    cliff.
169–74 The more I looked closely at her beautiful face, after I had (first)
    noticed her noble form, such heart-warming bliss came to me as had
    been little accustomed to do before where she was concerned. Delight
    urged me to call her, but the shock of surprise gave my heart a blow.

175 I sey hyr in so strange a place,   *saw*
    Such a burre myght make myn herte blunt.
    Thenne veres ho up her fayre frount,   *raises; forehead*
    Hyr vysayge whyt as playn yvore;   *face; polished ivory*
    That stonge myn hert, ful stray atount,
180 And ever the lenger, the more and more.

IV

    More then me lyste my drede aros;   *than I wanted; fear*
    I stod ful stylle and dorste not calle;   *dared*
    Wyth yyen open and mouth ful clos   *eyes*
    I stod as hende as hawk in halle.   *still*
185 I hoped that gostly was that porpose;
    I dred on ende quat schulde byfalle,
    Lest ho me eschaped that I ther chos,
    Er I at steven hir moght stalle.
    That gracios gay wythouten galle,   *lovely one; blemish*
190 So smothe, so smal, so seme slyght,   *beautifully dainty*
    Ryses up in hir araye ryalle,   *royal*
    A precios pyece in perles pyght.   *thing; set*

    Perles pyghte of ryal prys,
    There moght mon by grace haf sene,
195 Quen that frech as flor-de-lys
    Doun the bonke con bowe bydene.   *came directly*
    Al blysnande whyt was hir beau bys,
    Upon at sydes and bounden bene
    Wyth the myryeste margarys, at my devyse,

---

176 Such a blow might (well) make my heart stop.

179 That (action) stung my heart, (which was) utterly lost in bewilderment.

185-8 I thought the matter was of supernatural import; I feared what might happen in the end, lest she whom I saw there escaped from me before I might keep her back to meet me (lit. at a meeting).

193-5 There by (God's) grace a man might have seen pearls of royal excellence set (in her clothes), when that one who was as fresh as fleur-de-lis.

197-9 Her fine linen gown was all shining white, open at the sides and trimmed beautifully with the loveliest pearls, in my opinion.

200 That ever I sey yet with myn yyen;   *saw; eyes*
    Wyth lappes large, I wot and I wene,
    Dubbed with double perle and dyghte,
    Her cortel of self sute schene
    Wyth precios perles al umbepyghte.

205 A pyght coroune yet wer that gyrle
    Of mariorys and non other ston,
    Highe pynakled of cler quyt perle,
    Wyth flurted flowres perfet upon;
    To hed hade ho non other werle.

210 Her lere-leke al hyr umbegon,
    Her semblaunt sade for doc other erle,
    Her ble more blaght then whalles bon.
    As schorne golde schyr her fax thenne schon,
    On schylderes that leghe unlapped lyghte.

215 Her depe colour yet wonted non
    Of precios perle in porfyl pyghte.

    Pyght was poyned and uche a hemme   *wristband; every*
    At honde, at sydes, at overture,   *opening (of neck)*
    Wyth whyte perle and non other gemme,

220 And bornyste quyte was hyr vesture.   *shining; dress*
    Bot a wonder perle wythouten wemme   *wondrous; flaw*
    Inmyddes hyr breste was sette so sure;   *in the middle of*
    A mannes dom moght dryyly demme
    Er mynde moght malte in hit mesure.

225 I hope no tong moght endure

201–16 With broad hanging sleeves, I know full well, adorned and
embellished with double rows of pearls, her matching kirtle bright with
precious pearls set all round (it). That girl also wore a decorated crown
of pearls and no other stone, with high pinnacles of clear white pearl,
with perfect figured flowers on it; she had no other attire on her head.
Her wimple went all round her (face), her expression (was) grave
enough for a duke or earl, her complexion whiter than whale's bone.
Her hair, that lay lightly unbound on her shoulders, shone then like
bright cut gold. Her deep colour (of white) lacked nothing even by
comparison with the precious pearls set in the embroidered border (of
her wimple).

223–8 A man's reason might be utterly eclipsed before his mind could
take its measure. I believe no tongue might suffice to utter any

No saverly saghe say of that syght,
So was hit clene and cler and pure,
That precios perle ther hit was pyght.

Pyght in perle, that precios pyse   *thing*
230 On wyther half water com doun the   *the opposite side of*
    schore.
No gladder gome hethen into Grece   *man from here to*
Then I, quen ho on brymme wore.   *brink; was*
Ho was me nerre then aunte or nece;   *nearer to me than*
My joy forthy was much the more.   *therefore*
235 Ho profered me speche, that special spyce, *precious creature*
Enclynande lowe in wommon lore,   *bowing; fashion*
Caghte of her coroun of grete tresore   *took off*
And haylsed me wyth a lote lyghte.
Wel was me that ever I was bore   *born*
240 To sware that swete in perles pyghte!   *answer; sweet one*

V

'O perle,' quoth I, 'in perles pyght,
Art thou my perle that I haf playned,   *mourned*
Regretted by myn one on nyghte?   *grieved for on my own*
Much longeyng haf I for the layned,   *you; endured*
245 Sythen into gresse thou me aglyghte.   *since; slipped from*
Pensyf, payred, I am forpayned,   *worn out; in great pain*
And thou in a lyf of lykyng lyghte,   *easy pleasure*
In Paradys erde, of stryf unstrayned.   *land; untouched*
What wyrde has hyder my juel vayned,   *fate; sent*
250 And don me in thys del and gret daunger? *put; grief; distress*
Fro we in twynne wern towen and twayned,
I haf ben a joyles juelere.'   *jeweller*

That juel thenne in gemmes gente   *noble*
Vered up her vyse wyth yyen graye,

---

meaningful words about that sight, it was so bright and clear and pure,
that precious pearl in its setting.
238 And greeted me with a gracious utterance.
251 From the time that we were parted and separated.
254 Lifted up her face with its grey-blue eyes.

255 Set on hyr coroun of perle orient,   *put*
    And soberly after thenne con ho say: *gravely; said*
    'Sir, ye haf your tale mysetente,   *misconceived*
    To say your perle is al awaye,
    That is in cofer so comly clente
260 As in this gardyn gracios gaye,
    Hereinne to lenge for ever and play,   *stay; rejoice*
    Ther mys nee mornyng com never nere.
    Her were a forser for the, in faye,
    If thou were a gentyl jueler.   *good*

265 'Bot, jueler gente, if thou schal lose   *good*
    Thy joy for a gemme that the was lef,   *dear*
    Me thynk the put in a mad porpose,   *I think you are set*
    And busyes the aboute a raysoun bref.
    For that thou lestes was bot a rose   *that (which); lost*
270 That flowred and fayled as kynde hyt gef;
    Now thurgh kynde of the kyste that hyt con close
    To a perle of prys hit is put in pref,
    And thou has called thy wyrde a thef,   *fate*
    That oght of noght has mad the cler.
275 Thou blames the bote of thy meschef;   *cure; trouble*
    Thou art no kynde jueler.'   *true*

    A juel to me then was thys geste,   *creature*
    And jueles wern hyr gentyl sawes.   *noble words*
    'Iwyse,' quoth I, 'my blysfol beste,   *indeed; blessed dear* (one)
280 My grete dystresse thou al todrawes.   *dispel*
    To be excused I make requeste;
    I trawed my perle don out of dawes.
    Now haf I fonde hyt, I schal ma feste,   *make merry*

259–60 That is so fittingly enclosed in a casket such as this pleasant and
    delightful garden.

262–3 Where neither sorrow nor grief ever come near. Here indeed
    would be a casket for you (to appreciate).

268 And trouble yourself about a trivial matter.

270–2 That flowered and failed as Nature (*or* its nature) required (lit.
    gave to it). Now through the nature of the casket which encloses it it is
    proved (in fact) to be a pearl of (great) value.

274 That plainly has made something out of nothing for you.

282 I thought my pearl's days were over (i.e. that she was dead).

And wony wyth hyt in schyr   *live; bright*
    wod-schawes,   *groves*
285 And love my Lorde and al his lawes   *praise*
That has me broght thys blys ner.   *near*
Now were I at yow byyonde thise wawes,   *with you; waves*
I were a joyfol jueler.'

'Jueler,' sayde that gemme clene,   *bright*
290 'Wy borde ye men? So madde ye be!   *do you men jest*
Thre wordes has thou spoken at ene;
Unavysed, for sothe, wern alle thre.   *ill-considered, in truth*
Thou ne woste in worlde quat on dos mene;
Thy worde byfore thy wytte con fle.
295 Thou says thou trawes me in this dene,   *believe; valley*
Bycawse thou may wyth yyen me se;   *eyes*
Another thou says, in thys countré   *a second thing*
Thyself schal won wyth me ryght here;   *dwell*
The thrydde, to passe thys water fre –   *noble river*
300 That may no joyfol jueler.

VI

'I halde that jueler lyttel to prayse   *consider; be praised*
That leves wel that he ses wyth yye,   *believes*
And much to blame and uncortayse   *discourteous*
That leves oure Lorde wolde make a lyye,   *lie*
305 That lelly hyghte your lyf to rayse,
Thagh fortune dyd your flesch to dyye.   *caused; die*
Ye setten hys wordes ful westernays,   *askew*
That leves nothynk bot ye hit syye,
And that is a poynt o sorquydryye,
310 That uche god mon may evel byseme,

---

291 You have said three things (lit. words) all at once.
293–4 You do not know at all what one (of them) means; your words
    have flown ahead of your understanding.
305 Who faithfully promised to raise you (from the dead).
308–14 (You) who believe nothing unless you see it, and that is a mark
    of pride, that ill becomes a (lit. each) good man, to find no statement

To leve no tale be true to tryye
Bot that hys one skyl may dem.

'Deme now thyself if thou con dayly
As man to God wordes schulde heve.
315 Thou says thou schal won in this bayly;   *live; domain*
Me thynk the burde fyrst aske leve,   *you ought to*
And yet of graunt thou myghtes fayle.
Thou wylnes over thys water to weve;   *wish; pass*
Er moste thou cever to other counsayl;
320 Thy corse in clot mot calder keve,
For hit was forgarte at Paradys greve;
Oure yorefader hit con mysseyeme.
Thurgh drwry deth bos uch man dreve,
Er over thys dam hym Dryghtyn deme.'

325 'Demes thou me,' quoth I, 'my swete,   *if you condemn*
To dol agayn, thenne I dowyne.   *grief; pine away*
Now haf I fonte that I forlete,   *found; lost*
Schal I efte forgo hit er ever I fyne?   *again; die*
Why schal I hit bothe mysse and mete? *lose; find*
330 My precios perle dos me gret pyne.   *causes; pain*
What serves tresor bot gares men grete,
When he hit schal efte wyth tenes tyne?
Now rech I never for to declyne,
Ne how fer of folde that man me fleme.
335 When I am partles of perle myne,   *deprived*
Bot durande doel what may men deme?'

---

to be true (lit. to believe no statement to be true when put to the test)
except that which his unaided reason may understand. Now judge (for)
yourself whether you have spoken in the way that a man should offer
up words to God.

317 And even so you might fail to get permission.

319–24 Before that you must take other counsel; your body must go
down, colder (than it is now), into the earth, for it was ruined in the
garden of Paradise (i.e. Eden); our forefather (Adam) mistreated it.
Every man must go through cruel death before the Lord will allow him
over this water.

331–4 What use is treasure but to make a man weep, when he must lose
it again with pangs of sorrow? Now I do not care if I lose my
prosperity, nor how far from (my) land men shall drive me.

336–7 'What may men judge (that to be) but lifelong grief?' 'You speak

'Thow demes noght bot doel-dystresse,'
Thenne sayde that wyght, 'why dos thou so?   *being*
For dyne of doel of lures lesse
340 Ofte mony mon forgos the mo.
The oghte better thyselven blesse,
And love ay God, in wele and wo,
For anger gaynes the not a cresse;   *profits you; jot*
Who nedes schal thole be not so thro.
345 For thogh thou daunce as any do,
Braundysch and bray thy brathes breme,
When thou no fyrre may to ne fro
Thou moste abyde that he schal deme.

'Deme Dryghtyn, ever hym adyte,
350 Of the way a fote ne wyl he wrythe.
Thy mendes mountes not a myte,
Thagh thou for sorwe be never blythe.   *happy*
Stynt of thy strot and fyne to flyte,
And sech hys blythe ful swefte and swythe.
355 Thy prayer may hys pyté byte,   *pierce*
That mercy schal hyr craftes kythe.
Hys comforte may thy langour lythe   *grief; soothe*
And thy lures of lyghtly fleme;
For, marre other madde, morne and mythe,
360 Al lys in hym to dyght and deme.'

---

of nothing but painful sorrow.'

339–42 Because of (his) noise of lamentation for lesser losses, often many a man loses the greater (rewards). You ought rather to show favour to yourself (*or* cross yourself), and praise God always, in joy and sorrow.

344–8 Let him who must suffer be not so impatient. For though you dance about (in anguish) like any (wounded) doe, flaunt and cry your fierce agonies, when you may go no further to and fro you must endure what He shall decree.

349–51 (Though you) censure the Lord, accuse Him for ever, He will not turn aside from the way (i.e. His chosen course) one foot. Your favour (in His eyes) increases not a jot.

353–4 Stop your wrangling and cease to grumble, and seek His mercy swiftly and earnestly.

356 So that mercy shall (then) show her skills.

358–60 And quickly put your sorrow to flight. For (though you may) lament or rage, mourn and fret, all lies with Him to dispose and decree.

VII

Thenne demed I to that damyselle: *said; young lady*
'Ne worthe no wraththe unto my Lorde,
If rapely I rave, spornande in spelle.
My herte was al wyth mysse remorde,   *loss; afflicted*
365 As wallande water gos out of welle.   *gushing; spring*
I do me ay in hys myserecorde.   *put myself; mercy*
Rebuke me never wyth wordes felle,   *cruel*
Thagh I forloyne, my dere endorde,   *err; dear adored (one)*
Bot kythes me kyndely your coumforde,
370 Pytosly thenkande upon thysse:
Of care and me ye made acorde,
That er was grounde of alle my blysse.

'My blysse, my bale, ye han ben bothe,   *sorrow*
Bot much the bygger yet was my mon;   *grief*
375 Fro thou was wroken fro uch a wothe,
I wyste never quere my perle was gon.   *knew*
Now I hit se, now lethes my lothe   *softens; pain*
And, quen we departed, we wern at on;   *parted; at one*
God forbede we be now wrothe,   *angry*
380 We meten so selden by stok other ston.   *seldom; stump or*
Thagh cortaysly ye carp con,   *can speak*
I am bot mol and maneres mysse;
Bot Crystes mersy, and Mary and Jon,
Thise arn the grounde of alle my blisse.

385 'In blysse I se the blythely blent,   *joyfully placed*
And I a man al mornyf mate.
Ye take theron ful lyttel tente,
Thagh I hente ofte harmes hate.

362–3 May it not cause any offence to my Lord if I rave rashly, stumbling
   in (my) speech.
369–72 But kindly (*also* as it is your nature to do) show me your
   comfort, thinking with pity upon this: you made accord between
   sorrow and me, you who were once the ground of all my happiness.
375 From the time that you were banished from every peril (of this
   world).
382 I am but dust and lack (good) manners.
386–8 And I (am) a man all sad and dejected. You take very little notice
   of that, though I often endure burning sorrows.

Bot now I am here in your presente,   *presence*
390 I wolde bysech, wythouten debate,   *argument*
Ye wolde me say in sobre asente
What lyf ye lede erly and late.   i.e. *day and night*
For I am ful fayn that your astate   *glad; condition*
Is worthen to worschyp and wele, iwysse;
395 Of alle my joy the hyghe gate   *road*
Hit is, and grounde of alle my blysse.'

'Now blysse, burne, mot the bytyde,'
Then sayde that lufsoum of lyth and lere,
'And welcum here to walk and byde,   *stay*
400 For now thy speche is to me dere.
Maysterful mod and hyghe pryde,   *an arrogant nature*
I hete the, arn heterly hated here.   *promise; fiercely*
My Lorde ne loves not for to chyde,
For meke arn alle that wones hym nere;   *live*
405 And when in hys place thou schal apere,
Be dep devote in hol mekenesse.
My Lorde the Lamb loves ay such chere,   *always; demeanour*
That is the grounde of alle my blysse.   *who*

'A blysful lyf thou says I lede;
410 Thou woldes knaw therof the stage.   *degree of it*
Thow wost wel when thy perle con schede   *know; fell down*
I was ful yong and tender of age.
Bot my Lorde the Lombe, thurgh hys godhede,   *goodness*
He toke myself to hys maryage,   *as His bride*
415 Corounde me quene in blysse to brede   *flourish*
In lenghe of dayes that ever schal wage;
And sesed in alle hys herytage
Hys lef is – I am holy hysse.

---

391 That you would tell me in quiet agreement.
394 Is turned to (one of) honour and prosperity, indeed.
397–8 'Now may happiness, sir, be yours,' then said that one lovely of
    limb and face.
403 My Lord does not like grumbling (in others).
406 Be deeply devout in utter humility.
416–19 For a length of days that shall endure for ever; and His beloved
    is possessed of all His heritage – I am wholly His. His worth, His
    excellence and His high lineage.

Hys prese, hys prys, and hys parage
420 Is rote and grounde of alle my blysse.'   *root*

VIII

'Blysful' quoth I, 'may thys be trwe?   *said*
Dyspleses not if I speke errour.   *do not be displeased*
Art thou the quene of hevenes blwe,
That al thys worlde schal do honour?
425 We leven on Marye that grace of grewe,
That ber a barne of vyrgyn flour;
The croune fro hyr quo moght remwe
Bot ho hir passed in sum favour?
Now, for synglerty o hyr dousour,   *uniqueness of; sweetness*
430 We calle hyr Fenyx of Arraby,   *Phoenix*
That freles flewe of hyr fasor,   *flawless; from; creator*
Lyk to the quen of cortaysye.'   *courtesy*

'Cortayse quen,' thenne sayde that gaye,   *beautiful one*
Knelande to grounde, folde up hyr face,   *her face upturned*
435 'Makeles Moder and myryest may,
Blessed bygynner of uch a grace!'   *every*
Thenne ros ho up and con restay,   *paused*
And speke me towarde in that space: *spoke to me then*
'Sir, fele here porchases and fonges pray,
440 Bot supplantores none wythinne thys place.
That emperise al hevens has,
And urthe and helle in her bayly;   *earth, dominion*
Of erytage yet non wyl ho chace,
For ho is quen of cortaysye.

445 'The court of the kyndom of God alyve   *the living God*
Has a property in hytself beyng.   *inherent in itself*

425–8 We believe in Mary from whom grace grew, who bore a child in
   the flower of her virginity. Who might take the crown away from her
   unless she surpassed her in some gracious attribute?
435 Matchless mother and most beautiful maiden.
439–41 Sir, many here strive for and win a prize, but there are no
   usurpers in this place. That empress has all the heavens.
443 Yet she will oust none from their heritage (i.e. their title to the
   heavenly crown).

Alle that may therinne aryve
Of alle the reme is quen other kyng,   *realm; or*
And never other yet schal depryve,
450 Bot uchon fayn of otheres hafyng,
And wolde her corounes wern worthe tho fyve,
If possyble were her mendyng.
Bot my lady of quom Jesu con spryng,   *sprang*
Ho haldes the empyre over uus ful hyghe;
455 And that dyspleses non of oure gyng,   *company*
For ho is quene of cortaysye.

'Of courtaysye, as says Saynt Poule,   *through*
Al arn we membres of Jesu Kryst;
As heved and arme and legg and naule   *head; navel*
460 Temen to hys body ful trwe and tryste,
Ryght so is uch a Krysten sawle   *just; every; soul*
A longande lym to the Mayster of myste.
Thenne loke what hate other any gawle
Is tached other tyyed thy lymmes bytwyste;
465 Thy heved has nauther greme ne gryste,
On arme other fynger thagh thou ber byghe.
So fare we alle wyth luf and lyste
To kyng and quene, by cortaysye.'

'Cortaysé,' quoth I, 'I leve,   *believe*
470 And charyté grete, be yow among.
Bot my speche that yow ne greve,

.   .   .   .   .   .

Thyself in heven over hygh thou heve,   *too; raise*

449–52 And yet never shall one deprive another, but each is glad of what
the others have, and would wish that their crowns were five times as
precious, if their betterment was possible.

454 She holds supreme sway over us.

460 Are joined to their body most firmly and securely.

462–8 A limb belonging to the Master of spiritual mysteries. Then
consider what hatred or bitterness exists (lit. is attached or tied)
between your bodily parts; your head feels neither anger nor resent-
ment, even though you wear a ring on your arm or finger. In the same
way we all behave with love and joy towards king and queen (i.e. to
the other inhabitants of Heaven), through courtesy.

471 But may my speech not offend you.

To make the quen that was so yonge.
475 What more honour moghte he acheve
That hade endured in worlde stronge,   *steadfastly*
And lyved in penaunce hys lyves longe,   *all his life long*
Wyth bodyly bale hym blysse to byye?
What more worschyp moght he fonge
480 Then corounde be kyng, by cortaysé?

IX

'That cortaysé is to fre of dede,   *too free in action*
Yyf hyt be soth that thou cones saye.   *true; you have said*
Thou lyfed not two yer in oure thede;   *land*
Thou cowthes never God nauther plese ne pray,
485 Ne never nawther pater ne crede –
And quen mad on the fyrst day!   *made*
I may not traw, so God me spede,   *believe; help*
That God wolde wrythe so wrange away.   *go so far wrong*
Of countes, damysel, par ma fay,
490 Wer fayr in heven to halde asstate,
Other elles a lady of lasse aray.   *else; lesser degree*
Bot a quene! – hit is to dere a date.'   *too high a rank*

'Ther is no date of hys godnesse,'   *limit to*
Then sayde to me that worthy wyghte,   *noble creature*
495 'For al is trawthe that he con dresse,   *has ordained*
And he may do nothynk bot ryght,
As Mathew meles in your messe,   *says; mass*
In sothfol gospel of God almyght.   *true; almighty*
In sample he can ful graythely gesse,
500 And lyknes hit to heven lyghte: *bright Heaven*
"My regne," he says, "is lyk on hyght   *kingdom; on high*

---

474 To make yourself a queen, you who were so young.
478–80 So as to buy himself bliss with (his) bodily pain? What greater
honour might he receive than to be crowned king, through courtesy?
484–5 You never knew how to please God or pray to Him, nor (did you
ever know) the Paternoster (i.e. Lord's Prayer) or (Apostles') Creed.
489–90 On my word, young lady, it would be good (for you) to hold the
position of countess in Heaven.
499 He most aptly pictured it (i.e. His limitless goodness) in a parable.

To a lorde that hade a vyne, I wate.   *vineyard; believe*
Of tyme of yere the terme was tyght;
To labor vyne was dere the date.

505 "That date of yere wel knawe thys   *know; the labourers*
        hyne.
The lorde ful erly up he ros
To hyre werkmen to hys vyne,   *for*
And fyndes ther summe to hys porpos.   *purpose*
Into acorde thay con declyne
510 For a pené on a day, and forth thay gos,   *penny; go*
Wrythen and worchen and don gret pyne,
Kerven and caggen and man hit clos.
Aboute under the lorde to marked tos,
And ydel men stande he fyndes therate.
515 'Why stande ye ydel?' he sayde to thos;
'Ne knawe ye of this day no date?'

   "'Er date of daye hider arn we wonne;'
So was al samen her answar soght.
'We haf standen her syn ros the sunne,   *stood; since*
520 And no mon byddes uus do ryght noght.'
'Gos into my vyne, dos that ye conne,'   *go; do what*
So sayde the lorde, and made hit toght.   *settled (it) with them*
'What resonabele hyre be naght be runne
I yow pay in dede and thoghte.'
525 Thay wente into the vyne and wroghte,   *worked*
And al day the lorde thus yede his gate,   *went his way*
And nw men to hys vyne he broghte   *new*
Welnegh wyl day was passed date.

503–4 With respect to the time of year the appointed season had come;
    the time was right to work (in) the vineyard.
509 They settled on an agreement.
511–14 They toil and labour and make great effort, cut and tie and make
    it (i.e. the vineyard and the vines) secure. About the third hour (i.e. 9
    a.m.) the lord goes to the market, and there he finds men standing idle.
516–18 'Do you not know any beginning to this day?' 'We came here
    before the beginning of the day,' so they gave (their) answer all together.
520 And no one asks us to do anything at all.
523–4 Whatever reasonable wages may have accrued by night time I
    will pay you in full (lit. 'in deed and thought', a legal formula).
528 Until the (time of the) day was nearly over.

"At the date of day of evensonge,   *time*
530 On oure byfore the sonne go doun,   *one hour; goes*
He sey ther ydel men ful stronge   *saw*
And sade to hem wyth sobre soun,
'Wy stonde ye ydel thise dayes longe?'   *all day long*
Thay sayden her hyre was nawhere boun.
535 'Gos to my vyne, yemen yonge,   *workmen*
And wyrkes and dos that at ye moun.'   *do what you are able*
Sone the worlde bycom wel broun;   *very dark*
The sunne was doun and hit wex late.   *grew*
To take her hyre he mad sumoun;
540 The day was al apassed date.

X

"The date of the daye the lorde con knaw,   *time; knew*
Called to the reve: 'Lede, pay the meyny.
Gyf hem the hyre that I hem owe,   *wages*
And fyrre, that non me may reprené,   *further; reproach*
545 Set hem alle upon a rawe   *in a line*
And gyf uchon inlyche a peny.   *each one alike*
Bygyn at the laste that standes lowe,
Tyl to the fyrste that thou atteny.'   *reach*
And thenne the fyrst bygonne to pleny   *complain*
550 And sayden that thay hade travayled sore: *toiled hard*
'These bot on oure hem con streny;
Uus thynk uus oghe to take more.

"'More haf we served, uus thynk so,
That suffred han the dayes hete,   *have; heat*
555 Thenn thyse that wroght not houres two,   *worked*
And thou dos hem uus to counterfete.'

---

532 And said to them in a grave tone of voice.
534 They said there was no employment ready for them anywhere.
539-40 He summoned them to receive their wages; the day(-time) was
all over.
542 Called to the steward: 'Sir, pay the (group of) workmen.'
551-3 These (others) have laboured for just one hour; we think we ought
to get more. We have deserved more, so it seems to us.
556 And (yet) you make them equal to us.

Thenne sayde the lorde to on of tho: *one of them*
'Frende, no waning I wyl the yete;
Take that is thyn owne, and go.
560 And I hyred the for a peny agrete,   *if; in total*
Quy bygynnes thou now to threte?   *complain*
Was not a pené thy covenaunt thore?   *on that occasion*
Fyrre then covenaunde is noght to plete.
Wy schalte thou thenne ask more?

565 "'More, wether louyly is me my gyfte,
To do wyth myn quat-so me lykes?
Other elles thyn yye to lyther is lyfte
For I am goude and non byswykes?
'Thus schal I,' quoth Kryste, 'hit skyfte: *apportion*
570 The laste schal be the fyrst that strykes,   *who comes*
And the fyrst the laste, be he never so swyft;
For mony ben called, thagh fewe be mykes.'"   *chosen ones*
Thus pore men her part ay pykes,   *share; get*
Thagh thay com late and lyttel wore;
575 And thagh her sweng wyth lyttel atslykes,
The merci of God is much the more.

'More haf I of joye and blysse hereinne,
Of ladyschyp gret and lyves blom,
Then alle the wyyes in the worlde myght wynne   *than; people*
580 By the way of ryght to aske dome.
Whether welnygh now I con bygynne –
In eventyde into the vyne I come –   *vineyard; came*
Fyrst of my hyre my Lorde con mynne;

---

558 Friend, I do not want to propose (to you) any reduction (of your
     wages).
563 It is not right to claim more than the agreement.
565-8 Moreover, is not my giving lawful (to me), to do whatever pleases
     me with what is mine? Or else is your eye turned to evil (i.e. are you
     angry) because I am righteous and cheat no one?
574-5 Though they came late and were of little account; and though
     their labour is spent with little result.
578 Of high lady's state and bloom of life.
580-1 By asking for reward according to justice. Even though I began
     almost now.
583 My Lord remembered *my* wages first.

I was payed anon of al and sum.   *at once in full*
585 Yet other ther werne that toke more tom,
    That swange and swat for long yore,
    That yet of hyre nothynk thay nom,
    Paraunter noght schal to-yere more.'

Then more I meled and sayde apert: *spoke; plainly*
590 'Me thynk thy tale unresounable.   *words*
    Goddes ryght is redy and evermore rert,   *justice; active*
    Other Holy Wryt is bot a fable.   *or else*
    In Sauter is sayd a verce   *Psalter*
        overte   *of unmistakable meaning*
    That spekes a poynt determynable: *incontrovertible*
595 "Thou quytes uchon as hys desserte,   *reward; according to*
    Thou hyghe kyng ay pertermynable."   *supreme in judgment*
    Now he that stod the long day stable,
    And thou to payment com hym byfore,
    Thenne the lasse in werke to take more able,
600 And ever the lenger the lasse, the more.'

XI

'Of more and lasse in Godes ryche,'   *kingdom*
That gentyl sayde, 'lys no joparde,   *there is no question*
For ther is uch mon payed inlyche,   *alike*
Whether lyttel other much be hys rewarde.   *or; due*
605 For the gentyl Cheventayn is no chyche,
    Quether-so-ever he dele nesch other harde;
    He laves hys gyftes as water of dyche,
    Other gotes of golf that never charde.

585–8 Yet there were others who took more time, who toiled and
    sweated for long enough, who yet got nothing by way of wages, and
    perhaps shall get nothing more this year (i.e. for a long time to come,
    for ever).
597–600 Now he who stood steadfast (in his work) the whole day long,
    if you came to receive payment ahead of him, then (it would follow
    that) the less (done) in work the more qualified to take (payment), and
    always the greater the shortfall (in work), the more (the payment).
605–11 For the noble Ruler is no niggard, whether He deals gently or
    harshly (with people); He pours out His gifts like water from a ditch,
    or streams from a deep source that has never stopped flowing. That

Hys fraunchyse is large that ever dard
610 To Hym that mas in synne rescoghe.
No blysse bes fro hem reparde,
For the grace of God is gret inoghe.

'Bot now thou motes, me for to mate,
That I my peny haf wrang tan here;   *wrongly taken*
615 Thou says that I that come to late   *came too*
Am not worthy so gret fere.   *great reward*
Where wystes thou ever any bourne abate
Ever so holy in hys prayere
That he ne forfeted by sumkyn gate
620 The mede sumtyme of hevenes clere?
And ay the ofter the alder thay were;
Thay laften ryght and wroghten woghe.
Mercy and grace moste hem then stere,   *must; guide*
For the grace of God is gret innoghe.

625 'Bot innoghe of grace has innocent.
As sone as thay arn borne, by lyne   *in due order*
In the water of babtem thay dyssente;   *baptism; descend*
Then arne thay boroght into the vyne.
Anon the day, wyth derk endente
630 The niyght of deth dos to enclyne.
That wroght never wrang er thenne thay wente,
The gentyle Lorde thenne payes hys hyne.
Thay dyden hys heste, thay wern thereine;
Why schulde he not her labour alow –

---

man's privilege is great who has always submitted to Him who rescues (people) in sin. No happiness shall be withheld from them.
613 But now you argue, in order to shame me.
617–22 Where did you ever know of any mortal (lit. fallen) man so consistently holy in his prayers that he did not forfeit in one way or another the reward of the bright heavens on occasion? And always the older they were the more often (they forfeited); they abandoned right and did evil.
625 But the innocent (person) has grace enough.
628–35 Then they are brought into the vineyard (i.e. Christian life). Soon the day, edged with darkness, sinks down to the night of death. The noble Lord then pays His labourers, those who never did wrong before they departed (from the vineyard, in death, i.e. He pays those who died too young to do wrong). They did His bidding, they were in that place (i.e. the vineyard); why should He not recognise their labour

635 Yys, and pay hem at the fyrst fyne?
For the grace of God is gret innoghe.

'Inoghe is knawen that mankyn grete
Fyrste was wroght to blysse parfyt;
Oure forme fader hit con forfete   *first father; forfeited*
640 Thurgh an apple that he upon con byte.   *bit*
Al wer we dampned for that mete
To dyye in doel, out of delyt,
And sythen wende to helle hete,
Therinne to won wythoute respyt.   *live*
645 Bot theron com a bote astyt;
Ryche blod ran on rode so roghe,   *cross; cruel*
And wynne water then at that plyt;
The grace of God wex gret innoghe.   *grew*

'Innoghe ther wax out of that welle,   *flowed*
650 Blod and water of brode wounde.   *from the wide*
The blod uus boght fro bale of helle,   *bought; pain*
And delyvered uus of the deth secounde.   *from*
The water is baptem, the sothe to telle, *truth*
That folwed the glayve so grymly grounde,
655 That wasches away the gyltes felle   *deadly sins*
That Adam wyth inne deth uus dround.e
Now is ther noght in the worlde rounde   *nothing*
Bytwene uus and blysse bot that he wythdrow,
And that is restored in sely stounde;
660 And the grace of God is gret innogh.

– yes, and pay them first, in full?

637–8 It is well known that proud mankind was first created to perfect
   bliss.

641–3 Because of that food we were all condemned to die in pain,
   deprived of delight, and afterwards go to Hell's heat.

645 But a remedy for that came soon.

647 And precious water too in that (hard) plight.

654 That followed the spear so cruelly sharpened.

656 With which Adam drowned us in death.

658–9 Between us and bliss that He did not take away, and that (bliss),
   is restored in a blessed hour.

XII

   'Grace innogh the mon may have
   That synnes thenne new, yif him repente,   *anew; if he repents*
   Bot wyth sorw and syt he mot hit crave,   *sorrow; grief*
   And byde the payne therto is bent.
665 Bot resoun, of ryght that con noght rave,
   Saves evermore the innossent;
   Hit is a dom that never God gave,   *judgment*
   That ever the gyltles schulde be schente.   *destroyed*
   The gyltyf may contryssyoun hente   *guilty; come to*
670 And be thurgh mercy to grace thryght;   *brought*
   Bot he to gyle that never glente,
   As inoscente is saf and ryghte.

   'Ryght thus I knaw wel in this cas
   Two men to save is god by skylle.
675 The ryghtwys man schal se hys face,   *righteous; see*
   The harmles hathel schal com hym tylle.   *innocent man; to*
   The Sauter hyt sas thus in a pace:
   "Lorde, quo schal klymbe thy hygh hylle,
   Other rest wythinne thy holy place?"   *or*
680 Hymself to onsware he is not dylle:
   "Hondelynges harme that dyt not ille,
   That is of hert bothe clene and lyght,
   Ther schal hys step stable stylle."
   The innosent is ay saf by ryght.

685 'The ryghtwys man also sertayn   *certainly*

664–6 And endure the penalty that is attached to it (i.e. do penance for
  his sins). But reason, which cannot stray from right, always saves the
  innocent.
671–4 But he who never succumbed to guile is safe and sound as an
  innocent. Just so I know well in this matter that it is good according to
  reason to save two kinds of men.
677 The Psalter puts it thus in a (certain) passage.
680–4 He (i.e. the Psalmist) himself is not slow to answer (*or* he is not
  slow to reply to himself): 'He who did not wickedly do harm with his
  hands, who is both clean and pure of heart, his step shall be firm there
  for ever (i.e. he shall be there for ever).' The innocent is always safe (*or*
  saved) as of right.

Aproche he schal that proper pyle,   *excellent stronghold*
That takes not her lyf in vayne,
Ne glaveres her nieghbor wyth no gyle.
Of thys ryghtwys sas Salamon playn
690 How Koyntise onoure con aquyle;
By wayes ful streght he con hym strayn,
And scheued hym the rengne of God awhyle,
As quo says: "Lo, yon lovely yle!   *as (one) who; land*
Thou may hit wynne if thou be wyghte."   *strong*
695 Bot hardyly, wythoute peryle,   *assuredly; doubt*
The innocent is ay save by ryghte.   *safe (or saved) as of right*

'Anende ryghtwys men yet says a gome,
David in Sauter, if ever ye sey hit:
"Lorde, thy servaunt draw never to dome,
700 For non lyvyande to the is justyfyet."
Forthy to corte quen thou schal com,   *and so*
Ther alle oure causes schal be tryed,   *where*
Alegge the ryght, thou may be innome
By thys ilke spech I have asspyed –   *same; noted*
705 Bot he on rode that blody dyed,   *unless; cross*
Delfully thurgh hondes thryght,   *grievously; pierced*
Gyve the to passe, when thou arte tryed,
By innocens and not by ryghte.

'Ryghtwysly quo con rede,
710 He loke on bok and be awayed
How Jesus hym welke in arethede,
And burnes her barnes unto hym brayde.

687–92 Who does not spend his life in folly, nor deceive his neighbour
with any trickery. Concerning this righteous man Solomon says plainly
how Wisdom obtained honour (for him); He guided him by most
narrow paths, and showed him for a time the kingdom of God.

697–700 Concerning righteous men a (certain) man says further, David
in the Psalter, if ever you saw it: 'Lord, never bring your servant to
judgment, for no living man is justified before you.'

703 (If you) plead righteousness, you may be caught.

707–16 Should allow you to go free, when you are tried, through (your)
innocence and not through righteousness. He who can read rightly, let
him look at the Bible and be instructed how Jesus walked among the
people of ancient times and (how) people brought their children to

For happe and hele that fro hym yede
To touch her chylder thay fayr hym prayed.
715 His dessypeles wyth blame let be hem bede,
And wyth her resounes ful fele restayed.
Jesus thenne hem swetely sayde: *to them*
"Do way, let chylder unto me tyght;   *cease; come*
To suche is hevenryche arayed."
720 The innocent is ay saf by ryght.   *safe (or saved) as of right*

XIII

'Jesus con calle to hym hys mylde,   *called; gentle (disciples)*
And sayde hys ryche no wyy myght wynne   *kingdom; man*
Bot he com thyder ryght as a chylde,
Other elles nevermore com therinne.   *or else*
725 Harmles, trwe, and undefylde,   *guiltless*
Wythouten mote other mascle of sulpande synne –
Quen such ther cnoken on the bylde,   *knock; dwelling*
Tyt schal hem men the yate unpynne.   *quickly; unfasten*
Ther is the blys that con not blynne   *cease*
730 That the jueler soghte thurgh perré pres,   *a precious stone*
And solde alle hys goud, bothe wolen and lynne,
To bye hym a perle was mascelles.   *that was spotless*

'This makelles perle, that boght is dere,
The joueler gef fore alle hys god,
735 Is lyke the reme of hevenesse clere;
So sayde the Fader of folde and flode.   *land; sea*
For hit is wemles, clene, and clere,   *spotless, pure*
And endeles rounde, and blythe of mode,
And commune to alle that ryghtwys were.   *common*
740 Lo, even inmyddes my breste hit   *exactly in the middle of*
    stode.

Him. Because of the blessing and healing that came from Him they
asked him courteously to touch their children. His disciples reproach-
fully ordered them to stop, and kept back very many by their speech.
719 The kingdom of Heaven is prepared for such (as they are).
726 Without spot or stain of polluting sin.
731 And sold all his goods, both woollen and linen.
733–4 This matchless pearl, which is dear bought, for which the jeweller
    gave all his goods, is like the realm of bright Heaven.
738 And round without end, and beautiful in appearance.

My Lorde the Lombe, that schede hys blode,
He pyght hit there in token of pes.   *set; peace*
I rede the forsake the worlde wode   *advise you to; mad*
And porchace thy perle maskelles.'

745 'O maskeles perle in perles pure,
That beres,' quoth I, 'the perle of prys,   *wears; of great value*
Quo formed the thy fayre fygure?   *for you*
That wroght thy wede, he was ful wys.
Thy beauté com never of nature;   *from*
750 Pymalyon paynted never thy vys,   *Pygmalion; face*
Ne Arystotel nawther by hys lettrure
Of carped the kynde these propertés.
Thy colour passes the flour-de-lys,   *surpasses*
Thyn angel-havyng so clene cortes.
755 Breve me, bryght, quat kyn offys
Beres the perle so maskelles?'

'My makeles Lambe that al may bete,'
Quoth scho, 'my dere destyné,
Me ches to hys make, althagh unmete
760 Sumtyme semed that assemblé.
When I wente fro yor worlde wete,   *dismal* (lit. *wet*)
He calde me to hys bonerté: *blessedness*
"Cum hyder to me, my lemman swete,   *beloved* (*one*)
For mote ne spot is non in the."   *stain; none*
765 He gef me myght and als bewté;   *gave; power; also*
In hys blod he wesch my wede on dese,
And coronde clene in vergynté,
And pyght me in perles maskelles.'   *set*

---

748 He who made your clothes was most skilful.
751–2 Nor did Aristotle in his writings speak of the nature of these
    attributes.
754–6 Your angelic bearing (is) so perfectly refined. Tell me, beautiful
    one, what kind of office does the pearl so spotless hold?
757 My matchless Lamb, who may make amends for everything.
759–60 Chose me as His bride, although at one time that union would
    have seemed unfitting (i.e. while she was alive).
766–7 In His blood He washed my clothes on the dais (i.e. where His
    heavenly throne was), and crowned me pure in (my) virginity.

'Why, maskelles bryd, that bryght con flambe,
770 That reiates has so ryche and ryf,
Quat kyn thyng may be that Lambe   *kind of*
That the wolde wedde unto hys vyf?   *as His wife*
Over alle other so hygh thou clambe   *climbed*
To lede wyth hym so ladyly lyf.   *so queenly a*
775 So mony a comly anunnder cambe
For Kryst han lyved in much stryf,
And thou con alle tho dere out dryf
And fro that maryag al other depres,
Al only thyself so stout and styf,
780 A makeles may and maskelles.'

XIV

'Maskelles,' quoth that myry quene,   *lovely*
'Unblemyst I am, wythouten blot,   *stain*
And that may I wyth mensk menteene;   *honour; maintain*
Bot "makeles quene" thenne sade I not.   *said*
785 The Lambes vyves in blysse we bene,   *wives; are*
A hondred and forty thowsande flot,   *in company*
As in the Apocalyppes hit is sene.
Sant John hem syy al in a knot   *saw; group*
On the hyl of Syon, that semly clot;   *beautiful knoll*
790 The apostel hem segh in gostly drem   *saw; spiritual vision*
Arayed to the weddyng in that hyl-coppe,
The nwe cyté o Jerusalem.   *of*

'Of Jerusalem I in speche spelle;   *tell*
If thou wyl knaw what kyn he be,   *want to; kind (of man)*
795 My Lombe, my Lorde, my dere juelle,
My joy, my blys, my lemman fre,   *beloved (one); noble*

769–70 Why, spotless bride, who shines so brightly, who has such rich
  and abundant royal honours.
775–80 So many lovely ladies (lit. many a lovely one under comb) have
  lived in great hardship for Christ, and you are able to drive out all
  those worthy ones and exclude all others from that marriage, yourself
  being the only one sufficiently firm and resolute, a peerless and spotless
  maiden.
791 Arrayed for the wedding on that hill top.

The profete Ysaye of hym con melle   *Isaiah; spoke*
Pitously of hys debonerté: *compassionately; gentleness*
"That gloryous gyltles that mon con quelle
800 Wythouten any sake of felonye,
As a schep to the slaght ther lad was he;   *slaughter; led*
And, as lombe that clypper in hande   *shearer; took hold of*
   nem,
So closed he hys mouth fro uch query,
Quen Jues hym jugged in Jerusalem."

805 'In Jerusalem was my lemman slayn,
And rent on rode wyth boyes bolde.   *torn; cross by ruffians*
Al oure bales to bere ful bayn,   *sorrows; willing*
He toke on hymself oure cares colde.   *bitter*
Wyth boffetes was hys face flayn   *blows; torn*
810 That was so fayr on to byholde.   *to look on*
For synne he set hymself in vayn,
That never hade non hymself to wolde.
For uus he lette hym flyye and folde,
And brede upon a bostwys bem;
815 As meke as lomp that no playnt tolde,
For uus he swalt in Jerusalem.   *died*

'In Jerusalem, Jordan, and Galalye,   *Galilee*
Ther as baptysed the goude Saynt Jon,   *(there) where*
His wordes acorded to Ysaye.   *agreed with*
820 When Jesus con to hym warde gon,   *went towards him*
He sayde of hym thys professye: *prophecy*
"Lo, Godes Lombe as trwe as ston,   *true*
That dos away the synnes dryye   *takes; heavy*
That alle thys worlde has wroght upon."   *has committed*

799–800 That glorious innocent who was killed without any charge of felony (being proved against Him).

803 So He closed His mouth against every complaint (i.e. He refused to answer the charges made against Him).

811–15 For sin He set himself at nought, (He) who never had any (sin) Himself (lit. never had any Himself to possess). For us He let Himself be scourged and twisted, and stretched upon a rough beam; as meek as a lamb that made no complaint.

825 Hymself ne wroght never yet non;
    Whether on hymself he con al clem.
    Hys generacyoun quo recen con,
    That dyyed for uus in Jerusalem?   *who*

    'In Jerusalem thus my lemman swete
830 Twyes for lombe was taken thare,
    By trw recorde of ayther prophete,
    For mode so meke and al hys fare.
    The thryde tyme is therto ful mete,
    In Apokalypes wryten ful yare.
835 Inmydes the trone, there sayntes sete,   *in the midst of; sat*
    The apostel John hym saw as bare,   *most plainly*
    Lesande the boke with leves sware   *opening; square*
    There seven syngnettes wern sette in seme.
    And at that syght uche douth con dare   *every host cowered*
840 In helle, in erthe, and Jerusalem.

XV

    'Thys Jerusalem Lombe hade never pechche   *blemish*
    Of other huee bot quyt jolyf,
    That mot ne masklle moght on streche,
    For wolle quyte so ronk and ryf.
845 Forthy uche saule that hade never teche   *and so; stain*
    Is to that Lombe a worthyly wyf;   *honoured*
    And thagh uch day a store he feche,   *(new) supply; brings*
    Among uus commes nouther strot ne stryf,   *dispute*
    Bot uchon enlé we wolde were fyf –
850 The mo the myryer, so God me blesse.   *more*

825–7 He Himself never indeed committed any; yet He claimed all (sins)
    for himself. Who of His generation paid any heed?
830–4 Was twice taken for a Lamb there, by the true testimony of both
    prophets (i.e. Isaiah and John the Baptist), because of His meek
    appearance and His whole demeanour. The third time is fully consistent
    with those (two), described (in writing) very clearly in the Apocalypse.
838 Where seven seals were attached to the edge.
842–4 Of any other colour but beautiful white that neither speck nor
    stain might adhere to, because of the white wool, so rich and abundant.
849 But we would wish that every single one were five.

In compayny gret our luf con thryf,   *thrives*
In honour more and never the lesse.

'Lasse of blysse may non uus bryng
That beren thys perle upon oure bereste,
855 For thay of mote couthe never mynge
Of spotles perles that beren the creste.
Althagh oure corses in clottes clynge,   *bodies decay in earth*
And ye remen for rauthe wythouten reste,   *cry out; pain*
We thurghoutly haven cnawyng;
860 Of on dethe ful oure hope is drest.
The Lombe uus glades, oure care is   *gladdens*
    kest;   *taken away*
He myrthes uus alle at uch a mes.   *rejoices; every feast*
Uchones blysse is breme and beste,
And never ones honour yet never the les.

865 'Lest les thou leve my tale farande,
In Appocalyppece is wryten in wro: *passage*
"I seghe," says John, "the Loumbe hym   *saw*
    stande   *standing*
On the mount of Syon, ful thryven and thro,   *splendid; noble*
And wyth hym maydennes an hundrethe thowsande,
870 And fowre and forty thowsande mo.   *more*
On alle her forhedes wryten I fande   *found*
The Lombes nome, hys Faderes also.   *name*
A hue fro heven I herde thoo,   *shout; then*
Lyk flodes fele laden runnen on resse,
875 And as thunder throwes in torres blo –
That lote, I leve, was never the les.

_____

852–6 In greater honour (given and received), not less. No one may
    bring less bliss to us who wear this pearl upon our breast, for those
    who wear the badge of spotless pearls may never think of quarrelling.

859–60 We have understanding in full; our hope is entirely based on one
    death (i.e. Christ's).

863–5 Everyone's happiness is glorious and supreme, and yet no one's
    honour is any the less (i.e. they still honour each other). In case you
    think my fine words false.

874–8 Like many brimming rivers running in spate, and as thunder rolls
    in dark thunderclouds – that sound, I believe, was in no way less.

'"Nautheles, thagh hit schowted scharpe,
And ledden loude althagh hit were,
A note ful nwe I herde hem warpe,   *utter*
880 To lysten that was ful lufly dere.
As harpores harpen in her harpe,
That nwe songe thay songen ful cler,   *clearly*
In sounande notes a gentyl carpe.
Ful fayre the modes thay fonge in fere,
885 Ryght byfore Godes chayere,   *throne*
And the fowre bestes that hym obes,   *beasts; bowed to*
And the aldermen so sadde of chere –   *elders; grave; face*
Her songe thay songen never the les.   *sang*

'"Nowthelese non was never so quoynt,
890 For alle the craftes that ever thay knewe,
That of that songe myght synge a poynt,
Bot that meyny the Lombe that swe.
For thay arn boght, fro the urthe aloynte,
As newe fryt to God ful due,   *first fruits*
895 And to the gentyl Lombe hit arn anjoynt,   *they are joined*
As lyk to hymself of lote and hwe;   *bearing; appearance*
For never lesyng ne tale untrwe
Ne towched her tonge for no dysstresse.
That moteles meyny may never remwe
900 Fro that maskeles mayster, never the les."'

'Never the les let be my thonc,'
Quoth I, 'my perle, thagh I appose.

Nevertheless, though it rang resoundingly, and although it was a loud
sound.
880 That was most delightful to listen to.
883–4 A noble song in sonorous notes. They sang the melodies together
most beautifully.
889–93 Nevertheless there was none so skilful, for all the arts they ever
knew, who might sing a (single) phrase of that song, except for that
company who follow the Lamb. For they are redeemed, taken away
from the earth.
897–910 'For no lie or untrue words ever touched their tongue in any
circumstances. That spotless company may never be parted from that
spotless Lord, whatever the situation.' 'May my gratitude not be
(thought to be) at all the less,' I said, 'my pearl, although I question
you. I ought not to presume to test your excellent wisdom, you who
are chosen for Christ's bridal chamber. I am only muck and dust mixed

I schulde not tempte thy wyt so wlonc,
To Krystes chambre that art ichose.
905 I am bot mokke and mul among,
And thou so ryche, a reken rose,
And bydes here by thys blysful bonc
Ther lyves lyste may never lose.
Now, hynde, that sympelnesse cones enclose,
910 I wolde the aske a thynge expresse,
And thagh I be bustwys as a blose,   *rude; churl*
Let my bone vayl neverthelese.   *prayer prevail*

XVI

'Neverthelese cler I yow bycalle,   *clearly; call upon*
If ye con se hyt be to done;
915 As thou art gloryous, wythouten galle,   *spot (of impurity)*
Wythnay thou never my ruful bone.   *refuse; piteous*
Haf ye no wones in castel-walle,   *dwelling*
Ne maner ther ye may mete and won?   *manor where; dwell*
Thou telles me of Jerusalem the ryche ryalle,   *royal kingdom*
920 Ther David dere was dyght on trone;   *noble; set*
Bot by thyse holtes hit con not hone,   *woods; be situated*
Bot in Judee hit is, that noble note.   *Judaea; place*
As ye ar maskeles under mone,
Your wones schulde be wythouten mote.   *blemish*

925 'Thys moteles meyny thou cones of mele,
Of thousandes thryght so gret a route,
A gret ceté, for ye arn fele,
Yow byhod have, wythouten doute.
So cumly a pakke of joly juele
930 Wer evel don schulde lyy theroute;

---

together, and you (are) so noble, a lovely rose, and (you) live here by
this delightful bank where life's pleasure may never fade. Now, gracious
one, who are given to gentleness, I want to ask you one thing plainly.'
914 If you can see your way to doing it.
923 As you are altogether spotless (lit. spotless under moon).
925–30 This spotless retinue which you speak of, so great a company of
thousands crowded together, ought to have a great city, without doubt,
because you are (so) many. It would be wrong for so fine a crowd of
beautiful jewels to sleep out of doors.

And by thyse bonkes ther I con gele   *slopes; where I linger*
I se no bygyng nawhere aboute.   *dwelling anywhere*
I trowe alone ye lenge and loute,
To loke on the glory of thys gracious gote. *beautiful stream*
935 If thou has other bygynges stoute,
Now tech me to that myry mote.'

'That mote thou menes in Judy londe,'
That specyal spyce then to me spakk,   *precious person*
'That is the cyté that the Lombe con fonde   *sought out*
940 To soffer inne sor for manes sake,
The olde Jerusalem to understonde,
For there the olde gulte was don to slake.
Bot the nwe, that lyght of Godes sonde,
The apostel in Apocalyppce in theme con take.

945 The Lompe ther wythouten spottes blake   *Lamb; black*
Has feryed thyder hys fayre flote;   *brought; company*
And as hys flok is wythouten flake,   *blemish*
So is hys mote wythouten moote.   *city; stain*

'Of motes two to carpe clene –
950 And Jerusalem hyght bothe nawtheles –
That nys to yow no more to mene
Bot "ceté of God" other "syght of pes".
In that on oure pes was mad at ene;
Wyth payne to suffer the Lombe hit chese.
955 In that other is noght bot pes to glene   *to be gleaned*
That ay schal laste wythouten reles.   *ever; without end*
That is the borgh that we to pres   *city; hasten to*
Fro that oure flesch be layd to rote,   *after; rot*

---

933 I believe you stay here alone and hide.
935–7 'If you have fine buildings somewhere else, direct me now to that
    splendid city.' 'That city you mean in the land of Judea.'
940–4 To suffer pain in for mankind's sake, that is to say, the old
    Jerusalem, for there the old guilt (of Adam and Eve) was brought to an
    end. But the new (city), which came down (from Heaven) through
    God's sending, the Apostle took as his subject in the Apocalypse.
949–54 To speak plainly of these two cities – and both nevertheless are
    called Jerusalem – that (name) means no more to you than 'city of God'
    or 'vision of peace'. In the one our peace was made secure; the Lamb
    chose it (as a place in which) to suffer in pain.

Ther glory and blysse schal ever encres   *where; increase*
960 To the meyny that is wythouten mote.'   *for the company*

'Moteles may so meke and mylde,'   *spotless maid*
Then sayde I to that lufly flor,   *flower*
'Bryng me to that bygly bylde   *pleasant dwelling*
And let me se thy blysful bor.'   *bower*
965 That schene sayde: 'That God wyl schylde;
Thou may not enter wythinne hys tor.   *stronghold*
Bot of the Lombe I have the aquylde
For a syght therof thurgh gret favor.
Utwyth to se that clene cloystor
970 Thou may, bot inwyth not a fote;
To strech in the strete thou has no vygour,   *walk; power*
Bot thou wer clene wythouten mote.   *unless*

XVII

'If I this mote the schal unhyde,   *reveal*
Bow up towarde thys bornes heved,
975 And I anendes the on this syde   *opposite*
Schal sue, tyl thou to a hil be veved.'   *follow; brought*
Then wolde I no lenger byde,   *wait*
Bot lurked by launces so lufly leved,
Tyl on a hyl that I asspyed
980 And blusched on the burghe, as I forth dreved,
Byyonde the brok fro me warde keved,
That schyrrer then sunne wyth schaftes schon.
In the Apokalypce is the fasoun preved,   *manner (of it) shown*
As devyses hit the apostel Jhon.   *describes*

985 As John the apostel hit syy wyth syght,   *saw it*
I syye that cyty of gret renoun,

---

965 That lovely one said: 'God will forbid that.'
967–70 But I have obtained permission from the Lamb for you to have a
sight of it, out of (His) great kindness; you may see that bright enclosure
from the outside, but not (go) a single foot inside.
974 Go up towards the source of this stream.
978–82 But made my way past boughs so beautifully covered in leaves,
until I caught sight of the city and gazed on it as I went, (it having)
come down (from Heaven) on the far side of the brook from me,
shining with beams of light brighter than the sun.

Jerusalem so nwe and ryally dyght,   *royally adorned*
As hit was lyght fro the heven adoun.   *descended*
The borgh was al of brende golde bryght,   *city; pure*
990 As glemande glas burnist broun,   *gleaming; burnished bright*
Wyth gentyl gemmes anunder pyght,   *noble; set underneath*
Wyth banteles twelve on basyng boun,
The foundementes twelve of riche tenoun.
Uch tabelment was a serlypes ston;
995 As derely devyses this ilk toun   *well describes; same*
In Apocalyppes the apostel John.

As John thise stones in writ con nemme,   *scripture; named*
I knew the name after his tale.
Jasper hyght the fyrst gemme   *was called*
1000 That I on the fyrst basse con wale;   *foundation; saw*
He glente grene in the lowest hemme.   *it glinted; band*
Saffer helde the secounde stale;   *sapphire; place*
The calsydoyne thenne wythouten wemme   *chalcedony; flaw*
In the thryd table con purly pale.   *shone purely and palely*
1005 The emerade the furthe so grene of scale;   *fourth; surface*
The sardonyse the fyfthe ston;   *sardonyx*
The sexte the rybé he con hit wale   *sixth; ruby*
In the Apocalyppce, the apostel John.

Yet joyned John the crysolyt,   *added; chrysolite*
1010 The seventhe gemme in fundament;   *foundation*
The aghtthe the beryl cler and quyt;   *eighth; white*
The topasye twynne-hew the nente endent;
The crysopase the tenthe is tyght;
The jacynght the enleventhe gent;
1015 The twelfthe, the gentyleste in uche a plyt,
The amatyst purpre wyth ynde blente.

992-4 With twelve courses arranged on a base, the twelve layers of the
   foundation (being) of rich jointing. Each tier was a particular stone.
997 I knew the name (of them) by his enumeration.
1012-18 The bi-coloured topaz (is) mounted in the ninth; the chryso-
   prase is set in the tenth, the noble jacinth the eleventh; the twelfth, the
   most comforting in every difficulty, (is) the amethyst of purple and
   indigo mixed. The wall set above the courses (was) of jasper that shone
   gleaming like glass.

The wal abof the bantels bent
O jasporye, as glas that glysnande schon.
I knew hit by his devysement   *description*
1020 In the Apocalyppes, the apostel John.

As John devysed yet saw I thare;   *still (more)*
Thise twelve degres wern brode and stayre.   *steps; steep*
The cyté stod abof ful sware,   *square*
As longe as brode as hyghe ful fayre;   *exactly*
1025 The stretes of golde as glasse al bare,   *clear*
The wal of jasper that glent as glayr.
The wones wythinne enurned ware
Wyth alle kynnes perré that moght repayre.
Thenne helde uch sware of this manayre
1030 Twelve forlonge space, er ever hit fon,
Of heght, of brede, of lenthe to cayre,
For meten hit syy the apostel John.

XVIII

As John hym wrytes yet more I syye;
Uch pane of that place had thre yates,   *side; gates*
1035 So twelve in poursent I con asspye,
The portales pyked of rych plates,   *(were) adorned with*
And uch yate of a margyrye,   *with a pearl*
A parfyt perle that never fates.   *fades*
Uchon in scrypture a name con plye
1040 Of Israel barnes, folewande her dates,
That is to say, as her byrth-whates;

1026–32 The wall of jasper that shone like white of egg (used in
  illuminating manuscripts). The buildings within were adorned with all
  kinds of precious stones that might be present. And so each square side
  of this dwelling measured twelve furlongs (lit. contained ... twelve
  furlongs' space ... to traverse) in height, breadth, and length before it
  ever came to an end, for the apostle John saw its measurements (lit.
  saw it be measured).

1033 I saw still more of what John describes.

1035 So I saw twelve in the surrounding wall.

1039–41 Each (gate) had on it in inscribed lettering a name of the
  children of Israel, following their dates, that is to say, according to
  their birth-dates.

The aldest ay fyrst theron was done.   *oldest; inscribed*
Such lyght ther lemed in alle the strates   *shone; streets*
Hem nedde nawther sunne ne mone.   *they needed*

1045 Of sunne ne mone had thay no nede;
The self God was her lambe-lyght,
The Lombe her lantyrne, wythouten drede;   *doubt*
Thurgh hym blysned the borgh al bryght.   *shone; city*
Thurgh wowe and won my lokyng yede;
1050 For sotyle cler noght lette no lyght.
The hyghe trone ther moght ye hede   *observe*
Wyth alle the apparaylmente umbepyghte,
As John the appostel in termes tyghte;   *described in words*
The hyghe Godes self hit set upone.
1055 A rever of the trone ther ran outryghte
Was bryghter then bothe the sunne and mone.

Sunne ne mone schon never so swete
As that foysoun flode out of that flet;
Swythe hit swange thurgh uch a strete   *swiftly; rushed*
1060 Wythouten fylthe other galle other glet.   *or impurity or slime*
Kyrk therinne was non yete,
Chapel ne temple that ever was set.
The Almyghty was her mynyster mete,
The Lombe the sakerfyse ther to refet.
1065 The yates stoken was never yet,
Bot evermore upen at uche a lone;   *open; roadway*
Ther entres non to take reset   *no one; refuge*
That beres any spot anunder mone.

1046 God Himself was their lamp light.
1049–50 My gaze went through wall and building; because of the
    transparent clarity, nothing obstructed the light.
1052 Set round with all its adornments.
1054–6 The great God Himself sat upon it. A river ran there directly out
    of the throne that was brighter than both the sun and moon.
1058 As that copious flood (that flowed) out of that ground.
1061–5 Moreover there was no church in that place, no chapel or temple
    that was ever built; the Almighty was their fitting minister, the Lamb
    (was) the sacrifice to give refreshment there. The gates were never yet
    shut.

The mone may therof acroche no myghte;
1070 To spotty ho is, of body to grym,
And also ther ne is never nyght.
What schulde the mone ther compas clym,
And to even wyth that worthly lyght
That schynes upon the brokes brym?   *river's surface*
1075 The planetes arn in to pover a plyght,   *too poor a state*
And the self sunne ful fer to dym.   *sun itself; far too*
Aboute that water arn tres ful schym,   *bright*
That twelve frytes of lyf con bere ful sone;
Twelve sythes on yer thay beren ful frym,
1080 And renowles nwe in uche a mone.

Anunder mone so gret merwayle   *marvel*
No fleschly hert ne myght endeure,   *endure*
As quen I blusched upon that baly,   *looked; castle wall*
So ferly therof was the fasure.   *marvellous; appearance*
1085 I stod as stylle as dased quayle   *dazed quail*
For ferly of that frech fygure,
That felde I nawther reste ne travayle,
So was I ravyste wyth glymme pure.
For I dar say wyth conciens sure,   *conviction*
1090 Hade bodyly burne abiden that bone,
Thagh alle clerkes hym hade in cure,
His lyf wer loste anunder mone.

1069–73 The moon may take no power from there; she is too spotty,
too ugly of body, and also there is never any night there. Why should
the moon rise in her circuit there, and compete with that noble light?

1078–80 That bear twelve fruits of life very quickly (one after another);
twelve times a year they bear most abundantly, and renew themselves
again each month.

1086–8 In amazement at that vivid vision, so that I felt no bodily
sensations (lit. neither rest nor toil), so enraptured was I by the pure
radiance.

1090–2 Had any man in the body experienced that heavenly vision,
though all the learned men (in the world) had had him in their care, his
life would have been utterly lost.

XIX

Ryght as the maynful mone con rys
Er thenne the day-glem dryve al doun,
1095 So sodanly on a wonder wyse   *marvellous manner*
I was war of a prosessyoun.   *aware*
This noble cité of ryche enpryse   *splendour*
Was sodanly ful wythouten sommoun   *summons*
Of such vergynes in the same gyse   *guise*
1100 That was my blysful anunder croun.
And coronde wern alle of the same fasoun,   *crowned; fashion*
Depaynt in perles and wedes qwyte;   *adorned; white clothes*
In uchones breste was bounden boun   *fastened; firmly*
The blysful perle wyth gret delyt.   *most delightfully*

1105 Wyth gret delyt thay glod in fere   *went together*
On golden gates that glent as glasse.   *streets; shone*
Hundreth thowsandes I wot ther were,
And alle in sute her livrés wasse;
Tor to knaw the gladdest chere.
1110 The Lombe byfore con proudly passe,
Wyth hornes seven of red golde cler;   *bright*
As praysed perles his wedes wasse.   *precious*
Towarde the throne thay trone a tras;   *they made their way*
Thagh thay wern fele, no pres in plyt,
1115 Bot mylde as maydenes seme at mas,   *seem; mass*
So drow thay forth wyth gret delyt.   *moved; forward*

Delyt that hys come encroched,
To much hit were of for to melle.
Thise aldermen, quen he aproched,   *the elders*
1120 Grovelyng to his fete thay felle.   *prostrate*
Legyounes of aungeles, togeder voched,   *summoned*

1093–4 Just as the resplendent moon rises before the light of day fully
    subsides.

1100 As was my beautiful one under her crown.

1107–10 I know there were a hundred thousand, and their dress was all
    alike; it was hard to know who had the happiest demeanour. The Lamb
    went proudly before (them).

1114 Though they were many, (there was) assuredly no crowding.

1117–18 It would be too much (i.e. impossible) to tell of the delight
    which His coming brought.

Ther kesten ensens of swete smelle.   *scattered incense*
Then glory and gle was nwe abroched;
Al songe to love that gay juelle.   *sang; praise; bright*
1125 The steven moght stryke thurgh the urthe to helle   *sound*
That the Vertues of heven of joye endyte.
To love the Lombe his meyny in melle
Iwysse I laght a gret delyt.

Delit the Lombe for to devise
1130 Wyth much mervayle in mynde went.
Best was he, blythest, and moste to pryse,
That ever I herde of speche spent;
So worthly whyt wern wedes hys,   *gloriously; clothes*
His lokes symple, hymself so gent.   *mild; gracious*
1135 Bot a wounde ful wyde and weete con wyse   *wet; showed*
Anende hys hert, thurgh hyde torente;
Of his quyte syde his blod outsprent.   *white; gushed out*
Alas, thoght I, who did that spyt?   *evil deed*
Ani breste for bale aght haf forbrent
1140 Er he therto hade had delyt.

The Lombe delyt non lyste to wene;
Thagh he were hurt and wounde hade,
In his sembelaunt was never sene,
So wern his glentes gloryous glade.
1145 I loked among his meyny schene   *retinue; shining*
How thay wyth lyf wern laste and lade;
Then saw I ther my lyttel quene   *girl and queen*

1123 Then praise and rejoicing burst forth anew.
1126–32 That the Virtues (i.e. one of the nine orders of angels) of
Heaven make for joy. Indeed *I* conceived a great desire to praise the
Lamb among His retinue. Delight in gazing upon the Lamb went
together in my mind with great wonder. He was the best, most gracious,
and most to be praised that ever I heard tell of.
1136 Close to His heart, through the torn skin.
1139–41 Any (man's) breast ought to have burnt up for sorrow before
he took pleasure in that. No one saw fit to doubt the Lamb's delight.
1143–4 That was never seen in His demeanour, so gloriously joyful were
His looks.
1146 (And saw) how they were laden and filled to overflowing with life.

That I wende had standen by me in sclade.
Lorde, much of mirthe was that ho made
1150 Among her feres that was so quyt!
That syght me gart to thenk to wade
For luf-longyng, in gret delyt.

XX

Delyt me drof in yye and ere;
My manes mynde to maddyng malte.
1155 Quen I sey my frely, I wolde be there,   *saw; lovely (one)*
Byyonde the water thagh ho were walte.   *set*
I thoght that nothyng myght me dere
To fech me bur and take me halte,
And to start in the strem schulde non me stere,
1160 To swymme the remnaunt, thagh I ther swalte.
Bot of that munt I was bitalt;   *out of; intention; shaken*
When I schulde start in the strem astraye,
Out of that caste I was bycalt –
Hit was not at my Prynces paye.   *to; liking*

1165 Hit payed hym not that I so flonc   *pleased; flung (myself)*
Over mervelous meres, so mad arayde.
Of raas thagh I were rasch and ronk,
Yet rapely therinne I was restayed.
For, ryght as I sparred unto the bonc,   *just; ran; bank*

1148–52 That I thought had stood by me in the valley. Lord, great was
the rejoicing that she made among her companions, she who was so
white! That sight made me think of wading (across the river), because
of my love-longing, in (a state of) great delight (*and* desire).

1153–4 Delight (*and* desire) poured into me through eye and ear; my
man's mind gave way (lit. melted) to madness.

1157–60 I thought that nothing might hinder me from gathering my
strength and taking possession (of the Maiden) for myself, and that no
one should hold me back from plunging into the stream to swim the
rest (of the way), even though I should die there.

1162–3 When I was about to plunge wildly into the stream, I was called
away from that purpose.

1166–8 Over the marvellous waters, in such a state of frenzy. Though I
was rash and impetuous in rushing forward, yet I was quickly checked
in that course.

1170 That braththe out of my drem me brayde.
     Then wakned I in that erber wlonk;   *garden; lovely*
     My hede upon that hylle was layde
     Ther as my perle to grounde strayd.   *where; slipped*
     I raxled, and fel in gret affray,
1175 And, sykyng, to myself I sayd: *sighing*
     'Now al be to that Prynces paye.'

     Me payed ful ille to be outfleme
     So sodenly of that fayre regioun,   *from*
     Fro alle tho syghtes so quyke and queme.   *vivid; pleasant*
1180 A longeyng hevy me strok in swone,
     And rewfully thenne I con to reme: *sorrowfully; cried out*
     'O perle,' quoth I 'of rych renoun,   *noble splendour*
     So was hit me dere that thou con deme
     In this veray avysyoun.
1185 If hit be veray and soth sermoun
     That thou so stykes in garlande gay,
     So wel is me in thys doel-doungoun
     That thou art to that Prynses paye.'

     To that Prynces paye hade I ay bente,
1190 And yerned no more then was me gyven,
     And halden me ther in trwe entent,
     As the perle me prayed that was so thryven,
     As helde, drawen to Goddes present,
     To mo of his mysterys I hade ben dryven.

1170 That impetuous action startled me out of my dream.
1174 I roused myself, and fell into (a state of) great consternation.
1177 It greatly displeased me to be flung out.
1180 A heavy longing overcame me (lit. struck me into a swoon).
1183–7 It was very precious to me, what you spoke of in this true vision.
     If it is a true and correct statement (of your situation) that you are thus
     set in a bright garland, then it is well with me in this dungeon of
     sorrow.
1189–96 Had I always submitted myself to that Prince's pleasure, and
     yearned for no more than was given to me, and held myself in that
     (course) with steadfast purpose, as the pearl that was so lovely had
     urged me, (then) in all likelihood, drawn into God's presence, I would
     have been brought to more of His mysteries. But men always want to

1195 Bot ay wolde man of happe more hente
       Then moghte by ryght upon hem clyven.
       Therfore my joye was sone toriven,   *shattered*
       And I kaste of kythes that lastes aye.
       Lorde, mad hit arn that agayn the   *they are; against you*
            stryven,
1200 Other proferen the oght agayn thy paye.

       To pay the Prince other sete saghte
       Hit is ful ethe to the god Krystyin;   *easy; Christian*
       For I haf founden hym, bothe day and naghte,   *night*
       A God, a Lorde, a frende ful fyin.   *most excellent*
1205 Over this hyul this lote I laghte,
       For pyty of my perle enclyin,
       And sythen to God I hit bytaghte
       In Krystes dere blessyng and myn,   *precious*
       That in the forme of bred and wyn
1210 The preste uus schewes uch a daye.   *every*
       He gef uus to be his homly hyne
       Ande precious perles unto his pay.
                          Amen. Amen.

---

    take hold of more good fortune than is theirs by right (lit. than might
    adhere to them).
1198 And I cast out from lands that endure for ever.
1200–1 Or offer you anything contrary to your pleasure. To please the
    Prince or be reconciled (to Him).
1205–7 Upon this mound I had this experience, lying prostrate out of
    sorrow for my pearl, and then I committed it (i.e. the pearl) to God.
1211–12 May He grant us to be his lowly servants (*and* servants of the
    household), and precious pearls to His liking.

CLEANNESS

I

Clannesse who-so kyndly cowthe comende,
And rekken up alle the resouns that ho by right askes,
Fayre formes myght he fynde in forthering his speche,
And in the contraré kark and combraunce huge.

5 For wonder wroth is the wyy that wroght alle thinges
Wyth the freke that in fylthe folwes hym after,
As renkes of relygioun that reden and   *men; read in church*
   syngen
And aprochen to hys presens, and prestes arn called.

Thay teen unto his temmple and temen to hymselven;
10 Reken with reverence thay rychen his   *suitably; prepare*
   auter;
Thay hondel ther his aune body, and
   usen hit bothe.   *partake of it also*
If thay in clannes be clos, thay cleche gret mede,

Bot if they conterfete crafte and cortaysye wont,   *virtue; lack*
As be honest utwyth and inwith alle fylthes,
15 Then ar thay synful hemself, and sulped altogeder
Bothe God and his gere, and hym to greme cachen.

1–6 He who was able to praise cleanness appropriately, and reckon up
all the justifications that are hers as of right, might expect to find
excellent examples to help him in his discourse, and in doing the
contrary great trouble and difficulty. For the One who made all things
is very angry with the man who serves Him in a state of filth.

9 They go to His temple and attach themselves to Him.

12 If they are full of cleanness, they obtain great reward.

14–16 As to be clean outwardly, and inwardly all filthiness, then they
(themselves) are sinful, and both God and His vessels are utterly defiled,
and they drive Him to anger.

He is so clene in his courte. the kyng that al weldes,   *rules*
And honeste in his housholde, and hagherlych   *fittingly*
  served
With angeles enourled in alle that is clene   *by; steeped in*
20 Bothe withinne and withouten, in wedes ful bryght.

Nif he nere scoymus and skyg and non scathe lovied,
Hit were a mervayl to much, hit moght not falle.
Kryst kydde hit hymself in a carp ones,
Ther as he hevened aght happes and hyght hem her medes.

25 Me mynes on one amonge other, as Mathew   *I remember*
  recordes,
That thus of clannesse uncloses a ful cler speche: *sets forth*
'The hathel clene of his hert hapenes ful fayre,
For he schal loke on oure Lorde with a
  loue chere.'   *humble countenance*

As so says, to that syght seche schal he never
30 That any unclannesse has on, auwhere abowte;
For he that flemus uch fylthe fer fro his hert
May not byde that burre, that hit his body neghe.

Forthy hyy not to heven in hateres totorne,
Ne in the harlates hod and handes   *beggar's hood*
  unwaschen.
35 For what urthly hathel that hygh honour   *earthly; rank*
  haldes
Wolde lyke if a ladde com lytherly attyred,   *badly*

20–4 Both inside and outside, dressed in bright clothes. If He were not
  fastidious and particular and loved no wrong, it would be too great a
  marvel, it might not be. Christ made it clear Himself in a speech once,
  where He exalted eight blessed states and assigned them their rewards.
27 The man clean of heart gains good fortune.
29–33 That is to say that the man who has any uncleanness on him,
  anywhere about him, shall never come to that sight; for He who drives
  all filth far from His heart may not endure the shock of its coming near
  His person. Therefore do not hasten to Heaven in torn clothes.

When he were sette solempnely in a sete ryche,   *seated*
Abof dukes on dece, with dayntys served?   *dais*
Then the harlot with haste helded to the table   *if then; went*
40 With rent cokres at the kne, and his clutte trasches,

And his tabarde totorne, and his totes oute,
Other ani on of alle thyse, he schulde be   *or; one*
   halden utter,   *thrown out*
With mony blame ful bygge, a boffet peraunter,
Hurled to the halle dore and harde theroute schowved,

45 And be forboden that borghe, to bowe thider never,
On payne of enprysonment and puttyng in stokkes;
And thus schal he be schent for his   *punished*
   schrowde feble,   *clothes*
Thagh never in talle ne in tuch he trespas more.

And if unwelcum he were to a worthlych prynce,   *noble*
50 Yet hym is the hyghe kyng harder in heven;   *on him*
As Mathew meles in his masse of that man ryche
That made the mukel mangerye to marie his here dere,

And sende his sonde then to say that thay samne schulde,
And in comly quoyntis to com to his feste: *fine clothes*
55 'For my boles and my bores arn bayted and slayne,
And my fedde foules fatted with sclaght;

40-1 With leggings torn at the knee, and his patched old shoes, and his
   tabard torn, and the toes of his shoes out of shape.
43 With many a sharp rebuke, perhaps a blow.
45 And be forbidden to go to that great house ever again.
48 Though he should never again offend either in general appearance or
   in detail of dress.
51-3 As Matthew speaks in his gospel (read at mass) of that rich man
   who made the great banquet to marry his dear son, and then sent his
   messengers to say that men should assemble.
55-7 For my bulls and my boars are baited (by dogs, to improve the
   flavour of the meat) and killed, and my well-fed fowls are fattened for

My polyle that is penne-fed, and partrykes bothe,
Wyth scheldes of wylde swyn, swanes, and   *shoulders*
  crones,   *cranes*
Al is rotheled and rosted ryght to the sete;
60 Comes cof to my corte, er hit colde worthe.'   *quickly; gets*

When thay knewen his cal that thider com schulde,
Alle excused hem by the skyly he scape by moght.
On hade boght hym a borgh, he sayde by hys trawthe:
'Now turne I theder als tyd the toun to byholde.'

65 Another nayed also and nurned this cawse: *refused; offered*
'I haf yerned and yat yokkes of oxen,   *desired; got*
And for my hywes hem boght, to bowe haf I mester;
To see hem pulle in the plow aproche me byhoves.'   *I must*

'And I haf wedded a wyf,' so wer hym the thryd,   *excused*
70 'Excuse me at the court, I may not com there.'
Thus thay drow hem adrey with daunger uchone,
That non passed to the place, thagh he prayed were.

Thenne the ludych lorde lyked ful ille,
And hade dedayn of that dede – ful dryyly he carpes.
75 He says: 'Now for her owne sorwe thay forsaken habbes;
More to wyte is her wrange then any wylle gentyl.

---

slaughter; my poultry that is fed in a pen, and partridges as well.
59 Everything is broiled and roasted ready for the men to sit down.
61–4 When those who were invited received his summons, each man
excused himself by a pretext which enabled him to escape. One had
bought himself an estate, he said on his honour: 'Now I am going there
at once to see the property.'
67 And because my servants bought them, I need to go.
71–6 Thus each one of them drew back disdainfully, so that none,
though entreated, went to the house. Then the noble lord was much
displeased, and took offence at their behaviour – most gravely he
spoke. He says: 'Now it is to their own sorrow that they have refused;
their wrongdoing is more to be blamed than any gentile wilfulness.'

Thenne gos forth, my gomes, to the grete   *servants*
    streetes,   *roads*
And forsettes on uche a syde the ceté aboute
The wayferande frekes, on fote and on hors,   *people*
80 Bothe burnes and burdes, the better and the   *men; women*
    wers.

Lathes hem alle luflyly to lenge at my fest,
And brynges hem blythly to borghe as barounes   *graciously*
    thay were,
So that my palays platful be pyght al aboute;
Thise other wreches iwysse worthy noght wern.'   *indeed; not*

85 Then thay cayred and com that the cost waked,
Broghten bachleres hem wyth that thay by bonkes metten,
Swyeres that swyftly swyed on blonkes,
And also fele upon fote, of fre and of bonde.

When thay com to the courte, keppte wern thay   *received*
    fayre,
90 Styghtled with the stewarde, stad in the halle,
Ful manerly with marchal mad for to sitte,
As he was dere of degré dressed his seete.

Thenne segges to the soverayn sayden   *servants; lord*
    therafter:
'Lo, lorde, with your leve, at your lege   *sovereign*
    heste   *command*
95 And at thi banne we haf broght, as thou beden habbes,
Mony renischche renkes, and yet is roum   *outlandish men*
    more.'

---

78 And waylay on every side of the city.
81 Invite them all courteously to be present at my feast.
83 So that every part of my palace will be filled to overflowing.
85–8 Then they went to and fro, rousing the countryside, brought young
    knights with them that they met by the way, squires who came swiftly
    on horses, and also many on foot, bondmen and free.
90–2 Looked after by the steward, given a place in the hall, most
    courteously made to sit down by the marshal (the officer in charge of
    the feast), a man's place at table being assigned him according to his
    rank.
95 And by your edict we have brought, as you have asked.

Sayde the lorde to tho ledes: 'Laytes yet ferre,
Ferre out in the felde, and feches mo gestes;
Waytes gorstes and greves, if ani gomes lygges;
100 What kyn folk so ther fare, feches hem hider.

Be thay fers, be thay feble, forlotes none,
Be thay hol, be thay halt, be thay on-yyed,
And thagh thay ben bothe blynde and balterande   *hobbling*
   cruppeles,
That my hous may holly by halkes by fylled.

105 For certes thyse ilk renkes that me renayed habbe,
And denounced me noght now at this tyme,   *honoured*
Schul never sitte in my sale my soper to fele,   *hall; taste*
Ne suppe on sope of my seve, thagh thay swelt schulde.'

Thenne the sergauntes at that sawe swengen theroute,
110 And diden the dede that demed as he devised hade,
And with peple of alle plytes the palays thay fyllen;   *kinds*
Hit weren not alle on wyves sunes, wonen with on fader.

Whether thay wern worthy other wers, wel   *or not so worthy*
   wern thay stowed,   *seated*
Ay the best byfore and bryghtest atyred,   *always; in front*
115 The derrest at the hyghe dese, that dubbed wer fayrest,
And sythen on lenthe biloogh ledes inogh;

97–102 Said the lord to those servants: 'Search still further afield, far out
in the countryside, and bring more guests; search scrublands and
thickets, to see if any men lie hidden; whatever people are there, bring
them to this place. Be they bold, be they timid, overlook none, be they
sound, be they lame, be they one-eyed.'

104–5 So that my house may be filled completely, every corner of it. For
certainly these men who have refused me.

108–10 'Nor swallow one mouthful of my stew, though they should die.'
Then the servants at that command went swiftly outside and performed
the task, making proclamation as he had ordained.

112 They were not all one wife's sons, begotten by one father (i.e. they
were many and varied).

115–17 The nobles, who were best dressed, on the high dais, and then
men in plenty down the hall below; and each man looked dignified in
his dress.

And ay a segge soberly semed by her wedes.
So with marschal at her mete mensked   *by; meal; honoured*
   thay were;
Clene men in compaynye forknowen wern lyte,
120 And yet the symplest in that sale was served to the fulle,

Bothe with menske and with mete and mynstrasy noble,
And alle the laykes that a lorde aght in londe schewe;
And thay bigonne to be glad that god drink haden,
And uch mon with his mach made hym at ese.   *companion*

125 Now inmyddes the mete the mayster hym bithoght   *decided*
That he wolde se the semblé that samned   *assembly; gathered*
   was there,
And rehayte rekenly the riche and the pover,
And cherisch hem alle with his cher, and chaufen her joye.

Then he bowes from his bour into the brode halle,
130 And to the best on the bench, and bede hym be myry,
Solased hem with semblaunt and syled fyrre,
Tron fro table to table and talkede ay myrthe.

Bot as he ferked over the flor he fande with his yye
Hit was, not for a halyday honestly arayed,
135 A thral thryght in the throng, unthryvandely clothed,
Ne no festival frok, bot fyled with werkkes.

119–22 Well-bred men in that company were by no means neglected, and yet the most lowly man in the hall was served unstintingly, with honours and food and excellent minstrelsy, and all the diversions that it was proper for a lord to provide.

127–38 And courteously pay his respects to the rich and the poor, and be hospitable towards them all, and encourage their merrymaking. Then he went from his chamber into the great hall, to the noblest at the table, and bade them be merry, cheered them with his friendliness and passed on, went from table to table always talking pleasantly. But as he moved over the floor he noticed that there was a fellow not properly dressed for a festival, poorly clothed in the midst of the throng; (he wore) no festive garment, but one stained by labours. The

The gome was ungarnyst with god men to dele,
And gremed therwith the grete lorde, and greve hym he
    thoght.
'Say me, frende,' quoth the freke, with a
    felle chere,   *grim countenance*
140 'Hou wan thou into this won in wedes so fowle? *came; house*

The abyt that thou has upon, no halyday   *garment; have on*
    hit menskes;   *honours*
Thou, burne, for no brydale art busked in wedes.
How was thou hardy this hous for thyn unhap neghe,
In on so ratted a robe, and rent at the   *so very ragged a*
    sydes?

145 Thow art a gome ungoderly in that goun febele;   *vile*
Thou praysed me and my place ful pover and ful nede,
That was so prest to aproche my presens hereinne.   *quick*
Hopes thou I be a harlot, thi erigaut to prayse?'

That other burne was abayst of his brothe   *abashed at; angry*
    wordes,
150 And hurkeles doun with his hede, the urthe he   *hangs*
    biholdes;
He was so scoumfit of his scylle, lest he skathe hent,
That he ne wyst on worde what he warp schulde.

Then the lorde wonder loude laled and cryed,   *very; spoke*
And talkes to his tormenttoures: 'Takes hym,' he   *torturers*
    biddes,
155 'Byndes byhynde at his bak bothe two his handes,
And felle fetteres to his fete festenes bylyve;   *at once*

---

man was not suitably dressed for dealing with decent men, and the
great lord was angry on that account, and thought to punish him.
142–3 You, sir, are dressed for no wedding feast. How dared you come
near this house, to your misfortune?
146 You set a very poor and meagre value on me and my house.
148 Do you take me for a beggar, (that you expect me) to admire your
garment?
151–2 He was so scared out of his wits, lest he should come to harm,
that he might not find a single word to say.

Stik hym stifly in stokes, and stekes hym   *securely; confine*
     therafter
Depe in my doungoun ther doel ever dwelles,   *where misery*
Greving and gretyng and gryspyng harde
160 Of tethe tenfully togeder, to teche hym be quoynt.'

Thus comparisunes Kryst the kyndom of heven   *compares*
To this frelych feste that fele arn to called;
For alle arn lathed luflyly, the luther and the better,
That ever wern fulwed in font that fest to have.   *baptised*

165 Bot war the wel, if thou wylt, thy wedes ben clene,   *take care*
And honest for the halyday, lest thou   *suitable*
     harme lache;   *come to*
For aproch thou to that prynce of parage noble,
He hates helle no more then hem that ar sowle.   *filthy*

Wich arn thenne thy wedes thou wrappes the inne,
170 That schal schewe hem so schene, schrowde of the best?
Hit arn thy werkes wyterly that thou wroght haves,
And lyned with the lykyng that lyye in thyn hert,

That tho be frely and fresch fonde in thy lyve,
And fetyse of a fayr forme to fote and to honde,
175 And sythen alle thyn other lymes lapped ful clene;
Thenne may thou se thy Savior and his sete ryche.   *throne*

159–60 Wailing and weeping and bitter gnashing of teeth in anguish, to
     teach him to be well-dressed.
162–3 To this splendid feast to which many are summoned; for all are
     courteously invited, the better and the worse.
167 For should you approach that prince of noble rank.
170–5 That must look so bright, the best of clothes? To be sure they are
     your deeds which you have performed, and (which you have) lined
     with the good disposition of your heart, so that they should be found
     fair and fresh in your life, neat and of attractive appearance for the
     hands and feet, and then all your other parts brightly attired.

For fele fautes may a freke forfete his blysse,   *many*
That he the Soverayn ne se; then for slauthe one,
As for bobaunce and bost and bolnande priyde,
180 Throly into the develes throte man thrynges bylyve;

For covetyse and colwarde and croked dedes,
For monsworne and mensclaght and to much drynk,
For thefte and for threpyng, unthonk may mon have,
For roborrye and riboudrye and resounes untrwe,

185 And dysheriete and depryve dowrie of wydoes,
For marryng of maryages and mayntnaunce of schrewes,
For traysoun and trichcherye and
      tyrauntyre bothe,   *tyranny also*
And for fals famacions and fayned lawes.   *rumours; spurious*

Man may mysse the myrthe that much is   *bliss*
      to prayse   *be prized*
190 For such unthewes as thise, and thole much   *sins; endure*
      payne,
And in the Creatores cort com never more,
Ne never see hym with syght, for such sour   *vile*
      tournes.   *doings*

178–86 So that he does not see the Sovereign; thus for sloth alone, just
as for vanity and boasting and overweening pride, a man at once
hurtles violently into the Devil's throat; for covetousness and villainy
and unjust deeds, for perjury and manslaughter and too much drink,
for theft and for quarrelling, one may incur displeasure, for robbery
and loose living and false statements, and misappropriating and stealing
widows' dowers, for adultery and supporting evildoers.

Bot I have herkned and herde of mony hyghe clerkes,
And als in resounes of ryght red hit myselven,   *true writings*
195 That that ilk proper prynce that Paradys   *excellent*
  weldes,   *rules*
  Is displesed at uch a poynt that plyes to scathe;

Bot never yet in no boke breved I herde
That ever he wrek so wytherly on werk that he made,
Ne venged for no vilté of vice ne synne,
200 Ne so hastyfly was hot for hatel of his wylle,

Ne never so sodenly soght unsoundely to weng,
As for fylthe of the flesch that foles han used;
For, as I fynde, ther he foryet alle his fre thewes,
And wex wod to the wrache for wrath at his hert.

205 For the fyrste felonye the falce fende wroght,   *Devil*
  Whyl he was hyghe in the heven, hoven upon lofte,   *raised up*
  Of alle thyse athel aungeles attled the   *glorious; created*
    fayrest,
  And he unkyndely as a karle kydde a reward.

He sey noght bot hymself, how semly he were,   *saw*
210 Bot his Soverayn he forsoke and sade thyse wordes: *said*
  'I schal telde up my trone in the tramountayne,   *raise; North*
  And by lyke to that Lorde that the lyft made.'   *be; heavens*

---

193 But I have heard from many great scholars.
196–204 Is displeased at everything that has to do with sin; but I have
  not yet found written down in any book that He ever punished His
  creation so fiercely, or exacted retribution (so fiercely) for any abomi-
  nation of vice or sin, or was so precipitately violent for the hatred in
  His mind, or was ever so abruptly concerned to take drastic vengeance,
  as for filth of the flesh that fools have indulged in; for I find that then
  He abandoned all His gracious ways, and became furious for revenge
  on account of the anger in His heart.
208 And he responded as ungratefully as a churl.

With this worde that he warp the wrake on hym lyght;
Dryghtyn with his dere dom hym drof to the abyme.
215 In the mesure of his mode his mes never-the-lasse;
Bot ther he tynt the tythe dool of his tour ryche.

Thagh the feloun were so fers for his fayre wedes,   *proud*
And his glorious glem that glent so bryght,   *radiance; shone*
As sone as Dryghtynes dome drof to hymselven,   *reached him*
220 Thikke thowsandes thro thrwen theroute;

Fellen fro the fyrmament fendes ful blake,   *black*
Sweved at the fyrst swap as the snaw thikke,
Hurled into helle-hole as the hyve swarmes.   *hurtled*
Fylter fenden folk forty dayes lencthe,

225 Er that styngande storme stynt ne myght;
Bot as smylt mele under smal sive smokes for thikke,
So fro heven to helle that hatel schor laste,
On uche syde of the worlde aywhere ilyche.

This hit was a brem brest and a byge wrache;
230 And yet wrathed not the wyy, ne the wrech saghtled,
Ne never wolde for wylnesful his worthy God knawe,
Ne pray hym for no pité, so proud was his wylle.

213–16 With this speech that he uttered the vengeance fell on him; the Lord with His stern judgement drove him to the pit. Nevertheless His blow was in keeping with the moderation of His nature; He struck down on that occasion only the tenth part of His splendid entourage.
220 Teeming thousands were violently flung out.
222 Fell at the first blow like thick snow.
224–31 The fiendish creatures tumbled for the space of forty days, before that venomous storm was allowed to cease; but as refined meal smokes thickly under a fine sieve, so that hateful shower reached from Heaven to Hell, everywhere the same on all sides of the universe. This was a fearful calamity and a mighty vengeance; and yet the man (i.e. God) did not become angry, nor did the wretch make his peace, or ever wish to acknowledge his glorious God, on account of his wilfulness.

Forthy thagh the rape were rank, the rawthe was lyttel;
Thagh he be kest into kare, he kepes no better.
235 Bot that other wrake that wex, on wyyes hit lyght,
Thurgh the faut of a freke that fayled in trawthe,   *loyalty*

Adam inobedyent, ordaynt to blysse,   *appointed*
Ther pryvely in Paradys his place was   *apart*
    devised,   *ordained*
To lyve ther in lykyng the lenthe of a   *in pleasure for a while*
    terme,
240 And thenne enherite that home that aungeles
    forgart.   *forfeited*

Bot thurgh the eggyng of Eve he ete of an apple   *urging*
That enpoysened alle peples that parted fro hem   *descended*
    bothe,
For a defence that was dyght of Dryghtyn selven,
And a payne theron put and pertly halden.

245 The defence was the fryt that the freke towched,   *fruit*
And the dom is the dethe that drepes uus alle;   *strikes down*
Al in mesure and methe was mad the vengiaunce,
And efte amended with a mayden that make had never.

Bot in the thryd was forthrast al that thryve schuld;
250 Ther was malys mercyles and mawgré much scheued.
That was for fylthe upon folde that the   *earth*
    folk used   *indulged in*
That then wonyed in the worlde withouten any   *lived*
    maysters.

233–5 And so though the fall was great, the remorse was small; though
    he is thrown into misfortune, he looks for nothing better. But the
    second vengeance that took place fell on men.
243–4 On account of a prohibition that was ordained by the Lord
    Himself, and a penalty put on it and manifestly kept to.
247–50 The vengeance was taken in all measure and moderation, and
    afterwards mitigated by a maiden who was without peer. But in the
    third (vengeance), everything that had life was destroyed; there merci-
    less anger and great hostility were displayed.

Hit wern the fayrest of forme and of face als,   *they were*
The most and the myriest that   *mightiest; most excellent*
    maked wern ever,
255 The styfest, the stalworthest that stod ever on fete,   *strongest*
And lengest lyf in hem lent of ledes alle other.

For hit was the forme foster that the folde bred,
The athel aunceteres sunes that Adam was called,
To wham God hade geven alle that gayn were,   *good*
260 Alle the blysse boute blame that bodi   *blameless; a man*
    myght have.

And those lykkest to the lede that lyved next after;
Forthy so semly to see sythen wern none.
Ther was no law to hem layd bot loke to kynde,
And kepe to hit and alle hit cors clanly fulfylle.

265 And thenne founden thay fylthe in fleschlych dedes,   *but*
And controeved agayn kynde contraré werkes,
And used hem unthryftyly uchon on other,
And als with other, wylsfully, upon a wrange wyse.

So ferly fowled her flesch that the fende loked
270 How the deghter of the douthe wern derelych fayre,
And fallen in felawschyp with hem on folken wyse,
And engendered on hem jeauntes with her   *giants; tricks*
    japes ille.   *vile*

256–8 And (they were) the most long-lived of all men. For they were the
first offspring that the earth bred, sons of the noble forefather named
Adam.

261–4 And those who lived immediately after him (Adam) were most
like him; and so there were none afterwards so seemly to look upon.
There was no law imposed on them except to pay heed to nature, and
keep to it and perform its functions in a clean manner.

266–71 And contrived immoral acts against nature, and practised them
wantonly one on another, and also with other creatures, wilfully, in a
perverted way. So thoroughly was their flesh defiled that the devils saw
the daughters of men as exceedingly beautiful, and coupled with them
in human fashion.

Those wern men metheles and maghty on   *violent; mighty*
   urthe,
That for her lodlych laykes alosed thay were;
275 He was famed for fre that feght loved best,
And ay the bigest in bale the best was halden.

And thenne eveles on erthe ernestly grewen,   *in earnest*
And multyplyed monyfolde inmonges   *many times*
   mankynde,
For that the maghty on molde so marre thise other
280 That the wyye that all wroght ful wrothly bygynnes.

When he knew uche contré coruppte in hitselven,   *country*
And uch freke forloyned fro the ryght wayes,   *gone astray*
Felle temptande tene towched his   *fierce distressing anger*
   hert;
As wyye wo hym withinne werp to hymselven:

285 'Me forthynkes ful much that ever I mon made;   *I repent*
Bot I schal delyver and do away that doten on this molde,
And fleme out of the folde al that flesch weres,
Fro the burne to the best, fro bryddes to fysches.   *man; beast*

Al schal doun and be ded and dryven out of erthe
290 That ever I sette saule inne, and sore hit me   *I regret deeply*
   rwes
That ever I made hem myself; bot if I may herafter,
I schal wayte to be war her wrenches to kepe.'

274-6 Who were renowned for their hateful practices; he who best
   loved strife was reputed good, and always the man most prominent in
   evil-doing was reckoned the best.
279-80 Inasmuch as the mighty ones on the earth so corrupt the others
   that the One who created all things begins to speak most angrily.
284 As one anguished inwardly He said to Himself.
286-7 But I shall purge and do away with those who act senselessly on
   this earth, and banish from the world everything that has flesh.
292 I shall try to be careful to observe their tricks.

Thenne in worlde was a wyye wonyande on lyve,   *living*
Ful redy and ful ryghtwys, and rewled hym fayre;
295 In the drede of Dryghtyn his dayes he uses,   *fear; passes*
And ay glydande wyth his God his grace was the more.

Hym was the name Noe, as is innogh knawen;   *his name was*
He had thre thryven sunes, and thay thre wyves;   *grown*
Sem sothly that on, that other hyght Cam,
300 And the jolef Japheth was gendered the thryd.

Now God in nwy to Noe con speke
Wylde wrakful wordes, in his wylle greved:
'The ende of alle kynes flesch that on urthe meves
Is fallen forthwyth my face, and forther hit I thenk.

305 With her unworthelych werk me wlates withinne;
The gore therof me has greved and the glette nwyed;
I schal strenkle my distresse and strye al togeder,
Bothe ledes and londe and alle that lyf habbes.

Bot make to the a mancioun, and that is my wylle,
310 A cofer closed of tres clanlych planed;
Wyrk wones therinne for wylde   *rooms; wild animals*
    and for tame,
And thenne cleme hit with clay comly withinne,   *caulk; well*

---

294 Most zealous and righteous, and he conducted himself properly.
296 And his grace (received from God) was the greater in that he was
    always walking with his God.
299–310 The first indeed was Shem, the second was called Ham, and the
    third-born was the worthy Japheth. Now God in fury spoke wild
    vengeful words to Noah, His mind full of anger: 'The end of creatures
    of all kinds that move on the earth has come before me, and I intend to
    hasten it. In my heart I am disgusted with their shameful behaviour;
    the vileness of it has angered me and the filth has distressed me. I shall
    put forth my power and destroy all at once, both people and land and
    everything that has life. But make a house for yourself, and that is my
    will, a closed-in Ark of smoothly-planed boards.'

And alle the endentur dryven daube withouten.
And thus of lenthe and of large that lome   *breadth; vessel*
  thou make:
315 Thre hundred of cupydes thou holde to the   *cubits; allow*
  lenthe,
Of fyfty fayre overthwert forme the brede,

And loke even that thyn ark have of heghthe thretté,
And a wyndow wyd uponande wroght upon lofte,
In the compas of a cubit kyndely sware,
320 A wel dutande dor don on the syde.

Haf halles therinne and halkes ful   *large rooms; cubicles*
  mony,
Bothe boskes and boures and wel bounden penes;
For I schal waken up a water to wasch alle the   *deluge*
  worlde,
And quelle alle that is quik with quavende flodes.

325 Alle that glydes and gos and gost of lyf habbes,
I schal wast with my wrath, that wons upon urthe;
Bot my forwarde with the I festen on this wyse,
For thou in reysoun has rengned and ryghtwys ben ever:

Thou schal enter this ark with thyn athel barnes,   *fine sons*
330 And thy wedded wyf with the thou take,
The makes of thy myry sunes – this meyny of aghte
I schal save of monnes saules, and swelt those other.

---

313 And daub on the outside all the riveted jointing.
316–20 Make the width exactly fifty (cubits) across, and see to it that
   your Ark has a height of exactly thirty, with a window that opens wide
   constructed above, exactly a cubit square, (and) a properly-closing
   door made in the side.
322 Cow-houses and stalls and well-secured pens.
324–8 And kill all live things with surging floods. I shall destroy in my
   anger everything that lives on the earth, that walks and moves and has
   the breath of life; but I shall make my agreement with you as follows,
   because you have lived by reason and have always been righteous.
331–2 (And) the wives of your worthy sons – this company of eight I
   shall save from amongst mankind, and destroy the rest.

Of uche best that beres lyf busk the a cupple;   *has; take*
Of uche clene comly kynde enclose seven makes,
335 Of uche horwed in ark halde bot a payre,   *unclean*
For to save me the sede of alle ser kyndes;   *various*

And ay thou meng with the males the mete ho-bestes,
Uche payre by payre, to plese ayther other.   *each other*
With alle the fode that may be founde frette thy cofer,   *stock*
340 For sustnaunce to yowself and also those other.'

Ful graythely gos this god-man and dos Godes   *promptly*
   hestes,   *commands*
In dryy dred and daunger, that durst do non other.
Wen hit was fettled and forged and to the fulle graythed,
Thenn con Dryghttyn hym dele dryyly thyse wordes:

345 'Now, Noe,' quoth oure Lorde, 'art thou al redy?
Hast thou closed thy kyst with clay alle   *caulked; Ark*
   aboute?'
'Ye, Lorde, with thy leve,' sayde the lede thenne,   *man*
'Al is wroght at thi worde, as thou me wyt   *gave me skill*
   lantes.'

'Enter in thenn,' quoth he, 'and haf thi wyf with the,
350 Thy thre sunes withouten threp, and her thre   *question*
   wyves;
Bestes, as I bedene have, bosk therinne   *commanded; drive*
   als,
And when ye arn staued styfly, stekes yow therinne.

---

334 Take in seven of each clean seemly species.
337 And always put in with the males the appropriate she-animals.
342–4 In great fear and awe, not daring to do otherwise. When it was prepared and built and quite made ready, then the Lord gravely spoke these words to him.
352–5 And when you are securely housed, shut yourselves up in it. After

Fro seven dayes ben seyed I sende out bylyve
Such a rowtande ryge that rayne schal swythe,
355 That schal wasch alle the worlde of werkes of fylthe;
Schal no flesch upon folde by fonden on lyve, *be found*

Outtaken yow aght in this ark staued, *except for*
And sed that I wyl save of thyse ser bestes.' *seed; various*
Now Noe never styntes – that niyght he bygynnes – *pauses*
360 Er al wer stawed and stoken as the steven wolde.

Thenne sone com the seventhe day, when samned wern alle,
And alle woned in the whichche, the wylde and the tame.
Then bolned the abyme and bonkes con ryse;
Waltes out uch walle-heved in ful wode stremes.

365 Was no brymme that abod unbrosten bylyve;
The mukel lavande logh to the lyfte rered.
Mony clustered clowde clef alle in clowtes,
Torent uch a rayn ryfte and rusched to the urthe,

Fon never in forty dayes, and then the flod ryses, *stopped*
370 Overwaltes uche a wod and the wyde *rolls over; wood*
feldes;
For when the water of the welkyn with the worlde *sky*
mette,
Alle that deth moght dryye *who were subject to death*
drowned therinne.

---

seven days have passed I shall send out straightway a most violent
storm, with heavy rain, that will cleanse all the world of deeds of filth.
360–8 Until all were housed and confined as the command required.
Then quickly came the seventh day, by which time all were assembled,
and all dwelt in the Ark, wild animals and tame. Then the depths of
the earth swelled and the land rose up; each spring gushed out in raging
streams. Soon there was no bank that remained unbroken; the great
surging flood rose to the sky. Many a massed cloud split into shreds,
every cataract burst open and poured to the earth.

Ther was moon for to make when meschef was cnowen,
That noght dowed bot the deth in the depe stremes.
375 Water wylger ay wax, wones that stryede,
Hurled into uch hous, hent that ther dowelled.

Fyrst feng to the flyght alle that fle myght;
Uuche burde with her barne the byggyng thay leves
And bowed to the hygh bonk ther brentest hit wern,
380 And heterly to the hyghe hylles thay aled on faste.

Bot al was nedles her note, for never cowthe stynt
The roghe raynande ryg, the raykande wawes,
Er uch bothom was brurdful to the bonkes egges,
And uche a dale so depe that demmed at the brynkes.

385 The moste mountaynes on mor thenne were no more dryye,
And theron flokked the folke for ferde of the wrake.
Sythen the wylde of the wode on the water flette;
Summe swymmed theron that save hemself
trawed,   *thought to*

Summe styye to a stud and stared to the   *climbed; high place*
heven,
390 Rwly wyth a loud rurd rored for drede;   *pitifully; noise*
Hares, herttes also, to the hyghe runnen,   *harts; high ground*
Bukkes, bausenes, and bules to the bonkkes   *badgers; bulls*
hyyed,   *hurried*

373–87 There was lamentation to be made when the worst was known,
that nothing had power but death in the deep streams. The water grew
ever wilder, destroying dwellings, rushed into each house, seized those
who lived there. First all who were able to flee took to flight; each
woman with her child left her home and went to the high slopes where
they were steepest, hurried on with all speed to the high hills. But all
their effort was useless, for the furious rainstorm, the advancing waves
showed no signs of abating till each valley was brimful to the tops of
its slopes, and all the deepest dales were overflowing at the brink. The
greatest mountains on earth were then no longer secure, but the people
flocked onto them for fear of the vengeance. Then the wild creatures of
the wood floated on the water.

And alle cryed for care to the kyng of heven;   *distress*
Recoverer of the Creator thay cryed uchone.   *relief; cried for*
395 That amounted the mase, his mercy was   *was pointless*
    passed,
And alle his pyté departed fro peple that he hated.

Bi that the flod to her fete flowed and waxed,
Then uche a segge sey wel that synk hym byhoved;
Frendes fellen in fere and fathmed togeder,
400 To dryy her delful deystyné and dyyen alle samen;

Luf lokes to luf, and his leve takes,   *lover*
For to ende alle at ones and for ever twynne.   *part*
By forty dayes wern faren, on folde no flesch styryed
That the flod nade al freten with feghtande wawes;

405 For hit clam uche a clyffe cubites fyftene,   *climbed up*
Over the hyghest hylle that hurkled on erthe.   *stood*
Thenne mourkne in the mudde most ful nede   *rot; must needs*
Alle that spyrakle inspranc – no sprawlyng awayled –

Save the hathel under hach and his here straunge,
410 Noe that ofte nevened the name of oure Lorde,   *called on*
Hym aghtsum in that ark, as athel God lyked,
Ther alle ledes in lome lenged druye.

The arc hoven was on hyghe with hurlande gotes,
Kest to kythes uncouthe the clowdes ful nere;
415 Hit waltered on the wylde flod, went as hit   *rolled*
    lyste,   *pleased*
Drof upon the depe dam – in daunger hit   *drove over; sea*
    semed,

397–400 When the flood ran and rose to their feet, then each man saw clearly that he must sink; friends came together and embraced each other, to meet their wretched fate and die all together.

403–4 By the time that forty days had passed, no creature stirred on the earth that the flood had not devoured with turbulent waves.

408–9 Everything in which sprang the breath of life – no death-throes availed – except for the man on shipboard and his strange household.

411–14 Him and seven others in that Ark, as glorious God desired, there in that vessel where all men remained dry. The Ark was raised on high by surging swells, hurled to unknown regions close to the clouds.

Withouten mast other myke other myry bawelyne,
Kable other capstan to clyppe to her ankres,   *attach*
Hurrok, other hande-helme hasped on rother,
420 Other any sweande sayl to seche after haven.

Bot flote forthe with the flyt of the felle   *it drifted; brawling*
    wyndes;
Whederwarde-so the water wafte, hit   *wherever; surged*
    rebounde.
Ofte hit roled on rounde and rered on ende;   *spun about*
Nyf oure Lorde hade ben her lodesmon, hem had lumpen
    harde.

425 Of the lenthe of Noe lyf to lay a lel date:
The sex hundreth of his age and none odde yeres,
Of secounde monyth the seventethe day ryghtes,
Towalten alle thyse welle-hedes and the water   *burst out*
    flowed,

And thryes fyfty the flod of folwande dayes.
430 Uche hille was ther hidde with ythes ful graye;   *waves*
Al was wasted that ther wonyed the worlde withinne,
Ther ever flote, other flwe, other on fote yede.

That roghly was the remnaunt that the rac dryves,
That alle gendres so joyst wern joyned wythinne.
435 Bot quen the Lorde of the lyfte lyked   *heavens; was pleased*
    hymselven
For to mynne on his mon his meth that abydes,

---

417 Without mast or crutch (for mast when lowered) or goodly bowline.
419-20 Rudder-band, or tiller fastened to the rudder, or any speeding
    sail with which to seek out harbour.
424-7 If our Lord had not been their steersman, they would have fared
    badly. To assign an exact date (for the beginning of the Flood) in terms
    of Noah's age: (in) the six hundredth year of his age, with none left
    over, (on) precisely the seventeenth day of the second month.
429 And the flood (flowed) for the next one hundred and fifty days.
431-4 Everything was destroyed that lived there in the world, (that) ever
    swam there, or flew, or went on foot. All that remained was that
    troubled vessel that the storm drove, in which all species were so tightly
    packed.
436 To remember His servant who hopes for His mercy.

Then he wakened a wynde on watteres to blowe;   *raised*
Thenne lasned the llak that large was are;
Then he stac up the stanges, stoped the welles,
440 Bed blynne of the rayn – hit batede as fast.

Thenne lasned the logh, lowkande   *flood; contracting*
    togeder,
After harde dayes wern out an hundreth and fyfté.   *over*
As that lyftande lome luged aboute
445 Where the wynde and the weder warpen hit wolde,

Hit saghtled on a softe day, synkande to   *settled; pleasant*
    grounde;
On a rasse of a rok hit rest at the laste,   *crevice*
On the mounte of Ararach, of Armene hilles,   *Armenian*
That otherwayes on Ebru hit hat the Thanes.

Bot thagh the kyste in the crages were closed to byde,
450 Yet fyned not the flod, ne fel to the bothemes;   *ended*
Bot the hyghest of the egges unhuled wern   *edges; uncovered*
    a lyttel,
That the burne bynne borde byhelde the bare   *man on board*
    erthe.

Thenne wafte he upon his wyndowe and wysed theroute
A message fro that meyny, hem moldes to seche.
455 That was the raven so ronk, that rebel was ever;   *wilful*
He was colored as the cole, corbyal untrwe.   *raven*

438–40 Then the flood, that was immense before, subsided; then He
    closed the cataracts, stopped up the wells, ordered the rain to cease – it
    abated instantly.
443–4 As that heaving vessel lurched about wherever the wind and the
    weather would drive it.
448–9 Which alternatively, in Hebrew, is called Thanes. But though the
    Ark was lodged in the crags.
453–4 Then he swung open his window and sent out a messenger from
    that company, to look for land for them.

And he fonges to the flyght and fannes on the wyndes,
Hales hyghe upon hyght to herken tythynges;
He croukes for comfort when carayne he fyndes,   *carrion*
460 Kast up on a clyffe ther costes lay drye.   *land*

He hade the smelle of the smach and   *stench*
    smoltes theder sone,   *goes there at once*
Falles on the foule flesch and fylles his wombe,
And sone yederly foryete yisterday steven,
How the chevetayn hym charged that the kyst yemed.

465 The raven raykes hym forth that reches ful lyttel
How alle fodes ther fare, elles he fynde mete;
Bot the burne bynne borde, that bod to hys come,   *awaited*
Banned hym ful bytterly, with bestes alle   *cursed*
    samen.   *together*

He seches another sondesmon and settes   *messenger; chooses*
    on the dove,
470 Brynges that bryght upon borde, blessed, and   *fair one; deck*
    sayde:
'Wende, worthelych wyght, uus wones to seche.
Dryf over this dymme water; if thou druye fyndes,

Bryng bodworde to bot, blysse to uus alle.   *message; boat*
Thagh that fowle be false, fre be thou ever.'   *bird; true*
475 Ho wyrles out on the weder on wynges ful scharpe,
Dreyly alle alonge day that dorst never lyght.

457-8 And he takes flight and glides on the winds, soars to a great height
    to survey the scene.
463-6 And soon entirely forgot the command of a short time before,
    how the lord who ruled the Ark had enjoined him. Off goes the raven,
    caring little how all the creatures there get on, so long as he might find
    food.
471-2 Go, noble creature, to look for a place for us to live. Press on over
    this dark water; if you should find dry land.
475-6 She flies out into the sky on swift wings, on and on all through
    the day, never daring to alight.

And when ho fyndes no folde her fote on to pyche,   *land; set*
Ho umbekestes the coste and the kyst seches.   *circles; region*
Ho hittes on the eventyde and on the ark sittes;   *finds it*
480 Noe nymmes hir anon and naytly hir staues.

Noe on another day nymmes efte the dove,   *again*
And byddes hir bowe over the borne efte bonkes to seche;
And ho skyrmes under skwe and skowtes aboute
Tyl hit was nyghe at the naght, and Noe then seches.

485 On ark on an eventyde hoves the dowve;   *alights*
On stamyn ho stod and stylle hym abydes.
What! ho broght in hir beke a bronch of olyve,   *look!*
Gracyously umbegrouen al with grene   *attractively covered*
leves.

That was the syngne of savyté that sende hem oure   *salvation*
Lorde,
490 And the saghtlyng of hymself with tho   *reconciliation*
sely bestes.   *innocent*
Then was ther joy in that gyn, where jumpred er dryyed,
And much comfort in that cofer that was clay-daubed.   *Ark*

Myryly on a fayr morn, monyth the fyrst,
That falles formast in the yer, and the fyrst day,
495 Ledes loghen in that lome, and loked theroute
How that watteres wern woned and the worlde dryed.

---

480 Noah takes her at once and lodges her well.
482–4 And bids her go over the water to look for land again; and she
moves swiftly about in the sky and scouts around until it is almost
nightfall, and then she seeks out Noah.
486 She perched on the prow and quietly waited for him.
491 Then there was joy in that vessel, where the motley company had
suffered before.
493–6 On a fair morning, the first day of the first month of the year,
men laughed happily in that vessel, and saw how outside the waters
were diminished and the world was made dry.

Uchon loved oure Lorde, bot lenged ay   *praised; remained*
   stylle,
Tyl thay had tythyng fro the tolke that tyned hem therinne.
Then Godes glam to hem glod that gladed hem alle,
500 Bede hem drawe to the dor, delyver hem he wolde.   *bade; go*

Then went thay to the wykket, hit walt upon sone;
Bothe the burne and his barnes bowed theroute;
Her wyves walkes hem wyth, and the wylde after,   *animals*
Throly thrublande in thronge, throwen ful thykke.

505 Bot Noe of uche honest kynde nem out an odde,
And hevened up an auter and halwed hit fayre,
And sette a sakerfyse theron of uch a ser kynde   *different*
That was comly and clene – God kepes   *seemly; recognises*
   non other.

When bremly brened those bestes and the brethe rysed,
510 The savour of his sacrafyse soght to hym even
That al spedes and spylles; he spekes with that ilke,
In comly comfort ful clos and cortays wordes:

'Now, Noe, no more nel I never wary   *will not; curse*
Alle the mukel mayny-molde for no mannes   *great world*
   synnes;
515 For I se wel that hit is sothe that alle segges   *true; men's*
   wyttes
To unthryfte arn alle thrawen with thoght of   *folly; turned*
   her herttes,

498–9 Until they had word from the One who had confined them there.
  Then God's speech came to them, cheering them all.
501–2 Then they went to the door, it swung open at once; the man and
  his children went outside.
504–6 Impatiently jostling in a throng, pressed together tightly. But
  Noah picked out (a single) one of each clean species, and raised up an
  altar and consecrated it properly.
509–12 When those beasts were burning vigorously and the smoke rose,
  the smell of His sacrifice went right up to the One who makes and mars
  everything; He speaks with that man, full of seemly cheer and courteous
  words.

And ay has ben and wyl be yet fro her barnage;   *childhood*
Al is the mynde of the man to malyce enclyned.   *evil*
Forthy schal I never schende so schortly at ones
520 As dysstrye al for manes synne, dayes of this erthe.

Bot waxes now and wendes forth and worthes to monye;
Multyplyes on this molde, and menske yow bytyde.
Sesounes schal yow never sese of sede ne of hervest,
Ne hete ne no harde forst, umbre ne droghthe,

525 Ne the swetnesse of somer, ne the sadde wynter,   *dismal*
Ne the nyght, ne the day, ne the newe yeres,   *succeeding*
Bot ever renne restles – rengnes ye therinne.'
Therwyth he blesses uch a best and bytaght hem this   *gave*
      erthe.

Then was a skylly skyvalde, quen scaped alle the wylde;
530 Uche fowle to the flyght that fytheres myght serve,   *wings*
Uche fysch to the flod that fynne couthe nayte,   *water; use*
Uche beste to the bent that bytes on erbes.   *field; grass*

Wylde wormes to her won wrythes in the erthe,
The fox and the folmarde to the fryth wyndes,
535 Herttes to hyghe hethe, hares to gorstes,   *scrublands*
And lyounes and lebardes to the   *leopards*
      lake ryftes.   *river-valleys*

519–24 Therefore I shall never, on account of man's sin, punish so
   decisively as to destroy all at once, for as long as the earth shall last.
   But prosper now and go forth and increase in numbers; multiply on the
   earth, and may grace befall you. Seasons of seed-time and of harvest
   shall never cease for you, neither heat nor hard frost, dull weather nor
   drought.
527 But they shall run ever-changing – hold sway therein (i.e. on earth).
529 Then there was a clear splitting-up, when all the animals escaped.
533–4 Wild snakes slither to their dwelling in the earth, the fox and the
   polecat go to the wood.

Hernes and havekes to the hyghe   *eagles; hawks*
   roches,   *crags*
The hole-foted fowle to the flod hyyes,   *web-footed; hastens*
And uche best at a brayde ther hym best lykes;
540 The fowre frekes of the folde fonges the empyre.

Lo, suche a wrakful wo, for wlatsum dedes,
Parformed the hyghe Fader on folke that he made;   *inflicted*
That he chysly hade cherisched he chastysed ful hardee,
In devoydynge the vylanye that venkquyst his thewes.

545 Forthy war the now, wyye, that worschyp desyres
In his comlych courte that kyng is of blysse,   *seemly*
In the fylthe of the flesch that thou be founden never,
Tyl any water in the worlde to wasche the fayly.

For is no segge under sunne so seme of his craftes,
550 If he be sulped in synne that syttes unclene,
On spec of a spote may spede to mysse
Of the syghte of the Soverayn that syttes so hyghe.

For that schewe me schale in tho schyre howses
As the beryl bornyst byhoves be clene,
555 That is sounde on uche a syde and no sem habes,
Withouten maskle other mote, as margerye-perle.

539–41 And each animal (hastens) forthwith to where it pleases him best; the four men assume the rule of the earth. Look, such a bitter misfortune, on account of loathsome deeds.

543–5 Those whom He had lovingly cherished He chastised most severely, in purging the evil that had overcome His good nature. Therefore take care now, sir, you who desire honour.

548–56 To the extent that any water in the world should fail to cleanse you. For there is no man under the sun so seemly in his manners (but that) if he is polluted by sin that remains uncleansed, one speck of a spot may be enough to (make him) forfeit the sight of the Sovereign who sits so high. For he who will make an appearance in those bright houses must be as clean as the burnished beryl, which is perfect everywhere and has no seam, without spot or blemish, like the pearl.

II

Sythen the Soverayn in sete so sore forthoght
That ever he man upon molde merked to lyvy.   *gave life to*
For he in fylthe was fallen, felly he venged,   *because; fiercely*
560 Quen fourferde alle the flesch that he formed hade.   *perished*

Hym rwed that he hem uprerde and raght hem lyflode,
And efte that he hem undyd, hard hit hym thoght;
For quen the swemande sorwe soght to his   *painful; touched*
   hert,
He knyt a covenaunde cortaysly with   *made; graciously*
   monkynde there,

565 In the mesure of his mode and methe of his wylle,
That he schulde never for no syt smyte al at ones,   *evil*
As to quelle alle quykes, for qued that myght falle,
Whyl of the lenthe of the londe lastes the terme.

That ilke skyl for no scathe ascaped hym never;
570 Wheder wonderly he wrak on wykked men after,
Ful felly for that ilk faute forferde a kyth ryche,
In the anger of his ire that arwed mony.   *terrified*

And al was for this ilk evel, that unhappen   *accursed*
   glette,   *sin*
The venym and the vylanye and the vycios fylthe
575 That bysulpes mannes saule in unsounde hert,   *defiles*
That he his Saveour ne see with syght of his yyen.   *eyes*

---

557 Then the Sovereign on His throne repented very deeply.
561-2 He regretted that He had raised them up and given them sustenance, but afterwards it seemed to Him hard that He had destroyed them.
565 In the moderation of His nature and the mildness of His heart.
567-71 So as to kill all living things, whatever mischief occurred, for as long as the world lasted. That purpose never left Him, not for any sin; yet afterwards He punished wicked men exceedingly, fiercely destroyed a mighty people for that same offence.

Thus alle illes he hates as helle that stynkkes;   *evils*
Bot non nuyes hym, on naght ne never upon dayes,
As harlottrye unhonest, hethyng of selven;
580 That schames for no schrewedschyp, schent mot he worthe!

Bot savour, mon, in thyself, thagh thou a   *consider*
    sotte lyvie,   *idiot*
Thagh thou bere thyself babel, bythenk the sumtyme
Whether he that stykked uche a stare in uche steppe yye,
Yif hymself be bore blynde, hit is a brod wonder,

585 And he that fetly in face fettled alle eres,   *skilfully; fixed*
If he has losed the lysten, hit lyftes mervayle;
Traue thou never that tale, untrwe thou hit fyndes.   *believe*
Ther is no dede so derne that dittes his yyen;

Ther is no wyye in his werk so war ne so stylle
590 That hit ne thrawes to hym thro er he hit thoght have;
For he is the gropande God, the grounde of alle   *searching*
    dedes,
Rypande of uche a ring the reynyes and hert.

And there he fyndes al fayre a freke wythinne,   *where*
That hert honest and hol, that hathel he   *whole; man*
    honoures,
595 Sendes hym a sad syght, to se his auen face,   *solemn; own*
And harde honyses thise other and of his erde flemes.

578–80 But none angers Him, neither by night nor by day, so much as
    unclean lewdness, contempt for one's person; he who is ashamed of no
    depravity, let him be destroyed!
582–4 Though you behave foolishly, take thought for once that if He
    who put the power of sight in each bright eye should Himself be born
    blind, that would be a great wonder.
586 If He has lost the power of hearing, that would be a marvellous
    thing.
588–90 There is no deed so hidden that He is prevented from seeing it
    (lit. that closes His eyes); there is no man so careful or secretive in what
    he does but that it flies to Him swiftly before he has so much as thought
    of it.
592 Probing the reins and heart (i.e. innermost being) of every man.
596–9 And harshly spurns the rest and drives them from His dwelling.

Bot of the dome of the douthe for dedes of schame,
He is so skoymos of that skathe he scarres bylyve;
He may not dryye to draw allyt bot drepes in hast,
600 And that was schewed schortly by a scathe ones.   *disaster*

Olde Abraham in erde ones he syttes,   *at home*
Even byfore his hous dore, under an oke grene.   *directly*
Bryght blykked the bem of the brode   *shone; sun's rays*
    heven;
In the hyghe hete therof Abraham bides.   *intense; sits*

605 He was schunt to the schadow under schyre leves;
Thenne was he war on the waye of wlonk wyyes thrynne;
If thay wer farande and fre and fayre to   *handsome; noble*
    beholde,
Hit is ethe to leve by the last ende.

For the lede that ther laye the leves anunder,   *man*
610 When he hade of hem syght he hyyes bylyve,   *hastens*
And as to God the good-mon gos hem agaynes,   *towards*
And haylsed hem in onhede, and sayde: 'Hende Lorde,

Yif ever thy mon upon molde merit disserved,   *reward*
Lenge a lyttel with thy lede, I lowly biseche;
615 Passe never fro thi povere, yif I hit pray durst,
Er thou haf biden with thi burne and under boghe restted.

But concerning the punishment of men for deeds of shame, He is so
revolted by that sin that He takes alarm at once; He cannot bear to
hold back but kills in haste.
605-6 He had retreated to the shade under the bright leaves. Then he
became aware of three lordly men on the road.
608 It is easy to conclude from the sequel.
612 And greeted them as one, and said: 'Gracious Lord.'
614-16 Stay for a little with your servant, I humbly beseech; do not
leave your lowly one, if I dare entreat it, until you have sat with your
servant and rested under the boughs.

And I schal wynne yow wyght of water a   *bring; quickly*
   lyttel,
And fast aboute schal I fare your fette wer waschene;
Resttes here on this rote and I schal rachche   *root; go to get*
   after
620 And brynge a morsel of bred to baume your hertte.'   *cheer*

'Fare forthe,' quoth the frekes, 'and fech as thou segges;
By bole of this brode tre we byde the here.'
Thenne orppedly into his hous he hyyed to   *quickly*
   Sare,   *Sarah*
Comaunded hir to be cof and quyk   *prompt*
   at this ones: *for this once*

625 'Thre mettes of mele menge, and ma kakes;
Under askes ful hote happe hem bylive;
Quyl I fete sumquat fat, thou the fyr bete,
Prestly, at this ilke poynte, sum polment to make.'

He cached to his couhous and a calf brynges   *went*
630 That was tender and not toghe, bed tyrve of the hyde,
And sayde to his servaunt that he hit sethe faste;   *cook*
And he dervely at his dome dyght hit bylyve.

The burne to be bare-heved buskes hym thenne,
Cleches to a clene clothe and kestes on the grene,
635 Thrwe thryftyly theron tho thre therve-kakes,
And brynges butter wythal and by the bred settes.   *sets it*

---

618 And I shall busy myself to wash your feet.
621–2 'Go forth,' said the men, 'and fetch them as you say; we shall wait
    for you here by the trunk of this great tree.'
625–8 Mix three measures of meal, and make loaves; cover them quickly
    under hot ashes; while I fetch something (i.e. an animal) which has
    been fattened (for the table), you kindle the fire promptly, now at this
    very moment, to make a stew.
630 Ordered the hide to be stripped off.
632–5 And at his bidding he prepared it at once with all speed. The man
    then hastens to be bare-headed, takes up a clean cloth and throws it on
    the grass, swiftly and with propriety places the three unleavened loaves
    on it.

Mete messes of mylke he merkkes bytwene,
Sythen potage and polment in plater honest;
As sewer in a gud assyse he served hem fayre,
640 Wyth sadde semblaunt and swete, of such as he hade.

And God as a glad gest mad god chere,
That was fayn of his frende and his fest   *pleased with*
    praysed;
Abraham, al hodles, with armes
    upfolden,   *uplifted (in prayer)*
Mynystred mete byfore tho men that myghtes al weldes.

645 Thenne thay sayden as thay sete samen alle   *together*
    thrynne,   *three*
When the mete was remued and thay of
    mensk speken: *made polite conversation*
'I schal efte hereaway, Abram,' thay sayden,   *again come here*
'Yet er thy lyves lyght lethe upon erthe;   *is extinguished*

And thenne schal Sare consayve and a sun bere,
650 That schal be Abrahames ayre, and after hym   *heir*
    wynne   *beget*
With wele and wyth worschyp the worthely peple
That schal halde in heritage that I haf men yarked.'

Thenne the burde byhynde the dor for   *woman*
    busmar laghed,   *scorn*
And sayde sotyly to hirself Sare the madde: *slyly; foolish*
655 'May thou traw for tykle that thou teme moghtes,
And I so hyghe out of age, and also my   *much over age*
    lorde?'

637-40 He placed appropriate milk dishes here and there, then pottage
    and stew in a worthy platter; in fitting manner, like a servant at table,
    he served them fully with such as he had, with dignified and pleasant
    bearing.
644 Served food before those men who wield all powers.
651-2 In blessedness and honour the noble race which shall inherit that
    which I have granted to men (i.e. in the Covenant).
655 Can you believe that you will conceive through wantonness.

For sothely, as says the Wryt, hit wern of sadde elde,
Bothe the wyye and his wyf, such werk was hem fayled;
Fro mony a brod day byfore ho barayn ay had bene,   *long*
660 That selve Sare withouten sede into that same tyme.   *up to*

Thenne sayde oure Syre ther he sete: 'Se! so Sare laghes,
Not trawande the tale that I the to   *matter*
    schewed.   *disclosed*
Hopes ho oght may be harde my hondes to work?
And yet I avow verayly the avaunt that I made;

665 I schal yeply ayayn and yelde that I hyght,
And sothely sende to Sare a soun and an hayre.'   *indeed*
Thenne swenged forth Sare and swer by hir   *rushed; swore*
    trawthe
That for lot that thay laused ho laghed never.   *words; uttered*

'Now innogh, hit is not so,' thenne nurned the   *declared*
    Dryghtyn,   *Lord*
670 'For thou laghed alow, bot let we hit one.'   *quietly; let it pass*
With that thay ros up radly as thay rayke schulde,
And setten toward Sodamas her syght alle at ones.

For that cité therbysyde was sette in a vale,   *nearby*
No myles fro Mambre mo then tweyne,
675 Where-so wonyed this ilke wyy that wendes with oure Lorde
For to tent hym with tale and teche hym the gate.

Then glydes forth God, the godmon hym folwes;
Abraham heldes hem wyth, hem to conveye   *goes; escort*
In towarde the cety of Sodamas that synned had thenne
680 In the faute of this fylthe; the Fader hem thretes,   *threatens*

---

657 For truly, as the Bible says, they were of advanced age.
658 Such activity had come to an end for them.
663–5 Does she think anything is difficult for my hands to do? But
    nevertheless I emphatically affirm the vow that I made: I shall quickly
    return and perform what I promised.
671–2 With that they stood up quickly in readiness to go, and together
    turned their eyes towards Sodom.
674–7 No more than two miles from Mamre, where this same man lived
    who goes with our Lord to engage Him in conversation and show Him
    the way. Then God goes forth, the master of the house follows Him.

And sayde thus to the segg that sued hym   *man; attended*
   after:
'How myght I hyde myn hert fro Habraham the trwe,
That I ne dyscovered to his corse my counsayl so dere,
Sythen he is chosen to be chef chyldryn fader,

685 That so folk schal falle fro to flete alle the worlde,
And uche blod in that burne blessed schal worthe?
Me bos telle to that tolk the tene of my wylle,
And alle myn atlyng to Abraham unhaspe bilyve.

The grete soun of Sodamas synkkes in myn eres,   *clamour*
690 And the gult of Gomorre gares me to wrath;
I schal lyght into that led and loke   *go down; people*
   myselven
If thay haf don as the dyne dryves on lofte.

Thay han lerned a lyst that lykes me ille,   *practice; pleases*
That thay han founden in her flesch of fautes the   *in that*
   werst;
695 Uch male mas his mach a man as hymselven,
And fylter folyly in fere on femmales wyse.

I compast hem a kynde crafte and kende hit hem derne,
And amed hit in myn ordenaunce oddely dere,
And dyght drwry therinne, doole alther-swettest;
700 And the play of paramores I portrayed myselven,

683–8 And not reveal to him my most stern purpose, since he is chosen
   to be the first father of the children of Israel, from whom people shall
   spring so as to fill all the world, and (since) each nation shall be blessed
   through him? I must tell that man of the anger in my mind, and disclose
   all my intention to Abraham at once.
690 And the sin of Gomorrah makes me angry.
692 To see if they have behaved as the noise is raised on high.
695–702 Each male takes as his mate a man like himself, and they join
   together wantonly in female fashion. I devised for them a natural skill
   and taught it to them privately, and valued it exceptionally highly in
   my plan of creation, establishing love, the sweetest of all gifts, in that
   skill; and I devised the dalliance of lovers, and contrived in that regard

And made therto a maner myriest of other.
When two true togeder had tyyed hemselven,
Bytwene a male and his make such merthe   *mate; pleasure*
   schulde come,
Welnyghe pure Paradys moght preve no better.   *itself; prove*

705 Elles thay moght honestly ayther other welde,
At a stylle stollen steven unstered wyth syght,
Luf-lowe hem bytwene lasched so hote
That alle the meschefes on mold moght hit not sleke.

Now haf thay skyfted my skyl and scorned   *altered; purpose*
   natwre,
710 And henttes hem in hethyng an usage   *adopt in contempt*
   unclene;
Hem to smyte for that smod smartly I thenk,   *filth*
That wyyes schal be by hem war worlde withouten   *warned*
   ende.'

Thenne arwed Abraham, and alle his   *was afraid*
   mod chaunged,   *mood*
For hope of the harde hate that hyght has oure Lorde.
715 Al sykande he sayde: 'Sir, with yor leve,   *sighing*
Schal synful and sakles suffer al on   *innocent; one*
   payne?   *penalty*

Wether ever hit lyke my Lorde to lyfte such domes,
That the wykked and the worthy schal on wrake   *punishment*
   suffer,
And weye upon the worre half that wrathed the never?
720 That was never thy won that wroghtes uus alle.   *custom*

---

the most pleasant practice of all. Whenever two virtuous people joined
themselves together.
705–8 As long as they used each other decently, at a quiet private
meeting with none to look on, the fire of love might flare up between
them so hotly that all the misfortunes in the world would be unable to
extinguish it.
714 In expectation of the severe punishment that our Lord had promised.
717 Does it please my Lord to pronounce such judgments?
719 And to weigh on the wrong side (of the balance) those who never
angered you?

Now fyfty fyn frendes wer founde in yonde toune,

In the cety of Sodamas, and also Gomorre,

That never lakked thy laue, bot loved   *offended against; law*
   ay trauthe,

And reghtful wern and resounable and redy the   *righteous*
   to serve,

725 Schal thay falle in the faute that other frekes wroght,

And joyne to her juggement, her juise to have?

That nas never thyn note, unnevened hit worthe,

That art so gaynly a God and of goste   *gracious; nature*
   mylde.'

'Nay, for fyfty,' quoth the Fader, 'and thy fayre speche,

730 And thay be founden in that folk of her fylthe clene,   *if; free*

I schal forgyve alle the gylt thurgh my grace one,   *alone*

And let hem smolt al unsmyten smothely at ones.'

'Aa! blessed be thow,' quoth the burne, 'so boner   *kind*
   and thewed,   *gracious*

And al haldes in thy honde, the heven and the   *you hold*
   erthe;

735 Bot, for I haf this talke, tas to non ille

Yif I mele a lyttel more, that mul am and askes.

What if fyve faylen of fyfty the noumbre,   *are wanting*

And the remnaunt be reken, how restes   *honest; stands*
   thy wylle?'

'And fyve wont of fyfty,' quoth God, 'I schal   *if*
   foryete alle,   *pardon*

740 And wythhalde my honde for hortyng on lede.'

---

721 If now fifty worthies were found in that town.

726-7 And be included in your judgment of them (i.e. the guilty), to
share their doom? That was never your way, may it (i.e. the judgment)
be retracted.

732 And let them go in peace at once, quite unharmed.

735-6 But, since I am engaged in this conversation, do not take it amiss
if I speak a little more, I who am dust and ashes.

740-4 'And restrain my hand, so as not to hurt a single person.' 'And

'And quat if faurty be fre and fauty thyse other?
Schalt thow schortly al schende and schape non other?'
'Nay, thagh faurty forfete, yet fryst I a whyle,
And voyde away my vengaunce, thagh me vyl thynk.'

745 Then Abraham obeched hym and lowly   *bowed to; humbly*
    him thonkkes:
'Now sayned be thou, Saviour, so symple in   *blessed; mild*
    thy wrath.
I am bot erthe ful evel and usle so blake,   *vile; ashes*
For to mele wyth such a mayster as myghtes has alle.   *powers*

Bot I have bygonnen wyth my God, and he hit gayn   *if; good*
    thynkes;
750 Yif I forloyne as a fol, thy fraunchyse may serve.
What if thretty thryvande be thrad in yon tounes?
What shall I leve of my Lorde, if he hem lethe   *think; save*
    wolde?'

Thenne the godlych God gef hym onsware: *gracious*
'Yet for thretty in throng I schal my thro steke, *wrath restrain*
755 And spare spakly of spyt, in space of my thewes,
And my rankor refrayne four thy reken wordes.' *restrain; for*

'What for twenty,' quoth the tolke, 'untwynes thou hem
    thenne?'
'Nay, yif thou yernes hit, yet yark I hem grace.   *grant*
If that twenty be trwe, I tene hem no more,   *harm*
760 Bot relece alle that regioun of her ronk   *absolve; vile*
    werkkes.'

---

what if forty be good, and the others sinful, will you destroy all directly
and have it no other way?' 'No, if forty are to be lost, I shall still hold
back, and forego my vengeance, disgusted though I am.'

750-1 If I should go astray like a fool, your generosity will serve. What
    if thirty worthy men should be punished in those towns?

755 And willingly refrain from anger, in the generosity of my good
    nature.

757 'What shall you do for twenty,' said the man, 'will you then destroy
    them?'

'Now, athel Lorde,' quoth Abraham,   *noble*
  'ones a speche,   *once more*
And I schal schape no more tho schalkkes   *endeavour; men*
  to helpe.
If ten trysty in toune be tan in thi werkkes,
Wylt thou mese thy mode and menddyng abyde?'

765 'I graunt,' quoth the grete God. 'Graunt   *consent; thank you*
  mercy,' that other;
And thenne arest the renk and raght no fyrre.
And Godde glydes his gate by those grene   *departs along*
  wayes,
And he conveyen hym con with cast of his yye.

And als he loked along there as oure Lorde passed,
770 Yet he cryed hym after with careful steven: *anxious voice*
'Meke mayster, on thy mon to mynne if the lyked,
Loth lenges in yon leede, that is my lef brother.

He syttes ther in Sodomis, thy servaunt so   *dwells*
  povere,   *lowly*
Among tho mansed men that han the much   *accursed*
  greved;   *angered*
775 Yif thou tynes that toun, tempre thyn yre   *will overthrow*
As thy mersy may malte, thy meke to spare.'

Then he wendes his way, wepande for care,
Towarde the mere of Mambre, mornande for   *border*
  sorewe;
And there in longyng al nyght he lenges in wones,
780 Whyl the Soverayn to Sodamas sende to   *sent messengers*
  spye.

763-4 If ten true men in the town should be found engaged in your
  works, will you moderate your anger and wait for improvement?
766 And then the man stopped and went no further.
768-9 And he followed Him with his glance. And as he looked to where
  our Lord passed.
771-2 Merciful Lord, if it should please you to remember your servant,
  Lot, who is my dear kinsman, lives amongst that people.
776 As much as your mercy is able to soften it, to spare your humble
  one.
779 And there he remains at home, in anxiety all night.

His sondes into Sodamas was sende in that tyme,   *embassy*
In that ilk eventyde, by aungels tweyne,
Mevande mekely togeder as myry men yonge,   *briskly*
As Loot in a loge dor lened hym alone,

785 In a porche of that place pyght to the yates,
That was ryal and ryche, so was the renkes selven.
As he stared into the strete, ther stout men played,
He syye ther swey in asent swete men tweyne.

Bolde burnes wer thay bothe, with berdles chynnes,
790 Royl rollande fax to raw sylk lyke,   *splendid flowing hair*
Of ble as the brere-flour, where-so the bare scheweed.
Ful clene was the countenaunce of her cler   *bright; glance*
    yyen;

Wlonk whit was her wede, and wel hit hem semed;
Of alle fetures ful fyn, and fautles bothe;
795 Was non aucly in outher, for aungels hit wern,
And that the yep underyede that in the yate syttes.

He ros up ful radly and ran hem to mete,   *swiftly*
And lowe he loutes hem to, Loth, to the grounde;   *bows*
And sythen soberly: 'Syres, I yow byseche   *earnestly*
800 That ye wolde lyght at my loge and lenge therinne.

Comes to your knaves kote, I crave at this ones;
I schal fette yow a fatte your fette for to wasche;   *fetch; tub*
I norne yow bot for on nyght neghe me to lenge,   *ask; with*
And in the myry mornyng ye may your waye take.'   *bright*

784–8 As Lot sat alone in the doorway of a lodge, in a gatehouse next
  to the gates of that city, which was splendid and rich, as the man was
  himself. As he looked into the road, where proud men came and went,
  he saw two comely men there, moving together.

791 Of complexion like the briar-rose, wherever the bare skin was
  revealed.

793–6 Their dress was of rich white, and well it suited them; they were
  pleasing in every feature, and faultless as well; there was no blemish in
  either, for they were angels, and the alert man who sat in the gateway
  realized that.

800–1 That you would stop at my house and lodge there. Come to your
  servant's cottage, I beg you, for this once.

805 And thay nay that thay nolde negh no howses,
    Bot stylly ther in the strete, as thay stadde wern,
    Thay wolde lenge the long naght, and logge theroute;
    Hit was hous innoghe to hem the heven upon lofte.

    Loth lathed so longe wyth luflych wordes,   *urged; courteous*
810 That thay hym graunted to go, and grught   *agreed; refused*
      no lenger.
    The bolde to his byggyng brynges hem   *house*
      bylyve,   *quickly*
    That was ryally arayed, for he was ryche ever.   *exceedingly*

    The wyyes wern welcom as the wyf couthe;
    His two dere doghteres devoutly hem haylsed,   *greeted*
815 That wer maydenes ful meke, maryed not yet,
    And thay wer semly and swete and swythe wel arayed.   *very*

    Loth thenne ful lyghtly lokes hym aboute,   *quickly*
    And his men amonestes mete for to dyght: *charges; prepare*
    'Bot thenkkes on hit be threfte, what thynk so ye make,
820 For wyth no sour ne no salt serves hym never.'   *leaven*

    Bot yet I wene that the wyf hit wroth to dyspyt,
    And sayde softely to hirself: 'This unsaveré   *unseasoned*
      hyne   *fellows*
    Loves no salt in her sauce, yet hit no skyl were
    That other burne be boute, thagh bothe be nyse.'

805-7 But they said they would not go near any houses, but would stay
    there quietly in the road all night, and lodge in the open as they found
    themselves.
813 The men were made welcome by his wife to the best of her ability.
819 But take care that it be unleavened, whatever you make.
821 But yet I fancy that the woman twisted it into a wrong.
823-4 But it would not be reasonable that others should be without,
    though they are both ill-bred.

825 Thenne ho saveres with salt her seves   *seasons; sauces*
    uchone,
    Agayne the bone of the burne that hit forboden   *command*
    hade,
    And als ho scelt hem in scorne that wel her skyl knewen.
    Why was ho, wrech, so wod? Ho wrathed   *mad; angered*
    oure Lorde.

    Thenne seten thay at the soper, wern served bylyve,
830 The gestes gay and ful glad, of glam   *speech*
    debonere,   *courteous*
    Wela wynnely wlonk, tyl thay waschen hade,
    The trestes tylt to the wowe, and the table bothe.

    Fro the segges haden souped, and seten bot a whyle,
    Er ever thay bosked to bedde, the borgh was al   *went; town*
    up,
835 Alle that weppen myght welde, the wakker and the   *wield*
    stronger,
    To umbelyye Lothes hous, the ledes to take.   *surround; men*

    In grete flokkes of folk thay fallen to his yates;   *rush at*
    As a scowte-wach scarred so the asscry rysed;
    With kene clobbes of that clos thay clater on the wowes,
840 And wyth a schrylle scharp schout thay schewe thys   *utter*
    worde:

    'If thou lovyes thy lyf, Loth, in thyse wones,   *this place*
    Yete uus out those yong men that yorewhyle   *get; recently*
    here entred,
    That we may lere hym of lof, as oure lyst   *teach; desire*
    biddes,
    As is the asyse of Sodomas to segges that passen.'   *custom*

---

827 And in this way she scorned those who well knew her purpose.
831–3 Most excellently polite, until they had washed (i.e. at the end of
    the meal), the trestles having been tilted against the wall, and the table
    as well. After the men had eaten supper, and had sat but a short while.
838 Clamour rose up as from a startled sentry-patrol; with great clubs
    they beat on the walls of that house.

845 Whatt! thay sputen and speken of so spitous fylthe;
What! thay yeyed and yolped of yestande sorwe,
That yet the wynd and the weder and the worlde stynkes   *air*
Of the brych that upbraydes those brothelych wordes.

The godman glyfte with that glam and gloped for noyse;
850 So scharpe schame to hym schot, he schrank at the hert.
For he knew the costoum that kythed those   *observed*
    wreches;
He doted never for no doel so depe in his mynde.

'Allas!' sayd hym thenne Loth, and lyghtly he   *to himself*
    ryses,
And bowes forth fro the bench into the brode yates.
855 What! he wonded no wothe of wekked knaves
That he ne passed the port the peril to abide.

He went forthe at the wyket and waft hit hym after,   *swung*
That a clyket hit cleght clos hym byhynde.
Thenne he meled to tho men mesurable wordes,   *moderate*
860 For harlotes with his hendelayk he hoped to chast:

'Oo, my frendes so fre, your fare is to strange;
Dos away your derf dyn, and deres never my gestes.
Avoy! hit is your vylaynye, ye vylen yourselven;
And ye ar jolyf gentylmen, your japes ar ille.

845-6 Listen! they talked together and spoke of such shameful sin;
listen! they shouted and boasted of festering filth.

848-50 Of the sin which throws up those wild words. The master of the
house winced at that uproar and was aghast at the noise; such deep
shame came over him that he recoiled inwardly.

852 Never for any distressing event was he in such confusion (of mind).

854-6 And goes forth from his seat into the main gateway. Look! he
feared no harm from evil men that would stop him passing through the
gate to face the danger.

858 So that a catch fastened it firmly behind him.

860-6 For he hoped to chasten the lechers by his courtesy: 'Oh my most
noble friends, your behaviour is too unnatural; cease your great
clamour, and do not harm my guests. For shame! it is to your disgrace,
you degrade yourselves; if you are worthy gentlemen, your tricks are

865 Bot I schal kenne yow by kynde a crafte that is better;
    I haf a tresor in my telde of tow my fayre deghter,
    That ar maydenes unmard for alle men yette;   *undefiled*
    In Sodamas, thagh I hit say, non semloker   *prettier*
      burdes.   *women*

    Hit arn ronk, hit arn rype, and redy to manne;
870 To samen wyth tho semly the solace is better;
    I schal biteche yow tho two that tayt arn and quoynt,
    And laykes wyth hem as yow lyst, and letes my gestes one.'

    Thenne the rebaudes so ronk rerd such a noyse,
    That awly hurled in his eres her harlotes   *fearsomely rang*
      speche:
875 'Wost thou not wel that thou wones here a wyye strange,
    An outcomlyng, a carle? – we kylle of thyn heved!

    Who joyned the be jostyse, oure japes to blame,
    That com a boy to this borgh, thagh thou be burne ryche?'
    Thus thay throbled and throng and thrwe umbe his eres,
880 And distresed hym wonder strayt with strenkthe in the prece,

    Bot that the yonge men so yepe yornen theroute,   *bold; ran*
    Wapped upon the wyket and wonnen hem tylle,
    And by the hondes hym hent and horyed hym   *took; hurried*
      withinne,
    And steken the yates ston-harde wyth   *fastened; very firmly*
      stalworth barres.

---

    vile. But I shall teach you a better skill, according to nature; I have a
    treasure in my house, my two fair daughters.'

869–73 'They are grown, they are ripe, and ready to be mastered; there
    is better pleasure in consorting with those pretty ones; I shall give the
    two of them to you, lively and attractive as they are, and play with
    them as it pleases you, and leave my guests alone.' Then the vile
    scoundrels raised such a din.

875–80 'Do you not know well that you live here as a foreigner, an
    alien, a churl – we shall knock off your head! Who appointed you to
    be a judge, to find fault with our games, you who came to this town as
    a man of no account, though you are now a rich man?' Thus they
    jostled and pushed and crowded close about him, and would have hurt
    him very severely by their violence in the press.

882 Flung open the wicket and made their way to them.

885 Thay blwe a boffet in blande that banned peple,
That thay blustered as blynde as Bayard was ever.
Thay lest of Lotes logging any lysoun to   *failed; opening*
    fynde,
Bot nyteled ther alle the nyght for noght at the   *blundered*
    last.

Thenne uch tolke tyght hem that hade of tayt fayled,
890 And uchon rotheled to the rest that he reche   *staggered; get*
    moght;
Bot thay wern wakned awrank that ther in won lenged,
Of on the uglokest unhap ever on erd suffred.

Ruddon of the day-rawe ros upon ughten,
When merk of the mydnyght moght no more last.   *darkness*
895 Ful erly those aungeles this hathel thay ruthen,   *man; rouse*
And glopnedly, on Godes halve, gart hym upryse.

Fast the freke ferkes up, ful ferd at his hert;
Thay comaunded hym cof to cach that he   *quickly; take*
    hade:
'Wyth thy wyf and thy wyyes and thy wlonc deghtters,   *fair*
900 For we lathe the, sir Loth, that thou thy lyf have.   *urge; save*

Cayre tid of this kythe, er combred thou worthe,
With alle thi here upon haste, tyl thou a hil fynde;   *household*
Foundes faste on your fete, bifore your face lokes,   *go on*
Bot bes never so bolde to blusch yow   *do not dare; look*
    bihynde.

885-6 They blew a blast amongst that accursed people, so that they
    stumbled about as blind as Bayard (a proverbially blind horse) ever
    was.
889 Then each man went away, having failed to find pleasure.
891-3 But they were wretchedly awakened, those who lived there in that
    town, by the very worst disaster ever experienced on earth. The redness
    of first light came up at daybreak.
896-7 And in alarming fashion they ordered him to get up, in God's
    name. Quickly the man starts up, very frightened at heart.
901 Go quickly from this land, before you are overwhelmed.

905 And loke ye stemme no stepe, bot streches on faste;
    Til ye reche to a reset, rest ye never;   *refuge*
    For we schal tyne this toun and traythely disstrye,
    Wyth alle thise wyyes so wykke wyghtly devoyde,

    And alle the londe with thise ledes we losen at ones;
910 Sodomas schal ful sodenly synk into grounde,
    And the grounde of Gomorre gorde   *foundations; plunge*
        into helle,
    And uche a koste of this kyth clater upon hepes.'   *part*

    Then laled Loth: 'Lorde, what is best?   *spoke*
    If I me fele upon fote that I fle moght,
915 Hou schulde I huyde me from hym that has his hate kynned,
    In the brath of his breth that brennes alle thinkes?

    To crepe fro my Creatour and know not wheder,
    Ne whether his fooschip me folwes bifore other bihynde!'
    The freke sayde: 'No foschip oure Fader has the schewed,
920 Bot highly hevened thi hele fro hem that arn combred.

    Nou wale the a wonnyng that the warisch myght,
    And he schal save hit for thy sake that has uus sende hider;
    For thou art oddely thyn one out of this fylthe,
    And als Abraham thyn eme hit at himself asked.'

---

905 And see to it that you do not stop, but move on quickly.
907–9 For we shall overthrow this town and pitilessly destroy it, do
    away with it in a moment together with all these evil men, and all the
    land with its people we shall ruin all at once.
914–18 If I should go forward on foot in order to escape, how should I
    hide myself from Him who has kindled His anger, who consumes all
    things in the violence of His fury? (How absurd) to steal away from my
    Creator and not know where to go, nor whether His enmity will seek
    me out from in front or behind!
920–1 But (He has) specially exalted your safety above those who are
    overwhelmed. Now choose a place for yourself which can protect you.
923–4 For you are absolutely the only one untouched by this filth, and
    also Abraham your uncle asked it of Him.

925 'Lorde, loved he worthe,' quoth Loth,   *may He be praised*
      'upon erthe!
   Ther is a cité herbisyde that Segor hit hatte;   *which is called*
   Hereutter on a rounde hil hit hoves hit one.
   I wolde, if his wylle wore, to that won scape.'

   'Thenn fare forth,' quoth that fre, 'and fyne thou never,
930 With those ilk that thow wylt, that threnge the after,
   And ay goande on your gate wythouten agayntote;
   For alle this londe schal be lorne longe er the sonne rise.'   *lost*

   The wyye wakened his wyf and his wlonk deghteres,
   And other two myri men tho maydenes schulde wedde;
935 And thay token hit as tayt and tented hit lyttel,   *joke; heeded*
   Thagh fast lathed hem Loth, thay   *earnestly urged*
      leyen ful stylle.

   The aungeles hasted thise other and awly hem   *fearsomely*
      thratten,   *threatened*
   And enforsed alle fawre forth at the yates.   *drove*
   Tho wern Loth and his lef, his luflyche   *dear one (wife)*
      deghter;
940 Ther soght no mo to savement of cities athel fyve.

   Thise aungeles hade hem by hande out at the yates,   *brought*
   Prechande hem the perile, and beden hem passe   *bade; go*
      fast:
   'Lest ye be taken in the teche of tyrauntes here,   *sin; evil men*
   Loke ye bowe now bi bot, bowes fast hence.'

927–31 'It stands on its own on a round hill outside this place. I would
   like to escape to that town, if it were His will.' 'Then go forth,' said the
   noble one, 'and do not stop, with those whom you want with you, who
   owe allegiance to you, always going on your way without a backward
   glance.'

934 And two other worthy men whom those maidens were to wed.

940 No more reached safety from the five proud cities.

944–5 'See that you go now quickly, go fast from this place.' And they

945 And thay kayre ne con and kenely flowen;
    Erly, er any heven-glem, thay to a hil   *glimmer of dawn*
       comen.

    The grete God in his greme bygynnes on lofte   *anger*
    To wakan wederes so wylde – the wyndes he calles,   *storms*

    And thay wrothely upwafte and wrastled   *fiercely rose*
       togeder,
950 Fro fawre half of the folde, flytande loude;
    Clowdes clustered bytwene, kesten up torres,
    That the thik thunder-thrast thirled hem ofte.

    The rayn rueled adoun, ridlande thikke,   *poured; sifting*
    Of felle flaunkes of fyr and flakes of soufre,
955 Al in smolderande smoke, smachande   *smothering; smelling*
       ful ille,
    Swe aboute Sodamas and hit sydes alle,   *fell; its environs*

    Gorde to Gomorra that the grounde laused,
    Abdama and Syboym – thise ceteis alle faure
    Al birolled wyth the rayn, rostted and brenned,
960 And ferly flayed that folk that in those fees lenged.

    For when that the helle herde the houndes of   *when Hell*
       heven,
    He was ferlyly fayn, unfolded bylyve;
    The grete barres of the abyme he barst up at ones,
    That alle the regioun torof in riftes ful grete,   *broke up*

---

    did not hesitate but swiftly fled.
949–2 From the four corners of the earth, contending loudly; clouds
    clustered at intervals, threw up hill-like masses, which the ever-present
    lightning often pierced.
954 Of terrible sparks of fire and lumps of sulphur.
957–8 Beat on Gomorrah so that the ground gave way, on Admah and
    Zeboim.
959–60 Were all enveloped by the rain, were roasted and burned, and
    the people who dwelt in those towns were exceedingly frightened.
962–3 He was utterly delighted, opened quickly; he burst the great bars
    of the abyss all at once.

965 And cloven alle in lyttel cloutes the clyffes aywhere,
As lauce leves of the boke that lepes in twynne.
The brethe of the brynston bi that hit blende were,
Al tho citees and her sydes sunkken to helle.

Rydelles wern tho grete rowtes of renkkes withinne,
970 When thay wern war of the wrake that no wyye achaped;
Such a yomerly yarm of yellyng ther rysed,   *doleful clamour*
Therof clatered the cloudes, that Kryst myght   *resounded*
     haf rawthe.   *pity*

The segge herde that soun to Segor that yede,   *sound; went*
And the wenches hym wyth that by the way folwed;
975 Ferly ferde was her flesch that flowen ay ilyche,
Trynande ay a hyghe trot that torne never dorsten.

Loth and tho luly-whit, his lefly two deghter,
Ay folwed here face, bifore her bothe yyen;
Bot the balleful burde, that never bode keped,
980 Blusched byhynden her bak that bale for to herkken.

Hit was lusty Lothes wyf, that over her lyfte schulder
Ones ho bluschet to the burghe; bot bod ho no lenger
That ho nas stadde a stiffe ston, a stalworth image,
Also salt as ani se – and so ho yet standes.   *as; sea*

965–70 And the cliffs everywhere shattered all in little pieces, as leaves
fly from a book that springs apart. By the time that the stench of the
brimstone had spread, all those cities and their environs were sinking
to Hell. The great crowds of people in those places were in despair,
when they became aware of the vengeance that no man might escape.

974–83 And the women with him, following along the road; they were
thoroughly frightened, fleeing ever onwards, always going at a fast
pace, never daring to turn round. Lot and those lily-white ones, his two
lovely daughters, went ever forward, both eyes before them; but the
wretched woman, who never did as she was told, looked behind her
(back) to see that disaster. That was worthy Lot's wife, who looked
once at the town over her left shoulder; but the moment she did so she
was turned into a hard stone, a solid image.

985 Thay slypped bi and syye hir not that wern hir   *saw*
    samenferes,   *companions*
Tyl thay in Segor wern sette, and sayned our   *arrived; blessed*
    Lorde;
Wyth lyght loves uplyfte thay loved hym swythe,
That so his servauntes wolde see and save of such wothe.

Al was dampped and don and drowned   *damned; destroyed*
    by thenne;
990 The ledes of that lyttel toun wern lopen   *people; had rushed*
    out for drede
Into that malscrande mere, marred   *charmed sea; killed*
    bylyve,
That noght saved was bot Segor that sat on a   *so that*
    lawe,   *hill*

The thre ledes therin, Loth and his deghter.
For his make was myst, that on the mount lenged
995 In a stonen statue that salt savor habbes,
For two fautes that the fol was founde in mistrauthe:

On, ho served at the soper salt bifore   *firstly*
    Dryghtyn,   *the Lord*
And sythen ho blusched hir bihynde, thagh hir forboden
    were.
For on ho standes a ston, and salt for that other,   *the one*
1000 And alle lyst on hir lik that arn on launde bestes.

Abraham ful erly was up on the morne,
That alle naght much niye hade nomen in   *anguish; endured*
    his hert,
Al in longing for Loth leyen in a wache;
Ther he lafte hade oure Lorde he is on lofte wonnen.

987-8 With eager hands uplifted they praised Him devoutly, He who
    would so look after His servants and save them from such danger.
994-6 For his wife was missing, remaining on the mountain as a stone
    statue which has a salt taste, for two offences in which the foolish
    woman was found to be faithless.
998 And then she looked behind her, though she was forbidden to do so.
1000 And all the beasts of the earth desire to lick her.
1003-4 Had lain awake in great anxiety for Lot; he went up to (the
    place) where he had left our Lord.

1005 He sende towards Sodomas the syght of his yyen, *sent*
That ever hade ben an erde of erthe the swettest,
As aparaunt to Paradis that plantted the Dryghtyn;
Nou is hit plunged in a pit like of pich fylled. *as though*

Suche a rothum of a reche ros fro the blake,
1010 Askes upe in the ayre and uselles ther flowen, *ashes; cinders*
As a fornes ful of flot that upon fyr boyles, *scum*
When bryght brennande brondes ar bet theranunder. *kindled*

This was a vengaunce violent that voyded thise *laid waste*
places,
That foundered has so fayr a folk and the folde
sonkken. *engulfed*
1015 There fyve citees wern set nou is a see called,
That ay is drovy and dym, and ded in hit kynde;

Blo, blubrande, and blak, unblythe to neghe,
As a stynkande stanc that stryed synne,
That ever of synne and of smach smart is to fele;
1020 Forthy the derk dede see hit is demed *and so; called*
evermore.

For hit dedes of dethe duren there yet; *its; continue*
For hit is brod and bothemles, and bitter as the galle,
And noght may lenge in that lake that any lyf beres, *stay*
And alle the costes of kynde hit combres uchone.

1006-7 That had always been a region which was the most pleasant on
earth, in that it was like Paradise which the Lord created.
1009 Such a pall of red smoke rose from the blackness.
1015-19 The place where five cities were situated is now a sea, which is
always murky and dark, and dead in its nature; livid, bubbling, and
black, unpleasant to approach – a stinking pool which destroyed sin,
which in its sin and its savour is always bitter to taste.
1024 And it overturns all of the laws of nature.

1025 For lay theron a lump of led and hit on loft fletes,   *surface*
     And folde theron a lyght fyther and hit to   *place*
       founs synkkes;   *bottom*
     And ther water may walter to wete any erthe,
     Schal never grene theron growe, gresse ne wod nawther.

     If any schalke to be schent wer schowved   *man; killed*
       therinne,
1030 Thagh he bode in that bothem brothely a monyth,
     He most ay lyve in that loghe, in losying evermore,
     And never dryye no dethe to dayes of ende.

     And as hit is corsed of kynde, and hit coostes als,
     The clay that clenges therby arn corsyes strong,
1035 As alum and alkaran, that angré arn bothe,   *bitumen; caustic*
     Soufre sour and saundyver and other such mony;

     And ther waltes of that water, in waxlokes grete,
     The spumande aspaltoun that spyseres sellen.
     And suche is alle the soyle by that se halves,   *sea's shores*
1040 That fel fretes the flesch and festres   *cruelly devours; rots*
       bones.

     And ther ar tres by that terne of traytoures,   *lakes; evildoers*
     And thay borgounes and beres blomes ful fayre,   *flourish*
     And the fayrest fryt that may on folde growe,
     As orenge and other fryt and apple-garnade,   *pomegranate*

1027-8 And wherever the water flows to wet a piece of ground,
   vegetation will never grow there, neither grass nor trees.
1030-4 Though he should remain wretchedly in that pit for a month, he
   must live on in that sea, in perdition for ever, and never suffer death
   till the end of the world. And as it is cursed in its nature, and its shores
   as well, the clay that clings there consists of strong corrosives.
1036-8 Bitter sulphur and glass-gall and many other such; and there the
   foaming asphalt that apothecaries sell is flung from that water in great
   wax-like curls.

1045 Al so red and so ripe and rychely hwed   *coloured*
     As any dom myght device, of dayntyes oute;
     Bot quen hit is brused other broken other byten in twynne,
     No worldes goud hit wythinne, bot wyndowande askes.

     Alle thyse ar teches and tokenes to trow upon yet,
1050 And wittnesse of that wykked werk, and the wrake after
     That oure Fader forthered for fylthe of those ledes;   *executed*
     Thenne uch wyye may wel wyt that he the wlonk lovies.

     And if he lovyes clene layk that is oure Lorde   *conduct*
       ryche,   *noble*
     And to be couthe in his courte thou coveytes   *known; desire*
       thenne,
1055 To se that semly in sete and his swete   *seemly one; throne*
       face,
     Clerrer counsayl con I non bot that thou clene   *know*
       worthe.   *be*

     For Clopyngnel in the compas of his clene Rose,
     Ther he expounes a speche to hym that spede wolde
     Of a lady to be loved: 'Loke to hir sone
1060 Of wich beryng that ho be, and wych ho best lovyes;

     And be ryght such in uch a borghe, of body and of dedes,
     And folw the fet of that fere that thou fre haldes.
     And if thou wyrkkes on this wyse, thagh   *act*
       ho wyk were,   *hostile*
     Hir schal lyke that layk that lyknes hir tylle.'

1046 As any wit might conceive, attractive on the outside.

1048-50 No goodness inside it at all, only swirling ashes. All these are
     signs and tokens to take note of still, and evidence of that evil
     behaviour, and the vengeance afterwards.

1052 And so all may see well that He loves what is clean.

1057-62 For Clopinel (Jean de Meun) in his clean Rose (*Le Roman de
     la Rose*) sets forth there a speech for the man who would succeed in
     love with a lady: 'Look to her without delay to see what her disposition
     is, and what she likes best; and in every place be just like her, in
     appearance and actions, and follow the footsteps of the mistress whom
     you hold dear.'

1064 That conduct which copies her will be pleasing to her.

1065 If thou wyl dele drwrye wyth Dryghtyn   *have love-dealings*
     thenne,
  And lelly lovy thy Lorde and his leef worthe,   *truly; dear one*
  Thenne confourme the to Kryst, and the clene make, *be like*
  That ever is polyced als playn as the perle selven.   *smooth*

  For loke, fro fyrst that he lyght withinne the lel mayden,
1070 By how comly a kest he was clos there,
  When venkkyst was no vergynyté, ne vyolence   *vanquished*
     maked,   *done*
  Bot much clener was hir corse God kynned therinne.

  And efte when he borne was in Bethelen the ryche,   *again*
  In wych puryté thay departed, thagh thay pover were.
1075 Was never so blysful a bour as was a bos thenne,   *manger*
  Ne no schroude-hous so schene as a schepon thare,

  Ne non so glad under God as ho that grone schulde;
  For ther was seknesse al sounde that sarrest is halden,
  And ther was rose reflayr where rote has   *scent; rottenness*
     ben ever,
1080 And ther was solace and songe wher sorw has ay cryed.   *joy*

  For aungelles with instrumentes of organes and pypes,
  And rial ryngande rotes, and the reken fythel,
  And alle hende that honestly moght an hert glade,
  Aboutte my lady was lent, quen ho delyver   *present; delivered*
     were.

1069–70 For see, from the moment He alighted within the true maiden, by how seemly a contrivance He was enclosed there.

1072 But much cleaner was her body in that God was conceived in it.

1074 In what purity they parted from each other, though they were poor.

1076–8 Nor any sacristy so beautiful as a cow-shed was there, nor anyone so glad on God's earth as she who must groan (in childbirth); for there that sickness, which is considered the most severe, was fully healed.

1082–3 And rich resonant stringed instruments, and the noble violin, and everything pleasant that might worthily gladden the heart.

1085 Thenne was her blythe barne burnyst so clene   *fair child*
     That bothe the ox and the asse hym
          hered at ones;   *worshipped together*
     Thay knewe hym by his clannes for kyng of nature,
     For non so clene of such a clos com never er   *dwelling*
          thenne.

     And yif clanly he thenne com, ful cortays therafter, *well-bred*
1090 That alle that longed to luther ful lodly he hated;
     By nobleye of his norture he nolde never towche   *nobility*
     Oght that was ungoderly other ordure was inne.

     Yet comen lodly to that lede, as lazares monye,
     Summe lepre, summe lome, and lomerande blynde,
1095 Poysened and parlatyk and pyned in fyres,
     Drye folk and ydropike, and dede at the laste.

     Alle called on that cortayse and claymed his grace;
     He heled hem wyth hynde speche of that thay ask   *gracious*
          after;   *about*
     For what-so he towched also tyd tourned to hele,
1100 Wel clanner then any crafte cowthe devyse.

     So clene was his hondelyng uche ordure hit schonied,
     And the gropyng so goud of God and man bothe
     That for fetys of his fyngeres fonded he never   *skill; troubled*
     Nauther to cout ne to kerve with knyf ne wyth egge.   *blade*

1090 In that everything that pertained to vileness He hated with great
     loathing.
1092–7 Anything that was bad or had filth inside it. Yet loathsome
     people came to that Lord, such as many who were sick, some leprous,
     some lame, and the stumbling blind, (some) poisoned and palsied and
     consumed by fevers, dry-humoured people and dropsical, and finally
     the dead. All appealed to that courteous one and claimed His grace.
1099–102 For whatever He touched became sound at once, much cleaner
     than any art could make it. So clean was His handling that every filthy
     thing fled from it, and so good was the touching of Him who was both
     God and man.

1105 Forthy brek he the bred blades wythouten,   *and so; broke*
    For hit ferde freloker in fete in his fayre honde,
    Displayed more pryvyly when he hit part schulde
    Thenne alle the toles of Tolowse moght tyght hit to kerve.

    Thus is he kyryous and clene that thou his cort askes;
1110 Hou schulde thou com to his kyth bot if thou clene   *kingdom*
    were?
    Nou ar we sore and synful and souly uchone,
    How schulde we se, then may we say, that Syre upon throne?

    Yis, that mayster is mercyable, thagh thou be man fenny,
    And al tomarred in myre whyl thou on molde   *astray; earth*
    lyvyes;
1115 Thou may schyne thurgh schryfte, thagh   *confession*
    thou haf schome served,   *given yourself to*
    And pure the with penaunce tyl thou a perle   *purify*
    worthe.   *become*

    Perle praysed is prys ther perré is schewed,
    Thagh ho not derrest be demed to dele for penies;
    Quat may the cause be called bot for hir clene hwes,
1120 That wynnes worschyp abof alle whyte stones?   *honour*

1106–9 For it fared better, indeed, in His fair hand, fell apart more
    cleanly when He came to divide it than all the tools of Toulouse might
    manage to cut it. Thus He whose court you seek is fastidious and clean.
1111 Since we are vile and sinful and filthy, each one of us.
1113 Yes we may, (for) that Lord is merciful, though you be foul.
1117–19 The pearl is deemed precious where jewels are displayed,
    though it is not considered to have the highest money-value; what may
    be the reason unless on account of its clean colouring?

For ho schynes so schyr that is of schap rounde,   *brightly*
Wythouten faut other fylthe, yif ho fyn were;   *impurity; fine*
And wax ho ever in the worlde in weryng so olde,
Yet the perle payres not whyle ho in pyese lasttes.

1125 And if hit cheve the chaunce uncheryst ho worthe,
That ho blyndes of ble in bour ther ho lygges,
Nobot wasch hir wyth wourchyp in wyn, as ho askes;
Ho by kynde schal becom clerer then are.

So if folk be defowled by unfre chaunce,
1130 That he be sulped in sawle, seche to schryfte;
And he may polyce hym at the prest, by penaunce taken,
Wel bryghter then the beryl other browden perles.   *linked*

Bot war the wel, if thou be waschen wyth   *take good care*
    water of schryfte,
And polysed als playn as parchmen   *smooth; parchment*
    schaven,   *scraped*
1135 Sulp no more thenne in synne thy saule therafter,
For thenne thou Dryghtyn dyspleses with dedes   *the Lord*
    ful sore,   *vile*

And entyses hym to tene more traythly then ever,
And wel hatter to hate then hade thou not   *more hotly*
    waschen;
For when a sawele is saghtled and sakred to   *reconciled*
    Dryghtyn,
1140 He holly haldes hit his, and have hit he wolde. *wholly counts*

1123–31 And however long it may be worn (in the world), yet the pearl
does not deteriorate during its lifetime. And if it happens to be uncared
for, so that it loses colour in the chamber where it lies, just wash it
with respect in wine, as it requires; by its nature it will then become
brighter than before. So if through evil fortune a man should be defiled,
so that he is corrupted in his soul, let him resort to confession; and he
may cleanse himself at the hands of the priest, by penance received.
1137 And you incite Him to be more violently angry than ever.

Thenne efte lastes hit likkes, he loses hit ille,
As hit were rafte wyth unryght and robbed wyth thewes.
War the thenne for the wrake, his wrath is achaufed,
For that that ones was his schulde efte be unclene.

1145 Thagh hit be bot a bassyn, a bolle other a scole,   *bowl; cup*
A dysche other a dobler, that Dryghtyn ones served,   *platter*
To defowle hit ever upon folde fast he forbedes,
So is he scoymus of scathe that scylful is ever.

And that was bared in Babyloyn in Baltazar tyme,   *shown*
1150 Hou harde unhap ther hym hent, and hastyly sone,
For he the vesselles avyled that vayled in   *defiled; were used*
    the temple
In servyse of the Soverayn sumtyme byfore.

Yif ye wolde tyght me a tom, telle hit I   *grant; opportunity*
    wolde,
Hou charged more was his chaunce that hem cherych nolde
1155 Then his fader forloyné, that feched hem wyth strenthe,
And robbed the relygioun of relykes   *faith; sacred objects*
    alle.

1141-4 If then it tastes sins again, He takes its loss badly, as if it were
wrongfully carried off and plundered by thieves. Look out then for
vengeance, His anger is kindled, that what was once His should again
be unclean.
1147-8 Sternly He forbids it to be defiled in any way at all, so revolted
is He by sin, He who is ever righteous.
1150 How dire disaster overtook him there, and very speedily.
1154-5 How the fate of that man who would not respect them was
more grievous than that of his erring father, who carried them off by
force.

III

Danyel in his dialokes devysed symtyme,
As yet is proved expresse in his profecies,
Hou the gentryse of Juise and Jherusalem the ryche
1160 Was disstryed wyth distres and drawen to the erthe.

For that folke in her fayth was founden untrwe,
That haden hyght the hyghe God to halde of hym ever;
And he hem halwed for his, and help at her nede
In mukel meschefes mony that mervayl were to here.

1165 And thay forloyne her fayth and folwed   *but; stray from*
    other goddes,
And that wakned his wrath and wrast hit so   *worked it up*
    hyghe
That he fylsened the faythful in the falce   *helped*
    lawe   *religion*
To forfare the falce in the faythe trwe.   *destroy*

Hit was sen in that sythe that Zedethyas   *time; Zedekiah*
    rengned
1170 In Juda, that justised the Juyne kynges;   *which; ruled; Jewish*
He sete on Salamones solie, on solemne   *throne; dignified*
    wyse,
Bot of leauté he was lat to his Lorde hende.

He used abominaciones of idolatrye,   *practised*
And lette lyght bi the lawe that he was lege tylle.
1175 Forthi oure Fader upon folde a foman hym wakned;
Nabigodenozar nuyed hym swythe.

1157–60 Daniel once described in his stories, as is also plainly shown in
    his prophecies, how the nobility of Israel and mighty Jerusalem was
    forcibly overthrown and laid low.
1162–4 Who had promised the high God to owe allegiance to Him for
    ever; and He set them apart as His, and helped them in their need in
    many great misfortunes that would be wonderful to hear about.
1172 But he was remiss in loyalty to his gracious Lord.
1174–6 And set little store by the religion that he owed allegiance to.
    And so our Father raised up an enemy against him on the earth;
    Nebuchadnezzar harassed him severely.

He pursued into Palastyn with proude men mony,   *advanced*
And ther he wast wyth werre the wones of thorpes;
He heryed up alle Israel and hent of the beste,
1180 And the gentylest of Judee in Jerusalem biseged,   *noblest*

Umbewalt alle the walles wyth wyyes ful   *surrounded*
    stronge,
At uche a dor a doghty duk, and dutte hem wythinne,
For the borgh was so bigge, baytayled alofte,
And stoffed wythinne with stout men to stalle hem   *halt*
    theroute.

1185 Thenne was the sege sette the ceté aboute;
Skete skarmoch skelt, much skathe lached;
At uch brugge a berfray on basteles wyse,
That seven sythe uch a day asayled the yates.

Trwe tulkkes in toures teveled wythinne,
1190 In bigge brutage of borde bulde on the walles.
Thay feght and thay fende of and fylter togeder
Til two yer overtorned, yet tok thay hit never.   *went by*

At the laste, upon longe, tho ledes wythinne,
Faste fayled hem the fode, enfaminied monie;
1195 The hote hunger wythinne hert hem   *hurt*
    wel sarre   *more severely*
Then any dunt of that douthe that dowelled theroute.

1178–9 And there he destroyed by warfare the sites of villages; he ravaged all Israel and took the best (it had to offer).

1182–3 A bold chieftain at every gate, and (he) shut them inside; for the city was so mighty, battlemented above.

1186–7 Quickly skirmishing broke out, much injury was sustained; at each drawbridge was a siege-tower in the form of a bastille (turret on wheels).

1189–91 Within the city, worthy men laboured in towers, inside strong wooden hoarding built on the walls. They attacked and defended and joined battle.

1193–4 In the end, after a long time, the people inside became desperately short of food, and many starved.

1196–8 Than any blow from that army that waited outside. Then the crowds in that great city were in despair; once food was lacking, they grew thin.

Thenne wern tho rowtes redles in tho ryche wones;
Fro that mete was myst, megre thay wexen;
And thay stoken so strayt that thay   *(were) confined; securely*
   ne stray myght
1200 A fote fro that forselet to forray no goudes.   *fortress; forage*

Thenne the kyng of the kyth a counsayl hym takes,
Wyth the best of his burnes, a blench for to make;
Thay stel out on a stylle nyght er any steven rysed,   *outcry*
And harde hurles thurgh the oste er enmies hit wyste.

1205 Bot er thay atwappe ne moght the wach wythoute,
Highe skelt was the askry the skewes anunder.
Loude alarom upon launde lulted was   *earth; sounded*
   thenne;
Ryche, ruthed of her rest, ran to here wedes;

Hard hattes thay hent and on hors lepes;   *helmets*
1210 Cler claryoun crak cryed on lofte.   *blast; sounded*
By that was alle on a hepe hurlande swythee,
Folwande that other flote, and fonde hem   *troop*
   bilyve.   *at once*

Overtok hem as tyd, tult hem of sadeles,   *immediately; tipped*
Tyl uche prynce hade his per put to the grounde.   *opponent*
1215 And ther was the kyng kaght wyth Caldé   *by Chaldean*
   prynces,
And alle hise gentyle forjusted on Jerico   *nobles; unhorsed*
   playnes,

And presented wern as presoneres to the prynce rychest,
Nabigodenozar, noble in his chayer;   *throne*
And he the faynest freke that he his fo hade,   *happiest of men*
1220 And speke spitously hem to, and spylt therafter.

1201-2 Then the king of the country takes a decision, with the best of
   his men, to play a trick.
1204-6 And rushed quickly through the host before their enemies knew
   of it. But before they might slip past the watch outside, the alarm was
   raised loudly under the heavens.
1208 Noblemen, roused from their sleep, ran to their clothes.
1211 By then all were charging forward in a body with all speed.
1220 And he spoke contemptuously to them, and afterwards killed them.

The kynges sunnes in his syght he slow everuchone,
And holkked out his auen yyen heterly bothe,
And bede the burne to be broght to Babyloyn the ryche,
And there in dongoun be don, to dreye ther his   *put; endure*
   wyrdes.   *fate*

1225 Now se! so the Soverayn set has his wrake.
     Nas hit not for Nabugo ne his noble nauther
     That other depryved was of pryde, with paynes stronge,
     Bot for his beryng so badde agayn his blythe Lorde.

     For hade the Fader ben his frende that hym bifore keped,
1230 Ne never trespast to him in teche of mysseleve,
     To colde wer alle Caldé and kythes of Ynde –
     Yet take Torkye hem wyth, her tene hade ben little.

     Yet nolde never Nabugo this ilke note leve
     Er he hade tyrved this toun and torne hit to   *overthrown*
       grounde.
1235 He joyned unto Jerusalem a gentyle duc   *despatched; noble*
       thenne –
     His name was Nabuzardan – to noye   *Nebuzaradan; harass*
       the Jues.

     He was mayster of his men and myghty himselven,   *captain*
     The chef of his chevalrye his chekkes to make.
     He brek the bareres as bylyve, and the burgh after,
1240 And enteres in ful ernestly in yre of his hert.   *wrathfully*

1222 And savagely gouged out both his own eyes.

1225–33 Now see! in this way the Sovereign has taken His revenge. It
   was not for Nebuchadnezzar or his nobles that the other (Zedekiah)
   was deprived of glory, with cruel torments, but for his bad behaviour
   towards his gracious Lord. For had the Father whom he once heeded
   been his friend, and had he never offended against Him in the sin of
   wrong faith, then all Chaldea and the lands of India would have been
   too weak (to do him any harm) – take Turkey with them as well, their
   hostility would have been of little account. Nebuchadnezzar still would
   not abandon this course of action.

1238–9 The leader of his (Nebuchadnezzar's) knights in carrying out his
   attacks. He breached the outworks at once, and the city afterwards.

What! the maysterry was mene, the men wern   *victory; poor*
   away;
The best bowed wyth the burne that the borgh   *went*
   yemed;   *ruled*
And tho that byden wer so biten with the bale hunger
That on wyf hade ben worthe the welgest fourre.

1245 Nabizardan noght forthy nolde not spare,
   Bot bede al to the bronde under bare egge.
   Thay slowen of swettest semlych burdes,
   Bathed barnes in blod and her brayn spylled,   *children*

   Prestes and prelates thay presed to dethe,
1250 Wyves and wenches her wombes tocorven
   That her boweles outborst aboute the diches,
   And al was carfully kylde that thay cach   *ignominiously*
   myght.

   And alle swypped unswolwed of the sworde kene,
   Thay wer cagged and kaght on capeles al bare,
1255 Festned fettres to her fete under fole wombes,
   And brothely broght to Babyloyn ther bale to suffer,

   To sytte in servage and syte that sumtyme wer gentyle.
   Now ar chaunged to chorles and charged wyth   *burdened*
   werkkes,   *labours*
   Bothe to cayre at the kart and the kuy mylke,   *drive; cow*
1260 That sumtyme sete in her sale syres and burdes.

1243-7 And those who remained were so wasted by terrible hunger that
one woman would have been worth the strongest four. Nebuzaradan
would not by any means spare them on that account, but ordered
everyone to be put to the bare blade of the sword. They killed there the
sweetest of fair ladies.

1250 Cut open the stomachs of women and girls.

1253-7 And all who escaped undevoured by the sharp sword were
bound and tied naked on horses, with fetters fastened to their feet
under the horses' bellies, and they, who had once been genteel, were
brought wretchedly to Babylon to endure misery there, to live in
bondage and sorrow.

1260 Those who once sat in their hall as lords and ladies.

And yet Nabuzardan nyl never stynt,   *pause*
Er he to the tempple tee wyth his tulkkes alle;   *go; men*
Betes on the barers, brestes up the yates,
Slouen alle at a slyp that served therinne,   *stroke; officiated*

1265 Pulden prestes bi the polle and plat of her   *crown; struck*
        hedes,
Dighten dekenes to dethe, dungen doun clerkkes,
And alle the maydenes of the munster maghtyly hokyllen
Wyth the swayf of the sworde that   *sweep*
        swolwed hem alle.   *devoured*

Thenne ran thay to the relykes as robbors   *sacred objects*
        wylde,
1270 And pyled alle the apparement that pented to the kyrke,
The pure pyleres of bras pourtrayd   *noble pillars; decorated*
        in golde,
And the chef chaundeler, charged with the lyght,

That ber the lamp upon lofte that lemed   *held; shone*
        evermore
Bifore the sancta sanctorum, ther   *Holy of Holies*
        selcouth was ofte.   *marvellous event*
1275 Thay caght away that condelstik and the   *took; lamp-stand*
        crowne als,
That the auter hade upon, of athel golde ryche,   *on it; fine*

The gredirne and the goblotes   *gridiron*
        garnyst of sylver,   *decorated with*
The bases of the bryght postes and bassynes   *pillars*
        so schyre,   *beautiful*
Dere disches of golde and dubleres fayre,   *precious; platters*
1280 The vyoles and the vesselment of vertuous stones.

1263 They beat on the barriers (in front of the gates), smash the gates.
1266–7 Put deacons to death, struck down clerics, and ruthlessly mowed
      down all the maidens of the Temple.
1270 And pillaged all the furniture that belonged to the church.
1272 And the great lamp-stand, entrusted with the light.
1280 The bowls for incense and the vessels of stones of special power.

Now has Nabuzardan nomen alle thyse noble thynges,   *taken*
And pyled that precious place and pakked those godes;   *holy*
The golde of the gazafylace, to swythe gret noumbre,
Wyth alle the urnmentes of that hous, he hamppred togeder.

1285 Alle he spoyled spitously in a sped whyle
     That Salomon so mony a sadde yer soght to make.   *long*
     Wyth alle the coyntyse that he cowthe clene to wyrke
     Devised he the vesselment, the vestures clene;

     Wyth slyght of his ciences, his Soverayn to love,
1290 The hous and the anournementes he   *furnishings*
        hyghtled togedere.   *embellished*
     Now has Nabuzardan nummen hit al samen,   *at once*
     And sythen bet doun the burgh and brend hit in askes.

     Thenne wyth legiounes of ledes over   *men*
        londes he rydes,   *countryside*
     Heryes of Israel the hyrne aboute;   *harries; hinterland*
1295 Wyth charged chariotes the cheftayn he fyndes,   *laden*
     Bikennes the catel to the kyng that he caght *delivers; treasure*
        hade,

     Presented him the presoneres in pray that thay   *as booty*
        token,
     Moni a worthly wyye whil her worlde laste,
     Moni semly syre soun, and swythe rych maydenes,
1300 The pruddest of the province, and prophetes childer,   *noblest*

1283–5 He put in cases the gold of the Temple treasury, to a very great
   sum, together with all the furnishings of that house. Contemptuously,
   in a short while, he plundered everything.
1287–9 With all the skill in fine workmanship that he possessed he
   fashioned the vessels, the splendid vestments; in the cunning of his arts,
   to glorify his Sovereign.
1292 And afterwards razed the city and burned it to ashes.
1298–9 Many a man of noble rank in his time, many a fair son of a lord,
   and very well-born maidens.

As Ananie and Azarie and als Mizael,
And dere Daniel also, that was devine   *worthy; prophet*
   noble,
With moni a modey moder chylde mo   *proud man; more*
   then innoghe.
And Nabugodenozar makes much joye,

1305   Nou he the kyng has conquest and the kyth wunnen,
And dreped alle the doghtyest and derrest in armes,
And the lederes of her lawe layd to the grounde,   *religion*
And the pryce of the profetie presoners   *best; prophets*
   maked.

Bot the joy of the juelrye, so gentyle and ryche,
1310   When hit was schewed hym so schene, scharp   *bright; great*
   was his wonder;
Of such vessel avayed, that vayled so huge,
Never yet nas Nabugodenozar er thenne.

He sesed hem with solemneté, the Soverayn he   *reverence*
   praysed
That was athel over alle, Israel Dryghtyn;
1315   Such god, such gounes, such gay vesselles
Comen never out of kyth to Caldee   *Chaldean*
   reames.   *realms*

1305–6 Now that he has conquered the king and taken the country, and killed all the boldest and bravest in arms.

1309 But the beauty of the treasure, so splendid and rich.

1311–12 Never until that time had Nebuchadnezzar been shown such vessels, of such great value.

1314–15 Who was excellent above all others, the Lord of Israel. Such goods, such vestments, such fine vessels.

He trussed hem in his tresorye in a tryed   *packed; chosen*
    place,
Rekenly, wyth reverens, as he ryght hade;
And ther he wroght as the wyse, as ye may wyt hereafter,
1320 For hade he let of hem lyght hym moght haf lumpen worse.

That ryche in gret rialté rengned his lyve;
As conquerour of uche a cost he cayser was hatte,
Emperour of alle the erthe, and also the saudan,   *sultan*
And als the god of the grounde was   *as; world*
    graven his name.   *inscribed*

1325 And al thurgh dome of Daniel, fro he devised hade
That alle goudes com of God, and gef hit hym bi samples,
That he ful clanly bicnu his carp bi the laste;
And ofte hit mekned his mynde, his maysterful werkkes.

Bot al drawes to dyye with doel upon ende;
1330 By a hathel never so hyghe, he heldes to   *be; man; falls*
    grounde;
And so Nabugodenozar, as he nedes moste,
For alle his empire so highe, in erthe is he   *power*
    graven.   *buried*

Bot thenn the bolde Baltazar, that was his   *Belshazzar*
    barn aldest,   *son*
He was stalled in his stud, and stabled the rengne
1335 In the burgh of Babiloyne, the biggest he trawed,
That nauther in heven ne on erthe hade no pere.

1318–22 Suitably, with reverence, as was proper for him to do; and in
    this he acted like a wise man, as you will see later, for had he set little
    store by them he might have fared worse. That mighty king reigned in
    great splendour for the rest of his life; as the conqueror of every land
    he was called master.
1325–9 And all through Daniel's advice, after he had explained that all
    things come from God, and made it clear to him in parables, so that in
    the end he fully accepted what he said; and often it softened his
    purpose, his imperious actions. But all come to die pitifully in the end.
1334–5 He was installed as his successor, and governed the kingdom in
    the city of Babylon, the mightiest (of men) as he thought.

For he bigan in alle the glori that hym the gome lafte,   *man*
Nabugodenozar, that was his noble fader;
So kene a kyng in Caldee com never er thenne.   *great*
1340 Bot honoured he not hym that in heven wonies,   *dwells*

Bot fals fantummes of fendes formed with handes,
Wyth tool out of harde tre, and telded on lofte,
And of stokkes and stones, he stoute goddes calls,
When thay ar gilde al with golde and gered wyth   *adorned*
   sylver.

1345 And there he kneles and calles and clepes after help;   *asks for*
And thay reden him ryght, rewarde he hem hetes,
And if thay gruchen him his grace, to gremen his hert,
He cleches to a gret klubbe and knokkes hem to   *takes up*
   peces.

Thus in pryde and olipraunce his empyre he   *arrogance*
   haldes,
1350 In lust and in lecherye and lothelych werkkes,   *hateful*
And hade a wyf for to welde, a worthelych   *enjoy: noble*
   quene,
And mony a lemman never-the-later   *mistress; nevertheless*
   that ladis wer called.

In the clernes of his concubines and curious wedes,
In notyng of nwe metes and of nice gettes,
1355 Al was the mynde of that man on misschapen thinges,
Til the Lorde of the lyfte liste hit abate.

1341–3 But he addresses as mighty gods false images of devils made by
   hand, with tools, out of hard wood and stocks and stones, and raised
   upright.
1346–7 If they will deal well with him, he promises them reward, but if
   they should refuse his boon, to make him angry at heart.
1353–4 In the beauty of his concubines and elegant clothes, in the
   appreciation of new dishes and of extravagant fashions.
1356–9 Until the Lord of the heavens was pleased to put an end to it.
   Then this bold Belshazzar decides on a certain occasion to give a
   display of his vainglory; to the wanton man it is not enough to indulge
   in all vile practices.

Thenne this bolde Baltazar bithenkkes hym ones
To vouche on avayment of his vayneglorie;
Hit is not innogh to the nice al noghty think use,
1360 Bot if alle the worlde wyt his wykked dedes.   *unless; know of*

Baltazar thurgh Babiloyn his banne gart crye,
And thurgh the cuntre of Caldee his callyng   *summons*
   con spryng,   *went out*
That alle the grete upon grounde schulde geder hem samen,
And assemble at a set day at the saudans fest.

1365 Such a mangerie to make the man was avised
That uche a kythyn kyng schuld com thider;
Uche duk wyth his duthe, and other dere lordes,   *retinue*
Schulde com to his court to kythe hym for lege,

And to reche hym reverens and his revel herkken,
1370 To loke on his lemanes and ladis hem calle.   *mistresses*
To rose hym in his rialty rych men soghtten,   *praise; came*
And mony a baroun ful bolde, to Babyloyn the noble.

Ther bowed toward Babiloyn burnes so mony,   *went*
Kynges, cayseres ful kene, to the court wonnen,
1375 Mony ludisch lordes that ladies broghten,   *noble*
That to neven the noumbre to much nye were.   *state; trouble*

For the bourgh was so brod, and so bigge alce,
Stalled in the fayrest stud the sterres anunder,
Prudly on a plat playn, plek alther-fayrest,
1380 Umbesweyed on uch a syde with seven grete   *surrounded*
   wateres;   *rivers*

1361 Had his edict proclaimed.

1363 That all the great men in the world should come together.

1365-6 The man was determined to prepare a banquet such that the kings of all countries should come to it.

1368-9 To acknowledge him as sovereign, and pay him their respects and attend to his revels.

1374 Kings, mighty emperors, made their way to the court.

1377-9 For the city was so large, and so strong also, situated in the fairest place under the stars, proudly on a level plain in the very best spot.

With a wonder wroght walle, wruxeled ful highe,
With koynt carneles above, corven ful clene,
Troched toures bitwene, twenty spere lenthe,
And thiker throwen umbethour with overthwenrt palle.

1385 The place that plyed the pursaunt wythinne
Was longe and ful large, and ever ilych sware,
And uch a syde upon soyle helde seven myle,
And the saudans sete sette in the myddes.   *abode*

That was a palayce of pryde, passande alle   *noble; surpassing*
   other,
1390 Bothe of werk and of wunder, and walled al aboute;
Heghe houses withinne, the halle to hit med;
So brod bilde, in a bay, that blonkkes myght renne.

When the terme of the tyde was towched of the feste,
Dere drowen therto and upon des metten,
1395 And Baltazar upon bench was busked to sete;
Stepe stayred stones of his stoute throne.

Thenne was alle the halle flor hiled with knyghtes,   *covered*
And barounes at the sidebordes bounet aywhere,
For non was dressed upon dece bot the dere selven,
1400 And his clere concubynes in clothes ful bryght.   *beautiful*

1381–7 With a wonderfully constructed wall, built up to a great height,
with skilfully-made battlements above, most excellently fashioned;
pinnacled towers at intervals of twenty spear-lengths, and horizontal
paling set round about at closer intervals. The area that the surrounding
wall enclosed was extensive in length and breadth, and square on all
sides, and each side measured seven miles along the ground.

1390–6 Both elaborate and wonderful, and walled all about; high
buildings inside, the hall in keeping with it; so spaciously built, in the
shape of a bay, that horses might run there. When the appointed time
for the feast arrived, noblemen went there and met on the dais, and
Belshazzar was made ready for his place at table; the precious stones of
his great throne gleamed brightly.

1398–9 And everywhere there were (present) barons at the side tables,
for none was seated on the dais but the great one himself.

When alle segges were ther set, then servyse bygynnes;   *seated*
Sturne trumpen strake, steven in halle;
Aywhere by the wowes wrasten krakkes,
And brode baneres therbi, blusnande of gold.

1405 Burnes berande the bredes upon brode skeles,
That were of sylveren syght, and seves therwyth;
Lyfte logges therover and on lofte corven,
Pared out of paper and poynted of golde;

Brothe baboynes abof, besttes anunder,
1410 Foles in foler flakerande bitwene,
And al in asure and ynde enaumayld ryche;
And al on blonkken bak bere hit on honde.

And ay the nakeryn noyse, notes of pipes;
Tymbres and tabornes tulket among,
1415 Symbales and sonetes sware the noyse,
And bougouns busch batered so thikke.

So was served fele sythe the sale alle aboute,
With solace at the sere course, bifore the self lorde.
Ther the lede and alle his love lenged at the table,
1420 So faste thay weghed to him wyne, hit warmed his   *brought*
    hert,

1402–19 (There was) a loud blast of trumpets, clamour in the hall;
everywhere along the walls flourishes burst out, and (there were) great
banners on the trumpets, gleaming of gold. Men (were) carrying the
roast meats on large platters, that were of silver appearance, and sauces
with them; high houses (as dish covers) over them, figured on the upper
part, cut out of paper and painted over with gold; fearsome grotesques
on top, beasts below, birds fluttering here and there in foliage, and
everything richly enamelled in azure and indigo; and all (the servants)
carried it in their hands on horseback. And always the noise of horns,
notes of pipes; tambourines and drums sounded constantly, cymbals
and bells answered the noise, and the rattle of drumsticks reverberated
rapidly. So the hall was served all round many times, with delight in
the various courses, in front of the lord himself. There where the prince
and all his loves were seated at the table.

And breythed uppe into his brayn and   *rushed; befuddled*
   blemyst his mynde,
And al waykned his wyt, and welneghe he foles;
For he waytes on wyde, his wenches he   *looks around*
   byholdes,
And his bolde baronage aboute bi the wowes.   *barons*

1425 Thenne a dotage ful depe drof to his hert,
   And a caytif counsayl he caght bi hymselven.
   Maynly his marschal the mayster upon calles,
   And comaundes hym cofly coferes to lauce,   *quickly; open*

And fech forth the vessel that his fader broght,   *vessels*
1430 Nabugodenozar, noble in his strenthe,
   Conquerd with his knyghtes and of kyrk rafte
   In Judé, in Jerusalem, in gentyle wyse: *respectful*

'Bryng hem now to my borde, of beverage hem   *table*
   fylles;   *fill*
Let thise ladyes of hem lape, I luf hem in hert.   *drink*
1435 That schal I cortaysly kythe, and thay schin knawe sone,
   Ther is no bounté in burne lyk Baltazar thewes.'

Thenne towched to the tresour this tale was sone,
And he with keyes uncloses kystes ful mony;   *chests*
Mony burthen ful bryght was broght into   *many a burden*
   halle,
1440 And covered mony a cupborde with clothes ful quite.

1422 And his reason was all enfeebled, and he became almost deranged.
1425-7 Then a most grievous folly entered his heart, and he conceived an evil plan that was all his own. Loudly the lord calls for his marshal.
1431 (That he) captured with his knights and carried off from the church.
1435-7 'I shall graciously demonstrate that, and they will soon see that there is no bounty in any man like the favour of Belshazzar.' Then this matter was quickly made known to the treasurer.
1440 And many a sideboard was covered with whitest cloths.

The jueles out of Jerusalem with gemmes ful bryght   *treasures*
Bi the syde of the sale were semely   *attractively*
   arayed;   *set out*
The athel auter of brasse was hade into place,
The gay coroun of golde gered on lofte.

1445 That hade ben blessed bifore wyth bischopes   *that which*
   hondes,
And wyth besten blod busily anoynted,
In the solempne sacrefyce that goud savor hade
Bifore the Lorde of the lyfte, in loving hymselven,

Now is sette for to serve Satanas the blake,
1450 Bifore the bolde Baltazar, wyth bost and wyth   *pomp*
   pryde.   *ceremony*
Hoven upon this auter was athel vessel,   *raised up; vessels*
That wyth so curious a crafte corven was wyly.

Salamon sete him seven yere and a sythe more,
With alle the syence that hym sende the soverayn Lorde,
1455 For to compas and kest to haf hem clene wroght.
For ther wer bassynes ful bryght of brende golde clere,

Enaumaylde with azer, and eweres of sute;
Covered cowpes foul clene, as casteles arayed,
Enbaned under batelment, with bantelles quoynt,
1460 And fyled out of fygures of ferlylé schappes.

1443-4 The noble altar of bronze was brought to its place, the bright
crown of gold set on top of it.

1446-8 And zealously consecrated with the blood of animals, in the
solemn sacrifice in His praise that smelt sweet to the Lord of the
heavens.

1452-98 That with so subtle an art were cunningly fashioned. Solomon
applied himself for seven years and more, with all the skill that the
sovereign Lord sent him, to set his wits to work to have them excellently
made. For there were very beautiful basins of pure bright gold,
enamelled with azure, and pitchers to match; most splendid lidded
cups, shaped like castles, machicolated (i.e. provided with an external
gallery) under the battlements, with skilfully-made stepped corbels, and
fashioned into figures of marvellous shapes. The ornamental tops of

The coperounes of the covacles that on the cuppe reres
Wer fetysely formed out in fylyoles longe;
Pinacles pyght ther apert that profert bitwene,
And al bolled abof with braunches and leves;

1465 Pyes and papejayes purtrayed withinne,
As thay prudly hade piked of pomgarnades;
For alle the blomes of the boghes were blyknande perles,
And alle the fruyt in tho formes of flaumbeande gemmes,

Ande safyres and sardiners and somely topace,
1470 Alabaundeirynes and amarauns and amastised stones,
Casydoynes and crysolytes and clere rubies,
Penitotes and pynkardines, ay perles bitwene.

So trayled and tryfled a-traverce wer alle,
Bi uche bekyr ande bolle, the brurdes al umbe;
1475 The gobelotes of golde graven aboute,
And fyoles fretted with flores and flees of golde.

Upon that auter was al aliche dresset;
The candelstik bi acost was cayred thider sone,
Upon the pyleres apyked that praysed hit mony,
1480 Upon hit bases of brasse that ber up the werkes.

The boghes bryght therabof, brayden of golde,
Braunches bredande theron, and bryddes ther seten
Of mony kyndes, of fele kyn hues,
As thay with wynge upon wynde hade waged her fytheres.

---

the lids that rose high on the cups were skilfully drawn out into long
turrets, with pinnacles elegantly set on them, projecting at intervals,
and all embossed on the surface with branches and leaves, amongst
which magpies and parrots were depicted, as though splendidly partak-
ing of pomegranates; for all the blooms on the boughs were shining
pearls, and all the fruit in those designs was of brilliant gems, sapphires
and sardine-stones and fair topaz, almandines and emeralds and stones
of amethyst, chalcedonies and chrysolites and beautiful rubies, peridots
and pinkardines, with pearls at intervals throughout. Thus all (the
vessels) had trailing designs and trefoils across them, on each beaker
and bowl, all round the edges; the goblets of gold were engraved round
the circumference, and the bowls for incense were inlaid with flowers
and butterflies of gold. Everything was placed without distinction on
the altar; the lamp-stand was quickly brought in alongside, set on the
pillars so that many admired it, on its bases of bronze that supported

1485 Inmong the leves of the launces lampes wer graythed,
     And other louflych lyght that lemed ful fayre,
     As mony morteres of wax, merkked withoute
     With mony a borlych best al of brende golde.

     Hit was not wonte in that wone to wast no serges,
1490 Bot in temple of the trauthe trwly to stonde,
     Bifore the sancta sanctorum, ther sothefast Dryghtyn
     Expouned his speche spiritually to special prophetes.

     Leve thou wel that the Lorde that the lyfte yemes
     Displesed much at that play in that plyt stronge,
1495 That his jueles so gent wyth javeles wer fouled,
     That presyous in his presens wer proved sumwhyle.

     Soberly in his sacrafyce summe wer anoynted,
     Thurgh the somones of himselfe that syttes so hyghe;
     Now a boster on benche bibbes therof   *drinks from them*
1500 Tyl he be dronkken as the devel, and dotes ther he   *drivels*
     syttes.

     So the worcher of this worlde wlates therwyth
     That in the poynt of her play he porvayes a mynde;
     Bot er harme hem he wolde in haste of his yre,
     He wayned hem a warnyng that wonder hem thoght.

---

the structure. The branches above were bright, embellished with gold, with small branches spreading out from them on which birds sat – birds of many kinds, of various colours – as if fluttering their feathers with their wings in the wind. Amongst the leaves of the branches lamps were set, and other beautiful lights that shone most excellently, such as many mortars of wax, figured on the outside with many a noble beast all of pure gold. It (the lamp-stand) was not accustomed to waste candles in that place, but to stand in the Temple of the true faith, as was proper, before the Holy of Holies, where the true God made spiritual utterance to chosen prophets. Be sure that the Lord who rules the heavens was much displeased at that sport in that alien setting, that His splendid treasures were defiled by louts, treasures which had formerly been established as holy in His presence. Some had been solemnly consecrated in sacrifice to Him, by command of the One who sits so high.

1501–4 The Creator of the world is so disgusted on that account that at the height of their revelry He formulates a purpose; but before he would harm them in the haste of His anger, he sent them a warning which amazed them.

1505 Nou is alle this guere geten glotounes   *equipment fetched*
         to serve,
      Stad in a ryche stal, and stared ful bryght.
      Baltazar in a brayd: 'Bede uus therof!
      Weghe wyn in this won! Wassayl!' he cryes.

      Swyfte swaynes ful swythe swepen thertylle,
1510 Kyppe kowpes in honde kynges to serve;
      In bryght bolles ful bayn birlen this other,
      And uche mon for his mayster machches alone.

      Ther was rynging on ryght of ryche metalles
      Quen renkkes in that ryche rok rennen hit to cache;
1515 Clatering of covacles that kesten tho burdes
      As sonet out of sauteray songe als myry.

      Then the dotel on dece drank that he myght,   *fool*
      And thenne arn dressed dukes and prynces,   *served*
      Concubines and knyghtes, bi cause of that merthe;
1520 As uchon hade hym in helde, he haled of the cuppe.

      So long likked thise lordes thise lykores swete,
      And gloryed on her falce goddes and her grace
         calles,   *ask for*
      That were of stokkes and stones, stille evermore; *silent*
      Never steven hem astel, so stoken is hor tonge.

1506–16 Set up in a splendid place, and it shone most brightly. Belshazzar forthwith: 'Serve us (drink) from it! Bring wine in this place! Wassail!' he cries. Nimble servants quickly rush to it, grasp cups to serve the kings; eagerly they offer drink to them in bright bowls, and each servant strives for his master alone. There was ringing indeed of rich metals when men in that splendid company ran to seize it; the clattering of the lids that the women threw away rang out as merrily as music from a psaltery.

1519–21 For the sake of that sport; as each man was aged, so he drank from the cup. For a long time these lords tasted these sweet liquors.

1524 No sound ever escaped them, their tongue was so stuck fast.

1525 Alle the goude golden goddes the gaules yet   *wretches*
       nevenen,   *call on*
     Belfagor, and Belyal, and Belssabub als,   *Baal-peor*
     Heyred hem as hyghly as heven wer   *worshipped; devoutly*
       thayres;
     Bot hym that alle goudes gives, that God thay   *(good) things*
       foryeten.   *forgot*

     For ther a ferly bifel that fele folk seyen; *marvel; many; saw*
1530 Fyrst knew hit the kyng, and alle the cort after;
     In the palays pryncipale, upon the   *royal*
       playn wowe,   *bare wall*
     In contrary of the candelstik, that clerest hit schyned,

     Ther apered a paume, with poyntel in fyngres,   *hand; stylus*
     That was grysly and gret, and grymly he wrytes;   *great*
1535 Non other forme bot a fust faylande the wryste
     Pared on the parget, purtrayed lettres.

     When that bolde Baltazar blusched to that neve, *looked; fist*
     Such a dasande drede dusched to his   *numbing; came over*
       hert
     That al falewed his face and fayled the chere;
1540 The stronge strok of the stonde strayned his joyntes.

     His cnes cachches to close and cluchches his hommes,
     And he with plattyng his paumes displayes his leres,
     And romyes as a rad ryth that rores for drede,
     Ay biholdand the honde til hit hade al graven,
1545 And rasped on the rogh wowe runisch saues.

1532 Opposite the lamp-stand, which shone most brightly.
1535–6 No other shape but a fist without the wrist carved on the plaster,
     formed letters.
1539–45 That his face grew all pale and his composure broke down; the
     strong impact of the blow afflicted his joints. His knees knock together
     and his legs double up, and he tears his cheeks by beating his fists
     (against them), and bellows like a frightened bull that roars for fear,
     continually looking up at the hand till it had finished engraving, and
     had scratched strange sayings on the rough wall.

When hit the scrypture hade scraped wyth a   *writing*
    scrof penne,   *rough*
As a coltour in clay cerves tho forwes,
Thenne hit vanist verayly and voyded of syght;
Bot the lettres bileved ful large upon plaster.   *remained*

1550 Sone so the kynge for his care carping myght wynne,
He bede his burnes bow to that wer bok-lered,
To wayte the wryt that hit wolde, and wyter hym to say:
'For al hit frayes my flesche, the fyngres so grymme.'

Scoleres skelten theratte the skyl for to fynde,
1555 Bot ther was never on so wyse couthe on worde rede,
Ne what ledisch lore ne langage nauther,
What tythyng ne tale, tokened tho draghtes.

Thenne the bolde Baltazar bred ner   *became almost*
    wode,   *mad*
And bede the ceté to seche segges thurghout
1560 That wer wyse of wychecrafte, and warlawes other   *sorcerers*
That con dele wyth demerlayk and devine lettres.

'Calle hem alle to my cort, tho Caldé   *Chaldean*
    clerkkes,   *scholars*
Unfolde hem alle this ferly that is bifallen   *make known to*
    here,
And calle wyth a highe cry: "He that the kyng   *loud*
    wysses   *instructs*
1565 In expounyng of speche that spredes in thise lettres,

1547–8 As a ploughshare cuts furrows in clay, then it vanished com-
    pletely and disappeared from sight.
1550–7 As soon as the king in his distress might find words, he
    commanded his learned men to approach, to examine what the writing
    meant, and to tell him plainly: 'For the grim fingers terrify me utterly.'
    At that scholars came hurrying to discover the meaning, but there was
    not one wise enough to make out a single word, nor what people's lore
    or language, what message or meaning, those characters represented.
1559 And commanded men to be sought throughout the city.
1561 Who dealt in magic arts and interpreted writings.
1565 In the interpretation of the language which is expressed in these
    writings.

And makes the mater to malt my mynde   *sense; penetrate*
   wythinne,
That I may wyterly wyt what that wryt menes,   *plainly know*
He schal be gered ful gaye in gounes of porpre,
And a coler of cler golde clos umbe his   *fastened round*
   throte.

1570 He schal be prymate and prynce of pure clergye,   *of religion*
And of my threvenest lordes the thrydde he schal,
And of my reme the rychest to ryde wyth myselven,
Outtaken bare two, and thenne he the   *except for only*
   thrydde."'

This cry was upcaste, and ther comen   *proclamation; uttered*
   mony
1575 Clerkes out of Caldye that kennest wer   *wisest*
   knauen,   *known to be*
As the sage sathrapas that sorsory couthe;
Wyches and walkyries wonnen to that sale,

Devinores of demorlaykes that dremes cowthe rede,
Sorsers of exorsismus, and fele such clerkes.
1580 And alle that loked on that letter, as   *writing*
   lewed thay were   *unenlightened*
As thay had loked in the lether of my lyft   *as if; left*
   bote.   *boot*

Thenne cryes the kyng and kerves his wedes;   *tears*
What! he corsed his clerkes and calde hem chorles: *look!*
To henge the harlotes he heyed ful ofte;   *rogues; threatened*
1585 So was the wyye wytles he wed wel ner.

1568 He shall be attired most richly in gowns of purple.
1571–2 And he shall be third amongst my noblest lords, the worthiest in
   my kingdom to ride with me.
1576–9 Such as learned sages who knew sorcery; wizards and enchanters
   made their way to that hall, practitioners of magic arts who could
   interpret dreams, exorcists, and many such scholars.
1585–6 The man was so distracted he was almost mad. She who was the

Ho herde hym chyde to the chambre that was the chef quene;
When ho was wytered bi wyyes what was the *informed*
  cause,
Suche a chaungande chaunce in the chef halle, *fortune; great*
The lady, to lauce that los that the lorde *alleviate; trouble*
  hade,
1590 Glydes doun by the grece and gos to the kyng. *stairway*

Ho kneles on the colde erthe and carpes to hymselven *speaks*
Wordes of worchyp wyth a wys speche: *respect*

'Kene kyng,' quoth the quene, 'kayser of urthe, *great*
Ever laste thy lyf in lenthe of dayes!
1595 Why has thou rended thy robe for redles *torn; in despair*
  hereinne,
Thagh those ledes ben lewed lettres to rede,

And has a hathel in thy holde, as I haf herde ofte,
That has the gostes of God that gyes alle sothes?
His sawle is ful of syence sawes to schawe,
1600 To open uch a hide thyng of aunteres uncowthe.

That is he that ful ofte has hevened thy fader
Of mony anger ful hote with his holy speche;
When Nabugodenozar was nyed in *troubled at*
  stoundes, *times*
He devysed his dremes to the dere *explained; innermost*
  trawthe.

---

chief queen heard him railing at the household.
1594 May the days of your life last for ever!
1596–602 Though those men are unable to interpret writings, when you have a man in your kingdom, as I have heard often, who has the spiritual powers of God who commands all truths? His soul is full of wisdom to explain sayings, to reveal every hidden thing concerning strange happenings. He is the one who often raised your father out of many a hot fit of anger with his holy speech.

1605 He kevered hym with his counsayl of caytyf wyrdes;
Alle that he spured hym in space he expowned clene,
Thurgh the sped of the spyryt that sprad hym withinne
Of the godelest goddes that gaynes aywhere.

For his depe divinité and his dere sawes,   *excellent sayings*
1610 Thy bolde fader Baltazar bede by his name,
That now is demed Danyel of derne   *called; secret*
    coninges,   *arts*
That caght was in the captyvidé in cuntré   *(Jewish) Captivity*
    of Jues.

Nabuzardan hym nome, and now is he here,   *captured*
A prophete of that province and pryce of the   *the best in*
    worlde.
1615 Sende into the ceté to seche hym bylyve,
And wynne hym with the worchyp to wayne the bote;

And thagh the mater be merk that merked is yender,
He schal declar hit also as hit on clay standes.'
That gode counseyl at the quene was   *from*
    cached as swythe;   *accepted at once*
1620 The burne byfore Baltazar was broght in a whyle.   *man*

When he com bifore the kyng and clanly had   *politely*
    halsed,   *greeted him*
Baltazar umbebrayde hym, and 'Leve sir,'   *embraced; dear*
    he sayde,
'Hit is tolde me bi tulkes that thou trwe were   *men*
Profete of that provynce that prayed my fader,   *ravaged*

1605–8 He saved him by his counsel from a wretched fate; all that in
course of time he asked him he expounded fully, through the power of
the spirit that was present in him – the spirit of the most excellent gods
(plural from Dan. v. 11) who have power everywhere.
1610 Your bold father commanded his name to be Belteshazzar.
1615–18 Send messengers into the city to look for him at once, and
prevail on him respectfully to give you assistance; and though the
matter written there may be obscure, he will explain it just as it stands
on the plaster.

1625 Ande that thou has in thy hert holy connyng,   *understanding*
     Of sapyence thi sawle ful, sothes to schawe;
     Goddes gost is the geven that gyes alle thynges,
     And thou unhyles uch hidde that heven-kyng myntes.

     And here is a ferly byfallen, and I fayn wolde   *marvel*
1630 Wyt the wytte of the wryt that on the wowe clyves,
     For alle Caldé clerkes han cowwardely   *have miserably*
         fayled;
     If thou with quayntyse conquere hit, I quyte the thy mede.

     For if thou redes hit by ryght and hit to resoun brynges,
     Fyrst telle me the tyxte of the tede lettres,
1635 And sythen the mater of the mode mene me therafter,
     And I schal halde the the hest that I the hyght have,

     Apyke the in porpre clothe, palle alther-fynest,
     And the byghe of bryght golde abowte thyn nekke;
     And the thryd thryvenest that thrynges me after,
1640 Thou schal be baroun upon benche, bede I the no lasse.'

     Derfly thenne Danyel deles thyse wordes: *boldly; speaks*
     'Ryche kyng of this rengne, rede the oure Lorde!
     Hit is surely soth, the Soverayn of heven   *true*
     Fylsened ever thy fader and upon folde cheryched,

1626–8 (You have) your soul full of wisdom, to reveal truths; the spirit
   of God, who rules all things, is given to you, and you uncover each
   hidden thing that the King of Heaven has in mind.

1630 Know the meaning of the writing that is fixed on the wall.

1632–40 If through your wisdom you succeed in deciphering it, I shall
   pay you your reward. Thus if you interpret it correctly and make sense
   of it, first tell me the wording of the fated letters, and then explain to
   me afterwards the sense of the thought, and I shall keep for you the
   promise that I have made to you, array you in purple cloth, the very
   finest material, and put the collar of bright gold round your neck; and
   you shall be a lord of the king's council, I promise you no less, the third
   most worthy who owes allegiance to me.

1642 Great king of this kingdom, may our Lord guide you!

1644–50 Always helped your father and looked after him on earth,
   made him the greatest of all rulers, and made all the world to be at his
   command, let him govern as it pleases him. Whoever he wished to be
   well off, good fortune befell him, and the man whose death he desired
   he killed immediately; whoever it pleased him to lift up was soon on
   high, and whoever it pleased him to lay low was quickly brought down.

1645 Gart hym grattest to be of governores alle,
And alle the worlde in his wylle, welde as hym lykes.
Who-so wolde wel do, wel hym bityde,
And quos deth so he dezyre he dreped als fast;

Who-so hym lyked to lyft, on lofte was he sone,
1650 And quo-so hym lyked to lay was lowed bylyve.
So was noted the note of Nabugodenozar;   *famed; practice*
Styfly stabled the rengne, bi the stronge Dryghtyn.

For of the hyghest he hade a hope in his   *Most High; belief*
  hert
That uche pouer past out of that prynce   *came from*
  even;   *directly*
1655 And whyle that was cleght clos in his hert,   *fixed firmly*
There was no mon upon molde of myght   *earth; as powerful*
  as hymselven.

Til hit bitide on a tyme towched hym pryde,   *one day*
For his lordeschyp so large and his lyf ryche;   *great*
He hade so huge an insyght to his aune dedes   *opinion of*
1660 That the power of the hyghe prynce he purely   *completely*
  foryetes.

Thenne blynnes he not of blasfemy, on to blame the
  Dryghtyn;
His myght mete to Goddes he made with his wordes: *equal*
"I am god of the grounde, to gye as me lykes,   *world; govern*
As he that hyghe is in heven, his aungeles that weldes.

1665 If he has formed the folde and folk therupone,
I haf bigged Babiloyne, burgh alther-rychest,
Stabled therinne uche a ston in strenkthe of myn armes;
Moght never myght bot myn make such another."

1652 He governed the kingdom firmly, with the help of the mighty Lord.
1661 Then he does not refrain from blasphemy, from uttering impiety
  against the Lord.
1666–70 'I have built Babylon, the mightiest city of all, have placed
  every stone therein with my own strength; no power except mine might

Was not this ilke worde wonnen of his mowthe
1670 Er thenne the Soverayn sawe souned in his eres:
"Now, Nabugodenozar,
   innoghe has spoken.   *you have said enough*
Now is alle thy pryncipalté past at ones,   *sovereignty*

And thou, remued fro monnes sunes, or mor most abide,
And in wasturne walk, and wyth the wylde dowelle,
1675 As best byte on the bent of braken and erbes,
With wrothe wolfes to won, and wyth wylde   *fierce; live*
   asses."

Inmydde the poynt of his pryde departed he there
Fro the soly of his solempneté – his solace he leves,
And carfully is outkast to contré unknawen,   *ignominiously*
1680 Fer into a fyr fryth there frekes never comen.

His hert heldet unhole, he hoped non other
Bot a best that he be, a bol other an oxe;
He fares forth on alle faure, fogge was his mete,
And ete ay as a horce when erbes were fallen.

1685 Thus he countes hym a kow, that was a kyng ryche,
Quyle seven sythes were overseyed someres, I trawe.
By that mony thik thyghe thryght umbe his lyre,
That alle was dubbed and dyght in the dew of heven;

---

ever make such another.' This speech was not out of his mouth before
the words of the Sovereign sounded in his ears.

1673–5 And you, banished from the sons of men, must live on the moor,
and walk in the wilderness, and dwell with the wild animals, feed like
a beast on pasture of bracken and grass.

1677–8 At the height of his glory he departed thither, from the seat of
his high estate – he leaves his comforts.

1680–704 Far into a remote wilderness where men never come. His
mind became unsound, he believed nothing else but that he was a beast,
a bull or an ox; he went about on all fours, coarse grass was his food,
and he ate hay like a horse when the grass was withered. Thus he
counts himself a cow, he who had been a great king, until seven
summers had passed away, as I believe. By then many a thick thigh
crowded about his flesh, which was all arrayed and adorned in the dew

Faxe fyltered and felt flosed hym umbe,
1690 That schad fro his schulderes to his schyre-wykes,
And twenty-folde twynande hit to his tos raght,
Ther mony clyvy as clyde hit clyght togeder.

His berde ibrad alle his brest to the bare urthe,
His browes bresed as breres aboute his brode chekes;
1695 Holwe were his yyen and under campe hores,
And al was gray as the glede, with ful grymme clawes,

That were croked and kene as the kyte paume;
Erne-hwed he was and al overbrawden,
Til he wyst ful wel who wroght alle myghtes,
1700 And cowthe uche kyndam tokerve and kever when hym
lyked.

Thenne he wayned hym his wyt that hade wo soffered,
That he com to knawlach and kenned hymselven.
Thenne he loved that Lorde, and leved in trawthe
Hit was non other then he that hade al in honde.

---

of Heaven; tangled and matted hair fell in strands about him, coming down from his shoulders to the middle of his body, and twisting round many times it reached to his toes, where many a bur stuck it together like a poultice. His beard overspread all his breast to the bare earth, his eyebrows bristled like briars about his broad cheeks; his eyes were hollow and under rough lashes, and he was all grey as the kite, with most grim claws, that were curved and sharp like the kite's talon; he was coloured like an eagle and all covered over (with plumage), until he understood fully who created all powers, and could destroy each kingdom and restore it when it pleased Him. Then He sent him his reason, the man who had endured adversity, so that he came to his senses and knew himself. Then he praised the Lord, and believed truly that it was none other than He who ruled all things.

1705 Thenne sone was he sende agayn, his sete   *returned; throne*
     restored;
  His barounes bowed hym to, blythe of his   *went*
     come;   *coming*
  Hagherly in his aune hwe his heved was covered,
  And so yeply was yarked and yolden his state.

  Bot thou, Baltazar, his barne and his bolde ayre,   *son; heir*
1710 Sey these syngnes with syght and set hem at lyttel,
  Bot ay has hofen thy hert agaynes the hyghe Dryghtyn,
  With bobaunce and with blasfamye bost at hym kest,

  And now his vessayles avyled in vanyté unclene,
  That in his hows hym to honour were hevened of fyrst;
1715 Bifore the barouns has hom broght, and byrled therinne
  Wale wyne to thy wenches in waryed stoundes.

  Bifore thy borde has thou broght beverage in thede   *vessels*
  That blythely were fyrst blest with bischopes   *zealously*
     hondes,
  Lovande theron lese goddes that lyf   *praising with them; false*
     haden never,
1720 Made of stokkes and stones that never styry moght.   *stir*

  And for that frothande fylthe, the Fader of heven   *festering*
  Has sende into this sale thise syghtes uncowthe,   *hall; strange*
  The fyste with the fyngeres that flayed thi hert,   *dismayed*
  That rasped renyschly the wowe with the rogh   *harshly*
     penne.

1707–8 He was properly restored to his own shape, and thus his high
    estate was quickly re-established.
1710–16 Saw these miraculous events and thought little of them, but
    you have always raised up your heart against the great Lord, have
    hurled defiance at Him with arrogance and blasphemy, and now with
    foul presumption you have defiled His vessels, which in the beginning
    were raised up in His house to honour Him; you have brought them
    before the barons, and in them you have served choice wine to your
    women in accursed times.

1725 Thise ar the wordes here wryten, withoute werk more,   *ado*
     By uch fygure as I fynde, as oure Fader lykes:
     Mane, Techal, Phares, merked in thrynne,
     That thretes the of thyn unthryfte upon thre wyse.

     Now expowne the this speche spedly I thenk:
1730 Mane menes als much as maynful Gode   *almighty*
     Has counted thy kyndam bi a clene noumbre,
     And fulfylled hit in fayth to the fyrre ende.

     To teche the of Techal, that terme thus menes:
     Thy wale rengne is walt in weghtes to heng,
1735 And is funde ful fewe of hit fayth dedes;
     And Phares folwes for those fawtes, to frayst the trawthe.

     In Phares fynde I for sothe thise felle sawes:
     Departed is thy pryncipalté, depryved thou worthes;
     Thy rengne rafte is the fro and raght is the Perses;
1740 The Medes schal be maysteres here, and thou of menske
        schowved.'

     The kyng comaunded anon to clethe that   *be clothed*
        wyse   *wise man*
     In frokkes of fyn cloth, as forward hit   *garments; agreement*
        asked;
     Thenne sone was Danyel dubbed in ful dere porpor,   *dressed*
     And a coler of cler golde kest umbe his swyre.   *placed; neck*

1726–9 Character by character as I understand them, as our Father
   permits; Mane, Tekel, Peres, written as three words, which threaten
   you on account of your folly in three ways. Now I intend to explain
   these words to you without delay.

1731–40 Has assessed your kingdom in a full reckoning, and brought it
   indeed to its final end. To instruct you concerning Tekel, that word
   means as follows: your noble reign is marked out to be weighed in the
   balance, and is found to be greatly lacking in honest works; and Peres
   comes next on account of those offences, to tell the truth. In Peres I
   find indeed these grim sayings: your principality is divided, you are
   deposed; your kingdom is taken away from you and given to the
   Persians; the Medes shall be masters here, and you shall be driven from
   your noble estate.

1745 Then was demed a decré bi the duk selven;   *proclaimed*
     Bolde Baltazar bed that hym bowe schulde
     The comynes al of Caldé that to the kyng longed,
     As to the prynce pryvyest preved the thrydde,

     Heghest of alle other, saf onelych tweyne,   *worthiest; only*
1750 To bow after Baltazar in borghe and in felde.
     Thys was cryed and knawen in cort als fast,
     And alle the folk therof fayn that folwed hym tylle.

     Bot how-so Danyel was dyght, that day overyede;
     Nyght neghed ryght now with nyes fol mony;
1755 For dawed never another day that ilk derk   *dawned; night*
          after,
     Er dalt were that ilk dome that Danyel devysed.

     The solace of the solempneté in that sale dured,
     Of that farand fest, tyl fayled the sunne.   *pleasant; set*
     Thenne blykned the ble of the bryght   *faded; colour*
          skwes,   *skies*
1760 Mourkenes the mery weder, and the myst dryves;

     Thorgh the lyst of the lyfte, bi the low medoes,
     Uche hathel to his home hyyes ful fast,
     Seten at her soper and songen therafter;   *(they) sat*
     Then foundes uch a felawschyp fyrre at forth naghtes.

1746–8 Bold Belshazzar ordered that all the people of Chaldea who
were subject to the king should owe allegiance to him, as to the prince
recognized as third most important.

1750–4 To pay homage to Belshazzar in town and country. This was
immediately proclaimed and made known in the court, and all the
people who owed allegiance to him were glad of it. But however Daniel
was dealt with, that day passed away; night approached swiftly with
many troubles.

1756–7 Before the doom that Daniel described was dealt out. The joy of
the festivity continued in that hall.

1760–2 The clear air darkens, and the mist drives in; through the edge
of the clear air, along the low meadows, each man (i.e. the ordinary
people of the town, not Belshazzar's guests) hastens to his home.

1764 Then later on in the night each party of guests departs.

1765 Baltazar to his bedd with blysse was *ceremony*
    caryed; *brought*
    Reche the rest as hym lyst, he ros never therafter;
    For his foes in the felde, in flokkes ful grete, *in battle; armies*
    That longe hade layted that lede, his londes to strye,

    Now are thay sodenly assembled at the self tyme; *very*
1770 Of hem wyst no wyye that in that won dowelled.
    Hit was the dere Daryus, the duk of thise Medes, *noble*
    The prowde prynce of Perce, and Porros of *Persia; Porus*
    Ynde,

    With mony a legioun ful large, with ledes of *men at*
    armes, *arms*
    That now has spyed a space to spoyle Caldees.
1775 Thay throngen theder in the thester on thrawen hepes,
    Asscaped over the skyre watteres and scaled the walles,

    Lyfte laddres ful longe and upon lofte wonen,
    Stelen stylly the toun er any steven rysed.
    Withinne an oure of the niyght an entré thay hade, *nightfall*
1780 Yet afrayed thay no freke – fyrre thay *alarmed; further*
    passen,

    And to the palays pryncipal thay aproched *royal*
    ful stylle. *quietly*
    Thenne ran thay in on a res, on rowtes ful *rush; crowds*
    grete;
    Blastes out of bryght brasse brestes so hyghe,
    Ascry scarred on the scue, that scomfyted mony.

1766 Let him take rest as it pleases him, he never rose afterwards.
1768 Who had long sought that prince, to destroy his lands.
1770 No man who lived in that city was aware of them.
1774–8 Who had now spied an opportunity to ravage the Chaldeans. They rushed there in the darkness in close-packed battalions, slipped over the bright rivers and scaled the walls, lifted up long ladders and made their way aloft, quietly took the town before any outcry arose.
1783–4 Blasts burst out loudly from bright brass trumpets, clamour flew up to the sky, throwing many into confusion.

1785 Segges slepande were slayne er thay slyppe   *men; escape*
          myght;
      Uche hous heyred was withinne a   *ransacked*
          hondewhyle.   *short time*
      Baltazar in his bed was beten to dethe,
      That bothe his blod and his brayn blende on the   *mingled*
          clothes.

      The kyng in his cortyn was kaght bi the heles,   *bedcurtain*
1790 Feryed out bi the fete and fowle   *brought*
          dispysed,   *maltreated*
      That was so doghty that day and drank of the vessayl;   *bold*
      Now is a dogge also dere that in a dych   *as precious*
          lygges.   *lies*

      For the mayster of thyse Medes on the morne ryses,
      Dere Daryous that day, dyght upon trone;   *placed*
1795 That ceté seses ful sounde, and saghtlyng makes
      Wyth alle the barouns theraboute, that bowed hym after.

      And thus was that londe lost for the lordes synne,
      And the fylthe of the freke that defowled hade   *defiled*
      The ornementes of Goddes hous that holy were maked.
1800 He was corsed for his unclannes and cached   *overtaken*
          therinne,   *in it*

      Done doun of his dyngneté for dedes   *struck*
          unfayre,   *unseemly*
      And of thyse worldes worchyp wrast out for   *honour; cast*
          ever,
      And yet of lykynges on lofte letted, I trowe;
      To loke on oure lofly Lorde late bitydes.

1795–6 Takes secure possession of that city, and makes peace with all
      the barons round about, who paid homage to him.
1799 The sanctified ornaments of God's house.
1803–5 And also deprived of delights in Heaven, as I believe; looking on
      our gracious Lord will be long deferred (for him). Thus in three ways I
      have shown you clearly.

1805 Thus upon thrynne wyses I haf yow thro schewed
 That unclannes tocleves in corage dere   *sticks; heart; noble*
 Of that wynnelych Lorde that wonyes in   *gracious; dwells*
  heven,
 Entyses hym to be tene, telled up his wrake.

 Ande clannes is his comfort, and coyntyse he lovyes,
1810 And those that seme arn and swete schyn se his face.
 That we gon gay in oure gere that grace he uus sende,
 That we may serve in his syght ther solace never blynnes.
             Amen.

1808–12 Incites Him to be angry, His hostility aroused. But cleanness is
 His delight, and He loves refinement, and those that are seemly and
 pleasant shall see His face. May He send us the grace to be well dressed,
 so that we may serve in His sight where bliss never ends.

PATIENCE

PROLOGUE

Pacience is a poynt, thagh hit displese ofte.   *virtue*
When hevy herttes ben hurt wyth hethyng other elles,
Suffraunce may aswagen hem and the swelme lethe,
For ho quelles uche a qued and quenches malyce.

5 For quo-so suffer cowthe syt, sele wolde folwe,
And quo for thro may noght thole, the thikker he sufferes.
Then is better to abyde the bur umbestoundes
Then ay throw forth my thro, thagh me thynk ylle.

I herde on a halyday, at a hyghe masse,   *holy day*
10 How Mathew melede that his mayster his   *said*
   meyny con teche;   *taught his followers*
Aght happes he hem hyght, and ucheon a mede
Sunderlupes for hit dissert upon a ser wyse.

Thay arn happen that han in hert poverté,   *blessed; have*
For hores is the hevenryche to holde for ever.
15 Thay ar happen also that haunte mekenesse,   *practise*
For thay schall welde this worlde and alle her wylle   *possess*
   have.

Thay ar happen also that for her harme wepes,   *sin*
For thay schal comfort encroche in kythes   *obtain; lands*
   ful mony.
Thay ar happen also that hungeres after ryght,
20 For thay schal frely be refete ful of alle gode.   *fed*

2–8 When heavy hearts are hurt by scorn or anything else, patience may
    soothe them and lessen the bitterness, for it subdues every evil and
    extinguishes malice. Prosperity follows for the man who is able to put
    up with misfortune, but he who may not endure, on account of his
    impatience, suffers the more. And so it is better for me to accept the
    blow when it falls than to be always giving vent to my impatience,
    though I may not like it.
11–12 Eight blessed states He decreed to them, and a reward for each in
    turn according to its merit.
14 For theirs is the kingdom of Heaven to have for ever.

Thay ar happen also that han in hert rauthe,   *pity*
For mercy in alle maneres her mede schal   *forms; reward*
    worthe.   *be*
Thay ar happen also that arn of hert clene,
For thay her Savyour in sete schal se with her   *throne*
    yyen.   *eyes*

25 Thay ar happen also that halden her pese,   *are peaceful*
For thay the gracious Godes sunes schal godly be   *fittingly*
    called.
Thay ar happen also that con her hert stere,   *govern*
For hores is the hevenryche, as I er sayde.   *before*

These arn the happes alle aght that uus bihyght   *promised*
    weren,
30 If we thyse ladyes wolde lof in lyknyng of thewes:
Dame Povert, dame Pitee, dame Penaunce the thrydde,
Dame Mekenesse, dame Mercy and miry Clannesse,   *fair*

And thenne dame Pes and Pacyence put in therafter;
He were happen that hade one, alle were the better.
35 Bot syn I am put to a poynt that poverté hatte,   *state; is called*
I schal me porvay pacyence and play me with bothe.

For in the tyxte there thyse two arn in teme layde,
Hit arn fettled in on forme, the forme and the laste,
And by quest of her quoyntyse enquylen on mede;
40 And als, in myn upynyoun, hit arn of on kynde,   *they*

For ther as povert hir proferes ho nyl be put utter,
Bot lenge wheresoever hir lyst, lyke other greme;
And there as povert enpresses, thagh mon pyne thynk,
Much, maugré his mun, he mot nede suffer.

---

30 If we would love these ladies by copying their virtues.
36-9 I shall take patience upon myself and cultivate both. For in the text
    (i.e. Matt. 5:3-10) where these two are spoken of, they are arranged
    first and last in a series, and by the judgment of their Lord they receive
    one reward.
41-4 For where poverty presents herself she will not be put outside, but
    shall stay wherever she pleases, like it or not; and where poverty is
    oppressive a man must suffer much, in spite of his resistance, though
    he should think it hard.

45 Thus poverté and pacyence arn nedes   *necessarily*
      playferes;   *playfellows*
   Sythen I am sette with hem samen, suffer me byhoves.
   Thenne is me lyghtloker hit lyke and her lotes prayse
   Thenne wyther wyth and be wroth and the wers have.   *resist*

   Yif me be dyght a destyné due to have,   *ordained; appointed*
50 What dowes me the dedayn other dispit make?
   Other yif my lege lorde lyst on lyve me to bidde
   Other to ryde other to renne to Rome in his ernde,

   What graythed me the grychchyng bot grame more seche?
   Much yif he me ne made, maugref my chekes,
55 And thenne thrat moste I thole and unthonk to mede,
   The had bowed to his bode bongré my hyure.

   Did not Jonas in Judé suche jape   *Judaea; folly*
      sumwhyle?   *once*
   To sette hym to sewrté, unsounde he hym feches.
   Wyl ye tary a lyttel tyne and tent me a   *moment; attend to*
      whyle,
60 I schal wysse yow therwyth as Holy Wryt telles.   *tell; about it*

46–7 Since I am beset by them together, I must endure them. Then it is
    better for me to make the best of it and praise their ways.

50–6 Of what use is indignation to me, or defiance? Or if my liege lord
    pleased to command me to go to Rome on his errand, what would
    grumbling do for me except to invite more trouble? It would be too
    good to be true if he did not compel me (to go), in spite of my
    objections, and then I must endure misery and displeasure for a reward,
    I who ought to have bowed to his bidding according to the terms of my
    hire.

58 In trying to achieve safety, he brings disaster upon himself.

I

Hit bitydde sumtyme in the termes of   *happened; boundaries*
   Judé
Jonas joyned was therinne jentyle prophete.
Goddes glam to hym glod that hym unglad   *speech; came*
   made,
With a roghlych rurd rowned in his ere:

65 'Rys radly,' he says, 'and rayke forth   *quickly; go*
   even;   *at once*
Nym the way to Nynyve wythouten other   *take; further*
   speche,
And in that ceté my sawes soghe alle aboute   *sayings; spread*
That in that place, at the poynt, I put in   *when the time comes*
   thi hert.

For iwysse hit arn so wykke that in that won   *indeed; city*
   dowelles,
70 And her malys is so much, I may not abide,   *endure it*
Bot venge me on her vilanye and venym bilyve.
Now sweye me thider swyftly and say me this arende.'

When that steven was stynt that stowned his mynde,
Al he wrathed in his wyt and wytherly he thoght:
75 'If I bowe to his bode and bryng hem   *bidding*
   this tale,   *message*
And I be nummen in Nunive, my nyes   *arrested; troubles*
   begynes.

He telles me those traytoures arn typped   *consummate*
   schrewes;   *villains*
I com wyth those tythynges, thay ta me   *tidings; take*
   bylyve,   *at once*
Pynes me in a prysoun, put me in stokkes,   *confine*
80 Wrythe me in a warlok, wrast out myn yyen.

---

62 That there Jonah was appointed prophet to the gentiles.
64 Breathed in his ear with a harsh sound.
71–4 'But must revenge myself at once on their villainy and venom. Now
   go there quickly and proclaim this message for me.' When that voice,
   which stunned his senses, was silent, he became very angry in himself
   and thought rebelliously.
80 Torture me in a foot-shackle, tear out my eyes.

This is a mervayl message a man for to preche   *marvellous*
Amonge enmyes so mony and mansed   *accursed*
   fendes,   *evildoers*
Bot if my gaynlych God such gref to me wolde,
For desert of sum sake, that I slayn were.

85 At alle peryles,' quoth the prophete, 'I aproche hit   *risks*
   no nerre;   *nearer*
I wyl me sum other waye that he ne   *will go*
   wayte after.   *watches over*
I schal tee into Tarce and tary there a whyle,   *go; Tarshish*
And lyghtly when I am lest he letes me alone.'   *perhaps; gone*

Thenne he ryses radly and raykes bilyve,   *quickly; goes*
90 Jonas toward port Japh, ay janglande for   *Jaffa; grumbling*
   tene   *indignation*
That he nolde thole for no thyng non of those   *endure*
   pynes,   *·afflictions*
Thagh the Fader that hym formed were fale of his hele.

'Oure Syre syttes,' he says, 'on sege so hyghe,   *throne*
In his glowande glorye, and gloumbes ful lyttel   *worries*
95 Thagh I be nummen in Nunnive and naked
   dispoyled,   *stripped*
On rode rwly torent with rybaudes mony.'

Thus he passes to that port his passage to seche,
Fyndes he a fayr schyp to the fare redy,   *for the voyage*
Maches hym with the maryneres, makes her paye
100 For to towe hym into Tarce as tyd as thay   *take; quickly*
   myght.

83–4 Unless my gracious God wished such harm to me as to want me
   killed, in punishment for some offence or other.
92 Were unconcerned about his welfare.
96 Pitifully torn to pieces on a cross by many evil men.
99 Settles with the mariners, gives them payment.

Then he tron on tho tres and thay her tramme ruchen,
Cachen up the crossayl, cables thay fasten,
Wight at the wyndas weyen her ankres,
Spynde spak to the sprete the spare bawelyne,

105 Gederen to the gyde-ropes – the grete cloth falles.
Thay layden in on laddeborde and the lofe wynnes;
The blythe brethe at her bak the bosum he fyndes,
He swenges me thys swete schip swefte fro the haven.

Was never so joyful a Jue as Jonas was thenne,
110 That the daunger of Dryghtyn so derfly ascaped.
He wende wel that that wyy that al the world planted
Hade no maght in that mere no man for to greve.

Lo, the wytles wrechche, for he wolde noght suffer,   *because*
Now has he put hym in plyt of peril wel more.   *state; greater*
115 Hit was a wenyng unwar that welt in his mynde,
Thagh he were soght fro Samarye, that God sey no fyrre.

101–8 Then he goes aboard (lit. stepped on the boards) and they get the
gear ready, hoist the square-sail, fasten cables, swiftly weigh the
anchors at the windlass, smartly fasten the bowline, carried in reserve,
to the bow-sprit, tug at the guy-ropes – the mainsail comes down (i.e.
as it unfurls). They lay in oars on the port side and gain the luff (i.e. a
position more or less against the wind in which the sail becomes
effective); the merry wind at their back finds the belly of the sail (i.e. as
the ship turns), and swings this sweet ship swiftly from the harbour.

110–12 Who had so boldly escaped the power of the Lord. He knew
well that the One who had created all the world had no power in that
sea to harm any man.

115–19 It was a foolish thought that turned in his mind, that though he
were gone from Samaria, God looked no further. Yes, He looked with
wide-open eyes, he should have been certain of that; he had been told
that often in the words which the king spoke, noble David on his
throne who uttered this speech.

Yise, he blusched ful brode, that burde hym by sure;
That ofte kyd hym the carpe that kyng sayde,
Dyngne David on des that demed this speche
120 In a psalme that he set the Sauter withinne: *Psalter*

'O foles in folk, feles otherwhyle,
And understondes umbestounde, thagh ye be stape fole.
Hope ye that he heres not that eres alle made?   *think*
Hit may not be that he is blynde that bigged uche   *created*
    yye.'   *eye*

125 Bot he dredes no dynt that dotes for elde,
For he was fer in the flod foundande to   *ocean; hurrying*
    Tarce.
Bot I trow ful tyd overtan that he were,   *believe; overtaken*
So that schomely to schort he schote of his ame.

For the welder of wyt that wot alle thynges,
130 That ay wakes and waytes, at wylle has he slyghtes.
He calde on that ilk crafte he carf with his hondes;
Thay wakened wel the wrotheloker for wrothely he cleped:

'Ewrus and Aquiloun that on est sittes,
Blowes bothe at my bode upon blo watteres.'   *dark*
135 Thenne was no tom ther bytwene his tale and   *delay; words*
    her dede,
So bayn wer thay bothe two his bone for to wyrk.

121-2 O fools amongst the people, be sensible now and then, and show understanding occasionally, though you are quite mad.

125 But he, foolish in his old age, fears no blow.

128-33 So that he shot shamefully too short of his mark. For the Lord of wisdom who knows all things, who always wakes and watches, has means at His command. He called on those powers He had made with His hands; they wakened the more angrily in that angrily He called: 'Eurus (an easterly wind) and Aquilon (a north-easterly wind) who sit in the East.'

136 So eager were they both to carry out His command.

Anon out of the north-est the noys bigynes,
When bothe brethes con blowe upon blo   *winds blew*
    watteres.
Rogh rakkes ther ros, with rudnyng anunder;
140 The see soughed ful sore, gret selly to here.

The wyndes on the wonne water so wrastel togeder
That the wawes ful wode waltered so highe,
And efte busched to the abyme, that breed fysches
Durst nowhere for rogh arest at the bothem.

145 When the breth and the brok and the bote metten,   *sea*
Hit was a joyles gyn that Jonas was inne,   *craft*
For hit reled on roun upon the roghe ythes;   *around; waves*
The bur ber to hit baft, that braste alle her gere.

Then hurled on a hepe the helme and the sterne;
150 Furst tomurte mony rop, and the mast after;   *broke*
The sayl sweyed on the see; thenne suppe   *collapsed; sup*
    bihoved   *must*
The coge of the colde water, and thenne the cry ryses. *ship*

Yet corven thay the cordes and kest al theroute;   *cut; threw*
Mony ladde ther forth lep to lave and   *leapt; bale*
    to kest,   *cast out*
155 Scopen out the scathel water that fayn scape wolde,
For be monnes lode never so luther, the lyf is   *burden; heavy*
    ay swete.

Ther was busy overborde bale to kest,   *eagerness; packages*
Her bagges and her fether-beddes and her bryght
    wedes,   *clothes*
Her kysttes and her coferes, her caraldes alle, *chests; casks*
160 And al to lyghten that lome, yif lethe wolde schape.

139–44 Ragged clouds came up, with red light under them; the sea
roared most dreadfully, awesome to hear. The winds so wrestled
together on the dark water that the waves in their anger rolled so high,
and so plunged back into the abyss, that nowhere were the terrified fish
able to remain quiet at the bottom, on account of the upheaval.

148–9 The gale took it abaft, so that all the gear was shattered. Then the
tiller and the stern crashed in a heap.

155 Scooped out the threatening water, desiring to save their lives.

160 And all to lighten that vessel, to see if relief would come.

Bot ever was ilyche loud the lot of the wyndes,   *just as; noise*
And ever wrother the water and wodder the   *angrier; wilder*
   stremes.   *seas*
Then tho wery forwroght wyst no bote,
Bot uchon glewed on his god that gayned hym   *called; helped*
   beste.

165 Summe to Vernagu ther vouched avowes solemne,
   Summe to Diana devout and derf Neptune,   *holy; mighty*
   To Mahoun and to Mergot, the mone and   *Mahomet; Magog*
      the sunne,
   And uche lede as he loved and layde had his hert.

   Thenne bispeke the spakest, dispayred wel nere: *wisest*
170 'I leve here be sum losynger, sum lawles wrech,   *think; traitor*
   That has greved his god and gos here amonge uus.   *offended*
   Lo, al synkes in his synne and for his sake marres.   *perishes*

   I louve that we lay lotes on ledes uchone,
   And who-so lympes the losse, lay hym theroute;
175 And quen the gulty is gon, what may gome   *man*
      trawe,   *believe*
   Bot he that rules the rak may rwe on those other?'

   This was sette in asent, and sembled thay   *agreed; assembled*
      were,
   Heryed out of uche hyrne to hent that falles;
   A lodesmon lyghtly lep under hachches
180 For to layte mo ledes and hem to lote bryng.

---

163 Then those men, worn out with work, saw no remedy.

165 Some there made solemn vows to Vernagu (a Saracen god).

168 Each man as he had faith and had committed his heart.

173–4 I suggest that we cast lots amongst all the men, and whoever
   loses, throw him overboard.

176 But that He who rules the storm may pity the rest?

178–86 Routed out of every corner to take what should befall; a
   steersman quickly leapt below deck to look for more men and bring
   them to the casting of lots. But no man was missing whom he might

Bot hym fayled no freke that he fynde myght,
Saf Jonas the Jwe, that jowked in derne;
He was flowen, for ferde of the flode lotes,
Into the bothem of the bot, and on a brede lyggede,

185 Onhelde by the hurrok, for the heven wrache,
Slypped upon a sloumbe-selepe, and sloberande he routes.
The freke hym frunt with his fot and bede hym   kicked
   ferk up;   get
Ther Ragnel in his rakentes hym rere of his dremes!

Bi the hasp-hede he hentes hym thenne,
190 And broght hym up by the brest and upon borde sette, deck
Arayned hym ful runyschly what raysoun questioned; roughly
   he hade
In such slaghtes of sorwe to slepe so faste.   desperate straits

Sone haf thay her sortes sette and serelych deled,
And ay the lote upon laste lymped on Jonas.
195 Thenne ascryed thay hym sckete and asked   berated; quickly
   ful loude:
'What the devel has thou don, doted wrech?   stupid

What seches thou on see, synful schrewe,
With thy lastes so luther to lose uus uchone?
Has thou, gome, no governour ne god on to   fellow; master
   calle,
200 That thou thus slydes on slepe when thou slayn
   worthes?   are about to be

---

expect to find except Jonah the Jew, who was sleeping in a hidden
place; he had fled, for fear of the roaring of the sea, into the bottom of
the boat, and was lying on a plank, huddled up by the rudder-band, to
escape Heaven's vengeance, sunk in a deep sleep, and slobbering as he
snored.

188-9 So may Ragnel (a devil) in his chains rouse him from his dreams!
   He seizes him then by the clasp (of his garment).

193-4 Soon they have prepared their lots and dealt them out in turn,
   and always the lot finally fell to Jonah.

197-8 Why are you trying to destroy us all on the sea with your foul
   crimes, you evil wretch?

Of what londe art thou lent, what laytes thou here,
Whyder in worlde that thou wylt, and what is thyn arnde?
Lo, thy dom is the dyght, for thy dedes ille;
Do gyf glory to thy godde, er thou glyde hens.'   *go hence*

205 'I am an Ebru,' quoth he, 'of Israyl borne;
That wyye I worchyp, iwysse, that wroght alle thynges,   *One*
Alle the worlde with the welkyn, the wynde and   *sky*
   the sternes,   *stars*
And alle that wones ther withinne, at a worde one   *lives*

Alle this meschef for me is made at thys tyme,   *trouble*
210 For I haf greved my God and gulty am founden;
Forthy beres me to the borde and bathes me theroute;
Er gete ye no happe, I hope forsothe.'

He ossed hym by unnynges that thay undernomen
That he was flawen fro the face of frelych Dryghtyn.
215 Thenne such a ferde on hem fel and flayed hem withinne
That thay ruyt hym to rowwe, and letten the rynk one.

Hatheles hyyed in haste with ores ful longe,   *men hurried*
Syn her sayl was hem aslypped, on sydes to rowe,
Hef and hale upon hyght to helpen hymselven.
220 Bot al was nedles note, that nolde not bityde;

In bluber of the blo flod bursten her ores.   *turbulence*
Thenne hade thay noght in her honde that hem help myght;
Thenne nas no coumfort to kever, ne counsel non other
Bot Jonas into his juis jugge bylyve.

201–3 What land have you come from, what are you looking for here,
where in the world are you going, and what is your errand? See, your
fate is decided, for your evil deeds.

211–16 'And so carry me to the side and throw me overboard; you will
get no good fortune before then, I am certain.' He showed them by
signs which they understood that he had fled from the face of the most
high Lord. Then such a fear fell on them and dismayed their hearts that
they bestirred themselves to row, and left the man alone.

218–20 Since their sail had escaped them, to row at the sides, to heave
and pull with all their might to help themselves. But all their effort was
useless, it was not to be.

223–4 Then there was no comfort to be had, nor any other counsel
except to consign Jonah to his doom at once.

225 Fyrst thay prayen to the prynce that prophetes serven
That he gef hem the grace to greven hym never
That thay in baleles blod ther blenden her handes,
Thagh that hathel wer his that thay here quelled.

Tyd by top and bi to thay token hym synne,
230 Into that lodlych loghe thay luche hym sone.
He was no tytter outtulde that tempest ne sessed;
The se saghtled therwith as sone as ho moght.

Thenne thagh her takel were torne that totered on ythes,
Styffe stremes and streght hem strayned a whyle,
235 That drof hem dryylych adoun the depe to serve,
Tyl a swetter ful swythe hem sweyed to bonk.

Ther was lovyng on lofte, when thay the londe wonnen,
To oure mercyable God, on Moyses wyse,
With sacrafyse upset and solempne vowes,   *raised up*
240 And graunted hym on to be God, and graythly non other.

Thagh thay be jolef for joye, Jonas yet dredes;   *light-hearted*
Thagh he nolde suffer no sore, his seele is on anter;
For what-so worthed of that wyye fro he in water dipped,
Hit were a wonder to wene, yif Holy Wryt nere.

226–38 That He should give them the grace never to offend Him by
   (their) steeping their hands in innocent blood, even if the man they
   killed there were His. Quickly then they took him by top and toe,
   pitched him at once into that fearsome sea. No sooner was he thrown
   out than the tempest stopped; with that the sea became calm as soon as
   it might. Then though the tackle of that ship, which tottered on the
   waves, was torn to pieces, strong and compelling currents took charge
   of them for a while, driving them along relentlessly in the power of the
   deep, until a more favourable one sped them swiftly to land. Praise was
   raised on high, when they reached land, to our merciful God, after the
   manner of Moses.

240 And they acknowledged that He alone was God, and truly no other.

242–4 Though he would not suffer hardship, his welfare is in doubt; for
   what became of that man after he plunged into the water would be
   difficult to believe, if it were not for Holy Writ.

II

245 Now is Jonas the Jwe jugged to drowne;   *doomed*
   Of that schended schyp men schowved hym sone.   *wrecked*
   A wylde walterande whal, as wyrde then schaped,
   That was beten fro the abyme, bi that bot flotte,

   And was war of that wyye that the water soghte,   *aware*
250 And swyftely swenged hym to swepe and his swolw opened.
   The folk yet haldande his fete, the fysch hym tyd hentes;
   Withouten towche of any tothe he tult in his throte. *tumbled*

   Thenne he swenges and swayves to the se   *swings; sweeps*
      bothem,
   Bi mony rokkes ful roghe and rydelande   *swirling*
      strondes,   *currents*
255 Wyth the mon in his mawe malskred in drede –   *dazed*
   As lyttel wonder hit was, yif he wo dreyed,   *was in distress*

   For nade the hyghe heven-kyng, thurgh his   *had not*
      honde myght,   *power*
   Warded this wrech man in warlowes   *guarded; monster's*
      guttes,
   What lede moght lyve, bi lawe of any kynde,
260 That any lyf myght be lent so longe hym withinne?

   Bot he was sokored by that Syre that syttes so   *succoured*
      highe,
   Thagh were wanles of wele in wombe of that fissche,
   And also dryven thurgh the depe, and in derk walteres.
   Lorde, colde was his cumfort, and his care huge!   *trouble*

247-8 A wild wallowing whale, as fate then brought it about, that was
   driven from the depths, was floating near the boat.
250-1 And swiftly swooped and opened its gullet. With the people still
   holding his feet, the fish quickly seizes him.
259-60 What man could believe that he might, by any natural law, be
   granted life for such a long time inside (the whale)?
262-3 Though he was without hope of well-being in the belly of that
   fish, and driven through the deep besides, and though he rolled about
   in the darkness.

265 For he knew uche a cace and kark that hym lymped,
    How fro the bot into the blober was with a best lachched,
    And thrwe in at hit throte withouten thret more,
    As mote in at a munster dor, so mukel wern his chawles.

    He glydes in by the giles thurgh glaymande glette,   *slimy filth*
270 Relande in by a rop, a rode that hym thoght,
    Ay hele over hed hourlande aboute,   *tumbling*
    Til he blunt in a blok as brod as a halle.   *stopped; cavern*

    And ther he festnes the fete and fathmes aboute,
    And stod up in his stomak that stank as the devel.
275 Ther in saym and in sorwe that savoured as helle,
    Ther was bylded his bour that wyl no bale suffer.

    And thenne he lurkkes and laytes where was le best
    In uche a nok of his navel, bot nowhere he fyndes
    No rest ne recoverer bot ramel ande myre,
280 In wych gut so-ever he gos – bot ever is God swete.

    And ther he lenged at the last and to the lede   *halted; Lord*
       called:
    'Now, prynce, of thy prophete pité thou have.
    Thagh I be fol and fykel and falce of my hert,   *foolish*
    Dewoyde now thy vengaunce, thurgh vertu of rauthe.

285 Thagh I be gulty of gyle, as gaule of prophetes,   *scum*
    Thou art God, and alle gowdes ar graythely   *things; truly*
       thyn owen;
    Haf now mercy of thy man and his mysdedes,
    And preve the lyghtly a lorde in londe and in water.'   *readily*

265–8 For he was aware of every misfortune and trouble that had
    befallen him, how he was seized by a monster out of the boat into the
    seething water, and how he sped in through its throat without more
    ado, like a mote in at a cathedral door, so great were its jaws.
270 Reeling in along a gut, that seemed to him a road.
273 And there he gets his footing and gropes about.
275–9 There in grease and filth that stank as Hell, there was made the
    bower of the man who would suffer no hardship. And then he creeps
    and looks for the best shelter in every corner of its gut, but nowhere
    does he find any rest or safety, only muck and mire.
284 Forego your vengeance now, through the power of your pity.

With that he hitte to a hyrne and helde hym therinne,
290 Ther no defoule of no fylthe was fest hym abute.
Ther he sete also sounde, saf for merk one,
As in the bulk of the bote ther he byfore sleped.   *hold*

So in a bouel of that best he bides on lyve,   *lives on*
Thre dayes and thre nyght, ay thenkande on Dryghtyn,
295 His myght and his merci, his mesure thenne;   *moderation*
Now he knawes hym in care that couthe not in sele.

Ande ever walteres this whal bi wyldren depe,
Thurgh mony a regioun ful roghe,
thurgh ronk of his wylle;   *in the pride*
For that mote in his mawe mad hym, I trowe,   *made*
300 Thagh hit lyttel were hym wyth, to wamel at his hert.

Ande as sayled the segge, ay sykerly he herde
The bygge borne on his bak and bete on his sydes.
Then a prayer ful prest the prophete ther maked;   *quickly*
On this wyse, as I wene, his wordes were mony: *believe*

III

305 'Lorde, to the haf I cleped in cares ful stronge;   *called*
Out of the hole thou me herde of hellen wombe;   *of Hell*
I calde, and thou knew myn uncler steven.   *voice*
Thou diptes me of the depe se into the dymme hert;

289–91 With that he came upon a nook and installed himself in it, where
no foulness of filth was near him. There he remained as secure, save
only for darkness.

296–7 Now in trouble he acknowledges Him, he who did not know how
to do so in prosperity. And still the whale wallows through the angry
deep.

300–2 (Made it) feel sick at heart, though it were tiny by comparison.
And as the man sailed on, he heard, always in safety, the mighty ocean
on its back and beating on its sides.

308 You plunged me into the dim heart of the deep sea.

The grete flem of thy flod folded me umbe;   *flow; around*
310 Alle the gotes of thy guferes and groundeles powles,
And thy stryvande stremes of stryndes so mony,
In on daschande dam dryves me over.

And yet I sayde, as I seet in the se bothem: *sat*
"Careful am I, kest out fro thy cler yyen,   *distressed; eyes*
315 And desevered fro thy syght; yet surely I hope   *cut off*
Efte to trede on thy temple and teme to thyselven."

I am wrapped in water to my wo stoundes;
The abyme byndes the body that I byde inne;
The pure poplande hourle playes on my heved;
320 To laste mere of uche a mount, man, am I fallen.

The barres of uche a bonk ful bigly me haldes,
That I may lachche no lont, and thou my lyf weldes;
Thou schal releve me, renk, whil thy ryght slepes,
Thurgh myght of thy mercy that mukel is to tryste.

325 For when th'acces of anguych was hid in my sawle,   *pang*
Thenne I remembred me ryght of my rych Lorde,   *duly; noble*
Prayande him for peté his prophete to here,
That into his holy hous myn orisoun moght entre.   *prayer*

310–12 All the surges of your whirlpools and bottomless deeps, and
your restless seas of many currents, drive over me in one overwhelming
flood.

316–24 'To walk in your temple and be yours again.' I am wrapped in
water to my pangs of woe (Jonah 2: 6: to the soul); the abyss binds the
body that I inhabit; the boiling sea-surge itself plays on my head; I am
fallen, Sir, to the last boundary of every mountain (Jonah 2: 7: to the
bottoms of the mountains). The bars of every land hold me strongly, so
that I may not reach the shore, and you rule my life; you must succour
me, Sir, while your justice sleeps, through the power of your mercy that
one may readily rely on.

I haf meled with thy maystres mony longe day,
330 Bot now I wot wyterly that those unwyse ledes,
That affyen hym in vanyté and in vayne thynges,   *trust in*
For think that mountes to noght her mercy forsaken.

Bot I dewoutly awowe, that verray bes halden,
Soberly to do the sacrafyse when I schal save worthe,
335 And offer the for my hele a ful hol gyfte,   *safety; proper*
And halde goud that thou me hetes, haf here my trauthe.'

Thenne oure Fader to the fysch ferslych   *sternly*
  biddes   *commands*
That he hym sput spakly upon spare drye.
The whal wendes at his wylle and a warthe fyndes,
340 And ther he brakes up the buyrne as bede hym oure Lorde.

Thenne he swepe to the sonde in sluchched clothes;
Hit may wel be that mester were his mantyle to wasche.
The bonk that he blosched to and bode hym bisyde
Wern of the regiounes ryght that he renayed hade.

345 Thenne a wynde of Goddes worde efte the wyye bruxles:
'Nylt thou never to Nunive bi no kynnes wayes?'
'Yisse, Lorde,' quoth the lede, 'lene me thy grace   *give*
For to go at thi gre; me gaynes non other.'

329-30 I have spoken with your men of learning for many a long day,
  but I now know for certain that those unwise men.
332-4 Give up the mercy that would be theirs for things that amount to
  nothing. But I solemnly promise, I who am considered truthful, to
  make sacrifice to you with propriety when I am saved.
336 And accept what you command me, you have my word here.
338-46 That it should quickly spit him out upon dry land. The whale
  goes at His will and finds a shore, and there it spews up the man as our
  Lord commanded. Then he swept to the shore in filthy clothes; it may
  well be that there was need for him to wash his mantle. The land that
  met his gaze, lying around him, belonged to the very country which he
  had renounced. Then a breath of God's word again upbraids the man:
  'Will you still not go to Nineveh, not by any route?'
348-50 'To go as you desire; no other course will profit me.' 'Rise, then

'Ris, aproche then to prech, lo, the place here!
350 Lo, my lore is in the loke, lauce hit therinne!'
Thenne the renk radly ros as he myght,   *quickly*
And to Ninive that naght he neghed ful even.

Hit was a ceté ful syde and selly of brede;
On to threnge therthurghe was thre dayes dede.
355 That on journay ful joynt Jonas hym yede,
Er ever he warpped any worde to wyye that he mette,   *spoke*

And thenne he cryed so cler that kenne myght   *understand*
  alle;
The trwe tenor of his teme he tolde on this   *purport; message*
  wyse:
'Yet schal forty dayes fully fare to an ende,
360 And thenne schal Ninive be nomen and to noght worthe.

Truly this ilk toun schal tylte to grounde;   *fall*
Up so doun schal ye dumpe depe to the abyme, *pell-mell; dive*
To be swolwed swyftly wyth the swart erthe,   *by; black*
And alle that lyvyes hereinne lose the swete.'   *life-blood*

365 This speche sprang in that space and spradde   *went out; place*
  alle aboute
To borges and to bacheleres that in that burgh lenged.
Such a hidor hem hent and a hatel drede
That al chaunged her chere and chylled at the hert.

---

approach this place here, look, to preach to it! Look, my teaching is
locked inside you, release it in that place!'
352–5 And he came very near to Nineveh that night. It was a most
extensive city and of wondrous breadth; to press on through it took
three days. Jonah travelled very quickly for one day's journey.
359–60 From this time shall forty days pass away, and then Nineveh
shall be taken and destroyed.
366–9 To the burgesses and the young men who lived in that town. Such
fright and cruel fear seized them that all were transformed and were
chilled at heart. Still the man did not cease, but said again and again.

The segge sesed not yet, bot sayde ever ilyche:
370 'The verray vengaunce of God schal voyde this   *destroy*
      place.'
      Thenne the peple pitosly pleyned   *lamented*
      ful stylle,   *continually*
      And for the drede of Dryghtyn doured in hert.   *were troubled*

      Heter hayres thay hent that asperly bited,
      And those thay bounden to her bak and to her bare sydes,
375 Dropped dust on her hede, and dymly bisoghten   *feebly*
      That that penaunce plesed him that playnes on   *complains of*
      her wronge.

      And ay he cryes in that kyth tyl the kyng herde;   *still; place*
      And he radly upros and ran fro his chayer.   *promptly; throne*
      His ryche robe he torof of his rigge naked,   *ripped from; back*
380 And of a hep of askes he hitte in the myddes.

      He askes heterly a hayre and hasped hym umbe,
      Sewed a sekke therabof, and syked ful colde.
      Ther he dased in that duste, with droppande   *lay stunned*
      teres,
      Wepande ful wonderly alle his wrange dedes.

385 Thenne sayde he to his serjauntes: 'Samnes yow bilyve;
      Do dryve out a decré, demed of myselven,
      That alle the bodyes that ben withinne this borgh quyk,
      Bothe burnes and bestes, burdes and childer,

---

373 They took rough hair-shirts that bit sharply.
380-2 And he set himself in the middle of a heap of ashes. Urgently he
      asked for a hair-shirt and clasped it round him, sewed a piece of
      sackcloth on it and sighed most woefully.
384-8 Weeping prodigiously for all his evil deeds. Then he said to his
      servants: 'Assemble at once; proclaim a decree, ordained by myself,
      that all living creatures in this town, men and animals, women and
      children.'

Uch prynce, uche prest, and prelates alle,
390 Alle faste frely for her falce werkes.   *shall fast willingly*
Seses childer of her sok, soghe hem so never,
Ne best bite on no brom, ne no bent nauther,

Passe to no pasture, ne pike non erbes,
Ne non oxe to no hay, ne no horse to water.
395 Al schal crye, forclemmed, with alle oure clere strenthe;
The rurd schal ryse to hym that rawthe schal have; *noise; pity*

What wote other wyte may yif the wyye lykes,
That is hende in the hyght of his gentryse?
I wot his myght is so much, thagh he be
    myssepayed,   *displeased*
400 That in his mylde amesyng he mercy may fynde. *gentleness*

And if we leven the layk of oure layth synnes, *practice; foul*
And stylle steppen in the styye he styghtles hymselven,
He wyl wende of his wodschip, and his wrath *turn from; fury*
    leve,
And forgif uus this gult, yif we hym God leven.' *believe*

405 Thenne al leved on his lawe and laften her synnes,
Parformed alle the penaunce that the prynce radde. *imposed*
And God thurgh his godnesse forgef as he sayde;
Thagh he other bihyght, withhelde his vengaunce.

391–3 Take children from the breast, no matter how much it may
distress them, nor shall any beast feed on broom, or grass either, go to
pasture, or crop plants.
395 Pinched with hunger, we must all cry out with all our full strength.
397–8 Who knows or may know whether God, who is gracious in the
excellence of His nobility, will not be pleased?
402 And walk quietly in the path that He Himself marks out.
405 Then all accepted his edict and abandoned their sins.
407–8 And God in His goodness forgave them, as the king had said He
would; although He had promised otherwise, God withheld His
vengeance.

IV

Muche sorwe thenne satteled upon segge Jonas;

410 He wex as wroth as the wynde towarde oure Lorde. *became*

So has anger onhit his hert, he calles *entered*

A prayer to the hyghe prynce, for pyne, on thys *anguish*
    wyse:

'I biseche the, Syre, now thou self jugge,

Was not this ilk my worde that worthen is nouthe,

415 That I kest in my cuntré, when thou thy carp sendes

That I schulde tee to thys toun thi talent to preche?

Wel knew I thi cortaysye, thy quoynt *wise*
    soffraunce, *patience*

Thy bounté of debonerté, and thy bene grace,

Thy longe abydyng wyth lur, thy late vengaunce;

420 And ay thy mercy is mete, be mysse never *sufficient; wrong*
    so huge.

I wyst wel, when I hade worded quat-so-ever I *knew*
    cowthe *could*

To manace alle thise mody men that in this mote dowelles,

Wyth a prayer and a pyne thay myght her pese *penance*
    gete, *make*

And therfore I wolde haf flowen fer into Tarce. *fled; far*

425 Now, Lorde, lach out my lyf, hit lastes to *take away; too*
    longe;

Bed me bilyve my bale stour and bryng me on ende;

For me were swetter to swelt as swythe, as me thynk,

Then lede longer thi lore, that thus me les makes.'

414–16 Was not this that has now happened the very thing I said would
    happen, (back) in my own country, when you sent word that I should
    go to this town to preach your purpose?

418–19 The bounty of your kindness, and your good grace, your long
    endurance of injury, your tardy vengeance.

422 To threaten all these insolent men who live in this city.

426–8 Give me my death-throes quickly and bring me to my end; for I
    would rather die at once, I think, than have anything more to do with
    your counsel, you who thus make me untruthful.

The soun of oure Soverayn then swey in his   *voice; sounded*
   ere,
430 That upbraydes this burne upon a breme wyse: *man; stern*
   'Herk, renk, is this ryght so ronkly to wrath   *sir; haughtily*
   For any dede that I haf don other demed   *ordained for you*
   the yet?'

Jonas al joyles and janglande upryses,   *grumbling*
And haldes out on est half of the hyghe place,
435 And farandely on a felde he fetteles hym to bide,
For to wayte on that won what schulde worthe after.

Ther he busked hym a bour, the best that he   *made himself*
   myght,
Of hay and of everferne and erbes a fewe,   *ditch-fern*
For hit was playn in that place for plyande greves,
440 For to schylde fro the schene other any schade   *bright sun*
   keste.   *cast*

He bowed under his lyttel bothe, his bak to the   *sat: arbour*
   sunne,
And ther he swowed and slept sadly   *fell asleep; soundly*
   al nyght,
The whyle God of his grace ded grow of that soyle   *did*
The fayrest bynde hym abof that ever burne wyste.   *vine; saw*

445 When the dawande day Dryghtyn con sende,   *dawning; did*
Thenne wakened the wyy under wodbynde,   *woodbine*
Loked alofte on the lef that lylled grene.   *leaves; shimmered*
Such a lefsel of lof never lede hade,

434–6 And goes out on the east side of the city, and he prepares to wait
    in comfort in a field, in order to watch what would happen in that city
    later on.
439 For that spot was bare of swaying groves.
448 Never did a man have such a fine bower.

For hit was brod at the bothem, boghted on   *vaulted above*
 lofte,
450 Happed upon ayther half, a hous as hit   *closed in; all sides*
 were,
A nos on the north syde and nowhere non elles,
Bot al schet in a schawe that schaded ful cole.

The gome glyght on the grene graciouse leves,
That ever wayved a wynde so wythe and so cole.
455 The schyre sunne hit umbeschon, thagh no schafte myght
The mountaunce of a lyttel mote upon that man schyne.

Thenne was the gome so glad of his gay logge,   *fine arbour*
Lys loltrande therinne lokande to toune;   *lies lounging*
So blythe of his wodbynde he balteres therunder   *capers*
460 That of no diete that day – the devel haf! – he roght.

And ever he laghed as he loked the loge alle aboute,
And wysched hit were in his kyth ther he wony schulde,
On heghe upon Effraym other Ermonnes hilles.
'Iwysse, a worthloker won to welde I never keped.'

465 And quen hit neghed to naght nappe hym bihoved;
He slydes on a sloumbe-slep sloghe under leves,
Whil God wayned a worme that wrot upe the rote,   *sent; dug*
And wyddered was the wodbynde bi that the   *withered; when*
 wyye wakned.   *man*

451-6 A doorway on the north side and none anywhere else, but all
 enclosed in a thicket that cast cool shade. The man looked at the lovely
 green leaves, that a wind, so mild and cool, continually agitated. The
 bright sun shone round it, though no ray, not so much as a speck,
 might shine on that man.
460 That he takes no thought for food that day – to the devil with it!
462-6 And wished it were in his land where he must live, high up on
 Mount Ephraim or the hills of Mount Hermon. 'Indeed, I never wished
 to own a better dwelling.' But when night approached he had to sleep;
 he slipped tiredly into a deep sleep under the leaves.

And sythen he warnes the west to waken ful softe,
470 And sayes unto Zeferus that he syfle warme,
That ther quikken no cloude bifore the cler sunne,
And ho schal busch up ful brode and brenne as a candel.

Then wakened the wyye of his wyl dremes,   *pleasant*
And blusched to his wodbynde that brothely was marred.
475 Al welwed and wasted tho worthelych leves;
The schyre sunne hade hem schent er ever the schalk wyst.

And then hef up the hete and heterly brenned;
The warm wynde of the weste wertes he   *plants*
   swythes.   *scorches*
The man marred on the molde that moght hym not hyde;
480 His wodbynde was away, he weped for sorwe.

With hatel anger and hot heterly he calles: *bitter*
'A, thou maker of man, what maystery the thynkes
Thus thy freke to forfare forbi alle other?
With alle meschef that thou may, never thou me spares.

485 I kevered me a cumfort that now is caght fro   *acquired; taken*
   me,
My wodbynde so wlonk that wered my heved.   *fine; protected*
Bot now I se thou art sette my solace to reve;
Why ne dyghttes thou me to diye? I dure to longe.'

469–72 And then He asks the west wind to waken quietly, and tells
Zephyr (the west wind) to blow warm, so that no cloud should form in
front of the bright sun, and it must rise unobscured and burn like a
candle.

474–7 And looked at his woodbine which was suddenly ruined. The
splendid leaves were all shrivelled and wasted; the bright sun had
destroyed them before the man knew it. And then the heat mounted
and burned fiercely.

479 The man grieved on the earth that offered him no shelter.

482–4 Ah, you maker of man, what kind of achievement does it seem to
you thus to ruin your man before all others? You never stop attacking
me with all possible mischief.

487–8 But now I see you are determined to rob me of my pleasure; why
do you not pronounce my death? I live too long.

Yet oure Lorde to the lede laused a speche: *uttered*
490 'Is this ryghtwys, thou renk, alle thy ronk   *right; rebellious*
     noyse,
   So wroth for a wodbynde to wax so sone?   *grow*
   Why art thou so waymot, wyye, for so lyttel?'   *irate*

   'Hit is not lyttel,' quoth the lede, 'bot lykker to ryght;
   I wolde I were of this worlde, wrapped in moldes.'
495 'Thenne bythenk the, mon, if the forthynk sore,
   If I wolde help my hondewerk, haf thou no wonder.

   Thou art waxen so wroth for thy wodbynde,
   And travayledes never to tent hit the tyme of an howre,
   Bot at a wap hit here wax and away at an other;
500 And yet lykes the so luther, thi lyf woldes thou tyne.

   Thenne wyte not me for the werk, that I hit wolde help,
   And rwe on tho redles that remen for synne.
   Fyrst I made hem myself of materes myn one,
   And sythen I loked hem ful longe and hem on lode hade.

505 And if I my travayl schulde tyne, of termes so longe,
   And type doun yonder toun when hit turned   *bring; repented*
     were,
   The sor of such a swete place burde synk to my   *pain; must*
     hert,
   So mony malicious mon as mournes therinne.

493–5 'But rather a matter of justice; I wish I were away from this
    world, buried in my grave.' 'Then consider, sir, if you are sorely
    displeased.'

498–505 And yet you never put in an hour's work to tend it, but it
    sprang up here at one stroke and was gone at another; and yet you take
    it so badly you wish to do away with your life. Then do not blame me
    for wanting to help my handiwork and take pity on those desperate
    people who cry out for their sins. First I made them out of primal
    matter, by myself alone, and then I looked after them for a long time
    and had them under my guidance. And if I should lose my labour, of
    such long duration.

508–15 There being so many sinful men who lament their sins there.

And of that soumme yet arn summe, such sottes formadde,
510 As lyttel barnes on barme that never bale wroght,
And wymmen unwytte, that wale ne couthe
That on hande fro that other for alle this hyghe worlde.

[Bitwene the stele and the stayre disserne noght cunen,
What rule renes in roun bitwene the ryght hande
515 And his lyfte, thagh her lyf schulde lost be therfor.]

And als ther ben doumbe bestes in the burgh   *also; town*
  mony,
That may not synne in no syt hemselven to greve.
Why schulde I wrath wyth hem, sythen wyyes wyl   *since*
  torne,
And cum and cnawe me for kyng, and my carpe leve?

520 Wer I as hastif as thou, heere, were harme lumpen;
Couthe I not thole bot as thou, ther thryved ful fewe.
I may not be so malicious and mylde be halden,
For malyse is nogh to mayntyne boute mercy withinne.'

And of that number there are some who are utter simpletons, such as little children at the breast who never did harm, and foolish women, unable to tell one hand from the other for al this great world. They cannot distinguish between the side of the ladder and the step, nor can they see what rule mysteriously divides the right hand from the left, though they should lose their lives thereby. (The poet may have intended to cancel lines 513–515; see note.)

517 That may not commit any sin to harm themselves.

519–23 And come and acknowledge me as king, and accept what I say? Were I as hasty as you, sir, it would be unfortunate; if I could endure only as you do, few would prosper. I may not be so severe and still be considered gentle, for severity is not to be practised without mercy in one's heart.

Be noght so gryndel, godman, bot go forth   *angry; good sir*
    thy wayes,
525 Be prevé and be pacient in payne and in joye;   *quiet*
For he that is to rakel to renden his clothes
Mot efte sitte with more unsounde to sewe hem togeder.

Forthy when poverté me enpreces and paynes innoghe,
Ful softly with suffraunce saghttel me bihoves.
530 Forthy penaunce and payne topreve hit in syght
That pacience is a nobel poynt, thagh hit displese ofte. *virtue*
                                                    Amen.

526–30 For he who is too hasty in tearing his clothes must afterwards
    put up with further annoyance in sewing them together. And so when
    poverty oppresses me and many sorrows, I must quietly make my peace
    with patience. And so suffering and sorrow prove it for all to see.

SIR GAWAIN AND THE
GREEN KNIGHT

I

Sithen the sege and the assaut was sesed at   *after; ended*
   Troye,
The borgh brittened and brent to brondes and askes,
The tulk that the trammes of tresoun ther wroght
Was tried for his tricherie, the trewest on erthe.
5 Hit was Ennias the athel and his highe kynde,
That sithen depreced provinces, and patrounes bicome
Welneghe of al the wele in the west iles.
Fro riche Romulus to Rome ricchis hym swythe
With gret bobbaunce that burghe he biges upon fyrst,
10 And nevenes hit his aune nome, as hit now hat.
Ticius to Tuskan, and teldes   *(goes to) Tuscany; houses*
   bigynnes,
Langaberde in Lumbardie lyftes up homes,   *raises*
And fer over the French flod Felix Brutus   *far*
On mony bonkkes ful brode Bretayn he settes *slopes; founds*
15   wyth wynne,   *joy*
   Where werre and wrake and wonder
   Bi sythes has wont therinne,
   And oft bothe blysse and blunder
   Ful skete has skyfted synne.

2–10 (With) the city destroyed and burnt to charred timbers and ashes,
the man who hatched treacherous plots there was tried for his treach-
ery, the most certain on earth. It was the noble Aeneas and his high-
born kindred, who afterwards conquered provinces, and became lords
of almost all the wealth in the western lands. As soon as noble Romulus
hastens to Rome he founds that city with great ceremony and gives it
his own name, by which it is now called.

13 *French flod* i.e. English Channel.

16–19 Where war and vengeance and strange events have happened
from time to time, and often joy and trouble have rapidly succeeded
each other ever since.

20 Ande quen this Bretayn was bigged bi this burn rych,
   Bolde bredden therinne, baret that lofden,
   In mony turned tyme tene that wroghten.
   Mo ferlyes on this folde han fallen here oft
   Then in any other that I wot, syn that ilk   *know; since; same*
       tyme.
25 Bot of alle that here bult of Bretaygne kynges   *lived; Britain's*
   Ay was Arthur the hendest, as I haf herde telle.   *ever; noblest*
   Forthi an aunter in erde I attle to schawe,
   That a selly in sight summe men hit holden,
   And an outtrage awenture of Arthures wonderes.
30 If ye wyl lysten this laye bot on littel quile,   *a little while*
   I schal telle hit astit, as I in toun herde,   *at once*
             with tonge,   *(recited) aloud*
         As hit is stad and stoken   *set down and fixed*
         In stori stif and stronge,   *bold and strong*
35   With lel letteres loken,
         In londe so has ben longe.

   This kyng lay at Camylot upon Krystmasse
   With mony luflych lorde, ledes of the best,   *fine; men*
   Rekenly of the Rounde Table alle tho rich brether,
40 With rych revel oryght and rechles merthes.
   Ther tournayed tulkes bi tymes ful mony,
   Justed ful jolilé thise gentyle knightes,   *jousted; gallantly; noble*
   Sythen kayred to the court, caroles to make.
   For ther the fest was ilyche ful fiften dayes,

20-3 And when this Britain was founded by this mighty man, bold men
   bred there who loved fighting, who made mischief in many a troubled
   time. More marvels have taken place here on this soil, again and again.
27-9 And so I intend to unfold a real adventure, such that some men
   consider it a supreme marvel, and a most strange adventure amongst
   the wonders of Arthur.
35-6 Linked with true letters, as it has long been in the land.
39-41 All those noble brethren of the Round Table, in fitting fashion,
   with splendid revels indeed and carefree pleasures. There knights on
   many occasions took part in tournaments.
43-4 Then they rode to the court to dance carols. (The 'carol' was a ring
   dance with singing). For there the feasting was continuous for fully
   fifteen days.

45 With alle the mete and the mirthe that men   *food*
    couthe avyse,   *could devise*
Such glaum ande gle glorious to here,   *noise; merriment*
Dere dyn upon day, daunsyng on nyghtes.   *cheerful din*
Al was hap upon heghe in halles and chambres
With lordes and ladies, as levest him thoght.
50 With all the wele of the worlde thay woned ther samen,
The most kyd knyghtes under   *renowned*
    Krystes selven,   *Christ Himself*
And the lovelokkest ladies that ever lif haden,   *loveliest*
And he the comlokest kyng that the court haldes;
For al was this fayre folk in her first age,
55   on sille,
    The hapnest under heven,
    Kyng hyghest mon of wylle.
    Hit were now gret nye to neven
    So hardy a here on hille.

60 Wyle Nw Yer was so yep that hit was nwe cummen,
That day doubble on the dece was the douth served.
Fro the kyng was cummen with knyghtes into the halle,   *after*
The chauntré of the chapel cheved to an ende,
Loude crye was ther kest of clerkes and other,
65 Nowel nayted onewe, nevened ful ofte.
And sythen riche forth runnen to reche hondeselle,

48–50 Good cheer was fully abroad in halls and chambers, amongst
lords and ladies, to their perfect contentment (lit. as seemed dearest to
them). With all the joy in the world they dwelt there together.

53–9 And he who holds court (is) the handsomest king; for this fair
company in the hall were all in their first youth, the most favoured
(people) in the world, the king a man of the noblest temperament. It
would now (i.e. in the poet's own time) be very difficult to identify so
brave a company in a castle (lit. on a castle-mound).

60–1 While New Year was so new that it was only just arrived, that day
the company on the dais was served with double portions (of food).

63–7 The singing of mass in the chapel having come to an end, loud cries
were uttered there by clerics and others, Christmas (was) celebrated
anew, called out by name again and again (i.e. 'Noel' was used as a
greeting, equivalent to 'Merry Christmas'). And then nobles ran for-
ward to give presents, cried aloud 'New Year's gifts', offered them by
hand.

Yeyed 'yeres yiftes' on high, yelde hem bi hond,
Debated busyly aboute tho giftes.   *eagerly*
Ladies laghed ful loude, thogh thay lost haden,   *had*
70 And he that wan was not wrothe, that may ye wel trawe.
Alle this mirthe thay maden to the mete tyme.   *until; meal*
When thay had waschen worthyly thay wenten to sete,
The best burne ay abof, as hit best semed;
Whene Guenore, ful gay, graythed in the myddes,
75 Dressed on the dere des, dubbed al aboute –
Smal sendal bisides, a selure hir over
Of tryed Tolouse, of Tars tapites innoghe,
That were enbrawded and beten wyth the   *embroidered; set*
    best gemmes
That myght be preved of prys wyth penyes to bye
80   in daye.
            The comlokest to discrye
            Ther glent with yyen gray;
            A semloker that ever he syye,
            Soth moght no mon say.

85 Bot Arthure wolde not ete til al were served,
He was so joly of his joyfnes, and sumquat childgered;
His lif liked hym lyght, he lovied the lasse
Auther to lenge lye or to longe sitte,
So bisied him his yonge blod and his brayn wylde.

---

70 And he who won was not angry, that you may well believe.
72–7 When they had washed (their hands) politely they went to their
    seats, the man of highest rank always more highly placed (i.e. they were
    seated in order of degree), as seemed best; Queen Guinevere, most
    beautiful, was placed in the midst, seated on the high dais, (which was)
    decorated all round – fine silk to the sides, a canopy over her of choicest
    Toulouse (i.e. a rich red fabric associated with Toulouse), many
    tapestries of Tharsian silk.
79–84 That ever money could buy (lit. that might be proved to be of
    value by buying them with money, on any day). The loveliest to behold
    looked (about her) with grey-blue eyes; no man might truthfully say
    that he had ever seen a more beautiful lady.
86–9 He was so light-hearted in his youthfulness, and somewhat boyish;
    his life pleased him (when it was) light, the less he liked either to lie for
    long (lit. longer) or sit for long, his young blood and restless brain
    stirred him so much.

90 And also another maner meved   *consideration moved*
       him eke,   *as well*
   That he thurgh nobelay had nomen he wolde never ete
   Upon such a dere day, er hym devised were
   Of sum aventurus thyng an uncouthe tale,
   Of sum mayn mervayle that he myght trawe,
95 Of alderes, of armes, of other aventurus;
   Other sum segg hym bisoght of sum siker knyght
   To joyne wyth hym in justyng, in jopardé to lay,
   Lede lif for lyf, leve uchon other,
   As fortune wolde fulsun hom the fayrer to have.
100 This was kynges countenaunce where he in court were,
    At uch farand fest, among his fre meny
           in halle.
       Therfore of face so fere   *proud*
       He stightles stif in stalle;
105   Ful yep in that Nw Yere,   *youthful*
       Much mirthe he mas with alle.   *makes; everyone*

   Thus ther stondes in stale the stif kyng hisselven,
   Talkkande bifore the hyghe table of trifles ful
       hende.   *courteous*
   There gode Gawan was graythed Gwenore   *good; seated*
       bisyde,
110 And Agravayn a la dure mayn on that other syde sittes,
    Bothe the kynges sister sunes and ful siker   *sister's; true*
        knightes.

91–102 (Namely) that he in his nobility had undertaken that he would
  never eat on such a holiday until he had been told a far-fetched tale of
  some adventurous exploit, of some great marvel which he might believe
  in, of princes, of (feats of) arms, of other adventures, or else (until)
  some man had asked him for a true knight to join with him in jousting,
  to place themselves in jeopardy, stake life against life, each to allow the
  other to have the better as fortune favoured them (i.e. they were each
  to accept the outcome of the joust). This was the king's custom
  wherever he held court, at every great feast, amongst his noble company
  in hall.

104 He stands upright in his place.

107 And so the bold king himself stands there in his place.

Bischop Bawdewyn abof bigines the table,
And Ywan, Uryn son, ette with hymselven.
Thise were dight on the des and   *seated*
    derworthly served,   *sumptuously*
115 And sithen mony siker segge at the sidbordes.
Then the first cors come with crakkyng   *course; came; flourish*
    of trumpes,
Wyth mony baner ful bryght that therbi   *from them*
    henged;   *hung*
Nwe nakryn noyse with the noble pipes;
Wylde werbles and wyght wakned lote,
120 That mony hert ful highe hef at her towches;
Dayntés dryven therwyth, of ful dere metes;
Foysoun of the fresche, and on so fele disches
That pine to fynde the place the peple biforne
For to sette the sylveren that sere sewes halden
125   on clothe.
            Iche lede as he loved hymselve
            Ther laght withouten lothe;
            Ay two had disches twelve,   *each pair*
            Good ber and bryght wyn bothe.   *beer*

130 Now wyl I of hor servise say yow no   *their (table-) service*
    more,
For uch wyye may wel wit no wont that ther were.
An other noyse ful newe neghed bilive,

112–13 Bishop Baldwin sits at the head of the table, and Ywain, Urien's
    son, ate with him. (The courtiers were served in pairs; see line 128.)
115 And afterwards many true men at the side-tables.
118–27 (There was) a new noise of horns with the noble pipes; wild and
    vigorous trillings wakened echoes, so that many hearts soared high at
    their strains; dainties (were) brought in with it (i.e. the music), made
    up of most excellent foods; (there was) an abundance of fresh meats,
    and on so many dishes that it was difficult to find room in front of the
    people to set on the cloth the silver that held the various stews. Each
    man as he desired helped himself (to food) there without restraint.
131–4 For everyone (i.e. in the poem's audience) may be sure that there
    was no lack of anything. Another quite new noise approached suddenly,
    so that the prince might be free to take food. For the noise (of the
    music) was scarcely at an end.

That the lude myght haf leve liflode to cach.
For unethe was the noyce not a whyle sesed,
135 And the fyrst cource in the court kyndely served,   *duly*
Ther hales in at the halle dor an aghlich mayster,
On the most in the molde on mesure hyghe,
Fro the swyre to the swange so sware and so thik,
And his lyndes and his lymes so longe and so grete,
140 Half etayn in erde I hope that he were;
Bot mon most I algate mynn hym to bene,
And that the myriest in his muckel that myght ride,
For of bak and of brest al were his bodi sturne,
Both his wombe and his wast were worthily smale,
145 And alle his fetures folwande in forme that he hade,
  ful clene.
  For wonder of his hwe men hade,
  Set in his semblaunt sene;
  He ferde as freke were fade,
150   And overal enker-grene.

Ande al graythed in grene this gome and his wedes –
A strayt cote ful streght that stek on his sides,
A mere mantile abof, mensked withinne,
With pelure pured apert, the pane ful clene,
155 With blythe blaunner ful bryght, and his hod bothe,
That was laght fro his lokkes and layde on   *thrown back from*
his schulderes;

136–50 (When) there comes in at the hall door a fearsome lord, the very
 biggest in the world in his tall stature, from the neck to the waist so
 square and so thick-set, and his sides and his limbs so long and so
 large, that I believe he may have been half giant indeed; but at any rate
 I consider him to be the biggest of men, and the handsomest of his size
 who might (ever) ride horse, for although in back and breast his body
 was strong, both his stomach and his waist were becomingly small, and
 all his parts (were) in keeping with his shape, without exception (lit.
 most completely). Men wondered at his colour, plain to see in his face;
 he bore himself like a man of battle, and he was bright green all over.
151–5 And all arrayed in green (were) this man and his clothes – (he
 wore) a straight coat, very tight, that fitted his sides, a splendid cloak
 over it, adorned on the inside, with close-trimmed fur exposed, the
 edging most elegant, very bright with beautiful ermine, and his hood as
 well.

Heme, wel-haled hose of that same grene,
That spenet on his sparlyr, and clene spures under
Of bryght golde, upon silk bordes barred ful ryche,
160 And scholes under schankes there the schalk rides.
And alle his vesture verayly was   *clothing indeed*
      clene verdure,   *bright green*
Bothe the barres of his belt and other blythe stones, *fine gems*
That were richely rayled in his aray clene   *set*
Aboutte hymself and his sadel, upon silk werkes, *embroidery*
165 That were to tor for to telle of tryfles the halve
That were enbrauded abof, wyth bryddes and flyyes,
With gay gaudi of grene, the golde ay inmyddes.
The pendauntes of his payttrure, the proude cropure,
His molaynes and alle the metail anamayld was thenne;
170 The steropes that he stod on stayned of the same,
And his arsouns al after and his athel scurtes,
That ever glemered and glent al of grene stones.
The fole that he ferkkes on fyn of that ilke,
      sertayn.
175   A grene hors gret and thikke,   *big; thick-set*
          A stede ful stif to strayne,   *strong; curb*
          In brawden brydel quik;   *embroidered; restive*
          To the gome he was ful gayn.   *man; obedient*

157–60 Neat, tightly-drawn hose of that same green, that clung to his
   calves, and elegant spurs beneath of bright gold, on most richly barred
   bands, and no shoes on his feet (lit. under his legs) where the man rides
   (in the stirrups).
165–74 So that it would be too hard to tell of half the details that were
   embroidered on it, with birds and butterflies, with bright ornamenta-
   tion of green, gold everywhere amongst it. The pendants of his horse's
   breast-harness, the splendid crupper (i.e. saddle-strap passing under tail
   of horse), his bit studs and all the metal (fittings) were enamelled
   (green) also; the stirrups that he stood on were coloured similarly, and
   his saddle-bows (were) all matching and (also) his splendid saddle-
   skirts, that ever gleamed and glinted all with green stones. The horse
   that he rides on (was) bright with the same (colour), unquestionably.

Wel gay was this gome gered in grene,
180 And the here of his hed of his hors swete.
Fayre fannand fax umbefoldes his schulderes;
A much berd as a busk over his brest henges,
That wyth his highlich here that of his hed reches
Was evesed al umbetorne abof his elbowes,
185 That half his armes therunder were halched in the wyse
Of a kynges capados that closes his swyre.
The mane of that mayn hors much to hit lyke,   *great*
Wel cresped and cemmed, wyth knottes ful   *curled; combed*
   mony
Folden in wyth fildore aboute the fayre grene,
190 Ay a herle of the here, an other of golde.
The tayl and his toppyng twynnen of a sute,
And bounden bothe wyth a bande of a bryght grene,
Dubbed wyth ful dere stones, as the dok lasted,
Sythen thrawen wyth a thwong, a thwarle-knot alofte,
195 Ther mony belles ful bryght of brende golde rungen.
Such a fole upon folde, ne freke that hym rydes,
Was never sene in that sale wyth syght er that tyme,
     with yye.
   He loked as layt so lyght,
200   So sayd al that hym syye;   *saw*
   Hit semed as no mon myght   *as though*
   Under his dynttes dryye.   *blows; survive*

179–86 Truly handsome was this man attired in green, and the hair of
his head matched that of his horse. Beautiful hair, fanning out, enfolds
his shoulders; a great beard like a bush hangs over his breast, which
together with his splendid hair reaching down from his head was
clipped all round above the elbows, so that half his arms were enclosed
underneath in the manner of a king's cape that fits round his neck.

189–99 Plaited in with gold thread round the beautiful green, always
one strand of the hair, another of gold. The tail and the forelock (were)
plaited to match, and both bound with a band of a bright green,
adorned with most precious stones, to the end of the tuft, then tied
tight with a thong, an intricate knot at the top, where many very bright
bells of pure gold jingled. Such an extraordinary horse, or man riding
it, was never seen in that hall before that time, by (any) eye. His glance
was as swift as lightning.

Whether hade he no helme ne hawbergh nauther,
Ne no pysan, ne no plate that pented to armes,
205 Ne no schafte, ne no schelde, to schwve ne to   *spear; thrust*
    smyte,
    Bot in his on honde he hade a holyn bobbe,   *one; holly spray*
    That is grattest in grene when greves ar bare,   *most; woods*
    And an ax in his other, a hoge and unmete,   *huge; monstrous*
    A spetos sparthe to expoun in spelle, quo-so myght.
210 The lenkthe of an elnyerde the large hede hade,
    The grayn al of grene stele and of golde hewen,
    The bit burnyst bryght, with a brod egge   *blade; edge*
    As wel schapen to schere as scharp rasores.   *fashioned; cut*
    The stele of a stif staf the sturne hit bi grypte
215 That was wounden wyth yrn to the wandes ende,
    And al bigraven with grene in gracios werkes;
    A lace lapped aboute, that louked at the hede,
    And so after the halme halched ful ofte,
    Wyth tryed tasseles therto tacched innoghe
220 On botouns of the bryght grene brayden ful ryche.
    This hathel heldes hym in and the halle entres,   *man goes in*
    Drivande to the heghe dece – dut he no wothe.
    Haylsed he never one, bot heghe he over loked.
    The fyrst word that he warp: 'Wher is,' he sayd,   *spoke*

203–4 Yet he had no helmet or coat of mail either, nor any throat-
armour, nor any plate that had to do with armour.

209–11 A cruel battle-axe to describe it in words, whoever might try to
do so. The great axe-head was an ell-rod (i.e. 45 inches) in length, the
stock (i.e. the upper part of the axe-head) entirely forged out of green
steel and of gold.

214–20 The stern knight gripped it by the handle of a strong shaft that
was wound round with iron to the shaft's end, and all carved with
pleasing designs in green; a cord was wrapped round it that was
fastened at the (axe-)head, and so looped along the shaft again and
again, with many splendid tassels attached to it (i.e. the cord) on
buttons of the (same) bright green, most richly embroidered.

222–3 Pressing forward to the high dais – he feared no danger. He
greeted no one, but looked high above (them).

225 'The governour of this gyng? Gladly I wolde   *ruler; company*
     Se that segg in syght, and with hymself speke
                    raysoun.'
              To knyghtes he kest his yye,   *cast; eye*
              And reled hym up and doun.
230   He stemmed, and con studie
              Quo walt ther most renoun.

     Ther was lokyng on lenthe, the lude to   *for a long time; man*
         beholde,
     For uch mon had mervayle quat hit mene   *everyone wondered*
         myght
     That a hathel and a horse myght such a hwe lach   *colour; take*
235 As growe grene as the gres and grener hit   *as to grow; grass*
         semed,
     Then grene aumayl on golde glowande bryghter.
     Al studied that ther stod, and stalked hym nerre,
     Wyth al the wonder of the worlde what he worch   *would do*
         schulde.
     For fele sellyes had thay sen, bot such never   *many marvels*
         are;   *before*
240 Forthi for fantoum and fayryye the folk there hit demed.
     Therfore to answare was arwe mony athel freke,
     And al stouned at his steven and stonstil seten
     In a swoghe sylence thurgh the sale riche;
     As al were slypped upon slepe so slaked hor lotes
245   in hyye.
              I deme hit not al for doute,   *think; fear*
              Bot sum for cortaysye;   *courtesy*

226–7 Set eyes on that man, and have speech with him.
229–31 And went quickly up and down (the hall). He stopped, and
    looked carefully to see who had the greatest renown there.
236–7 Glowing brighter than green enamel on gold. All who stood there
    stared, and moved cautiously closer to him.
240–5 And so the people there took it for illusion and magic. For that
    reason many a noble knight was afraid to answer, and all were
    dumbfounded at his voice and sat still as stone in a dead silence
    throughout the rich hall; as though all had slipped into sleep, so their
    noise died away suddenly.

       Bot let hym that al schulde loute
       Cast unto that wyye.

250 Thenn Arthour bifore the high dece that
     aventure byholdes,   *strange event*
    And rekenly hym reverenced, for rad was he never,
    And sayde: 'Wyye, welcum iwys to this place,   *sir; indeed*
    The hede of this ostel Arthour I hat.   *house; am called*
    Light luflych adoun and lenge, I the praye,
255 And quat-so thy wylle is we schal wyt after.'   *whatever; learn*
    'Nay, as help me,' quoth the hathel, 'he that on hyghe
       syttes,
    To wone any quyle in this won, hit was not myn ernde.
    Bot for the los of the, lede, is lyft up so hyghe,
    And thy burgh and thy burnes best ar holden,
260 Stifest under stel-gere on stedes to ryde,
    The wyghtest and the worthyest of the worldes kynde,
    Preve for to play wyth in other pure laykes –
    And here is kydde cortaysye, as I haf herd carp,   *shown; tell*
    And that has wayned me hider, iwyis, at this   *brought; indeed*
       tyme.
265 Ye may be seker bi this braunch that I bere here   *sure*
    That I passe as in pes, and no plyght seche.   *peace; trouble*
    For had I founded in fere, in feghtyng wyse,
    I have a hauberghe at home and a helme bothe,   *coat of mail*
    A schelde and a scharp spere, schinande bryght,
270 Ande other weppenes to welde, I wene wel, als.
    Bot for I wolde no were, my wedes ar softer.

248–9 But let (imperative) him to whom all must defer (i.e. Arthur) address himself to that man.

251 And greeted him courteously, for he was not at all afraid.

254 Kindly dismount and stay (with us), I pray you.

256–62 'No, so help me God (lit. He who dwells on high)', said the man, 'it was not my mission to stay any length of time in this place. But because your renown, sir, is lifted up so high, and your castle and your men are held to be the best, the mightiest in armour who ride steeds, the bravest and the worthiest of the world's creatures, fit to contend with in any noble sports.

267 For had I travelled in (warlike) company, in fighting fashion.

270–1 And other weapons to wield, as I well know, besides. But since I want no war, my clothes are softer.

Bot if thou be so bold as alle burnes tellen,   *men say*
Thou wyl grant me godly the gomen that I   *graciously; game*
  ask
        bi ryght.'   *as of right*
275   Arthour con onsware,   *answered*
      And sayd: 'Sir cortays knyght,
      If thou crave batayl bare,
      Here fayles thou not to fyght.'

'Nay, frayst I no fyght, in fayth I the telle;   *seek*
280 Hit arn aboute on this bench bot berdles chylder;
    If I were hasped in armes on a heghe stede,   *buckled*
    Here is no mon me to mach, for myghtes so wayke.
    Forthy I crave in this court a Crystemas gomen,   *and so; game*
    For hit is Yol and Nwe Yer, and here ar   *Yule*
      yep mony.   *many young men*
285 If any so hardy in this hous holdes hymselven,
    Be so bolde in his blod, brayn in hys hede,
    That dar stifly strike a strok for an other,
    I schal gif hym of my gyft thys giserne ryche,   *battle-axe*
    This ax, that is hevé innogh, to hondele as   *heavy; handle*
      hym lykes,
290 And I schal bide the fyrst bur, as bare as I sitte.
    If any freke be so felle to fonde that I telle,
    Lepe lyghtly me to, and lach this weppen;
    I quit-clayme hit for ever, kepe hit as his auen.
    And I schal stonde hym a strok, stif on this flet,

277–8 If you crave battle without armour, here you will not fail to get a
    fight.

280 There are only beardless children about on these benches.

282 Here is no man to match me, their strength is so weak.

285–7 If any in this house considers himself so bold in his temperament,
    so hot-headed, as to dare to strike fearlessly one stroke (in return) for
    another.

290–6 And I shall endure the first blow, unarmed as I sit (here). If any
    man is so bold as to put to the test what I propose, let him run quickly
    to me and seize this weapon; I give it up for ever, let him keep it as his
    own. And I shall stand a stroke from him, firm on this floor, provided
    that you will give me the right to deal him another, by agreement.

295 Elles thou wyl dight me the dom to dele hym an other,
        barlay.
            And yet gif hym respite   (I) *give*
            A twelmonyth and a day;
            Now hyye, and let se tite
300   Dar any herinne oght say.'

        If he hem stowned upon fyrst, stiller were   *stunned; at first*
            thanne
        Alle the heredmen in halle, the hygh and the lowe.   *courtiers*
        The renk on his rouncé hym ruched in his sadel,
        And runischly his rede yyen he reled aboute,
305   Bende his bresed browes, blycande grene,
        Wayved his berde for to wayte quo-so wolde ryse.
        When non wolde kepe hym with carp he coghed ful hyghe,
        Ande rimed hym ful richly, and ryght hym to speke:
        'What, is this Arthures hous,' quoth the hathel thenne,   *man*
310   'That al the rous rennes of thurgh ryalmes   *talk; realms*
            so mony?
        Where is now your sourquydrye and your conquestes,   *pride*
        Your gryndellayk and your greme and your   *fierceness; anger*
            grete wordes?
        Now is the revel and the renoun of the Rounde   *revelling*
            Table
        Overwalt wyth a worde of on wyyes   *overthrown; one man's*
            speche,
315   For al dares for drede withoute dynt schewed!'
        Wyth this he laghes so loude that the lorde greved;
        The blod schot for scham into his schyre   *shame; handsome*
            face

299–300 Now hurry, and let us see quickly if any here dare say anything.
303–8 The man on his horse turned in his saddle and fiercely rolled his
    red eyes about, wrinkled his bristling brows, shining green, swept his
    beard from side to side (i.e. turned his head) to see whoever would rise
    (from his seat). When no one would engage him in talk, he coughed
    very loudly, and drew himself up most grandly, and proceeded to
    speak.
315–16 'For all cower in fear without a blow being offered.' With this
    he laughs so loudly that the lord (i.e. Arthur) took offence.

	and lere.	*cheek*
	He wex as wroth as wynde;	*grew; angry*
320	So did alle that ther were.	*who were there*
	The kyng, as kene bi kynde,	
	Then stod that stif mon nere.	

	Ande sayde: 'Hathel, by heven thyn askyng is	*sir*
	nys,	*foolish*
	And as thou foly has frayst, fynde the behoves.	
325	I know no gome that is gast of thy grete wordes.	*man; afraid*
	Gif me now thy geserne, upon Godes halve,	
	And I schal baythen thy bone that thou boden habbes.'	
	Lyghtly lepes he hym to, and laght at his honde;	
	Then feersly that other freke upon fote lyghtis.	*man*
330	Now has Arthure his axe, and the halme grypes,	*handle*
	And sturnely stures hit aboute, that stryke wyth hit thoght.	
	The stif mon hym bifore stod upon hyght,	*stood upright*
	Herre then ani in the hous by the hede and more.	*taller*
	Wyth sturne schere ther he stod he stroked	*expression; where*
	his berde,	
335	And wyth a countenaunce dryye he drow	*unmoved; drew*
	doun his cote,	
	No more mate ne dismayd for hys mayn dintes	
	Then any burne upon bench hade broght hym to	*than if; man*
	drynk	
	of wyne.	
	Gawan, that sate bi the quene,	*sat*
340	To the kyng he can enclyne:	*bowed*
	'I beseche now with sawes sene	
	This melly mot be myne.'	

321–2 The king, as one brave by nature, then stood near that formidable man.

324 And as you have asked for folly, you deserve to find it.

326–8 'Give me your battle-axe now, for God's sake, and I shall grant you the boon that you have asked for.' Quickly he runs to him, and took hold of his hand (i.e. to help him dismount).

331 And grimly swings it about, intending to strike with it.

336 No more daunted or dismayed by his great blows (i.e. by Arthur's brandishing of the axe).

341–2 I implore (you) now in plain words that this quarrel might be mine.

'Wolde ye, worthilych lorde,' quoth   *if you would; honoured*
    Wawan to the kyng,
Bid me bowe fro this benche and stonde by yow there,   *go*
345 That I wythoute vylanye myght   *so that; discourtesy*
    voyde this table,   *leave*
And that my legge lady lyked not ille,
I wolde com to your counseyl bifore your cort   *to advise you*
    ryche.   *noble*
For me think hit not semly, as hit is soth knawen,
Ther such an askyng is hevened so hyghe in your sale,
350 Thagh ye yourself be talenttyf, to take hit to yourselven,
Whil mony so bolde yow aboute upon bench sytten,
That under heven, I hope, non hagherer of wylle,
Ne better bodyes on bent ther baret is rered.
I am the wakkest, I wot, and of wyt feblest,   *weakest; know*
355 And lest lur of my lyf, quo laytes the sothe.
Bot for as much as ye ar myn em, I am only to prayse;
No bounté bot your blod I in my bodé knowe.   *virtue*
And sythen this note is so nys that noght hit yow falles,
And I have frayned hit at yow fyrst, foldes hit   *asked; it falls*
    to me;
360 And if I carp not comlyly, let alle this cort rych,
        bout blame.'
      Ryche togeder con roun,   *nobles; whispered*

---

346 And provided that my liege lady was not displeased.

348–53 For it seems to me not fitting, as is manifestly evident, that where
such a request is voiced so loudly in your hall you should take it upon
yourself, even though you yourself may be willing, while many most
bold men sit around you on the benches, such that under the heavens,
I believe, there are none of readier courage, nor better men on the field
where battle is done.

355–6 And my life would be the smallest loss, to tell the truth (lit.
whoever wishes to know the truth). I am only to be esteemed inasmuch
as you are my uncle.

358 And since this business is so foolish that it is not at all proper for
you.

360–1 And if I do not speak fittingly, let all this noble court decide (the
matter), without blame.

And sythen thay redden alle same:
To ryd the kyng wyth croun,
365   And gif Gawan the game.

Then comaunded the kyng the knyght for to ryse,
And he ful radly up ros and ruchched hym fayre,
Kneled doun bifore the kyng, and caches that weppen;   *takes*
And he luflyly hit hym laft, and lyfte up his honde
370 And gef hym Goddes blessyng, and gladly hym biddes
That his hert and his honde schulde hardi be bothe.   *bold*
'Kepe the, cosyn,' quoth the kyng, 'that thou on kyrf sette,
And if thou redes hym ryght, redly I trowe
That thou schal byden the bur that he schal bede after.'
375 Gawan gos to the gome, with giserne in   *man; battle-axe*
        honde,
And he baldly hym bydes, he bayst never the helder.
Then carppes to Sir Gawan the knyght in the grene: *speaks*
'Refourme we oure forwardes er we fyrre passe.
Fyrst I ethe the, hathel, how that thou hattes,
380 That thou me telle truly, as I tryst may.'
'In god fayth,' quoth the goode knyght, 'Gawan
        I hatte,   *am called*
That bede the this buffet, quat-so bifalles after,
And at this tyme twelmonyth take at the another
Wyth what weppen so thou wylt, and wyth no wyy elles
385   on lyve.'
        That other onswares agayn: *answers (back)*

_____

363–4 And then they gave advice with one accord: to relieve the crowned king.
367 And he rose up most promptly and duly prepared himself.
369 And he graciously gave it up to him, and lifted up his hand.
372–4 'Take care, kinsman,' said the king, 'that you steady your blow, and if you manage him rightly, I fully believe that you will survive the blow that he will offer later.'
376 And he boldly waits for him, he was none the more dismayed.
378–80 Let us restate our agreement before we go further. First I entreat you, sir, to tell me truly how you are called, so that I may be sure (of you).
382–5 Who offers you this blow, whatever happens after, and who at this time twelve month's hence shall take another from you with whatever weapon you desire, and from no one else on earth.

'Sir Gawan, so mot I thryve,   *may; prosper*
As I am ferly fayn
This dint that thou schal dryve.'   *blow; strike*

390 'Bigog,' quoth the grene knyght, 'Sir Gawan, me lykes
That I schal fange at thy fust that I haf frayst here.
And thou has redily rehersed, bi resoun ful trwe,   *in words*
Clanly al the covenaunt that I the kynge   *correctly*
        asked,   *put to*
Saf that thou schal siker me, segge, bi thi trawthe,
395 That thou schal seche me thiself, where-so thou hopes *think*
I may be funde upon folde, and foch   *earth; take for yourself*
        the such wages
As thou deles me to-day bifore this douthe ryche.'   *company*
'Where schulde I wale the,' quoth Gauan, 'where is   *seek you*
        thy place?
I wot never where thou wonyes, bi hym that me wroght,
400 Ne I know not the, knyght, thy cort ne thi name.
Bot teche me truly therto, and telle me howe thou hattes,
And I schal ware alle my wyt to wynne me theder,
And that I swere the for sothe, and by my seker traweth.'
'That is innogh in Nwe Yer, hit nedes no more,'
405 Quoth the gome in the grene to Gawan the hende: *noble*
'Yif I the telle trwly, quen I the tape have
And thou me smothely has smyten, smartly I the teche
Of my hous and my home and myn owen nome;   *name*
Then may thou frayst my fare and forwardes holde.

---

388 I am exceedingly glad.
390–1 'By God,' said the green knight, 'Sir Gawain, it pleases me that I
    shall take at your hand what I have asked for here.'
394 Except that you must assure me, sir, by your word.
399 I do not know at all where you live, by Him who made me.
401–4 'But direct me faithfully to it and tell me how you are called, and
    I shall use all my wits to find my way there, and that I swear to you
    truly, and on my word of honour.' 'That is enough (talk) for New
    Year, no more is needed.'
406–7 If I assure you that when I have received the blow and you have
    duly struck me, I shall (then) promptly inform you.
409–11 Then you may try my hospitality and keep the agreement. And
    if I say nothing, then you will fare the better, for you may stay in your
    own land and look no further.

410 And if I spende no speche, thenne spedes thou the better,
    For thou may leng in thy londe and layt no fyrre –
          bot slokes!   *enough*
          Ta now thy grymme tole to the,   *take; weapon*
          And let se how thou cnokes.'   *strike*
415   'Gladly, sir, for sothe,'   *indeed*
          Quoth Gawan; his ax he strokes.

The grene knyght upon grounde graythely hym dresses,
A littel lut with the hede, the lere he discoveres;
His longe lovelych lokkes he layd over his croun,   *handsome*
420 Let the naked nec to the note schewe.   *in readiness*
Gauan gripped to his ax and gederes hit on hyght, *lifts; high*
The kay fot on the folde he before sette,   *left foot; ground*
Let hit doun lyghtly lyght on the naked,
That the scharp of the schalk schyndered the bones
425 And schrank thurgh the schyire grece and scade hit in
    twynne,
That the bit of the broun stel bot on the grounde.
The fayre hede fro the halce hit to the erthe,   *neck*
That fele hit foyned wyth her fete, there hit   *many; kicked*
    forth roled;
The blod brayd fro the body, that blykked on the grene.
430 And nawther faltered ne fel the freke never the helder,
Bot stythly he start forth upon styf schonkes,
And runyschly he raght out, there as renkkes stoden,
Laght to his lufly hed, and lyft hit up sone;   *seized; at once*
And sythen bowes to his blonk, the brydel he *then goes; horse*
    cachches,

417–18 The green knight at once takes up his stance, bent his head a little, (and) exposes the flesh.

423–6 Let it come down swiftly on the naked flesh, so that the sharp blade shattered the bones and sank through the white fat and cut it in two, so that the blade of bright steel bit on the ground.

429–32 The blood spurted from the body, shining on the green (flesh and clothes). And yet never the more for that did the man falter or fall, but strongly started forward on firm legs, and reached out roughly (*and* wierdly), as men stood there.

435 Steppes into stel-bawe and strydes alofte,   *stirrup*
And his hede by the here in his honde haldes.
And as sadly the segge hym in his sadel sette
As non unhap had hym ayled, thagh hedles nowe
            in stedde.
440   He brayde his bluk aboute,   *twisted; trunk*
       That ugly bodi that bledde;
       Moni on of hym had doute,   *a one; fear*
       Bi that his resouns were redde.

For the hede in his honde he haldes up even,   *plainly*
445 Toward the derrest on the dece he dresses the face;
And hit lyfte up the yye-lyddes, and loked
       ful brode,   *with a broad stare*
And meled thus much with his muthe, as ye may now here:
'Loke, Gawan, thou be graythe to go as thou   *ready*
       hettes,   *promise*
And layte als lelly til thou me, lude, fynde,
450 As thou has hette in this halle, herande   *in the hearing of*
       thise knyghtes.
To the grene chapel thou chose, I charge the, to   *go*
       fotte   *receive*
Such a dunt as thou has dalt – disserved thou   *blow; dealt*
       habbes   *have*
To be yederly yolden on Nw Yeres morn.   *promptly; repaid*
The knyght of the grene chapel men knowen me mony;
455 Forthi me for to fynde, if thou fraystes, fayles thou never.
Therfore com, other recreaunt be calde the behoves.'
With a runisch rout the raynes he tornes,   *rough jerk; reins*
Halled out at the hal-dor, his hed in his hande,   *went*
That the fyr of the flynt flawe fro fole hoves.
460 To quat kyth he becom knwe non there,   *land; went*

437–9 And the man sat himself in his saddle as steadily as though no
   mishap had afflicted him, though he was now headless there.
443 By the time he had had his say.
445 He turns the face towards the noblest (ones) on the dais.
447 And spoke with his mouth to this effect, as you may now hear.
449 And search for me as faithfully, sir, until you find me.
455–6 And so if you ask, you will never fail to find me. Come, therefore,
   or you deserve to be called a coward.
459 So that the flint-sparks flew from the horse's hooves.

Never more then thay wyste from quethen he was wonnen.
     What thenne?
     The kyng and Gawen thare   *there*
     At that grene thay laghe and grenne;
465   Yet breved was hit ful bare
     A mervayl among tho menne.

Thagh Arther the hende kyng at hert hade wonder,   *noble*
He let no semblaunt be sene, bot sayde ful hyghe *sign; loudly*
To the comlych quene, wyth cortays   *comely; courteous*
   speche:
470 'Dere dame, to-day demay yow never;   *do not be dismayed*
Wel bycommes such craft upon Cristmasse,
Laykyng of enterludes, to laghe and to syng,
Among thise kynde caroles of knyghtes and ladyes.
Never-the-lece to my mete I may me wel dres, *meal; proceed*
475 For I haf sen a selly, I may not forsake.'   *marvel; deny*
He glent upon Sir Gawen and gaynly he *looked; courteously*
   sayde:
'Now sir, heng up thyn ax, that has innogh   *hang; enough*
   hewen.'   *hewn*
And hit was don abof the dece, on doser to henge,
Ther alle men for mervayl myght on hit loke, *as a marvel*
480 And bi trwe tytel therof to telle the wonder.
Thenne thay bowed to a borde thise burnes *went; table; men*
   togeder,
The kyng and the gode knyght, and kene men hem   *bold*
   served
Of alle dayntyes double, as derrest myght falle,
Wyth alle maner of mete and mynstralcie   *kinds of food*
   bothe.

---

461 Any more than they knew where he had come from.
464-6 Laugh and grin at that green man; yet it was openly spoken of as
   a marvel amongst the people.
471-3 Such doings are entirely fitting at Christmas time, playing of
   interludes (i.e. dramatic entertainments between courses at a banquet),
   laughing and singing, amongst the pleasant carols of knights and ladies.
478 And it was placed above the dais, to hang on the wall-tapestry.
480 And on its true authority (i.e. with it as incontrovertible evidence)
   tell of the wondrous event.
483 A double portion of every delicacy, in the best manner.

485 Wyth wele walt thay that day, til worthed an ende
           in londe.   *in that place*
        Now thenk wel, Sir Gawan,
        For wothe that thou ne wonde
        This aventure for to frayn,
490   That thou has tan on honde.   *undertaken*

II

     This hanselle has Arthur of aventurus on fyrst
     In yonge yer, for he yerned yelpyng to here.
     Thagh hym wordes were wane when thay to sete
           wenten,   *lacking*
     Now ar thay stoken of sturne werk, stafful her hond.
495 Gawan was glad to begynne those gomnes in halle,   *games*
     Bot thagh the ende be hevy, haf ye no wonder;
     For thagh men ben mery in mynde quen thay han   *have*
        mayn drynk,   *strong*
     A yere yernes ful yerne, and yeldes never lyke;
     The forme to the fynisment foldes ful selden.
500 Forthi this Yol overyede, and the yere after,   *passed by*
     And uche sesoun serlepes sued after other.
     After Crystenmasse com the crabbed Lentoun,   *Lent*
     That fraystes flesch wyth the fysche and fode more   *tries*
        symple.
     Bot thenne the weder of the worlde wyth wynter hit   *weather*
        threpes,   *contends*
505 Colde clenges adoun, cloudes uplyften,   *shrinks; lift*
     Schyre schedes the rayn in schowres ful warme,   *bright falls*
     Falles upon fayre flat, flowres there   *meadow*
        schewen;   *appear*

---

485 They passed that day in enjoyment, until it came to an end.
488-9 That you do not shrink because of danger from pursuing this
     adventure.
491-4 Arthur has (received) this gift of marvels at the beginning of the
     young year, because he yearned to hear brave talk. Though they (i.e.
     Arthur and Gawain) lacked words when they went to their seats, now
     they are saddled with difficult work, their hands cram-full.
498-9 A year passes very quickly, and never gives back the same; the
     beginning is very seldom like the end.
501 And each season in turn followed after the other.

Bothe groundes and the greves, grene ar her wedes.
Bryddes busken to bylde, and bremlych syngen   *hasten; loudly*
510 For solace of the softe somer that sues therafter   *joy; follows*
      bi bonk.   *on the slopes*
      And blossumes bolne to blowe   *swell; bloom (vb.)*
      Bi rawes rych and ronk;   *hedgerows; luxuriant*
      Then notes noble innoghe   *most noble*
515   Ar herde in wod so wlonk.   *glorious*

After the sesoun of somer wyth the soft wyndes,
Quen Zeferus syfles hymself on sedes and erbes,
Wela wynne is the wort that waxes theroute,
When the donkande dewe dropes of the leves,   *moistening*
520 To bide a blysful blusch of the bryght sunne.   *await; gleam*
Bot then hyyes hervest, and hardenes hym sone,
Warnes hym for the wynter to wax ful rype;
He dryves wyth droght the dust for to ryse,   *drought*
Fro the face of the folde to flyye ful hyghe.   *earth; fly*
525 Wrothe wynde of the welkyn wrasteles with the sunne,
The leves laucen fro the lynde and lyghten on   *fall; (lime-) tree*
      the grounde,
And al grayes the gres that grene was ere.
Thenne al rypes and rotes that ros upon fyrst,
And thus yirnes the yere in yisterdayes mony,
530 And wynter wyndes ayayn, as the worlde askes,
        no fage.   *in truth*
      Til Meghelmas mone   *Michaelmas moon*
      Was cumen wyth wynter wage;   *pledge of winter*
      Then thenkkes Gawan ful sone
535   Of his anious vyage.   *anxious journey*

---

508 Green are the clothes of both fields and woods.

517–18 When Zephyrus (the west wind) blows on seeds and grasses,
very beautiful is the plant that grows from them (i.e. the seeds).

521–2 But then autumn hastens, and soon hardens it (i.e. toughens the
plant, *also* makes it hard with fruit), tells it to grow fully ripe on
account of the winter.

525 Angry winds in the sky wrestle with the sun.

527–30 And the grass all withers that was green before. Then all ripens
and rots that sprang up at first, and thus the year passes in many
yesterdays, and winter comes round again, as the world requires.

Yet quyl Al-hal-day with Arther he lenges,
And he made a fare on that fest, for the frekes sake,
With much revel and ryche of the Rounde Table.   *revelry*
Knyghtes ful cortays and comlych ladies   *courteous; comely*
540 Al for luf of that lede in longynge thay were,
Bot never-the-lece ne the later thay nevened bot merthe;
Mony joyles for that jentyle japes ther maden.
For aftter mete with mournyng he meles to his eme,
And spekes of his passage, and pertly he   *journey; openly*
     sayde:
545 'Now, lege lorde of my lyf, leve I yow ask.   *leave (to go)*
Ye knowe the cost of this cace, kepe I no more
To telle yow tenes therof, never bot trifel;
Bot I am boun to the bur barely to-morne,
To sech the gome of the grene, as God wyl me   *seek; man*
     wysse.'   *guide*
550 Thenne the best of the burgh bowed togeder,   *castle went*
Aywan and Errik and other ful mony,   *Ywain*
Sir Doddinaval de Savage, the duk of Clarence,
Launcelot and Lyonel and Lucan the gode,
Sir Boos and Sir Bydver, big men bothe,   *Bors; Bedivere; strong*
555 And mony other menskful, with Mador de la Port.   *nobles*
Alle this compayny of court com the kyng nerre,   *near*
For to counseyl the knyght, with care at her hert.
There was much derne doel driven in the sale,
That so worthé as Wawan schulde wende on that   *one so; go*
     ernde,   *mission*
560 To dryye a delful dynt, and dele no   *endure a grievous blow*
     more
          wyth bronde.   *sword*

536-7 Yet until All Saint's Day (1 November) he stays with Arthur, and
   he (i.e. Arthur) made a feast on that festival day, for the knight's sake.
540-3 Were distressed all for the sake of that man, but nevertheless they
   talked of pleasant things only; many who were joyless on account of
   that gentle knight made jokes there. For after dinner he speaks with
   sorrow to his uncle.
546-8 You know the nature of this business, I do not wish to say any
   more about the difficulties that go with it, they are nothing but a trifle;
   but I am bound for the blow without fail tomorrow morning.
558 There was much secret sorrow suffered in the hall.

The knyght mad ay god chere,
And sayde: 'Quat schuld I wonde?   *why; hesitate*
Of destinés derf and dere
565   What may mon do bot fonde?'

He dowelles ther al that day, and dresses on the morn,   *stays*
Askes erly hys armes, and alle were thay broght.   *asks for*
Fyrst a tulé tapit, tyght over the flet,
And miche was the gyld gere that glent ther alofte.
570 The stif mon steppes theron, and the stel   *bold; steel*
        hondeles,   *handles (vb.)*
Dubbed in a dublet of a dere tars,   *clad; precious Tharsian silk*
And sythen a crafty capados, closed aloft,
That wyth a bryght blaunner was   *bright white fur*
        bounden withinne.   *trimmed*
Thenne set thay the sabatouns upon the   *steel shoes*
        segge fotes,   *man's feet*
575 His leges lapped in stel with luflych greves,   *fine shin-pieces*
With polaynes piched therto, policed ful clene,
Aboute his knes knaged wyth knotes of golde.   *fastened*
Queme quyssewes then, that coyntlych closed
His thik thrawen thyghes, with thwonges to tachched;
580 And sythen the brawden bryné of bryght   *linked coat of mail*
        stel rynges
Vmbeweved that wyy, upon wlonk stuffe,
And wel bornyst brace upon his bothe   *burnished arm-pieces*
        armes,
With gode cowters and gay, and gloves   *elbow-pieces; bright*
        of plate,   *(steel) plate*
And alle the godlych gere that hym gayn schulde   *good; benefit*
585   that tyde.   *time*

562 The knight always remained cheerful.
564–5 What may a man do but make trial of painful and pleasant
destinies (alike)?
568–9 First a carpet of red silk, spread over the floor, and there was
much gilded armour that gleamed upon it.
572 And then a skilfully-made cape, fastened at the neck.
576 With knee-pieces attached to them, polished very clean.
578–9 Then fine thigh-pieces, which neatly enclosed his thick muscular
thighs, secured with thongs.
581 Enveloped that knight, over (a tunic made of) splendid material.

            Wyth ryche cote-armure,
            His gold spores spend with pryde,   *fastened*
            Gurde wyth a bront ful sure   *girt; sword*
            With silk sayn umbe his syde.

590 When he was hasped in armes, his harnays   *buckled; armour*
        was ryche;
    The lest lachet other loupe lemed of golde.
    Al harnayst as he was he herknes his masse,   *armoured; hears*
    Offred and honoured at the heghe auter.   *and celebrated*
    Sythen he comes to the kyng and to his
        cort-feres,   *companions at court*
595 Laches lufly his leve at lordes and ladyes;   *takes; courteously*
    And thay hym kyst and conveyed,   *escorted*
        bikende hym to Kryst.   *commending*
    Bi that was Gryngolet grayth, and gurde with a sadel
    That glemed ful gayly with mony golde frenges,   *fringes*
    Ayquere naylet ful nwe, for that note ryched;
600 The brydel barred aboute, with bryght golde bounden.
    The apparayl of the payttrure and of the proude skyrtes,
    The cropore and the covertor, acorded wyth the arsounes,
    And al was rayled on red ryche golde nayles,
    That al glytered and glent as glem of the sunne.   *shone*
605 Thenne hentes he the helme, and hastily hit kysses, *takes; helmet*
    That was stapled stifly, and stoffed wythinne.
    Hit was hyghe on his hede, hasped bihynde,   *fastened*
    Wyth a lyghtly urysoun over the aventayle,

---

589 With a silk girdle round his waist.
591 The smallest latchet or loop gleamed of gold.
597 By that time Gryngolet (i.e. Gawain's horse) was ready.
599–603 Newly studded all over, made for that occasion; the bridle
    barred round, trimmed with bright gold. The adornment of the breast-
    harness and of the splendid skirts, the crupper (i.e. saddle-strap passing
    under tail of horse) and the horse-cloth matched the saddle-bows, and
    everywhere, set upon a red ground, were rich gold nails.
606 That was strongly stapled, and padded inside.
608–14 With a light silk band over the neck-guard, embroidered and
    adorned with the best gems on a broad silken hem, and (figures of)
    birds on the seams, such as parrots depicted amongst periwinkles, (and
    with) turtledoves and true-love-knots portrayed so thickly (that it was)
    as if many a lady had been working seven years on it at court.

Enbrawden and bounden wyth the best gemmes
610 On brode sylkyn borde, and bryddes on semes,
As papjayes paynted pervyng bitwene,
Tortors and trulofes entayled so thyk
As mony burde theraboute had ben seven wynter
          in toune.
615   The cercle was more o prys   *circlet; even finer*
           That umbeclypped hys croun,   *ringed; head*
           Of diamauntes a devys   *diamonds; of the best*
           That bothe were bryght and broun.   *dark*

Then thay schewed hym the schelde, that was of
          schyr goules,   *bright gules (i.e. red)*
620 Wyth the pentangel depaynt of pure golde hwes.
He braydes hit by the bauderyk, aboute the hals kestes;
That bisemed the segge semlyly fayre.
And quy the pentangel apendes to that prynce   *why; belongs*
          noble
I am intent yow to telle, thof tary hyt me   *though; delay*
          schulde.
625 Hit is a syngne that Salamon set sumquyle
In bytoknyng of trawthe, bi tytle that hit habbes,
For hit is a figure that haldes fyve poyntes,
And uche lyne umbelappes and loukes in other,
And ayquere hit is endeles, and Englych hit callen   *everywhere*
630 Overal as I here, the endeles knot.   *in all parts*
Forthy hit acordes to this knyght and to his cler armes,
For ay faythful in fyve and sere fyve sythes
Gawan was for gode knawen and, as golde pured,
Voyded of uche vylany, wyth vertues ennourned

620-2 With the pentangle (i.e. five-pointed star) painted on it in pure
     gold colours. He takes it by the baldric (i.e. strap for shield etc. hung
     from shoulder to opposite hip), slings it round his neck; it suited the
     man most becomingly.

625-6 It is a symbol that Solomon once devised as a token of truth, on
     account of the properties it has.

628 And each line overlaps and joins in another.

631-4 And so it befits this knight and his bright armour, for always
     faithful in five ways and five times in each way Gawain was known as
     a good knight and, like refined gold, free from every impurity, adorned
     with virtues.

635   in mote.   *castle*
               Forthy the pentangel nwe
               He ber in schelde and cote,   *surcoat*
               As tulk of tale most trwe,   *man; word*
               And gentylest knyght of lote.   *noblest; bearing*

640 Fyrst he was funden fautles in his fyve wyttes,   *senses*
     And efte fayled never the freke in his fyve   *secondly; man*
        fyngres,
     And alle his afyaunce upon folde was in the   *trust; earth*
        fyve woundes
     That Cryst kaght on the croys, as the crede telles.
     And quere-so-ever thys mon in melly was stad,
645 His thro thoght was in that, thurgh alle other thynges,
     That alle his forsnes he fong at the fyve joyes
     That the hende heven quene had of hir chylde.   *gracious; in*
     At this cause the knyght comlyche hade
     In the inore half of his schelde hir ymage depaynted,
650 That quen he blusched therto his belde never payred.
     The fyft fyve that I finde that the frek   *fifth (group of) five*
        used   *practised*
     Was fraunchyse and felawschyp forbe al   *liberality; above*
        thyng;
     His clannes and his cortaysye croked were never,   *purity; awry*
     And pité, that passes alle poyntes – thyse pure fyve
655 Were harder happed on that hathel then on any other.
     Now alle these fyve sythes, for sothe, were   *sets (of five)*
        fetled on this knyght,   *settled*
     And uchone halched in other, that non ende hade,

643–6 That Christ received on the cross, as the (Apostle's) Creed tells.
   And wherever this man was hard-pressed in battle, his steadfast thought
   was that, above all other things, he should take all his fortitude from
   the five joys.

648–50 For this reason the knight had her image beautifully painted on
   the inside of his shield, so that when he looked at it his courage never
   failed.

654–5 And pity (*also* piety), that surpasses all virtues – these excellent
   five were more firmly attached to that knight than to any other.

657–9 And each one (was) joined to another, so that none had (any) end,
   and (they were) fixed on five points that never failed, nor did any come
   together anywhere, or come apart either.

And fyched upon fyve poyntes that fayld never,
Ne samned never in no syde, ne sundred nouther,
660 Withouten ende at any noke I noquere   point; anywhere
    fynde,
    Whereever the gomen bygan or glod to an ende.   game; came
    Therfore on his schene schelde schapen was   bright; fashioned
    the knot
    Ryally wyth red golde upon rede gowles,   royally; gules
    That is the pure pentaungel wyth the peple called
665   with lore.
             Now graythed is Gawan gay,   made ready; handsome
             And laght his launce ryght thore,   he took; there
             And gef hem alle goud day –
             He wende, for ever more.   (as) he thought

670 He sperred the sted with the spures, and sprong on   spurred
    his way
    So stif that the ston-fyr stroke out therafter.
    Al that sey that semly syked in hert,
    And sayde sothly al same segges til other,
    Carande for that comly: 'Bi Kryst, hit is scathe
675 That thou, leude, schal be lost, that art of lyf noble!   sir
    To fynde hys fere upon folde, in fayth, is not ethe.   equal; easy
    Warloker to haf wroght had more wyt bene,
    And haf dyght yonder dere a duk to have worthed.
    A lowande leder of ledes in londe hym wel semes,
680 And so had better haf ben then britned to noght,
    Hadet wyth an alvisch mon, for angardes pryde.
    Who knew ever any kyng such counsel to take
    As knyghtes in cavelaciouns on Crystmasse gomnes?'

664–5 That is called by learned people the true pentangle.
671–4 So strongly that sparks flew out of the stones behind him. All
    who saw that seemly one sighed in their hearts, and men said quietly to
    each other, all together, grieving for that excellent knight: 'By Christ, it
    is a pity.'
677–83 It would have been wiser to have acted more cautiously, and to
    have appointed that noble knight to be a duke. It well suits him to be a
    glorious leader of men, and better had he been so than brought down
    to nothing, beheaded by an elvish man, for the sake of overweening
    pride. Who knew any king ever to take such counsel as knights give in
    quibbles over Christmas games?

Wel much was the warme water that waltered of   *flowed*
    yyen,   *eyes*
685 When that semly syre soght fro tho wones
        thad daye.   *that*
      He made non abode,   *delay*
      Bot wyghtly went hys way;   *quickly*
      Mony wylsum way he rode,   *devious*
690   The bok as I herde say.

Now rides this renk thurgh the ryalme   *knight; realm*
    of Logres,   *Britain*
Sir Gauan, on Godes halve, thagh hym no gomen thoght.
Oft leudles alone he lenges on   *companionless; remains*
    nyghtes,
Ther he fonde noght hym byfore the fare that he lyked.
695 Hade he no fere bot his fole bi frythes and dounes,
Ne no gome bot God bi gate wyth to karp,
Til that he neghed ful neghe into the Northe Wales.
Alle the iles of Anglesay on lyft half he haldes,   *left side*
And fares over the fordes by the forlondes,   *goes; headlands*
700 Over at the Holy Hede, til he hade eft bonk
In the wyldrenesse of Wyrale – wonde ther bot lyte
That auther God other gome wyth goud hert lovied.
And ay he frayned, as he ferde, at frekes that he met,
If thay hade herde any karp of a knyght grene,   *talk*
705 In any grounde theraboute, of the grene chapel;   *region*
And al nykked hym wyth nay, that never in her lyve
Thay seye never no segge that was of suche hwes   *saw; man*

---

685 When that fine knight went from that dwelling.
690 As I heard the story say.
692 Sir Gawain, in God's name, though it seemed no game to him.
694–7 Where he found no food that he liked (set) in front of him. He
    had no companion but his horse through woods and hills, nor any man
    but God to talk to on the way, until he approached very close to North
    Wales.
700–3 Till he reached the shore again in the wilderness of Wirral – few
    lived there who loved either God or man with a good heart. And
    always as he went he asked of people that he met.
706 And they all said to him no, that never in their lives.

> of grene.
> The knyght tok gates straunge   *ways*
710 In mony a bonk unbene;
> His cher ful oft con chaunge,   *mood*
> That chapel er he myght sene.   *before; see*

Mony klyf he overclambe in contrayes straunge,   *climbed over*
Fer floten fro his frendes fremedly he rydes.
715 At uche warthe other water ther the wyye passed
He fonde a foo hym byfore, bot ferly hit were,
And that so foule and so felle that feght hym byhode.
So mony mervayl bi mount ther the mon   *among the hills*
> fyndes,
Hit were to tore for to telle of the tenthe dole.   *hard; part*
720 Sumwhyle wyth wormes he werres, and with   *dragons; fights*
> wolves als,   *also*
Sumwhyle wyth wodwos that woned in the knarres,
Bothe wyth bulles and beres, and bores   *boars*
> otherquyle,   *at other times*
And etaynes that hym anelede of the heghe felle.
Nade he ben dughty and dryye, and Dryghtyn had served,
725 Douteles he hade ben ded and dreped ful ofte,   *done for*
For werre wrathed hym not so much that   *fighting troubled*
> wynter was wors,
When the colde cler water fro the cloudes schadde,   *fell*
And fres er hit falle myght to the fale erthe.   *froze; pale*
Ner slayn wyth the slete he sleped in his yrnes   *sleet; armour*
730 Mo nyghtes then innoghe in naked rokkes,   *more*
Ther as claterande fro the crest the colde borne rennes,
And henged heghe over his hede in hard ysse-ikkles.   *hung*
Thus in peryl and payne and plytes ful harde   *hardships*

---

710 On many an inhospitable slope.
714-17 Far removed from his friends he rides as a stranger. At each ford
> or stretch of water where the knight passed it was a wonder if he did
> not find a foe waiting for him, and one so foul and so fierce that he had
> to fight him.
721 Sometimes with trolls who lived in the crags.
723-4 And giants who pursued him from the high fell. If he had not
> been brave and enduring, and had not served God.
731 Where clattering from the crest the cold burn runs.

Bi contray caryes this knyght tyl   *over the land; rides*
Krystmasse even,   *eve*
735   al one.   *alone*
     The knyght wel that tyde   *at that time*
     To Mary made his mone,   *complaint*
     That ho hym red to ryde,
     And wysse hym to sum wone.

740 Bi a mounte on the morne meryly he rydes   *hill; stoutly*
Into a forest ful dep, that ferly was wylde,
Highe hilles on uche a halve, and holtwodes under
Of hore okes ful hoge a hundreth togeder.   *grey; hundred*
The hasel and the hawthorne were
     harled al samen,   *all tangled together*
745 With roghe raged mosse rayled aywhere,
With mony bryddes unblythe upon bare twyges,   *unhappy*
That pitosly ther piped for pyne of the colde.   *piteously; pain*
The gome upon Gryngolet glydes hem under   *man; goes*
Thurgh mony misy and myre, mon al hym one,
750 Carande for his costes, lest he ne kever schulde
To se the servyse of that syre, that on that self nyght
Of a burde was borne, oure baret to quelle.
And therfore sykyng he sayde: 'I beseche the, Lorde,   *sighing*
And Mary, that is myldest moder so dere,
755 Of sum herber ther heghly I myght here   *lodging; devoutly*
     masse
Ande thy matynes to-morne, mekely I ask,
And therto prestly I pray my pater and ave
     and crede.'
     He rode in his prayere,
760   And cryed for his mysdede;

738–9 That she should guide his riding, and direct him to some dwelling.

741–2 Into a very deep forest, that was wonderfully wild, (with) high hills on every side, and woods below.

745 Covered all over with rough shaggy moss.

749–52 Through many a bog and mire, a man all alone, concerned about his religious duties, lest he should not succeed in seeing the service of that Lord who on that very night was born of a maiden, to end our strife.

757–8 And to this end promptly I pray my Paternoster (i.e. Lord's Prayer), Ave (Maria), and (Apostles') Creed.

He sayned hym in sythes sere
And sayde: 'Cros Kryst me spede!'

Nade he sayned hymself, segge, bot thrye,
Er he was war in the wod of a won in a mote,
765 Abof a launde, on a lawe, loken under boghes
Of mony borelych bole aboute bi the diches –
A castel the comlokest that ever knyght aghte,   *finest; owned*
Pyched on a prayere, a park al aboute,   *set; meadow*
With a pyked palays, pyned ful thik,
770 That umbeteye mony tre mo then two myle.
That holde on that on syde the hathel avysed,
As hit schemered and schon thurgh the schyre okes.   *bright*
Thenne has he hendly of his helme, and heghly he thonkes
Jesus and sayn Gilyan, that gentyle ar bothe,   *St Julian; kind*
775 That cortaysly hade hym kydde and his cry herkened.
'Now bone hostel,' cothe the burne, 'I beseche yow yette!'
Thenne gerdes he to Gryngolet with the gilt   *he spurs on*
   heles,   *spurs*
And he ful chauncely has chosen to the chef gate,
That broght bremly the burne to the bryge ende
780   in haste.
    The bryge was breme upbrayde,   *firmly drawn up*
    The yates wer stoken faste,   *shut*
    The walles were wel arayed –   *constructed*
    Hit dut no wyndes blaste.   *feared*

761–2 He crossed himself several times and said: 'May Christ's cross help me!'
763–6 The knight had scarcely crossed himself three times before he was aware in the wood of a dwelling inside a moat, above an open space, on a mound, shut in under the boughs of many massive trees in and about the ditches (of the moat).
769–71 With a spiked palisade, most thickly set, which enclosed many trees for more than two miles (round). The knight gazed at that stronghold on the one side.
773 Then he respectfully removes his helmet and devoutly thanks.
775–6 Who had shown him courtesy and listened to his cry. 'Now good lodging,' said the knight, 'I beseech you to grant.'
778–9 And he most fortunately has found the main path that swiftly brought the knight to the end of the drawbridge.

785 The burne bode on blonk, that on bonk hoved,
Of the depe double dich that drof to the place.   *surrounded*
The walle wod in the water wonderly depe,   *went into*
Ande eft a ful huge heght hit haled upon lofte,
Of harde hewen ston up to the tables,
790 Enbaned under the abataylment in the best lawe;
And sythen garytes ful gaye gered bitwene,
Wyth mony luflych loupe that louked ful clene.
A better barbican that burne blusched   *fortification; looked*
upon never.
And innermore he behelde that halle ful hyghe,   *further in*
795 Towres telded bytwene, trochet ful thik,
Fayre fylyoles that fyyed, and ferlyly long,
With corvon coprounes craftyly sleye.
Chalkwhyt chymnees ther ches he innoghe,   *discerned; many*
Upon bastel roves that blenked ful quyte.
800 So mony pynakle payntet was poudred ayquere
Among the castel carneles, clambred so thik,
That pared out of papure purely hit semed.
The fre freke on the fole hit fayre innoghe thoght,
If he myght kever to com the cloyster wythinne,
805 To herber in that hostel whyl halyday   *lodge; religious festival*
lested,
          avinant.   *pleasantly*
       He calde, and sone ther com

---

785 The knight remained on his horse, which halted on the bank.
788–92 And it rose up again a huge height into the air, made of hard
hewn stone up to the cornices, machicolated (i.e. provided with an
external gallery) under the battlements in the best style; and then there
were splendid turrets fashioned at intervals (along the walls), with
many excellent loopholes (i.e. for shooting arrows) that fastened (with
shutters) most neatly.
795–7 Towers built at intervals, thickly tined, handsome pinnacles that
fitted exactly (to the towers), and wonderfully tall, with carved orna-
mental tops, exquisitely intricate (in workmanship).
799–804 On the roofs of turrets that gleamed all white. So many painted
pinnacles were scattered everywhere among the battlements of the
castle, clustered so thickly, that it looked exactly as though it was cut
out of paper. The noble knight on the horse thought it handsome
enough, if only he might manage to come inside the wall.

A porter pure plesaunt.
On the wal his ernd he nome,   *message; took*
810   And haylsed the knyght erraunt.   *greeted; journeying*

'Gode sir,' quoth Gawan, 'woldes thou go myn ernde
To the hegh lorde of this hous, herber to crave?'   *lodging*
'Ye, Peter,' quoth the porter, 'and purely I trowee
That ye be, wyye, welcum to won quyle yow lykes.'   *stay*
815 Then yede the wyye yerne, and com ayayn swythe,
And folke frely hym wyth, to fonge the   *readily; receive*
      knyght.
Thay let doun the grete draght and derely out yeden,
And kneled doun on her knes upon the colde erthe
To welcum this ilk wyy, as worthy hom thoght.
820 Thay yolden hym the brode yate, yarked up wyde,
And he hem raysed rekenly and rod over the   *raised graciously*
      brygge.
Sere segges hym sesed by sadel, quel he lyght,
And sythen stabeled his stede stif men innoghe.
Knyghtes and swyeres comen doun thenne   *squires*
825 For to bryng this buurne wyth blys into halle.   *man*
Quen he hef up his helme, ther hiyed innoghe *lifted; hastened*
For to hent hit at his honde, the hende to   *take; noble man*
      serven;
His bronde and his blasoun bothe thay token.   *sword; shield*
Then haylsed he ful hendly tho hatheles uchone,
830 And mony proud mon ther presed, that   *pressed (forward)*
      prynce to honour.

---

808 A most agreeable gatekeeper.
811 'Good sir,' said Gawain, 'would you go on an errand for me.'
813–15 'Yes, by St Peter,' said the gatekeeper, 'and I truly believe that
      you will be welcome, sir, to stay as long as it pleases you.' Then the
      man quickly went away, and came back at once.
817 They let down the great drawbridge and courteously went out.
819–20 To welcome this same knight in a way that seemed to them
      worthy. They yielded him (i.e. allowed him through) the great gate,
      (which was) thrown wide open.
822–3 Several men held his saddle while he dismounted, and then many
      stalwart men led his horse to the stable.
829 Then most courteously he greeted each of those knights.

Alle hasped in his hegh wede to halle thay hym wonnen,
Ther fayre fyre upon flet fersly   *hearth; fiercely*
        brenned.   *burned*
Thenne the lorde of the lede loutes fro his chambre
For to mete wyth menske the mon on the flor.   *honour*
835 He sayde: 'Ye ar welcum to wone as yow lykes;
    That here is, al is yowre awen, to have at yowre wylle
                and welde.'
                'Graunt mercy,' quoth Gawayn,   *thank you*
                'Ther Kryst hit yow foryelde.'
840   As frekes that semed fayn   *men; glad (to meet)*
                Ayther other in armes con felde.

Gawayn glyght on the gome that godly hym   *looked at; man*
    gret,   *greeted*
And thught hit a bolde burne that the burgh   *castle*
    aghte,   *owned*
A hoge hathel for the nones, and of hyghe eldee.
845 Brode, bryght was his berde, and al bever-   *beaver-coloured*
    hwed,
Sturne, stif on the stryththe on stalworth schonkes,
Felle face as the fyre, and fre of hys speche;
And wel hym semed for sothe, as the segge thught,
To lede a lortschyp in lee of leudes ful gode.
850 The lorde hym charred to a chambre, and   *took*
    chefly cumaundes   *quickly*
To delyver hym a leude, hym lowly to serve.

---

831 They brought him, all buckled in his noble armour, into the hall.
833 Then the lord of the household comes down from his chamber (i.e.
    private sitting-room).
835-7 You are welcome to stay as long as it pleases you; what is here is
    all your own, to have and use as you please.
839 May Christ reward you for it.
841 Each took the other in his arms.
844 A huge man indeed, and of mature age.
846-9 Stern, standing firm on stalwart legs, a face bold as fire, and free
    of his speech. And it truly suited him well, so the knight (i.e. Gawain)
    thought, to lead a household of good men in a castle.
851 That a man should be assigned to him, to serve him humbly.

And there were boun at his bode burnes   *ready; command*
    innoghe
That broght hym to a bryght boure, ther beddying
    was noble,
Of cortynes of clene sylk, wyth cler golde hemmes,
855 And covertores ful curious with comlych panes
Of bryght blaunmer above, enbrawded bisydes,
Rudeles rennande on ropes, red golde rynges,
Tapytes tyght to the wowe, of Tuly and Tars,
And under fete, on the flet, of folwande sute.
860 Ther he was dispoyled, wyth speches   *relieved*
    of myerthe,   *cheerful*
The burn of his bruny and of his bryght   *coat of mail*
    wedes.   *clothes*
Ryche robes ful rad renkkes hym broghten,   *promptly; men*
For to charge and to chaunge and chose   *put on; change (into)*
    of the best.
Sone as he on hent, and happed therinne,
865 That sete on hym semly, wyth saylande skyrtes,
The ver by his visage verayly hit semed
Welnegh to uche hathel, alle on hwes,
Lowande and lufly alle his lymmes under,
That a comloker knyght never Kryst made,
870   hem thoght.
        Whethen in worlde he were,   *from wherever*
        Hit semed as he moght   *might*
        Be prynce withouten pere   *peer*
        In felde ther felle men foght.   *fierce; fought*

853-9 Who brought him to a bright bedchamber, where the bed-
trappings were noble, (consisting of) coverlets most skilfully made with
beautiful panels of bright ermine on top, embroidered at the sides,
curtains running on cords, (with) red gold rings, tapestries of Toulouse
and Turkestan attached to the wall, and similar ones underfoot on the
floor.

864-70 As soon as he had taken one and wrapped himself in it, one that
suited him well, with flowing skirts, (then) to everyone it seemed almost
to be truly springtime, all colourful as he was, (with) all his limbs
underneath glowing and graceful, so that Christ never made a more
handsome knight, as it seemed to them.

875 A cheyer byfore the chemné, ther charcole   *chair; fireplace*
    brenned,
  Was graythed for Sir Gawan graythely with clothes,
  Whyssynes upon queldepoyntes that koynt wer bothe.
  And thenne a meré mantyle was on that mon cast   *splendid*
  Of a broun bleeaunt, enbrauded ful ryche,   *silk; embroidered*
880 And fayre furred wythinne with felles of the   *beautifully; skins*
  best,
  Alle of ermyn in erde, his hode of the same.
  And he sete in that settel semlych ryche,
  And achaufed hym chefly, and thenne his cher mended.
  Sone was telded up a tabil on trestes ful fayre,
885 Clad wyth a clene clothe that cler quyt schewed,
  Sanap and salure and sylverin spones.
  The wyye wesche at his wylle, and went to his mete.
  Segges hym served semly innoghe   *men; most handsomely*
  Wyth sere sewes and sete, sesounde of the best,
890 Double-felde, as hit falles, and fele kyn fisches,
  Summe baken in bred, summe brad on the gledes,
  Summe sothen, summe in sewe savered with spyces,
  And ay sawses so sleye that the segge lyked.
  The freke calde hit a fest ful frely and ofte   *man; freely*
895 Ful hendely, quen alle the hatheles rehayted hym at ones
      as hende:
        'This penaunce now ye take,

876–7 Was promptly prepared for Sir Gawain with coverings, (namely) cushions upon quilted cloths that were both skilfully made.

881–7 All of finest ermine, his hood of the same (material). And he sat in that splendidly rich seat and warmed himself quickly, and then his mood improved. Soon a table was set up on most excellent trestles, covered with a clean cloth that was of pure white appearance, (with) over-cloth and salt-cellar and silver spoons. The man washed (his hands) at his good pleasure and went to his meal.

889–93 With varied and excellent soups, seasoned in the best manner, in double portions, as was fitting, and many kinds of fish, some baked in bread, some grilled on the embers, some poached, some in stew flavoured with spices, and always (with) sauces so subtle that the man was pleased.

895–8 Most courteously, when all the men together rallied (i.e. teasingly encouraged) him politely: 'You are taking this penance now, and later it will improve.'

And eft hit schal amende.'
That mon much merthe con make,   *made*
900 For wyn in his hed that wende.   *because of; went to*

Thenne was spyed and spured upon spare wyse,
Bi prevé poyntes of that prynce, put to hymselven,
That he beknew cortaysly of the court that he were,
That athel Arthure the hende haldes hym one,
905 That is the ryche ryal kyng of the Rounde Table;
And hit was Wawen hymself that in that won syttes,   *· house*
Comen to that Krystmasse, as case hym then lymped.
When the lorde hade lerned that he the leude hade,   *knight*
Loude laghed he therat, so lef hit hym   *laughed; delightful*
     thoght,
910 And alle the men in that mote maden much joye   *castle*
To apere in his presense prestly that tyme,   *promptly*
That alle prys and prowes and pured thewes
Apendes to hys persoun, and praysed is ever;
Byfore alle men upon molde his mensk is the   *earth; honour*
     most.
915 Uch segge ful softly sayde to his fere: *companion*
'Now schal we semlych se sleghtes of thewes
And the teccheles termes of talkyng noble.
Wich spede is in speche unspurd may we lerne,
Syn we haf fonged that fyne fader of nurture.
920 God has geven uus his grace godly for sothe,   *generously*

901–4 Then enquiry was tactfully made, by discreet questions put to
   that prince, such that he courteously acknowledged that he was of the
   court that noble Arthur the gracious alone presides over.
907 (Having) come to that Christmas festival, as chance befell him then.
912–13 In that all excellence and prowess and refined manners belong to
   his person, and he is esteemed at all times.
916–19 Now we shall see in seemly fashion the arts of good manners
   and the polished phrases of noble conversation. We shall learn without
   asking what profit there is in speech, since we have captured that
   excellent master of (good) breeding.

That such a gest as Gawan grauntes uus to have,
When burnes blythe of his burthe schal sitte
                and synge.
            In menyng of maneres mere
925   This burne now schal uus bryng.
            I hope that may hym here
            Schal lerne of luf-talkyng.'

Bi that the diner was done and the dere up,
Hit was negh at the niyght neghed the tyme.
930 Chaplaynes to the chapeles chosen the gate,   *made their way*
Rungen ful rychely, ryght as thay schulden,   *rang (bells)*
To the hersum evensong of the hyghe tyde.
The lorde loutes therto, and the lady als;   *goes; also*
Into a cumly closet coyntly ho entres.
935 Gawan glydes ful gay and gos theder sone;
The lorde laches hym by the lappe and *catches; fold (of gown)*
        ledes hym to sytte,
And couthly hym knowes and calles hym his nome,
And sayde he was the welcomest wyye of the worlde;   *man*
And he hym thonkked throly, and ayther halched other,
940 And seten soberly samen the servise-quyle.
Thenne lyst the lady to loke on the knyght;   *it pleased*
Thenne com ho of hir closet with mony cler   *lovely*
        burdes.   *women*
Ho was the fayrest in felle, of flesche and of lyre,

921–7 Who allows us to have such a guest as Gawain, (at this time)
    when men joyful at His birth shall sit and sing. This man will now
    bring us to an understanding of noble manners. I believe that whoever
    hears him will learn about courteous conversation.

928–9 By the time dinner was finished and the noble company risen, it
    was nearly night-time.

932 To the solemn evensong of the festive season.

934–5 She gracefully enters a beautiful closed pew. Gawain goes most
    cheerfully and proceeds there (i.e. to the chapel) soon after.

937 And greets him familiarly and calls him by his name.

939–40 And he thanked him heartily, and each embraced the other, and
    they sat quietly together while the service lasted.

943–6 She was the most beautiful of all (others) in skin, in flesh and

And of compas and colour and costes, of alle other,
945 And wener then Wenore, as the wyye thoght.
He ches thurgh the chaunsel to cheryche that hende.
An other lady hir lad bi the lyft honde,   *led; left*
That was alder then ho, an auncian hit   *older; old woman*
    semed,
And heghly honowred with hatheles aboute.
950 Bot unlyke on to loke tho ladyes were,
For if the yonge was yep, yolwe was that   *fresh; withered*
    other.
Riche red on that on rayled ayquere,
Rugh ronkled chekes that other on rolled.
Kerchofes of that on, wyth mony cler perles,
955 Hir brest and hir bryght throte bare displayed,
Schon schyrer then snawe that schedes on
    hilles.
That other wyth a gorger was gered over the swyre,
Chymbled over hir blake chyn with chalk-quyte vayles,
Hir frount folden in sylk, enfoubled ayquere,
960 Toret and treleted, with tryfles aboute,
That noght was bare of that burde bot the blake   *lady*
    browes,
The tweyne yyen and the nase, the naked lyppes,   *eyes; nose*
And those were soure to se and sellyly blered.   *exceedingly*
A mensk lady on molde mon may hir calle,   *fine lady indeed*
965   for Gode!   *by*

---

complexion, in shape and colour and bearing, and more beautiful than
Guinevere, as the knight thought. He went through the chancel to greet
that noble lady.

949 And highly honoured with men in attendance.

952–60 Rich red (colouring) was everywhere on the one, rough wrinkled
cheeks rolled on the other. The kerchiefs of the one, with many lustrous
pearls, displayed her breast and her lovely neck uncovered, (and they)
shone brighter than snow that falls on hills. The other was wrapped
about the neck with a gorget (i.e. neckerchief for the throat), her
swarthy chin swathed in chalk-white veils, her forehead enveloped in
silk, muffled up everywhere, (the silk) edged and latticed, with trefoils
all over.

Hir body was schort and thik,
Hir buttokes balw and brode;   *round*
More lykkerwys on to lyk   *tasty to taste*
Was that scho hade on lode.

970 When Gawayn glyght on that gay, that graciously loked,
Wyth leve laght of the lorde he lent hem ayaynes.
The alder he haylses, heldande ful lowe;
The loveloker he lappes a lyttel in armes.
He kysses hir comlyly and knyghtly he   *courteously*
    meles;   *speaks*
975 Thay kallen hym of aquoyntaunce, and he hit quyk askes
To be her servaunt sothly, if hemself lyked.
Thay tan hym bytwene hem, wyth talkyng hym leden   *take*
To chambre, to chemné, and chefly thay   *fireplace; promptly*
    asken   *ask for*
Spyces, that unsparely men speded   *spiced cakes; unstintingly*
    hom to bryng,
980 And the wynnelych wyne therwith uche tyme.   *cheering*
The lorde luflych aloft lepes ful ofte,
Mynned merthe to be made upon mony sythes,
Hent heghly of his hode, and on a spere henged,
And wayned hom to wynne the worchip therof
985 That most myrthe myght meve that Crystenmas whyle.
'And I schal fonde, bi my fayth, to fylter wyth the best

---

969 Was the one she had in tow.
970-3 When Gawain saw that beautiful one, who looked graciously (on
    him, cf. l. 941), with permission obtained from the lord he went to
    meet them. He greets the elder, bowing very low; the lovelier he folds a
    little in his arms.
975-6 They beg his acquaintance, and he quickly asks to be their true
    servant, if it so pleased them.
981-8 Very often the lord springs up enthusiastically, urged mirth to be
    made many a time, spiritedly took off his hood and hung it on a spear,
    and called on those to win the honour of (having) it who provided
    most entertainment during that Christmas: 'And I shall try, on my
    honour, to contend with the best before I shall go without this garment,
    with the help of my friends.' So with laughing words the lord makes
    merry.

Er me wont the wede, with help of my frendes.'
Thus wyth laghande lotes the lorde hit tayt makes,
For to glade Sir Gawayn with gomnes in halle *gladden; games*
990   that nyght.
         Til that hit was tyme
         The lord comaundet lyght;   *lights*
         Sir Gawen his leve con nyme   *took*
         And to his bed hym dight.   *took himself*

995 On the morne, as uch mon mynes that   *morrow; remembers*
      tyme
    That Dryghtyn for oure destyné to deye was   *the Lord; die*
      borne,
    Wele waxes in uche a won in worlde for his sake.
    So did hit there on that day thurgh dayntés mony; *delights*
    Bothe at mes and at mele, messes ful quaynt
1000 Derf men upon dece drest of the best.
    The olde auncian wyf heghest ho syttes;
    The lorde lufly her by lent, as I trowe.
    Gawan and the gay burde togeder thay   *beautiful lady*
      seten   *sat*
    Even inmyddes, as the messe metely come;
1005 And sythen thurgh al the sale, as hem best semed,
    Bi uche grome at his degré graythely was served.
    Ther was mete, ther was myrthe, ther was much joye, *food*
    That for to telle therof hit me tene were,
    And to poynte hit yet I pyned me paraventure.
1010 Bot yet I wot that Wawen and the wale   *know; lovely*
      burde   *lady*
    Such comfort of her compaynye caghten togeder

---

997 Joy flourishes in every dwelling on earth for His sake.
999-1000 Both at dinner and at other meals, stalwart men on the dais
    served most exquisite dishes in the best manner.
1002 The lord courteously took his place beside her, as I believe.
1004-6 Right in the middle, where the food fittingly came (first of all);
    and afterwards (it went) through all the hall, in the way that seemed
    best to them, until each man according to his degree was duly served.
1008-9 Such that it would be difficult for me to tell of it (in general
    terms), and to describe it in detail I would perhaps *still* be troubling
    myself (to do it).
1011-15 Together took such pleasure in each other's company, through

Thurgh her dere dalyaunce of her derne wordes,
Wyth clene cortays carp closed fro fylthe,
That hor play was passande uche prynce gomen,
1015   in vayres.
  Trumpes and nakerys,   *trumpets; horns*
  Much pypyng ther repayres;   *is present*
  Uche mon tented hys, *minded his own (business)*
  And thay two tented thayres.

1020 Much dut was ther dryven that day and that other,
And the thryd as thro thronge in therafter.
The joye of sayn Jones day was gentyle to here, *pleasant*
And was the last of the layk, leudes ther thoghten;
Ther wer gestes to go upon the gray morne.   *guests*
1025 Forthy wonderly thay woke, and the wyn dronken,
Daunsed ful dreyly wyth dere caroles.
At the last, when hit was late, thay lachen her leve, *take*
Uchon to wende on his way that was wyye strange.
Gawan gef hym god day, the godmon hym lachches,
1030 Ledes hym to his awen chambre, the
  chymné bysyde,   *beside the fireplace*
And there he drawes hym on dryye, and derely hym thonkkes
Of the wynne worschip that he hym *for; great honour*
  wayved hade,   *shown*
As to honour his hous on that hyghe tyde, *festive season*
And enbelyse his burgh with his bele chere.

---

the pleasant dalliance of their private speech, with refined courteous talk free from grossness, that their play surpassed every princely sport, in truth.

1020–1 Much merriment was made there that day and the next, and the third (day) just as crowded (with pleasure) pressed in afterwards.

1022 *sayn Jones day*, St John's Day (27 December).

1023 And was the last of the festivities, as people there realised.

1025–6 And so they revelled prodigiously through the night, and drank wine, danced on and on with pleasant carols.

1028–9 Everyone ready to go on his way who was not of the household. Gawain said goodbye to him, the host seizes hold of him.

1031 And there he detains him, and courteously thanks him.

1034–5 And embellish his castle with his good company. 'Indeed, sir, as long as I live, I shall be the better for it.'

1035 'Iwysse, sir, quyl I leve, me worthes the better
       That Gawayn has ben my gest at Goddes awen fest.'
       'Grant merci, sir,' quoth Gawayn, 'in god fayth hit   *thank you*
          is yowres,
       Al the honour is your awen – the heghe kyng yow   *High King*
          yelde!   *reward*
       And I am, wyye, at your wylle, to worch youre hest,
1040 As I am halden therto, in hyghe and in lowe,
                 bi right.'
                 The lorde fast can hym payne   *tried hard*
                 To holde lenger the knyght;
                 To hym answres Gawayn
1045   Bi non way that he myght.

       Then frayned the freke ful fayre at himselven
       Quat derve dede had hym dryven at that dere tyme
       So kenly fro the kynges kourt to kayre al his one,
       Er the halidayes holly were halet out of toun.
1050 'For sothe, sir,' quoth the segge, 'ye sayn bot   *knight; speak*
          the trawthe,
       A heghe ernde and a hasty me hade fro tho wones,
       For I am sumned myselfe to sech to a place,
       I ne wot in worlde whederwarde to wende hit to fynde.
       I nolde bot if I hit negh myght on Nw Yeres morne
1055 For alle the londe inwyth Logres, so me oure Lorde help!
       Forthy, sir, this enquest I require yow here,   *question; ask*
       That ye me telle with trawthe if ever ye tale herde   *mention*
       Of the grene chapel, quere hit on grounde stondes,
       And of the knyght that hit kepes, of colour of grene.

1039–41 And I am, sir, at your command, to do your bidding, as I am
     required to do, in great things and in small, by bounden duty.
1045 That he might by no means (stay longer).
1046–9 Then the man very politely asked him what grim deed had
     driven him at that festive season to ride out all on his own so boldly
     from the king's court, before the holidays were wholly over and done
     with.
1051–5 A great and urgent mission took me from that house, for I myself
     am summoned to go to a (certain) place, and I do not know where in
     the world (to go) to find it. I would not fail to come to it on New
     Year's morning (lit. I would not wish otherwise than that I might come
     near it) for all the land in Britain, so help me our Lord!

1060 Ther was stabled bi statut a steven uus bytwene
     To mete that mon at that mere, yif I myght last;
     And of that ilk Nw Yere bot neked now wontes,
     And I wolde loke on that lede, if God me let wolde,   *man*
     Gladloker, bi Goddes sun, then any god welde.
1065 Forthi, iwysse, bi yowre wylle, wende me bihoves;
     Naf I now to busy bot bare thre dayes,
     And me als fayn to falle feye as fayly of myyn ernde.'
     Thenne laghande quoth the lorde: 'Now leng   *laughing; stay*
          the byhoves,   *you must*
     For I schal teche yow to that terme bi the tymes ende;
1070 The grene chapayle upon grounde greve yow
          no more.
     Bot ye schal be in yowre bed, burne, at thyn ese,   *sir*
     Quyle forth dayes, and ferk on the fyrst of the yere,
     And cum to that merk at mydmorn, to   *appointed place*
          make quat yow likes   *do*
                in spenne.   *there*
1075   Dowelles whyle New Yeres daye,   *stay until*
          And rys and raykes thenne.   *go*
          Mon schal yow sette in waye;
          Hit is not two myle henne.'   *hence*

     Thenne was Gawan ful glad, and gomenly he   *cheerfully*
          laghed: *laughed*
1080 'Now I thonk yow thryvandely thurgh alle other thynge;
     Now acheved is my chaunce, I schal   *accomplished; adventure*
          at your wylle
     Dowelle, and elles do quat ye demen.'   *otherwise; think fit*

1060–2 An appointment was fixed by solemn agreement between us (for
     me) to meet that man at that appointed place, if I might live (till then);
     and there is but little time left till that same New Year.

1064–7 More gladly, by God's Son, than own any good thing. And so,
     indeed, by your leave, I am obliged to go; I have barely three days in
     which to bestir myself, and I would rather fall down dead than fail in
     my mission.

1069–70 For I shall direct you to that appointed place by the end of the
     time; let the whereabouts of the green chapel trouble you no more.

1072 Until well on in the day, and go on the first day of the year.

1077 A man shall put you on the (right) path.

1080 Now I thank you with all my heart (for this) above all else.

Thenne sesed hym the syre and set hym bysyde,
Let the ladies be fette, to lyke hem the better.
1085 Ther was seme solace by hemself stille;
The lorde let for luf lotes so myry,
As wyy that wolde of his wyte, ne wyst quat he myght.
Thenne he carped to the knyght, criande loude: *said*
'Ye han demed to do the dede that I bidde;   *agreed*
1090 Wyl ye halde this hes here at thys ones?'
'Ye, sir, for sothe,' sayd the segge trwe,   *knight*
'Whyl I byde in yowre borghe, be bayn to yowre hest.'
'For ye haf travayled,' quoth the tulk, 'towen fro ferre,
And sythen waked me wyth, ye arn not wel waryst
1095 Nauther of sostnaunce ne of slepe, sothly I knowe.
Ye schal lenge in your lofte and lyye in your ese   *stay; room*
To-morn quyle the messe-quyle, and to mete wende
When ye wyl, wyth my wyf, that wyth yow schal sitte
And comfort yow with compayny, til I to cort   *(my) court*
    torne.   *return*
1100   Ye lende,   *stay*
        And I schal erly ryse;
        On huntyng wyl I wende.'
        Gauayn grantes alle thyse,
        Hym heldande, as the hende.

1105 'Yet firre,' quoth the freke, 'a forwarde we make:

1083-7 Then the lord seized hold of him and seated him beside him, had the ladies fetched the better to please them. They had excellent entertainment by themselves in private; the lord in delight uttered such joyous cries as though he was (a man who was) likely to lose his wits, and did not know what he might do.

1090 Will you keep this promise here and now?

1092-5 'While I stay in your castle, I shall be obedient to your command.' 'As you have had a hard journey,' said the man, '(and have) come from afar, and afterwards revelled through the night with me, you are not well supplied with either sustenance or sleep, I know (that) for certain.'

1097 Tomorrow until the time for mass, and go to your meal.

1103-4 Gawain consents to all these things, bowing to him, like the courteous man he was.

1105 'Yet further,' said the man, 'let us make an agreement.'

Quat-so-ever I wynne in the wod, hit worthes to   *shall be*
   youres;
And quat chek so ye acheve, chaunge me therforne.
Swete, swap we so – sware with trawthe –
Quether, leude, so lymp lere other better.'
1110 'Bi God,' quoth Gawayn the gode, 'I grant thertylle,
And that yow lyst for to layke, lef hit me thynkes.'
'Who brynges uus this beverage, this bargayn is maked,'
So sayde the lorde of that lede. Thay laghed   *household*
   uchone,
Thay dronken and daylyeden and dalten untyghtel,
1115 Thise lordes and ladyes, quyle that hem lyked;
And sythen with frenkysch fare and fele fayre lotes
Thay stoden and stemed and stylly speken,
Kysten ful comlyly and kaghten her leve.   *decorously; took*
With mony leude ful lyght and lemande torches,
1120 Uche burne to his bed was broght at the laste   *man*
           ful softe.   *quietly*
      To bed yet er thay yede,   *before; went*
      Recorded covenauntes ofte;   *they repeated*
      The olde lorde of that leude   *household*
1125   Cowthe wel halde layk alofte.

III

Ful erly bifore the day the folk up rysen;
Gestes that go wolde hor gromes thay calden,   *servants*

1107–12 And whatever fortune you gain, give it me in exchange for it.
   Good sir, let us swap in this way – answer on your honour – whether,
   sir, it turns our worse or better.' 'By God,' said good Gawain, 'I agree
   to that; if it pleases you to play, that seems excellent to me.' 'Once
   someone brings us a drink (i.e. to seal the bargain), this bargain is
   made.'
1114 They drank and dallied and enjoyed themselves without restraint.
1116–17 And then with elaborate (lit. French-style) courtesy and many
   polite words they stood and lingered and spoke quietly.
1119 With many most prompt attendants and gleaming torches.
1125 Knew well how to keep a game going.

And thay busken up bilyve blonkkes to sadel,
Tyffen her takles, trussen her males.
1130 Richen hem the rychest, to ryde alle arayde,
Lepen up lyghtly, lachen her brydeles,   *take hold of*
Uche wyye on his way ther hym wel lyked.
The leve lorde of the londe was not the last   *esteemed*
Arayed for the rydyng, with renkkes ful mony;   *men*
1135 Ete a sop hastyly, when he hade herde   *(he) ate a light meal*
masse.
With bugle to bent-felde he buskes   *hunting-field; hastens*
bylyve;   *eagerly*
By that any daylyght lemed upon   *by (the time that); shone*
erthe,
He with his hatheles on hyghe horsses weren.   *men*
Thenne thise cacheres that couthe cowpled hor houndes,
1140 Unclosed the kenel dore and calde hem theroute,
Blwe bygly in bugles thre bare mote;   *strongly; single notes*
Braches bayed therfor and breme noyse maked,
And thay chastysed and charred on chasyng that went,
A hundreth of hunteres, as I haf herde telle,
1145   of the best.
          To trystors vewters yod,
          Couples huntes of kest;
          Ther ros for blastes gode   *on account of horn-blasts*
          Gret rurd in that forest.   *noise*

1150 At the fyrst quethe of the quest quaked the wylde;
Der drof in the dale, doted for drede,

1128–30 And they hurry forward at once to saddle horses, prepare their
equipment, pack their bags. The guests of highest rank make themselves
ready, all dressed to ride.
1132 Each man (went) on his way to where it best pleased him.
1139 Then huntsmen who knew their business coupled their hounds (i.e.
leashed them together in pairs).
1142–3 Hounds bayed in response and made fierce din, and they
whipped and turned back those that went chasing off.
1146–7 Keepers of hounds went to their hunting stations, huntsmen cast
off the leashes.
1150–3 At the first sound of baying (of hounds on the trail) the wild
creatures trembled; deer swarmed in the valley, crazed for fear, rushed

Hiyed to the hyghe – bot heterly thay were
Restayed with the stablye, that stoutly ascryed.
Thay let the herttes haf the gate, with the   *let the stags go*
   hyghe hedes,
1155 The breme bukkes also with hor brode paumes; *fierce; antlers*
For the fre lorde hade defende in fermysoun tyme
That ther schulde no mon meve to the male dere.
The hindes were halden in with 'hay!' and 'war!'   *held*
The does dryven with gret dyn to the depe slades.   *valleys*
1160 Ther myght mon se, as thay slypte, slentyng of arwes;
At uche wende under wande wapped a flone,
That bigly bote on the broun with ful brode hedes.
What! thay brayen and bleden, bi bonkkes thay   *bray*
   deyen,   *die*
And ay rachches in a res radly hem folwes.
1165 Hunteres wyth hyghe horne hasted hem after,   *loud*
Wyth such a crakkande kry as klyffes haden brusten.
What wylde so atwaped wyyes that schotten
Was al toraced and rent at the resayt,
Bi thay were tened at the hyghe and taysed to the wattres.
1170 The ledes were so lerned at the lowe trysteres,
And the grehoundes so grete, that geten hem bylyve
And hem tofylched as fast as frekes myght loke,
      ther ryght.

---

to the high ground – but they were roughly turned back by the ring of
   beaters, who shouted loudly.

1156–7 For the noble lord had forbidden that any man should interfere
   with the male deer in the close season.

1160–2 There a man might see the slanting flight of arrows as they were
   loosed; at each turning in the wood an arrow flew, (arrows) that bit
   hard on the brown hides with very broad heads.

1164 And all the time the hounds pursue them headlong.

1166–73 With such an ear-splitting cry it was as though the cliffs had
   shattered. Whatever wild creature escaped the archers was all savaged
   and torn (by the hounds) at the receiving stations, when they were
   harried on the high ground and driven to the streams. The men at the
   low receiving stations were so expert, and their greyhounds so big, that
   they quickly caught and tore them down as fast as men might look,
   right there.

The lorde for blys abloy   *transported with pleasure*
1175   Ful oft con launce and lyght,
And drof that day wyth joy   *passed*
Thus to the derk nyght.   *till*

Thus laykes this lorde by lynde-wodes eves,
And Gawayn the god mon in gay bed lyges,   *beautiful; lies*
1180 Lurkkes quyl the daylyght lemed on the wowes,
Under covertour ful clere, cortyned aboute.   *coverlet; bright*
And as in slomeryng he slode, sleyly he herde
A littel dyn at his dor, and dernly upon;
And he heves up his hed out of the clothes,   *heaves*
1185 A corner of the cortyn he caght up a lyttel,   *caught*
And waytes warly thiderwarde quat hit be myght.
Hit was the ladi, loflyest to beholde,   *loveliest*
That drow the dor after hir ful dernly and stylle,
And bowed towarde the bed; and the burne   *moved; man*
schamed,   *was embarrassed*
1190 And layde hym doun lystyly and let as he   *craftily; pretended*
slepte.
And ho stepped stilly and stel to his bedde,   *softly; stole*
Kest up the cortyn and creped withinne,   *lifted*
And set hir ful softly on the bed-syde,   *herself; gently*
And lenged there selly longe, to loke quen he   *stayed; very; see*
wakened.
1195 The lede lay lurked a ful longe quyle,   *man; with eyes closed*
Compast in his concience to quat that cace myght
Meve other amount – to mervayle hym thoght,
Bot yet he sayde in hymself: 'More semly hit were
To aspye wyth my spelle in space quat ho wolde.'

1175 Rode forward and dismounted very often.
1178 Thus this lord enjoys himself along the edges of the forest.
1180 Lies low while the daylight gleamed on the walls.
1182-3 And as he drifted in light sleep he heard slyly a little sound at his
    door, and heard it stealthily open.
1186 And looks warily towards it (the door) to see what it might be.
1188 Who closed the door after her most stealthily and quietly.
1196-9 Turned over in his mind what that matter might come to or
    amount to – it seemed very strange to him, but yet he said to himself:
    'It would be more fitting (than my lying here) for me to find out
    through (my) speech at once what she wants.'

1200 Then he wakenede and wroth and   *stretched (himself)*
     to-hir-warde torned,
    And unlouked his yye-lyddes and let as hym wondered,
    And sayned hym, as bi his sawe the saver to worthe,
        with hande.
        Wyth chynne and cheke ful swete,
1205   Bothe quit and red in blande,   *white; together*
        Ful lufly con ho lete,
        Wyth lyppes smal laghande.   *laughing*

    'God moroun, Sir Gawayn,' sayde that gay lady,   *morning*
    'Ye ar a sleper unslyye, that mon may slyde hider.
1210 Now ar ye tan astyt; bot true uus may schape,
    I schal bynde yow in your bedde, that be ye   *be sure of that*
     trayst.'
    Al laghande the lady lauced tho   *uttered those*
     bourdes.   *pleasantries*
    'Goud moroun, gay,' quoth Gawayn the blythe,   *cheerful*
    'Me schal worthe at your wille, and that me wel lykes,
1215 For I yelde me yederly and yeye after grace,
    And that is the best, be my dome, for me byhoves nede.'
    And thus he bourded ayayn with mony a   *jested in return*
     blythe laghter.   *laugh*
    'Bot wolde ye, lady lovely, then leve me grante,   *permission*
    And deprece your prysoun and pray   *release; prisoner; ask*
     hym to ryse,
1220 I wolde bowe of this bed and busk me better;   *leave; dress*
    I schulde kever the more comfort to karp yow wyth.'
    'Nay, for sothe, beau sir,' sayd that swete,   *indeed; good sir*
    'Ye schal not rise of your bedde, I rych yow better.   *counsel*

1201-3 And opened his eyelids and pretended to be surprised, and
   crossed himself with his hand, as though to make himself the safer by
   his prayer.
1206 She spoke most graciously.
1209-10 You are a careless sleeper, that one may steal here. Now you
   are captured at once; unless we can make a truce.
1214-16 It shall be with me as you desire, and that pleases me greatly,
   for I promptly surrender myself and cry for mercy, and that is best, in
   my opinion, for I must needs (do it).
1221 I should get the more pleasure from talking to you.

I schal happe yow here that other half als,
1225 And sythen karp wyth my knyght that I kaght have.
For I wene wel, iwysse, Sir Wowen ye are,   *know well; indeed*
That alle the worlde worchipes, quere-so   *honours; wherever*
          ye ride;
Your honour, your hendelayk is hendely   *courtesy; highly*
          praysed
With lordes, wyth ladyes, with alle that lyf bere.   *by*
1230 And now ye ar here, iwysse, and we bot oure   *by ourselves*
          one;
My lorde and his ledes ar on lenthe faren,   *men; gone away*
Other burnes in her bedde, and my burdes als,   *ladies too*
The dor drawen and dit with a derf haspe.
And sythen I have in this hous hym that al lykes,
1235 I schal ware my whyle wel, quyl hit lastes,
          with tale.
               Ye ar welcum to my cors,
               Yowre awen won to wale;
               Me behoves of fyne force
1240   Your servaunt be, and schale.'

'In god fayth,' quoth Gawayn, 'gayn hit me thynkkes,
Thagh I be not now he that ye of speken;
To reche to such reverence as ye reherce here
I am wyye unworthy, I wot wel myselven.
1245 Bi God, I were glad and yow god thoght
At sawe other at servyce that I sette myght
To the plesaunce of your prys – hit were a pure joye.'

1224–5 I shall close you in here on the other side as well, and then talk with my knight whom I have caught.

1233–40 The door closed and fastened with a strong bolt. And since I have in this house the man whom everyone admires, I shall use my time well, while it lasts, with speech. You are welcome to me (lit. to my body), to do with as you please (lit. to choose your own pleasure); I must of absolute necessity be your servant, and I shall be.

1241–7 'In truth,' said Gawain, 'that seems to me a good thing, though I am not indeed the man you speak of; to attain to such honour as you talk of here I am an unworthy person, I know (that) well myself. By God, I would be glad if you thought it good that I might devote myself, with words or with service, to pleasing you – it would be a pure joy (to me).'

'In god fayth, Sir Gawayn,' quoth the gay lady,
'The prys and the prowes that pleses al other,   *excellence*
1250 If I hit lakked other set at lyght, hit were littel daynté.
Bot hit ar ladyes innoghe that lever wer nowthe
Haf the, hende, in hor holde, as I the habbe here,
To daly with derely your daynté wordes,
Kever hem comfort and colen her cares,
1255 Then much of the garysoun other golde that thay haven.
Bot I louve that ilk lorde that the lyfte haldes,
I haf hit holly in my honde that al desyres,
          thurghe grace.'
          Scho made hym so gret chere,
1260   That was so fayr of face;
          The knyght with speches skere
          Answared to uche a cace.

'Madame,' quoth the myry mon, 'Mary yow yelde,
For I haf founden, in god fayth, yowre fraunchis nobele,
1265 And other ful much of other folk fongen for hor dedes.
Bot the daynté that thay delen for my disert nys ever;
Hit is the worchyp of yourself that noght bot wel connes.'
'Bi Mary,' quoth the menskful, 'me thynk hit   *noble lady*
     another;   *otherwise*
For were I worth al the wone of wymmen alyve,   *multitude*
1270 And al the wele of the worlde were in my honde,   *wealth*

1250–62 'If I disparaged or made light of it, it would be small courtesy.
  But there are many ladies who would rather now have you, good sir,
  in their hold, as I have you here, to make pleasant play with your
  courteous words, find solace for themselves and assuage their sorrows,
  than much of the treasure or gold that they have. But I praise that
  (same) Lord who rules the heavens (that) I have it wholly in my hand
  what everyone desires, through (His) grace.' She behaved very warmly
  towards him, she who was so fair of face; the knight, with immaculate
  speeches, answered (her) every remark.

1263–7 'Madam,' said the good man, 'may Mary reward you, for I have
  found in truth your generosity to be noble, and (indeed) others receive
  a great deal (of respect) from other people for their deeds. But the
  respect that they give (me) is not at all for my merit; it is (due to) your
  own sense of honour, (you) who know nothing but good.'

And I schulde chepen and chose to cheve me a lorde,
For the costes that I haf knowen upon   *qualities; seen in*
    the, knyght, here,   *you*
Of bewté and debonerté and blythe semblaunt,
And that I haf er herkkened and halde hit here trwee,
1275 Ther schulde no freke upon folde bifore yow be chosen.'
'Iwysse, worthy,' quoth the wyye, 'ye haf waled wel better;
Bot I am proude of the prys that ye put on me,   *value*
And, soberly your servaunt, my soverayn I holde yow,
And yowre knyght I becom, and Kryst yow foryelde!'   *reward*
1280 Thus thay meled of muchquat til   *talked; many things*
    mydmorn paste,
And ay the lady let lyk a hym loved mych;
The freke ferde with defence, and feted ful fayre.
Thagh ho were burde bryghtest the burne in mynde hade,
The lasse luf in his lode, for lur that he soght
1285   boute hone –
        The dunte that schulde hym deve,   *blow; strike down*
        And nedes hit most be done.
        The lady thenn spek of leve,   *spoke; leaving*
        He granted hir ful sone.   *immediately*

1290 Thenne ho gef hym god day, and wyth a glent laghed,   *glance*
And as ho stod ho stonyed hym wyth ful   *stunned*
    stor wordes: *strong*
'Now he that spedes uche spech this disport yelde yow!'

1271 And I should bargain and choose to find myself a husband.
1273–6 'Of beauty and courtesy and cheerful demeanour, and that which I have heard of before and here hold (it) to be true, there would be no man on earth chosen before you.' 'Indeed, good lady,' said the knight, 'you have chosen much better.'
1278 And, respectfully your servant, I hold you as my sovereign lady.
1281–5 And always the lady acted as though she loved him greatly; the knight defended himself, and behaved most courteously. Even though she was the most beautiful woman the knight knew of, there was the less warmth in his manner on account of (his preoccupation with) the doom that he was going to without delay.
1292 Now may He who prospers every speech reward you for this entertainment!

Bot that ye be Gawan, hit gos not in *is hard to believe*
    mynde.'
'Querfore?' quoth the freke, and freschly he *why; eagerly*
    askes,
1295 Ferde lest he hade fayled in fourme of his castes.
Bot the burde hym blessed, and bi this skyl sayde:
'So god as Gawayn gaynly is halden,
And cortaysye is closed so clene in hymselven,
Couth not lyghtly haf lenged so long wyth a lady
1300 Bot he had craved a cosse, bi his courtaysye,
Bi sum towch of summe tryfle at sum tales ende.'
Then quoth Wowen: 'Iwysse, *indeed*
    worthe as yow lykes; *be it as you please*
I schal kysse at your comaundement, as a knyght falles, *befits*
And fire, lest he displese yow, so plede hit no *further*
    more.'
1305 Ho comes nerre with that, and caches hym in armes, *nearer*
Loutes luflych adoun and the leude kysses.
Thay comly bykennen to Kryst ayther other;
Ho dos hir forth at the dore withouten dyn more.
And he ryches hym to ryse and rapes hym sone,
1310 Clepes to his chamberlayn, choses his wede, *calls; clothes*
Bowes forth, quen he was boun, blythely to *goes; ready*
    masse,
And thenne he meved to his mete that menskly hym keped,
And made myry al day til the mone rysed, *rose*
    with game. *revelry*
1315   Was never freke fayrer fonge
    Bitwene two so dyngne dame, *such worthy ladies*

1295-1301 Afraid that he had failed in the etiquette of his behaviour.
But the lady wished him well, and gave this as the reason: 'A man as
good as Gawain is rightly held to be, and one in whom courtesy is so
completely embodied, might not easily have stayed so long with a lady
without craving a kiss, through his courtesy, by some touch of light
speech at the end of a conversation.'

1306-9 Bends down graciously and kisses the knight. They courteously
commend each other to Christ; she goes out at the door without more
speech. And he prepares himself to get up and at once makes haste.

1312 And then he went to his meal that fittingly awaited him.

1315 Never was man better entertained.

The alder and the yonge;   *older; younger*
Much solace set thay same.

And ay the lorde of the londe is lent on his gamnes,
1320 To hunt in holtes and hethe at hyndes barayne.
Such a sowme he ther slowe bi that the sunne heldet,
Of dos and of other dere, to deme were wonder.
Thenne fersly thay flokked in, folk at the laste,   *eagerly*
And quykly of the quelled dere a querré thay maked.
1325 The best bowed therto with burnes innoghe,
Gedered the grattest of gres that ther were,
And didden hem derely undo as the dede askes.
Serched hem at the asay summe that ther were;
Two fyngeres thay fonde of the fowlest of alle.
1330 Sythen thay slyt the slot, sesed the erber,
Schaved wyth a scharp knyf and the schyre knitten.
Sythen rytte thay the foure lymmes and rent of the hyde,
Then brek thay the balé, the boweles out token
Lystily for laucyng the lere of the knot.
1335 Thay gryped to the gargulun and graythely departed
The wesaunt fro the wynt-hole, and walt out the guttes.
Then scher thay out the schulderes with her scharp   *cut*
knyves,

1318 They had much pleasure together.

1319–22 And all the time the lord of the land is off on his games,
hunting the barren hinds in woods and heath. He had killed there such
a number by the time the sun slanted low, of does and of other kinds
of deer, that it would be a wonderful thing to reckon them.

1324–36 And quickly they made a heap of the slaughtered deer. The
highest in rank went up to it with many attendants, collected those
with the greatest amount of fat that were there, and cut them up
properly as the operation requires. Some who were there examined
them at the assay (a ceremonial testing of the quality of the game); they
found two fingers' breadth of fat on the poorest of all. Then they slit
the slot (i.e. the hollow at the base of the throat), seized the gullet,
scraped it with a sharp knife and tied up the white flesh. Next they cut
off the four legs and tore off the hide, then they opened the belly, took
the bowels out carefully to guard against undoing the ligature of the
knot. They took hold of the throat and quickly separated the gullet
from the windpipe, and flung out the guts.

Haled hem by a lyttel hole, to have hole sydes.
Sithen britned thay the brest and brayden hit in twynne.
1340 And eft at the gargulun bigynes on thenne,
Ryves hit up radly ryght to the byght,
Voydes out the avanters, and verayly therafter
Alle the rymes by the rybbes radly thay lauce.
So ryde thay of by resoun bi the rygge bones
1345 Evenden to the haunche, that henged alle samen,
And heven hit up al hole and hwen hit of there –
And that thay neme for the noumbles bi nome, as I trowe,
        bi kynde.
        Bi the byght al of the thyghes
1350   The lappes thay lauce bihynde.
        To hewe hit in two thay hyyes,
        Bi the bakbon to unbynde.

Bothe the hede and the hals thay hwen of thenne,   *neck*
And sythen sunder thay the sydes swyft fro the   *part*
    chyne,   *backbone*
1355 And the corbeles fee thay kest in a greve.
Thenn thurled thay ayther thik side thurgh bi the rybbe,
And henged thenne ayther bi hoghes of the fourches,
Uche freke for his fee as falles for to have.
Upon a felle of the fayre best fede thay   *skin; excellent beast*
    thayr houndes

1360 Wyth the lyver and the lyghtes, the lether of the   *lungs; lining*
         paunches,   *stomachs*
      And bred bathed in blod blende   *mixed*
         ther-amonges.   *with them*
      Baldely thay blw prys, bayed thayr rachches;
      Sythen fonge thay her flesche, folden to home,
      Strakande ful stoutly mony stif motes.
1365 Bi that the daylyght was done, the douthe was al wonen
      Into the comly castel, ther the knyght bides   *splendid; waits*
                  ful stille.   *quietly*
            Wyth blys and bryght fyr bette,
            The lorde is comen thertylle;   *to that place*
1370   When Gawayn wyth hym mette,
            Ther was bot wele at wylle.

      Thenne comaunded the lorde in that sale to samen alle the
         meny,
      Bothe the ladyes on loghe to lyght with her burdes.
      Bifore alle the folk on the flette, frekes he beddes
1375 Verayly his venysoun to fech hym byforne,
      And al godly in gomen Gawayn he called,
      Teches hym to the tayles of ful tayt bestes,
      Schewes hym the schyree grece schorne upon rybbes.
      'How payes yow this play? Haf I prys wonnen?
1380 Have I thryvandely thonk thurgh my craft served?'

1362-5 Boldly they blew the capture, their hounds bayed; then they took
   their game, made their way home, sounding most vigorously many
   loud notes. By the time that the daylight was done, the company had
   all come.
1368 With festivity and with a bright fire kindled.
1371 There was nothing but unbounded pleasure.
1372-82 Then the lord commanded all the household to gather in the
   hall, both the ladies to come downstairs with their women. In front of
   all the people on the floor he duly orders men to bring his venison in
   before him, and all good-humouredly, in sport, he called Gawain,
   draws his attention to the tails (i.e. tally) of prime beasts, shows him
   the white fat cut from the ribs. 'How does this sport please you? Have
   I won the prize? Have I well and truly deserved thanks through my
   skill?' 'Yes, indeed,' said that other man, 'here is the best

'Ye, iwysse,' quoth that other wyye, 'here is wayth fayrest
That I sey this seven yere in sesoun of wynter.'
'And al I gif yow, Gawayn,' quoth the gome thenne,   *man*
'For by acorde of covenaunt ye crave hit as   *terms; may claim*
    your awen.'   *own*
1385 'This is soth,' quoth the segge, 'I say yow   *true; knight*
    that ilke;   *the same*
And I haf worthyly wonnen this wones wythinne,
Iwysse with as god wylle hit worthes to youres.'
He hasppes his fayre hals his armes wythinne,   *clasps; neck*
And kysses hym as comlyly as he couthe   *graciously; might*
    awyse: *manage*
1390 'Tas yow there my chevicaunce, I cheved no more;
I wowche hit saf fynly, thagh feler hit were.'
'Hit is god,' quoth the godmon, 'grant mercy therfore.
Hit may be such, hit is the better and ye me breve wolde
Where ye wan this ilk wele bi wytte of yorselven.'
1395 'That was not forward,' quoth he, 'frayst me   *agreement; ask*
    no more;
For ye haf tan that yow tydes, trawe ye non other
            ye mowe.'
            Thay laghed and made hem blythe   *made merry*
            Wyth lotes that were to lowe.
1400   To soper thay yede as swythe,   *went at once*
            Wyth dayntés nwe innowe.   *in plenty*

And sythen by the chymné in chamber thay   *then; fireplace*
    seten;   *sat*

---

spoils that I have seen for seven years (i.e. for a long time) in the winter
    season.'
1386-7 If I have won something worthy in this house, indeed with as
    good a will it shall be yours.
1390-4 'Take there my gain, I achieved no more; I give it freely, (and
    would do so) though there were more of them.' 'It is good,' said the
    lord of the household, 'thank you for that. It may be (so) that it would
    be the better if you would tell me where you won this good fortune by
    your skill.'
1396-7 As you have taken what is owing to you, be sure you may have
    nothing else.
1399 With excellent talk (lit. with words that were to be praised).

Wyyes the walle wyn weghed to hem   *men; choice; brought*
    oft,
And efte in her bourdyng thay baythen in the morn
1405 To fylle the same forwardes that thay byfore maden –
That chaunce so bytydes, hor chevysaunce to chaunge,
What nwes so thay nome, at naght quen thay metten.
Thay acorded of the covenauntes byfore the court   *agreed*
    alle;
The beverage was broght forth in bourde at that tyme.   *jest*
1410 Thenne thay lovelych leghten leve at the   *courteously took*
    last,
Uche burne to his bedde busked bylyve.   *man; went quickly*
Bi that the coke hade crowen and cakled bot thryse
The lorde was lopen of his bedde, the leudes uch one,
So that the mete and the masse was metely delyvered,
1415 The douthe dressed to the wod, er any day sprenged,
        to chace.
      Hegh with hunte and hornes   *proudly; huntsmen*
      Thurgh playnes thay passe in space;
      Uncoupled among tho thornes
1420   Raches that ran on race.

Sone thay calle of a quest in a ker syde;
The hunt rehayted the houndes that hit fyrst mynged,
Wylde wordes hym warp wyth a wrast noyce.
The howndes that hit herde hastid thider swythe   *swiftly*
1425 And fellen as fast to the fuyt, fourty at ones.   *fell quickly; trail*

1404–7 And again in their jesting they agreed to carry out the next day
the same covenant that they had made before – whatever fortune might
bring, to exchange their winnings, whatever new thing they obtained,
when they met at night.

1412–16 By the time that the cock had crowed and cackled just three
times the lord had leapt from his bed, and all the men, so that the meal
and the mass were duly despatched and the company gone to the wood
before any daylight appeared, to the hunt.

1418–20 They pass through fields shortly; they unleashed amongst the
thorns hounds that ran headlong.

1421–3 Soon they pick up a scent at the edge of a marsh; the huntsmen
urged on the hounds that first noticed it, shouted wild words to them
with loud clamour.

Thenne such a glaver ande glam of gedered rachches
Ros that the rocheres rungen aboute;
Hunteres hem hardened with horne and wyth muthe.
Then al in a semblé sweyed togeder   *pack; rushed*
1430 Bitwene a flosche in that fryth and a foo cragge.
In a knot bi a clyffe, at the kerre syde,   *thicket; marsh*
Ther as the rogh rocher unrydely was fallen,
Thay ferden to the fyndyng, and frekes hem after.
Thay umbekesten the knarre and the knot bothe,
1435 Wyyes, whyl thay wysten wel wythinne hem hit were,
The best that ther breved was wyth the blodhoundes.
Thenne thay beten on the buskes and bede hym up ryse,
And he unsoundyly out soght segges overthwert.
On the sellokest swyn swenged out there,
1440 Long sythen fro the sounder that soght for olde;
For he was breme, bor alther grattest,
Ful grymme quen he gronyed. Thenne greved mony,
For thre at the fyrst thrast he thryght to the erthe,
And sped hym forth good sped boute spyt more.
1445 Thise other halowed 'hyghe!' ful hyghe, and
         'hay! hay!' cryed,
Haden hornes to mouthe, heterly rechated.
Mony was the miyry mouthe of men and of houndes

1426–8 Then such a babble and din rose from the assembled hounds
   that the rocks round about rang; hunters encouraged them with horn
   and voice.
1430 Between a pool in that wood and a forbidding crag.
1432–47 There where the rugged crag was fallen in rough confusion,
   they went to the finding (of the quarry), and men after them. Men
   surrounded both the crag and the thicket until they knew for certain
   that it was in there, the animal whose presence had been announced by
   the bloodhounds. Then they beat on the bushes and called on him to
   rouse himself, and he came out dangerously across the (line of) men.
   The most wondrous boar of all charged out there, long since gone from
   the herd because of his age; for he was savage, the very greatest of
   boars, most fierce when he grunted. Then many were dismayed, for he
   threw three to the ground at the first thrust, and sped off at a good
   speed without more ado. Others shouted 'hi!' very loudly, and cried
   'hey! hey!', put horns to mouths, quickly blew the rally. Many were the
   joyful cries of men and of hounds.

That buskkes after this bor with bost and   *hurry; clamour*
    wyth noyse,
          to quelle.   *to the kill*
1450   Ful oft he bydes the baye   *stands at bay*
    And maymes the mute inn melle;
    He hurtes of the houndes, and thay   *some of*
    Ful yomerly yaule and yelle.   *piteously yowl*

Schalkes to schote at hym schowen to thenne,
1455 Haled to hym of her arewes, hitten hym   *loosed arrows at him*
    oft.
Bot the poyntes payred at the pyth that pyght in his scheldes,
And the barbes of his browe bite non wolde;
Thagh the schaven schaft schyndered in   *smooth; shattered*
    peces,
The hede hypped ayayn were-so-ever hit hitte.   *rebounded*
1460 Bot quen the dyntes hym dered of her dryye strokes,
    Then, braynwod for bate, on burnes he rases,
    Hurtes hem ful heterly ther he forth hyyes,
    And mony arwed therat and on lyte drowen.
    Bot the lorde on a lyght horce launces hym   *swift; gallops*
    after,
1465 As burne bolde upon bent his bugle he blowes;
    He rechated and rode thurgh rones ful thyk,
    Suande this wylde swyn til the sunne schafted.
    This day wyth this ilk dede thay dryven on this wyse,
    Whyle oure luflych lede lys in his bedde,   *courteous knight*
1470 Gawayn graythely at home, in geres   *pleasantly; bedclothes*
    ful ryche
          of hewe.

1451 And injures the pack in the midst (of it).

1454 Then men pressed forward to shoot at him.

1456–7 But the points failed at the sinew that was set in his shoulders, and none would pierce the bristles of his brow.

1460–3 But when the blows of their unceasing attacks hurt him, then, maddened by the baiting, he charges at the men, wounds them most viciously as he rushes out, and many were afraid at that and drew back.

1465–8 As a bold huntsman he blows his bugle; he sounded the rally and rode through very thick brushwood, pursuing this wild boar until the sun sank low. They pass the day in this way in this same occupation.

The lady noght foryate,   *did not forget*
Com to hym to salue;   *came; greet*
Ful erly ho was hym ate   *with him*
1475   His mode for to remwe.   *mood; change*

Ho commes to the cortyn and at the knyght totes.   *peeps*
Sir Wawen her welcumed worthy on fyrst,   *courteously*
And ho hym yeldes ayayn, ful yerne of hir wordes,
Settes hir sofly by his syde, and swythely ho   *gently; quickly*
   laghes,
1480 And wyth a luflych loke ho layde hym thyse   *amorous; spoke*
   wordes:
'Sir, yif ye be Wawen, wonder me thynkkes,
Wyye that is so wel wrast alway to god,
And connes not of compaynye the costes undertake,
And if mon kennes yow hom to knowe, ye kest
   hom of your mynde.
1485 Thou has foryeten yederly that yisterday I   *quickly what*
   taghtte
Bi alder-truest token of talk that I cowthe.'
'What is that?' quoth the wyghe, 'iwysse I wot never.
If hit be sothe that ye breve, the blame is myn awen.'
'Yet I kende yow of kyssyng,' quoth the   *taught*
   clere thenne,   *beautiful lady*
1490 'Quere-so countenaunce is couthe, quikly to clayme;
That bicumes uche a knyght that cortaysy   *every*
   uses.'   *practises*
'Do way,' quoth that derf mon, 'my dere, that speche,
For that durst I not do, lest I devayed were;   *dare; refused*

1478 And she replies to him, most eager with her words.
1481–4 Sir, if you are Gawain, it seems strange to me, a man who is
   always so well disposed to good things, and you do not know how to
   practise the usages of polite society, and if someone teaches you to
   know them, you put them out of your mind.
1486–8 'By the truest possible lesson in words that I could manage.'
   'What (lesson) is that?' said the man, 'indeed I do not know. If what
   you say is true, the blame is my own.'
1490 Whenever (a lady's) favour is manifest, to claim it (i.e. a kiss)
   quickly.
1492 'Enough of that speech, my dear lady,' said that bold man.

If I were werned, I were wrang, iwysse, yif I profered.'

1495 'Ma fay,' quoth the meré wyf, 'ye may not be werned;
Ye ar stif innoghe to constrayne wyth strenkthe, yif   *strong*
   yow lykes,   *it pleases you*
Yif any were so vilanous that yow devaye wolde.'
'Ye, be God,' quoth Gawayn, 'good is your speche,
Bot threte is unthryvande in thede ther I lende,

1500 And uche gift that is geven not with goud wylle.
I am at your comaundement, to kysse quen yow lykes;
Ye may lach quen yow lyst, and leve quen yow thynkkes,
       in space.'   *in due course*
      The lady loutes adoun   *bends*
1505   And comlyly kysses his face;   *graciously*
      Much speche thay ther expoun
      Of druryes greme and grace.

'I woled wyt at yow, wyye,' that worthy ther sayde,
'And yow wrathed not therwyth, what were the skylle
1510 That so yong and so yepe as ye at this tyme,
So cortayse, so knyghtyly, as ye ar knowen oute –
And of alle chevalry to chose, the chef thyng alosed
Is the lel layk of luf, the lettrure of armes;

1494–5 'If I were refused, I would be wrong, indeed, if I offered.' 'Upon my word,' said the lovely lady, 'you may not be refused.'

1497 If any were so ill-bred as to deny you.

1499 But force is ignoble in the land where I live.

1502 You may take when it pleases you, and leave off when you think fit.

1506–7 They have much to say there concerning the pain and pleasure of love.

1508–29 'I would like to know from you, sir,' that noble lady said there, 'if it did not anger you, what the reason was that one so young and so bold as you are at this time, so courteous, so chivalrous, as you are known far and wide – and to choose from all chivalry, the chief thing praised is the noble practice of love, the lore of the knightly profession;

For to telle of this tevelyng of this trwe knyghtes,
1515 Hit is the tytelet token and tyxt of her werkkes,
How ledes for her lele luf hor lyves han auntered,
Endured for her drury dulful stoundes,
And after wenged with her walour and voyded her care,
And broght blysse into boure with bountees hor awen.
1520 And ye ar knyght comlokest kyd of your elde,
Your worde and your worchip walkes ayquere,
And I haf seten by yourself here sere twyes,
Yet herde I never of your hed-helde no wordes
That ever longed to luf, lasse ne more.
1525 And ye, that ar so cortays and coynt of your hetes,
Oghe to a yonke thynk yern to schewe
And teche sum tokenes of trweluf craftes.
Why, ar ye lewed, that alle the los weldes,
Other elles ye demen me to dille your dalyaunce to herken?
1530   For schame!
         I com hider sengel and sitte   *alone*
         To lerne at yow sum game;   *from*
         Dos teches me of your wytte,
         Whil my lorde is fro hame.'   *away from home*

---

for in telling of the deeds of true knights, it is the inscribed title and text of their works (i.e. it is the main subject of knightly romances) how men for their true love have ventured their lives, endured grievous trials for their love, and afterwards taken vengeance through their valour and done away with their trouble, and brought joy into the bower (of their lady) by their own merits. And you are known as the noblest knight of your generation, your reputation and your honour go everywhere, and I have sat by you here on two separate occasions, yet never heard any words fall from your lips that ever belonged in any way to love. And you, who are so courteous and polite in your vows (of service), ought to be eager to show and teach to a young person some examples of the arts of true love. Why, are you ignorant, (you) who have all the renown, or else do you think me too stupid to listen to your words of love?'

1533 Do teach me something of what you know.

1535 'In goud faythe,' quoth Gawayn, 'God yow foryelde!   *reward*
      Gret is the gode gle, and gomen to me huge,
      That so worthy as ye wolde wynne hidere,
      And pyne yow with so pover a mon, as   *trouble yourself; poor*
         play wyth your knyght
      With anyskynnes countenaunce – hit keveres me ese.
1540 Bot to take the torvayle to myself to trwluf expoun,
      And towche the temes of tyxt and tales of armes
      To yow that, I wot wel, weldes more slyght
      Of that art, bi the half, or a hundreth of seche
      As I am other ever schal, in erde ther I leve –
1545 Hit were a folé felefolde, my fre, by my trawthe.
      I wolde yowre wylnyng worche at my myght,
      As I am hyghly bihalden, and evermore wylle
      Be servaunt to yourselven, so save me Dryghtyn!'
      Thus hym frayned that fre and fondet hym   *tested; tempted*
         ofte,
1550 For to haf wonnen hym to woghe, what-so scho thoght elles;
      Bot he defended hym so fayr that no faut   *well*
         semed,   *was to be seen*
      Ne non evel on nawther halve, nawther thay wysten
                  bot blysse.

1536-7 It is my great good pleasure and a huge delight to me that one
       as noble as you are should want to come here.
1539-48 With any show of favour – it gives me delight. But to take the
        task upon myself to expound true love, and discourse on the main
        themes and stories of chivalry to you who, I well know, have more skill
        in that art by far than a hundred such as I am or ever shall be, for as
        long as I live in the world – it would be a manifold folly, my noble
        lady, upon my word. I would like to carry out your wishes to the best
        of my ability, as I am deeply obligated (to do), and I shall evermore be
        your servant, so help me God!
1550 In order to have brought him to harm, whatever she thought
     besides.
1552 Nor any evil on either side, nor did they know anything but
     pleasure.

Thay laghed and layked longe;   *amused themselves*

1555   At the last scho con hym kysse.   *she kissed him*

Hir leve fayre con scho fonge,

And went hir waye, iwysse.   *indeed*

Then ruthes hym the renk and ryses to the   *bestirs; knight*
masse,

And sithen hor diner was dyght and derely served.

1560   The lede with the ladyes layked alle day,

Bot the lorde over the londes launced ful ofte,   *galloped*

Swes his uncely swyn, that swynges bi the bonkkes

And bote the best of his braches the bakkes in   *bit; hounds*
sunder

Ther he bode in his bay, tel bawemen hit breken,

1565   And madee hym, mawgref his hed, for to mwe utter,

So felle flones ther flete when the folk gedered.

Bot yet the styffest to start bi stoundes he made,

Til at the last he was so mat he myght no more   *exhausted*
renne,   *run*

Bot in the hast that he myght he to a hole wynnes

1570   Of a rasse, bi a rokk ther rennes the boerne.

He gete the bonk at his bak, bigynes to   *got*
scrape;   *scrape (the ground)*

The frothe femed at his mouth unfayre bi the wykes,

Whettes his whyte tusches. With hym then irked

1556 She courteously took her leave.

1559-60 And afterwards their dinner was prepared and nobly served. The knight amused himself with the ladies all day.

1562 Pursues his malevolent boar, that rushes over the slopes.

1564-7 Where he stood at bay, till bowmen broke it (i.e. his stand) and made him move into the open, in spite of all he could do, such deadly arrows flew there when the men gathered together. But yet at times he made the bravest start aside.

1569-70 But with all the speed that he could muster he goes to a hole in a gully, by a rock where the burn runs.

1572-6 The froth foamed uglily at the corners of his mouth, (and) he whets his white tusks. Then all the bold men who stood round him

Alle the burnes so bolde that hym by stoden
1575 To nye hym on-ferum, bot neghe hym non durst
       for wothe.
      He hade hurt so mony byforne
      That al thught thenne ful lothe   *felt; loath*
      Be more wyth his tusches torne,   *torn*
1580   That breme was and braynwod bothe. *fierce; frenzied*

Til the knyght com hymself, kachande his   *came; urging on*
  blonk,   *horse*
Syy hym byde at the bay, his burnes bysyde.   *saw*
He lyghtes luflych adoun, leves his corsour,
Braydes out a bryght bront and bigly forth strydes,
1585 Foundes fast thurgh the forth ther the felle bydes.
The wylde was war of the wyye with weppen *wild beast; man*
  in honde,
Hef hyghly the here – so hetterly he fnast
That fele ferde for the freke, lest felle hym the worre.
The swyn settes hym out on the segge even,
1590 That the burne and the bor were bothe   *so that*
  upon hepes   *in a heap*
In the wyghtest of the water. The worre *swiftest; worst (of it)*
  hade that other,
For the mon merkkes hym wel, as thay mette fyrst,   *marks*
Set sadly the scharp in the slot even,
Hit hym up to the hult, that the hert   *hilt; heart*
  schyndered,   *shattered*

---

became tired of harassing him from a distance, but none dared go near
him because of the danger.

1583–5 He dismounts gracefully, leaves his horse, draws out a bright
sword and strides strongly forward, moves quickly through the ford
where the fiece beast waits.

1587–9 He made his bristles stand on end – so fiercely he snorted that
many were afraid for the man, in case he should get the worst of it.
The boar rushes out straight at the man.

1593 Firmly planted the sharp blade right in the hollow above the
breastbone.

1595 And he yarrande hym yelde, and yed doun the water
              ful tyt.
              A hundreth houndes hym hent,   *seized*
              That bremely con hym bite;   *fiercely bit him*
              Burnes him broght to bent   *bank*
1600   And dogges to dethe endite.   *do (him)*

      There was blawyng of prys in mony breme horne,
      Heghe halowing on highe with hatheles that myght.
      Brachetes bayed that best, as bidden the maysteres,
      Of that chargeaunt chace that were chef huntes.
1605 Thenne a wyye that was wys upon wodcraftes
      To unlace this bor lufly bigynnes.   *cut up; expertly*
      Fyrst he hewes of his hed and on highe settes,
      And sythen rendes him al roghe bi the rygge after,
      Braydes out the boweles, brennes hom on   *pulls; burns*
          glede,   *hot coals*
1610 With bred blent therwith his braches   *mixed with them*
          rewardes.
      Sythen he britnes out the brawen in bryght brode cheldes,
      And has out the hastlettes, as hightly bisemes;
      And yet hem halches al hole the halves togeder,
      And sythen on a stif stange stoutly hem henges.
1615 Now with this ilk swyn thay swengen to home;   *quickly go*
      The bores hed was borne bifore the burnes   *man himself*
          selven,

1595 And he surrendered snarling, and was very quickly swept
      downstream.
1601-5 There was blowing of the kill on many a glorious horn, loud
      hallooing on high by those men who were able to do so (i.e. those who
      had not been hurt by the boar). Hounds bayed at that beast, as the
      masters (of game), who were the chief huntsmen of that difficult chase,
      commanded. Then a man who was knowledgable in hunting practices.
1607-8 First he cuts off his head and sets it on high (i.e. on a stake), and
      then tears him all roughly along the backbone.
1611-14 Then he cuts out the brawn (i.e. boar's flesh) in broad shining
      slabs and takes out the entrails, in the right and proper manner; and
      then he joins the halves fully together, and afterwards hangs them
      securely on a strong pole.

That him forferde in the forthe thurgh forse of his honde
    so stronge.
   Til he sey Sir Gawayne   *saw*
1620 In halle hym thoght ful longe;   *it seemed to him*
   He calde, and he com gayn   *promptly*
   His fees ther for to fonge.   *dues; receive*

The lorde, ful lowde with lote and laghter myry *noise*
When he seye Sir Gawayn, with solace he spekes. *delight*
1625 The goude ladyes were geten, and gedered   *brought*
   the meyny;   *household*
He schewes hem the scheldes and schapes hem the tale
Of the largesse and the lenthe, the lithernes alse
Of the were of the wylde swyn in wod ther he fled.
That other knyght ful comly comended his dedes, *courteously*
1630 And praysed hit as gret prys that he proved hade;
For suche a brawne of a best, the bolde burne sayde,
Ne such sydes of a swyn segh he never are.
Thenne hondeled thay the hoge hed, the hende *courteous*
   mon hit praysed,
And let lodly therat the lorde for to here.
1635 'Now, Gawayn,' quoth the godmon, 'this gomen is your
   awen
Bi fyn forwarde and faste, faythely ye knowe.'
'Hit is sothe,' quoth the segge, 'and as siker trwe
Alle my get I schal yow gif agayn, bi my trawthe.'
He hent the hathel aboute the halse and hendely hym kysses,

1617–18 Who had destroyed him in the ford by the strength of his strong
 hand.
1626–8 He shows them the slabs (of boar's flesh) and tells them the
 story of the breadth and the length (of it), also the ferocity of the
 defence of the wild boar in the wood as he fled.
1630–2 And praised the great prowess (lit. praised it as great prowess)
 which he had shown; for the bold man said that he had never seen
 before such a (quantity of) brawn on a beast, nor such sides of a boar.
1634–40 And professed horror at it in order to praise the lord. 'Now,
 Gawain,' said the lord of the household, 'this quarry is yours by fully
 ratified and binding agreement, indeed you know this.' 'It is true,' said
 the man, 'and as surely true that I shall give you all my winnings in
 return, upon my word.' He clasped the man around the neck and kisses

1640 And eftersones of the same he served hym there.
      'Now ar we even,' quoth the hathel, 'in this eventide,
      Of alle the covenauntes that we knyt,   *in respect of; drew up*
         sythen I com hider,   *since*
                  bi lawe.'   *due process*
            The lorde sayde: 'Bi saynt Gile,   *Giles*
1645   Ye ar the best that I knowe;
            Ye ben ryche in a whyle,   *will be rich*
            Such chaffer and ye drowe.'

      Thenne thay teldet tables trestes   *set up tables on trestles*
         alofte,
      Kesten clothes upon; clere lyght thenne
1650 Wakned bi wowes, waxen torches.
      Segges sette, and served in sale al aboute.   *set tables; hall*
      Much glam and gle glent up therinne
      Aboute the fyre upon flet, and on fele wyse,
      At the soper and after, mony athel songes,   *noble*
1655 As coundutes of Krystmasse and caroles newe,
      With alle the manerly merthe that mon may of telle.
      And ever oure luflych knyght the lady bisyde;   *courteous*
      Such semblaunt to that segge semly ho made,
      Wyth stille stollen countenaunce, that stalworth to plese,
1660 That al forwondered was the wyye, and wroth
         with hymselven;
      Bot he nolde not for his nurture nurne hir ayaynes,

---

him courteously, and a second time he served him there in the same
manner (i.e. he kissed him twice).
1647 If you carry on such trade.
1649–50 Threw cloths upon them; bright lights then came to life along
the walls, torches of wax.
1652–3 Much mirth and glad cheer arose in that place around the fire in
the hall, and in great variety.
1655–6 Such as Christmas part-songs and new carols (i.e. ring-dances
with singing), with all the seemly entertainment a man might tell of.
1658–63 She adopted such a becoming manner towards that man, with
secret stolen looks of favour, to please that stalwart, that he (lit. the
man) was all astonished, and angry within himself; but he would not
repulse her on account of his good breeding, but dealt with her in all
courtesy, however the matter might turn out awry.

Bot dalt with hir al in daynté, how-se-ever the dede turned
      towrast.
    Quen thay hade played in halle
1665   As longe as hor wylle hom last,
    To chambre he con hym calle,
    And to the chemné thay past.   *fireplace; proceeded*

Ande ther thay dronken and dalten, and demed eft nwe
To norne on the same note on Nwe Yeres even;
1670 Bot the knyght craved leve to kayre on the morn,   *depart*
For hit was negh at the terme that he to schulde.
The lorde hym letted of that, to lenge hym resteyed,
And sayde: 'As I am trwe segge, I siker my   *give my*
  trawthe   *word*
Thou schal cheve to the grene chapel, thy   *get*
  charres to make,   *business; do*
1675 Leude, on Nw Yeres lyght, longe bifore pryme.
Forthy thow lye in thy loft and lach thyn ese,
And I schal hunt in this holt and halde the   *forest; keep*
  towches,   *terms of agreement*
Chaunge wyth the chevisaunce, bi that I charre hider;
For I haf fraysted the twys, and faythful I fynde the.   *tested*
1680 Now "thrid tyme throwe best," thenk on the morne;
Make we mery quyl we may, and mynne upon joye,   *think*
For the lur may mon lach when-so mon lykes.'
This was graythely graunted, and   *readily*
  Gawayn is lenged;   *made to stay*

1665–6 For as long as they desired, he (i.e. the lord of the castle) called
him to his private sitting-room.

1668–9 And there they drank and talked, and proposed once more to
continue in the same way on New Year's Eve.

1671–2 For it was near to the appointed time when he must go. The lord
dissuaded him from that, prevailed on him to stay.

1675–6 Sir, at dawn on New Year's Day, long before prime (i.e. 9 a.m.).
And so you lie in your room and take your ease.

1678 Exchange winnings with you, when I return here.

1680 Now tomorrow think 'third time lucky' (lit. 'third time throw best',
at dice).

1682 For a man may find sorrow whenever he likes.

Blithe broght was hym drynk, and thay to   *joyfully; to them*
   bedde yeden   *went*
1685   with light.   *lights*
      Sir Gawayn lis and slepes
      Ful stille and softe al night;
      The lorde that his craftes kepes,
      Ful erly he was dight.   *ready*

1690 After messe a morsel he and his men   *mass; small meal*
   token;   *took*
   Miry was the mornyng, his mounture he askes.   *fine; mount*
   Alle the hatheles that on horse schulde helden   *men; follow*
   hym after
   Were boun busked on hor blonkkes   *ready prepared; horses*
   bifore the halle yates.
   Ferly fayre was the folde, for the forst clenged;
1695 In rede rudede upon rak rises the sunne,
   And ful clere castes the clowdes of the welkyn.
   Hunteres unhardeled bi a holt   *unleashed (the hounds); forest*
   syde,
   Rocheres roungen bi rys for rurde of her hornes.
   Summe fel in the fute ther the fox bade,
1700 Trayles ofte a traverse bi traunt of her wyles.
   A kenet kryes therof, the hunt on hym calles,
   His felawes fallen hym to, that fnasted ful thike,
   Runnen forth in a rabel in his ryght fare.
   And he fyskes hem byfore; thay founden hym sone,   *scampers*
1705 And quen thay seghe hym with syght thay   *saw*
   sued hym fast,   *pursued*

1688 The lord, attending to his pursuits.
1694–6 The earth was very beautiful, for the frost clung; the fiery sun
   rises in a red sky on drifting cloud, and, very bright, drives the clouds
   from the sky.
1698–1703 Rocks rang in the woods with the noise of their horns. Some
   (of the hounds) fell upon the track where the fox lay low, trail often
   from side to side in the practice of their wiles. A small hound gives
   tongue at it (i.e. on picking up the scent), the hunters call on him, his
   fellows fall in with him, panting hard, run forward in a rabble on the
   right trail.

Wreyande hym ful weterly with a wroth noyse;
And he trantes and tornayees thurgh mony tene greve,
Havilounes and herkenes bi hegges ful   *doubles back; listens*
    ofte.
At the last bi a littel dich he lepes over a spenné,   *fence*
1710 Steles out ful stilly bi a strothe rande,   *quietly; marsh edge*
Went haf wylt of the wode with wyles fro the houndes.
Thenne was he went, er he wyst, to a wale tryster,
Ther thre thro at a thrich thrat hym at ones,
          al graye.
1715   He blenched ayayn bilyve   *darted back quickly*
          And stifly start onstray;
          With alle the wo on lyve   *woe in the world*
          To the wod he went away.

Thenne was hit lof upon list to lythen the houndes
1720 When alle the mute hade hym met, menged togeder.
Suche a sorwe at that syght thay sette on his hede
As alle the clamberande clyffes hade clatered on hepes.
Here he was halawed when hatheles hym   *hallooed; men*
    metten,
Loude he was yayned with yarande speche;   *greeted; abusive*
1725 Ther he was threted and ofte thef called,   *threatened; thief*
And ay the titleres at his tayl, that tary he ne myght.   *hounds*
Ofte he was runnen at when he out   *made for the open*
    rayked,
And ofte reled in ayayn, so Reniarde was wylé.

1706–7 Vilifying him in no uncertain manner with an angry commotion;
    and he dodges and turns back through many a rough thicket.
1711–14 Thought to have escaped from the wood by his wiles, away
    from the hounds. Then he came before he knew it to a well-placed
    hunting station, where three fierce hounds in a rush attacked him
    together, all grey.
1716 And started off strongly in a new direction.
1719–22 Then it was a delight to the ear to hear the hounds when all the
    pack had found him, mingled together. At that sight they called down
    such an imprecation on his head it was as though all the towering cliffs
    had clattered in heaps.
1728–30 And often he turned suddenly in again, so wily was Reynard.

And ye, he lad hem bi lagmon, the lorde and his meyny,
1730 On this maner bi the mountes quyle myd-over-under,
Whyle the hende knyght at home holsumly   *noble; soundly*
    slepes
Withinne the comly cortynes, on the colde morne.
Bot the lady for luf let not to slepe,   *did not allow herself*
Ne the purpose to payre that pyght in hir hert,
1735 Bot ros hir up radly, rayked hir theder   *quickly; went*
In a mery mantyle, mete to the erthe,   *beautiful robe; reaching*
That was furred ful fyne with felles wel pured.
No hwes goud on hir hede, bot the hagher stones
Trased aboute hir tressour be twenty in clusteres,
1740 Hir thryven face and hir throte throwen al   *fair; exposed*
    naked,
Hir brest bare bifore, and bihinde eke.   *her back also*
Ho comes withinne the chambre dore and closes hit hir after,
Wayves up a wyndow and on the wyye   *throws open; man*
    calles,
And radly thus rehayted hym with hir riche wordes,
1745   with chere:
        'A! mon, how may thou slepe?
        This morning is so clere.'
        He was in drowping depe,   *troubled sleep*
        Bot thenne he con hir here.   *heard her*

1750 In drey droupyng of dreme draveled that noble,
As mon that was in mornyng of mony   *weighed down by*
    thro thoghtes,   *oppressive*
How that destiné schulde that day dele hym his wyrde   *fate*
At the grene chapel, when he the gome metes,   *man*

And yes, he led them a dance in this way among the hills, the lord and his company, until mid-afternoon.
1734 Nor (did she allow) the purpose that was fixed in her heart to weaken.
1737-9 That was finely furred with well-trimmed skins. No bright colours (were) on her head except for the skilfully-cut gems set round her head-band in clusters of twenty.
1744-5 And promptly rallied (i.e. teasingly encouraged) him thus with her ringing words, good-humouredly.
1750 In heavy troubled sleep that noble knight muttered in his dreams.

And bihoves his buffet abide withoute debate more.
1755 Bot quen that comly com he kevered his wyttes,
Swenges out of the swevenes and swares with hast.
The lady luflych com laghande swete,   *laughing sweetly*
Felle over his fayre face and fetly hym kyssed. *bent; gracefully*
He welcumes hir worthily with a wale chere; *pleasant manner*
1760 He sey hir so glorious and gayly atyred,   *saw*
So fautles of hir fetures and of so fyne hewes, *complexion*
Wight wallande joye warmed his hert.   *strong swelling*
With smothe smylyng and smolt thay smeten into merthe,
That al was blis and bonchef that breke *happiness; burst forth*
    hem bitwene,
1765   and wynne.   *joy*
    Thay lauced wordes gode,   *uttered; friendly*
    Much wele then was therinne;   *delight; in that place*
    Gret perile bitwene hem stod,   *stood*
    Nif Maré of hir knyght con mynne.

1770 For that prynces of pris depresed hym so thikke,
Nurned hym so neghe the thred, that nede hym bihoved
Other lach ther hir luf other lodly refuse.
He cared for his cortaysye, lest crathayn he were,
And more for his meschef, yif he schulde make synne
1775 And be traytor to that tolke that that telde aght.
'God schylde,' quoth the schalk, 'that schal not   *forbid; man*
    befalle!'
With luf-laghyng a lyt he layd hym bysyde
Alle the speches of specialté that sprange of   *affection*
    her mouthe.

1754-6 And must endure his blow without more ado. But when that
    beautiful woman came he recovered his wits, starts quickly out of his
    dreams and answers in haste.
1763 With pleasant and affable smiling they fell into cheerful speech.
1769 Unless Mary remembered her knight.
1770-5 For that noble princess pressed him so hard, pushed him so near
    the limit, that he must needs either take her love there or rudely refuse.
    He was anxious about his courtesy, lest he should be a boor, and more
    about his own harm, if he should commit sin and be traitor to the man
    who owned that house.
1777 With a little good-natured laughter he put aside.

Quoth that burde to the burne: 'Blame ye   *lady; knight*
  disserve,
1780 Yif ye luf not that lyf that ye lye nexte,   *person*
Bifore alle the wyyes in the worlde wounded in hert,
Bot if ye haf a lemman, a lever, that yow lykes better,
And folden fayth to that fre, festned so harde
That yow lausen ne lyst – and that I leve nouthe.
1785 And that ye telle me that now trwly, I pray yow;
For alle the lufes upon lyve, layne not the sothe
                          for gile.'
              The knyght sayde: 'Be sayn Jon,'   *St John*
              And smethely con he smyle,   *smiled pleasantly*
1790   'In fayth I welde right non,
              Ne non wil welde the quile.'

'That is a worde,' quoth that wyght, 'that worst is   *woman*
  of alle;
Bot I am swared for sothe, that sore me thinkkes.
Kysse me now comly, and I schal cach hethen.
1795 I may bot mourne upon molde, as may that much lovyes.
Sykande ho sweye doun and semly hym kyssed,   *sighing; bent*
And sithen ho severes hym fro, and says as ho stondes:
'Now, dere, at this departyng, do me this ese;   *comfort*
Gif me sumquat of thy gifte, thi glove if hit were,
1800 That I may mynne on the, mon, my mournyng to   *think of*
  lassen.'   *lessen*
'Now iwysse,' quoth that wyye, 'I wolde I hade here
The levest thing for thy luf that I in londe welde,

1781–4 (Who is) more than all the people in the world wounded in
   heart, unless you have a lover, a dearer one, who is more pleasing to
   you, and (you have) plighted your troth to that excellent lady, pledged
   (it) so firmly that you do not care to break it – and that I now believe.
1786–7 For all the loves there are, do not hide the truth through guile.
1790–1 Truly I have none at all, nor will I have anyone at present.
1793–5 But I am truly answered, in a way that grieves me. Kiss me now
   properly, and I shall go from here. I may do nothing on earth but
   mourn, as a woman who loves much.
1797 And then she parts from him, and says as she stands.
1799 Give me something as your gift, your glove perhaps.
1801–2 'Now indeed,' said that man, 'I wish I had here, for your sake,
   the most precious thing that I have in the world.'

For ye haf deserved, for sothe, sellyly   *in truth; exceedingly*
   ofte
More rewarde bi resoun then I reche myght;   *by rights; give*
1805 Bot to dele yow for drurye that dawed bot neked –
Hit is not your honour to haf at this tyme
A glove for a garysoun of Gawaynes giftes.
And I am here an erande in erdes   *on a mission; lands*
   uncouthe,   *strange*
And have no men wyth no males with   *bags*
   menskful thinges.   *beautiful*
1810 That mislykes me, ladé, for luf at this tyme;
Iche tolke mon do as he is tan, tas to non ille
       ne pine.'
      'Nay, hende of hyghe honours,'
      Quoth that lufsum under lyne,
1815   'Thagh I hade noght of youres,
      Yet schulde ye have of myne.'

Ho raght hym a riche rynk of red golde werkes,
Wyth a starande ston stondande alofte,
That bere blusschande bemes as the bryght sunne;
1820 Wyt ye wel, hit was worth wele ful hoge.
Bot the renk hit renayed, and redyly he sayde:
'I wil no giftes for Gode, my gay, at this tyme;
I haf none yow to norne, ne noght wyl I take.'   *offer*
Ho bede hit hym ful bysily, and he hir bode wernes,

1805–7 But to give you as a love-token something that was worth only a
little – it is not worthy of you (for you) to have, on this occasion, a
glove as a tribute, as a gift from Gawain.

1810–16 'I regret that, lady, for the sake of courtesy on this occasion;
each man must do as he is circumstanced, do not take it amiss or
grieve.' 'No, noble knight of high honour,' said that lovely lady (lit.
that lovely one under linen), 'though I had nothing of yours, yet you
ought to have something of mine.'

1817–22 She offered him a rich ring of red gold workmanship, with a
glittering stone set in it, that gave out shining beams like the bright sun;
be sure, it was worth huge amounts of money. But the man rejected it,
and promptly said: 'Before God I desire no gifts, my lovely one, on this
occasion.'

1824–5 She offered it to him most eagerly, and he refused her offer, and

1825 And swere swyfte by his sothe that he hit sese nolde;
And ho soré that he forsoke, and sayde   *(was) sorry; refused*
    therafter:
'If ye renay my rynk, to ryche for hit semes,
Ye wolde not so hyghly halden be to me,
I schal gif yow my girdel, that gaynes yow lasse.'   *profits*
1830 Ho laght a lace lyghtly that leke umbe hir sydes,
Knit upon hir kyrtel under the clere mantyle.
Gered hit was with grene sylke and with golde schaped,
Noght bot arounde brayden, beten with fyngres;
And that ho bede to the burne, and   *offered; man*
    blythely bisoght,   *cheerfully implored*
1835 Thagh hit unworthi were, that he hit take wolde.
And he nay that he nolde neghe in no wyse
Nauther golde ne garysoun, er God hym grace sende
To acheve to the chaunce that he hade chosen there.
'And therfore, I pray yow, displese yow noght,.
1840 And lettes be your bisinesse, for I baythe hit yow never
                    to graunte.
            I am derely to yow biholde   *deeply beholden*
            Bicause of your sembelaunt,   *(kind) behaviour*
            And ever in hot and colde   *in all circumstances*
1845   To be your trwe servaunt.'   *(I am bound) to be*

'Now forsake ye this silke,' sayde the burde thenne,   *refuse*
'For hit is symple in hitself? And so hit wel   *of little value*
    semes.
Lo! so hit is littel, and lasse hit is worthy.

---

swiftly swore on his word of honour that he would not take it.
1827–8 If you refuse my ring because it seems too costly, (and) you do
    not wish to be so deeply indebted to me.
1830–3 She quickly caught hold of a belt that was fastened round her
    waist, tied over her gown under the bright robe. It was made out of
    green silk and fashioned with gold, embroidered only around the edges,
    worked by hand.
1836–8 And he said that he would not on any account have to do with
    either gold or gift, before God sent him the grace to accomplish the
    adventure which he had undertaken there.
1840 And cease your importunity, for I shall never agree to grant it (i.e.
    what you want) to you.
1848 See, how small it is, and (still) less is it of value.

Bot who-so knew the costes that knit ar   *properties; woven*
   therinne,   *into it*
1850 He wolde hit prayse at more prys, paraventure;
For quat gome so is gorde with this grene lace,   *man; girt*
While he hit hade hemely halched aboute,   *closely fastened*
Ther is no hathel under heven tohewe hym   *man; cut down*
   that myght,
For he myght not be slayn for slyght   *by any stratagem*
   upon erthe.'   *at all*
1855 Then kest the knyght, and hit come to his   *pondered; came*
   hert
Hit were a juel for the jopardé that hym jugged were,
When he acheved to the chapel his chek for to fech;
Myght he haf slypped to be unslayn, the sleght were noble.
Thenne he thulged with hir threpe and tholed hir to speke,
1860 And ho bere on hym the belt and bede hit hym swythe,
And he granted, and ho hym gafe with a goud   *consented*
   wylle,
And bisoght hym, for hir sake, discever hit never,   *reveal*
Bot to lelly layne fro hir lorde. The   *loyally conceal (it)*
   leude hym acordes   *man agrees*
That never wyye schulde hit wyt, iwysse, bot thay twayne,
1865   for noghte.
     He thonkked hir oft ful swythe,   *profoundly*
     Ful thro with hert and thoght.   *earnestly*
     Bi that on thrynne sythe
     Ho has kyst the knyght so toght.

1870 Thenne lachches ho hir leve and leves hym there,   *takes*
For more myrthe of that mon moght ho not gete.   *pleasure*

1850 He would esteem it more highly, perhaps.
1856–60 It would be a jewel for the peril that had been decreed for him, when he came to the chapel to meet his fate; if he might escape alive, that would be an excellent trick. Then he bore with her importunity and allowed her to speak, and she pressed the belt on him and offered it to him eagerly.
1864–5 That no one should ever know of it, indeed, except the two of them, for any reason at all.
1868–9 By then she has kissed the bold knight three times.

When ho was gon, Sir Gawayn geres hym   *attires himself*
    sone,
Rises and riches hym in araye noble,   *dresses*
Lays up the luf-lace the lady hym raght,
1875 Hid hit ful holdely ther he hit eft fonde.
Sythen chevely to the chapel choses he the   *quickly; takes*
    waye,
Prevely aproched to a prest, and prayed hym there   *privately*
That he wolde lyfte his lyf and lern hym better   *lift up; teach*
How his sawle schulde be saved when he schuld
    seye hethen.   *go hence (i.e. die)*
1880 There he schrof hym schyrly and   *confessed himself fully*
    schewed his mysdedes
Of the more and the mynne, and merci beseches,
And of absolucioun he on the segge calles;
And he asoyled hym surely and sette hym so   *absolved; made*
    clene
As domesday schulde haf ben dight on the morn.
1885 And sythen he mace hym as mery among the fre ladyes,
With comlych caroles and alle kynnes joye,
As never he did bot that daye, to the derk nyght,
        with blys.
        Uche mon hade daynté thare
1890   Of hym, and sayde: 'Iwysse,
        Thus myry he was never are,
        Syn he com hider, er this.'

Now hym lenge in that lee, ther luf hym bityde!
Yet is the lorde on the launde, ledande his gomnes;

1874–5 Puts away the love-lace the lady had given him, hid it most
    carefully where he might find it again.

1881 The greater and the lesser, and begs for mercy, and calls on the
    man (i.e. the priest) for absolution.

1884–92 As if Doomsday had been appointed for the next day. And
    then he makes himself as merry amongst the noble ladies, with pleasant
    carols and all kinds of joy, as he never did except on that day, until the
    dark night, happily. Everyone there was pleased with him and said:
    'Truly, he was never as cheerful as this, since he came here, until now.'

1893–4 Now let him stay in that place of comfort, may friendship befall
    him! The lord is still in the field, engaged in his sport.

1895 He has forfaren this fox that he folwed longe. *killed; followed*
      As he sprent over a spenné to spye the schrewe,
      Ther as he herd the howndes that hasted hym swythe,
      Renaud com richchande thurgh a roghe greve,
      And alle the rabel in a res, ryght at his heles.   *rabble; rush*
1900 The wyye was war of the wylde and warly abides,
      And braydes out the bryght bronde and at the best castes,
      And he schunt for the scharp and schulde haf arered.
      A rach rapes hym to ryght er he myght,
      And ryght bifore the hors fete thay fel on hym alle   *horse's*
1905 And woried me this wyly wyth a wroth noyse.
      The lorde lyghtes bilyve and   *dismounts quickly*
            laches hym sone,   *seizes him at once*
      Rased hym ful radly out of the rach mouthes,
      Haldes heghe over his hede, halowes faste,
      And ther bayen hym mony brath houndes.   *bay at; fierce*
1910 Huntes hyyed hem theder with   *huntsmen; hurried there*
            hornes ful mony,
      Ay rechatande aryght til thay the renk seyen.
      Bi that was comen his compeyny noble,   *when*
      Alle that ever ber bugle blowed at ones, *carried; blew together*
      And alle thise other halowed, that hade no hornes. *the others*
1915 Hit was the myriest mute that ever men herde,
      The rich rurd that ther was raysed for Renaude saule
                  with lote.
            Hor houndes thay ther rewarde,

1896-8 As he jumped over a fence to spy out the villain, where he (i.e.
    the lord) heard the hounds pressing him hard, Reynard came running
    through a rough thicket.

1900-3 The man saw the wild creature and waits cautiously, and draws
    out his bright sword and strikes at the beast, and he turned aside on
    account of the sharp blade and would have retreated. A hound speeds
    to him before he might do so.

1905 And worried this wily one with a fierce clamour.

1907-8 Snatched him very quickly out of the mouths of the dogs, holds
    him high over his head, halloos loudly.

1911 Constantly sounding the recall in the correct manner until they saw
    the man.

1915-17 It was the most joyous sound of a hunt that ever men heard,
    the ringing clamour that was raised there for Reynard's soul, with
    (their) cries.

	Her hedes thay fawne and frote;	*fondle; stroke*
1920	And sythen thay tan Reynarde	*then; take*
	And tyrven of his cote.	*strip off*

	And thenne thay helden to home, for hit was	*made for*
	niegh nyght,	*nearly*
	Strakande ful stoutly in hor store hornes.	
	The lorde is lyght at the laste at hys lef home,	
1925	Fyndes fire upon flet, the freke ther-byside,	*hearth; knight*
	Sir Gawayn the gode that glad was withalle –	
	Among the ladies for luf he ladde much joye.	
	He were a bleaunt of blwe that bradde to the erthe;	
	His surkot semed hym wel that softe was forred,	
1930	And his hode of that ilke henged on his schulder –	
	Blande al of blaunner were bothe al aboute.	
	He metes me this godmon inmyddes the flore,	
	And al with gomen he hym gret, and goudly he sayde:	
	'I schal fylle upon fyrst oure forwardes nouthe,	
1935	That we spedly han spoken ther spared was no drynk.'	
	Then acoles he the knyght and kysses hym thryes,	*embraces*
	As saverly and sadly as he hem sette couthe.	
	'Bi Kryst,' quoth that other knyght, 'ye cach much sele	
	In chevisaunce of this chaffer, yif ye hade goud chepes.'	
1940	'Ye, of the chepe no charg,' quoth chefly that other,	
	'As is pertly payed the porchas that I aghte.'	
	'Mary,' quoth that other mon, 'myn is bihynde,	*by St Mary*
	For I haf hunted al this day, and noght haf I geten	*got*

1923–4 Sounding their great horns most vigorously. The lord has arrived at last at his splendid home.

1927–35 He was enjoying himself among the ladies with their friendship. He wore a blue mantle that reached to the ground; his surcoat, softly furred, suited him well, and his matching hood hung on his shoulder – both were trimmed all round with white fur. He meets the lord of the household in the middle of the floor, and greeted him most cheerfully, and said courteously: 'I shall first fulfil our agreement now, which we readily affirmed when the drink flowed freely.'

1937–41 As feelingly and firmly as he might plant them. 'By Christ,' said that other knight, 'you get much good fortune in obtaining this merchandise, if you paid a good price.' 'Now, no matter about the price,' the other said quickly, 'as the gain which I obtained is manifestly paid over (to you).'

Bot this foule fox felle – the fende haf the godes! –
1945 And that is ful pore for to pay for suche prys thinges
As ye haf thryght me here thro, suche thre cosses
        so gode.'
      'Inogh,' quoth Sir Gawayn,
      'I thonk yow, bi the rode.'
1950   And how the fox was slayn
      He tolde hym as thay stode.   *stood*

With merthe and mynstralsye, wyth metes at hor   *dishes*
  wylle,
Thay maden as mery as any men moghten.   *could*
With laghyng of ladies, with   *laughing*
  lotes of bordes,   *light-hearted words*
1955 Gawayn and the godemon so glad were thay bothe,
Bot if the douthe had doted other dronken ben other.
Bothe the mon and the meyny maden mony   *household*
  japes,   *jokes*
Til the sesoun was seyen that thay sever   *time; come; part*
  moste;
Burnes to hor bedde behoved at the laste.   *men; had to go*
1960 Thenne lowly his leve at the lorde fyrst
Fochches this fre mon, and fayre he hym thonkkes:
'Of such a selly sojorne as I haf hade here,
Your honour at this hyghe fest, the hyghe kyng yow yelde!
I yef yow me for on of youres, if yowreself lykes;
1965 For I mot nedes, as ye wot, meve to-morne,
And ye me take sum tolke to teche, as ye hyght,

1944–9 'But this vile fox skin – the Devil take the goods! – and that is
  most poor payment for such precious things as you have warmly
  pressed on me here, three such good kisses.' 'Enough,' said Sir Gawain,
  'I thank you, by the cross (of Christ).'
1955–6 Gawain and the lord of the household were both as happy as
  they could be, unless the company had been mad or else drunk.
1960–8 Then with deference the good man first (i.e. before he takes his
  leave of the ladies, cf. lines 1977–82) takes his leave of the lord, and
  thanks him courteously: 'For such an excellent stay as I have had here,
  (for) your hospitality at this high festival, may the High King reward
  you! I give myself to you (as your servant) in return for one of your
  men, if it pleases you; for as you know I must needs go tomorrow, if
  you will assign a man to me as you promised, to show the way to the

The gate to the grene chapel, as God wyl me suffer
To dele on Nw Yeres day the dome of my wyrdes.'
'In god faythe,' quoth the godmon, 'wyth a goud wylle –
1970 Al that ever I yow hyght, halde schal I redé.'
   Ther asyngnes he a servaunt to sett hym in the waye   *assigns*
   And coundue hym by the downes, that he no drechch had
   For to ferk thurgh the fryth and fare at the gaynest
              bi greve.
1975   The lorde Gawayn con thonk,
           Such worchip he wolde hym weve.
           Then at tho ladyes wlonk   *of; noble*
           The knyght has tan his leve.   *taken*

With care and wyth kyssyng he carppes hem tille,
1980 And fele thryvande thonkkes he thrat hom to have,
   And thay yelden hym ayayn yeply that ilk;
   Thay bikende hym to Kryst with ful colde sykynges.
   Sythen fro the meyny he menskly   *then; company; courteously*
      departes;
   Uche mon that he mette, he made hem a thonke   *thanked*
1985 For his servyse and his solace, and his sere pyne
   That thay wyth busynes had ben aboute hym to serve.
   And uche segge as sore to sever with hym there
   As thay hade wonde worthyly with that wlonk ever.
   Then with ledes and lyght he was ladde to his chambre,   *men*
1990 And blythely broght to his bedde to be at his rest   *courteously*

---

green chapel, (insofar) as God will allow me to receive on New Year's
Day the sentence of my fate.'
1970 All that I ever promised you I shall readily keep to.
1972–6 And conduct him through the hills, so that he had no delay in
   travelling through the woodland and going by the most direct route
   through the thickets. Gawain thanked the lord for doing him such
   honour (i.e. for providing him with a guide).
1979–82 He speaks to them with sorrow and with kissing, and he
   pressed them to accept many heartfelt thanks, and they promptly
   returned the same to him; they commended him to Christ with most
   grievous sighs.
1985–8 For his service and his kindness, and for the particular pains that
   they had taken to serve him diligently. And each man was as sorry to
   part with him there as if they had always lived in honour with that
   noble knight.

Yif he ne slepe soundyly say ne dar I,
For he hade muche on the morn to mynne, yif he wolde,
   in thoght.
  Let hym lyye there stille,
1995 He has nere that he soght;
  And ye wyl a whyle be stylle,   *if*
  I schal telle yow how thay wroght. *what they did*

IV

Now neghes the Nw Yere and the nyght passes, *draws near*
The day dryves to the derk, as Dryghtyn biddes.
2000 Bot wylde wederes of the worlde wakned theroute,
Clowdes kesten kenly the colde to the erthe,
Wyth nyye innoghe of the northe, the naked to tene.
The snawe snitered ful snart, that snayped the wylde;
The werbelande wynde wapped fro the hyghe
2005 And drof uche dale ful of dryftes ful grete. *drove*
The leude lystened ful wel, that ley in his bedde. *knight; lay*
Thagh he lowkes his liddes, ful lyttel he slepes; *shuts*
Bi uch kok that crue he knwe wel the steven. *crowed; time*
Deliverly he dressed up er the day sprenged,
2010 For there was lyght of a laumpe that lemed in his *from; shone*
 chambre.
He called to his chamberlayn, that cofly hym *promptly*
 swared,   *answered*
And bede hym bryng hym his bruny and his blonk sadel;
That other ferkes hym up and feches hym his *gets up*
 wedes,   *clothes*

1991-3 Whether he slept soundly I dare not say, for he had much to
 think about on the next day, if he wanted to.
1995 He has close at hand what he sought.
1999-2004 The day comes up on the darkness, as the Lord commands.
 But wild storms arose in the world outside, clouds keenly drove the
 cold (sleet) to the earth, with much evil (weather) from the north, to
 torment the naked. The snow sleeted down sharply, stinging the wild
 animals; the whistling wind blew in gusts from the high ground.
2009 Quickly he got up before the day dawned.
2012 And asked him to bring him his coat of mail and saddle his horse.

And graythes me Sir Gawayn upon a grett wyse.
2015 Fyrst he clad hym in his clothes, the colde for to
     were,   *ward off*
And sythen his other harnays, that holdely was keped,
Bothe his paunce and his plates, piked ful clene,
The rynges rokked of the roust of his riche bruny;
And al was fresch as upon fyrst, and he was fayn *at first; glad*
     thenne
2020   to thonk.   *give thanks*
          He hade upon uche pece,
          Wypped ful wel and wlonk.   *polished; splendid*
          The gayest into Grece
          The burne bede bryng his blonk.

2025 Whyle the wlonkest wedes he warp on hymselven –
His cote wyth the conysaunce of the clere werkes
Ennurned upon velvet, vertuus stones
Aboute beten and bounden, enbrauded semes,
And fayre furred withinne wyth fayre pelures.
2030 Yet laft he not the lace, the ladies gifte;   *left (off); girdle*
That forgat not Gawayn, for gode of hymselven.
Bi he hade belted the bronde upon his   *when; sword*
     balwe haunches,   *rounded hips*
Thenn dressed he his drurye double hym aboute,
Swythe swethled umbe his swange swetely that knyght.
2035 The gordel of the grene silke that gay wel bisemed,

2014 And dresses Sir Gawain in magnificent style.
2016–18 And then his other gear, that had been carefully kept, both his
    stomach-armour (of mail) and his pieces of plate, polished very clean,
    the rings of his rich coat of mail scraped clean of rust.
2021 (Then) he had every piece on him.
2023–4 The best-looking knight from here to Greece asked the man to
    bring him his horse.
2025–9 While he himself put on the richest garments – his surcoat with
    the device of bright embroidery worked on velvet, gems of special
    power inlaid and set round it, embroidered seams, and beautifully
    furred on the inside with fine fur-skins.
2033–46 Then he doubled his love-token about himself, lovingly the
    knight wound it tightly round his waist. The girdle of green silk suited

Upon that ryol red clothe that ryche was to schewe.
Bot wered not this ilk wyye for wele this gordel,
For pryde of the pendauntes, thagh polyst thay were,
And thagh the glyterande golde glent upon endes,
2040 Bot for to saven hymself when suffer hym byhoved,
To byde bale withoute dabate, of bronde hym to were
                    other knyffe.
            Bi that the bolde mon boun
            Wynnes theroute bilyve.
2045   Alle the meyny of renoun
            He thonkkes ofte ful ryve.

Thenne was Gryngolet graythe, that gret was and   *ready*
    huge,
And hade ben sojourned saverly and in a siker wyse;
Hym lyst prik for poynt, that proude hors thenne.
2050 The wyye wynnes hym to and wytes on his lyre,
And sayde soberly hymself and by his soth sweres:
'Here is a meyny in this mote that on menske thenkkes.
The mon hem maynteines, joy mot he have!
The leve lady on lyve, luf hir bityde!
2055 Yif thay for charyté cherysen a gest,

---

that handsome knight well, upon the splendid red cloth of rich appearance. But this (same) man did not wear this girdle for (its) costliness, (nor) for the fine appearance of the pendants, polished though they were, and though glittering gold gleamed at the ends (of the pendants), but in order to save himself when he had to submit, (had) to wait for death without resisting, without defending himself with sword or knife. By then the bold man, (now) ready, goes quickly outside. Again and again he thanks all the noble company most profusely (i.e. in their absence, cf. lines 2052–9).

2048–58 And had been stabled comfortably and securely; that proud horse then wanted to gallop, because of his fine condition. The man goes to him and looks at his coat, and said quietly to himself, swearing on his honour: 'Here is a company in this castle that is mindful of courtesy. The man who looks after them, joy may he have! The most dear lady, may friendship befall her! If (i.e. whenever) they entertain a

And halden honour in her honde, the hathel hem yelde
That haldes the heven upon hyghe, and also yow alle!
And yif I myght lyf upon londe lede any quyle,
I schuld rech yow sum rewarde redyly, if I   *give; willingly*
    myght.'
2060 Thenn steppes he into stirop and strydes alofte.
His schalk schewed hym his schelde; on schulder   *man; shield*
    he hit laght,   *slung*
Gordes to Gryngolet with his gilt heles,   *strikes G.; spurs*
And he startes on the ston – stod he no lenger
           to praunce.
2065   His hathel on hors was thenne,   *attendant*
     That bere his spere and launce.   *carried*
     'This kastel to Kryst I kenne –   *commend*
     He gef hit ay god chaunce!'

The brygge was brayde doun, and the   *drawbridge; lowered*
    brode yates
2070 Unbarred and born open upon bothe halve.   *laid; sides*
The burne blessed hym bilyve, and the bredes passed,
Prayses the porter bifore the prynce kneled,
Gef hym God and goud day, that Gawayn he save,
And went on his way with his wyye one,   *one attendant*
2075 That schulde teche hym to tourne to that tene place
Ther the ruful race he schulde resayve.
Thay bowen bi bonkkes ther boghes ar bare,   *went; boughs*
Thay clomben bi clyffes ther clenges the   *climbed; clings*
    colde.

---

guest out of kindness and dispense hospitality, may the Lord who rules
the heaven on high reward them, and all of you (i.e. all the household)
besides. And if I might live any length of time on this earth.'

2064 And he springs forward on the stone (of the courtyard) – he stood
prancing no longer.

2068 May He give it good fortune always.

2071–3 The man crossed himself quickly, and passed over the planks (of
the drawbridge); he commends the gatekeeper who knelt before the
prince, (who) gave him God and good day, that He (should) save
Gawain.

2075–6 Who was to teach him how to find his way to that perilous place
where he must receive the grievous blow.

The heven was up halt, bot ugly therunder;
2080 Mist muged on the mor, malt on the   *drizzled; dissolved*
           mountes.
     Uch hille hade a hatte, a myst-hakel huge.   *cloak of mist*
     Brokes byled and breke bi bonkkes aboute,
     Schyre schaterande on schores ther thay doun schowved.
     Wela wylle was the way ther thay bi wod schulden,
2085 Til hit was sone sesoun that the sunne ryses
                    that tyde.
           Thay were on a hille ful hyghe,
           The quyte snaw lay bisyde;   *white; round about*
           The burne that rod hym by   *beside him*
2090   Bede his mayster abide.   *asked; to stop*

'For I haf wonnen yow hider, wyye, at this tyme,   *brought; sir*
And now nar ye not fer fro that note place
That ye han spied and spuryed so specially after.
Bot I schal say yow for sothe, sythen I   *tell you truly; since*
     yow knowe,
2095 And ye ar a lede upon lyve that I wel lovy,
Wolde ye worch bi my wytte, ye worthed the better.
The place that ye prece to ful perelous is halden;   *hasten; held*
Ther wones a wyye in that waste, the worst upon   *lives; man*
     erthe,
For he is stiffe and sturne, and to strike lovies,
2100 And more he is then any mon upon myddelerde,   *bigger; earth*
And his body bigger then the best fowre   *stronger*

2079 The clouds were drawn up high, but ugly underneath.
2082–6 Brooks boiled and broke on the hillsides round about, dashing
     brightly against their banks as they flowed swiftly down. Most perplex-
     ing was the way they had to take through the wood, till it was soon the
     hour that the sun rises at that time of year.
2092–3 And now you are not far from that well-known place that you
     have enquired and asked about so particularly.
2095–6 And you are indeed a man whom I love well, if you would act
     according to my understanding (of the situation), you would be the
     better for it.
2099 For he is bold and grim, and loves to strike (blows).

That ar in Arthures hous, Hestor, other other.
He cheves that chaunce at the chapel grene
Ther passes non bi that place so proude in his armes
2105   That he ne dynges hym to dethe with dynt of his honde.
For he is a mon methles, and mercy non uses;   *ruthless; shows*
For be hit chorle other chaplayn that bi the chapel   *churl*
    rydes,
Monk other masseprest, other any mon elles,   *priest*
Hym thynk as queme hym to quelle as quyk go hymselven.
2110   Forthy I say the, as sothe as ye in sadel sitte,
Com ye there, ye be kylled, may the knyght rede;
Trawe ye me that trwely, thagh ye had twenty lyves   *believe*
    to spende.
    He has wonyd here ful yore,   *lived; a long while*
2115   On bent much baret bende.
    Ayayn his dyntes sore   *against; grievous*
    Ye may not yow defende.   *yourself*

'Forthy, goude Sir Gawayn, let the gome one,   *man alone*
And gos away sum other gate, upon Goddes halve!
2120   Cayres bi sum other kyth, ther Kryst mot yow spede!
And I schal hyy me hom ayayn, and hete yow fyrre
That I schal swere bi God and alle his gode halwes —

2102-5   That are in Arthur's house, (or) Hector (of Troy), or any others.
He brings it about at the green chapel that no one passes by that place
so proud in his armour that he does not strike him dead with a blow of
his hand.

2109-11   It seems to him as pleasant to kill him as to be alive himself.
And so I say to you, as surely as you sit in the saddle, come there and
you will be killed, if the knight has his way.

2115   (And has) caused much trouble by fighting (lit. caused much trouble
on the battlefield).

2119-39   'And go away (on) some other path, for God's sake! Ride some
other way, may Christ help you! And I shall take myself off home
again, and moreover I promise you that I shall swear by God and all
his good saints — "so help me God and the holy relics", and (other)

"As help me God and the halydam", and othes innoghe –
That I schal lelly yow layne, and lauce never tale
2125 That ever ye fondet to fle for freke that I wyst.'
'Grant merci,' quoth Gawayn, and gruchyng he sayde:
'Wel worth the, wyye, that woldes my gode,
And that lelly me layne I leve wel thou woldes.
Bot helde thou hit never so holde, and I here passed,
2130 Founded for ferde for to fle, in fourme that thou telles,
I were a knyght kowarde, I myght not be excused.
Bot I wyl to the chapel, for chaunce that may falle,
And talk wyth that ilk tulk the tale that me lyste,
Worthe hit wele other wo, as the wyrde lykes
2135   hit hafe.
             Thaghe he be a sturn knape
             To stightel, and stad with stave,
             Ful wel con Dryghtyn schape
             His servauntes for to save.'

2140 'Mary!' quoth that other mon, 'now thou so much spelles
That thou wylt thyn awen nye nyme to thyselven.
And the lyst lese thy lyf, the lette I ne kepe.

---

oaths in plenty – that I shall faithfully keep your secret, and never
breathe a word that you were ever minded to flee for (the sake of) any
man that I knew of.' 'Thank you,' said Gawain, and he spoke with
displeasure: 'Good fortune befall you, sir, who have my good at heart,
and I well believe that you would loyally keep my secret. But however
faithfully you kept it, if I went away from here, minded out of fear to
flee, in the way that you describe, I would be a cowardly knight, I
might not be excused. But I will go to the chapel, whatever may
happen, and speak whatever words I wish to that same man, whether
good or ill will come of it, as fate is pleased to have it. Though he may
be a grim fellow to deal with, and armed with a club, the Lord is well
able to bring it about that He saves His servants.'
2140–2 Now you as much as say that you will bring your own harm on
yourself. If it pleases you to lose your life, I shall not trouble to stop
you.

Haf here thi helme on thy hede, thi spere in thi   *helmet*
    honde,
And ryde me doun this ilk rake bi yon rokke syde,
2145 Til thou be broght to the bothem of the brem valay.   *wild*
Thenne loke a littel on the launde on thi lyfte honde,
And thou schal se in that slade the self chapel   *valley; very*
And the borelych burne on bent that hit kepes.
Now fares wel, on Godes half, Gawayn the   *in God's name*
    noble!
2150 For alle the golde upon grounde I nolde   *on earth; would not*
    go wyth the,
Ne bere the felawschyp thurgh this fryth on fote fyrre.'
Bi that the wyye in the wod wendes his brydel,
Hit the hors with the heles as harde as he myght,
Lepes hym over the launde, and leves the knyght there
2155   al one.
        'Bi Goddes self,' quoth Gawayn,
        'I wyl nauther grete ne grone;   *weep; complain*
        To Goddes wylle I am ful bayn,   *obedient*
        And to hym I haf me tone.'   *committed myself*

2160 Thenne gyrdes he to Gryngolet and gederes the rake,
Schowves in bi a schore at a schawe syde,
Rides thurgh the roghe bonk ryght to the dale.
And thenne he wayted hym aboute, and   *looked*
    wylde hit hym thoght,   *it seemed to him*
And seye no syngne of resette bisydes nowhere,

2144 And ride down this path here by the side of that rock.
2146 Then look a little distance across the open ground on your left side.
2148 And the man mighty in battle who guards it.
2151-2 'Nor keep you company through this wood one foot further.'
    With that the man in the wood turns his bridle.
2154-5 Gallops over the open ground, and leaves the knight there all
    alone.
2160-2 Then he strikes spurs into Gringolet and picks up the path,
    pushes in along a slope at the edge of a wood, rides through the rough
    (vegetation of the) slope right to the valley bottom.
2164 And he saw no sign of habitation anywhere about.

2165 Bot hyghe bonkkes and brent upon bothe halve,   *steep; sides*
     And rughe knokled knarres with knorned stones;
     The skwes of the scowtes skayned hym thoght.
     Thenne he hoved and wytthhylde his hors at *halted; held back*
          that tyde,   *time*
     And ofte chaunged his cher the chapel to seche.   *position*
2170 He sey non suche in no syde, and selly hym thoght,
     Save a lyttel on a launde, a lawe as hit were,
     A balw berw bi a bonke the brymme bysyde,
     Bi a forw of a flode that ferked thare;
     The borne blubred therinne as hit boyled hade.
2175 The knyght kaches his caple and com to the lawe,
     Lightes doun luflyly, and at a lynde taches
     The rayne and his riche with a roghe braunche.
     Thenne he bowes to the berwe, aboute hit he   *goes; mound*
          walkes,
     Debatande with hymself quat hit be myght.
2180 Hit hade a hole on the ende and on ayther syde,   *each*
     And overgrowen with gresse in glodes   *patches*
          aywhere;   *everywhere*
     And al was holw inwith, nobot an   *hollow inside; nothing but*
          olde cave,
     Or a crevisse of an olde cragge – he couthe hit noght deme
          with spelle.
2185   'We! Lorde,' quoth the gentyle knyght,   *ah!; noble*
             'Whether this be the grene chapelle?   *is this*

2166–7 And rough knuckled crags with gnarled stones; the clouds
     seemed to him to be grazed by the jutting rocks.
2170–7 He saw nothing like it on any side, and that seemed strange to
     him, except for, a little way off in an open space, a mound as it were, a
     rounded barrow by a cliff beside the water's edge, by the channel of
     a stream which flowed there; the burn bubbled in it as though it were
     boiling. The knight urges his horse and came to the mound, dismounts
     gracefully, and ties the reins and his noble horse to the rough branch of
     a tree.
2183–4 Or a crevice in an old crag; he could not describe it in words.

Here myght aboute mydnyght
The dele his matynnes telle!   *Devil; matins*

'Now iwysse,' quoth Wowayn, 'wysty is   *indeed; desolate*
here;
2190 This oritore is ugly, with erbes overgrowen.   *chapel; grass*
Wel bisemes the wyye wruxled in grene
Dele here his devocioun on the develes wyse.
Now I fele hit is the fende, in my fyve wyttes,   *Devil; senses*
That has stoken me this steven to strye me here.
2195 This is a chapel of meschaunce – that chekke hit bytyde!
Hit is the corsedest kyrk that ever I com inne.'   *most accursed*
With heghe helme on his hede, his launce in his honde,
He romes up to the roffe of tho rogh wones.
Thene herde he of that hyghe hil, in a harde roche
2200 Biyonde the broke, in a bonk, a wonder breme noyse.
Quat! hit clatered in the clyff as hit cleve schulde,
As one upon a gryndelston hade grounden a sythe.
What! hit wharred and whette, as water at a mulne.
What! hit rusched and ronge, rawthe to here.
2205 Thenne 'Bi Godde,' quoth Gawayn, 'that gere, as I trowe,
Is ryched at the reverence me, renk, to mete
     bi rote.
   Let God worche! "We loo" –
   Hit helppes me not a mote.
2210   My lif thagh I forgoo,
   Drede dos me no lote.'

2191–2 It would well suit the man dressed in green to perform his devotions here in the Devil's fashion.

2194 Who has imposed this tryst on me to destroy me here.

2195 This is a chapel of evil – may ill fortune befall it!

2198–211 He goes up to the roof of that rough dwelling. Then from that high hill he heard, (coming from) within a hard rock beyond the brook, in a hillside, an amazingly fierce noise. What! it clattered in the cliff as though it would split it in two, as though one were grinding a scythe on a grindstone. What! it whirred and made a whetting noise, like water at a mill. What! it rushed and rang, horrible to hear. Then 'By God,' said Gawain, 'that equipment, as I believe, is being prepared in my honour, sir, (for you) to meet me according to (your) custom. Let God have His way! (To say) "alas" helps me not a jot. Though I should lose my life, no noise makes me fear.'

Thenne the knyght con calle ful hyghe: *called; loudly*
'Who stightles in this sted, me steven to holde?
For now is gode Gawayn goande ryght here.   *present*
2215 If any wyye oght wyl, wynne hider fast,
Other now other never, his nedes to spede.'
'Abyde,' quoth on on the bonke aboven over   *wait; someone*
     his hede,
'And thou schal haf al in hast that I the hyght   *promised you*
     ones.'   *once*
Yet he rusched on that rurde rapely a throwe,
2220 And wyth quettyng awharf, er he wolde lyght.
And sythen he keveres bi a cragge and   *then; makes his way*
     comes of a hole,   *out of*
Whyrlande out of a wro wyth a felle weppen,   *corner; fierce*
A denes ax nwe dyght, the dynt with to yelde,
With a borelych bytte bende by the halme,
2225 Fyled in a fylor, fowre fote large –
Hit was no lasse, bi that lace that lemed ful bryght.
And the gome in the grene gered as   *man; attired as at first*
     fyrst,
Bothe the lyre and the legges, lokkes and berde,   *face; hair*
Save that fayre on his fote he foundes on the erthe,
2230 Sette the stele to the stone and stalked bysyde.
When he wan to the watter, ther he   *came; where*
     wade nolde,   *did not want to*
He hypped over on hys ax and orpedly   *hopped; boldly*
     strydes,

2213 Who rules in this place, to keep tryst with me?
2215–16 If any man wants anything let him come here quickly, now or
     never, to get on with his business.
2219–20 Yet he went on with that rushing noise briskly for a while, and
     turned away on account of his grinding, before he would come down.
2223–6 A Danish axe (i.e. battle-axe) newly prepared, (with which) to
     return the blow, with a huge blade fixed on the shaft, sharpened on a
     grindstone, four feet broad – it was no less, (measured) by that lace
     which shone so bright (i.e. a decorative lace was presumably wrapped
     round the shaft, cf. lines 217–18).
2229–30 Except that firm on his feet he walks on the ground, set the
     shaft to the stones and stalked alongside.

Bremly brothe, on a bent that brode was aboute,
           on snawe.
2235   Sir Gawayn the knyght con mete,   *met*
         He ne lutte hym nothyng lowe.
         That other sayde: 'Now, sir swete,
         Of steven mon may the trowe.

'Gawayn,' quoth that grene gome, 'God   *may God keep you!*
    the mot loke!
2240 Iwysse thou art welcom, wyye, to my place,   *certainly; sir*
     And thou has tymed thi travayl as truee mon   *journey; true*
         schulde.
     And thou knowes the covenauntes kest uus bytwene: *made*
     At this tyme twelmonyth thou toke that the falled,
     And I schulde at this Nwe Yere yeply the   *promptly*
         quyte.   *repay*
2245 And we ar in this valay verayly oure one;   *truly by ourselves*
     Here ar no renkes us to rydde, rele as uus likes.
     Haf thy helme of thy hede, and haf here thy pay.   *take; off*
     Busk no more debate then I the bede thenne
     When thou wypped of my hede at a wap   *struck; single blow*
         one.'
2250 'Nay, bi God,' quoth Gawayn, 'that me gost lante,
     I schal gruch the no grwe for grem that falles.
     Bot styghtel the upon on strok, and I schal stonde stylle
     And warp the no wernyng to worch as the lykes,
                 nowhare.'

2233–4 Exceedingly grim, on a piece of open ground that lay broad
       about, in the snow.
2236 He did not bow at all low to him.
2238 A man may trust you to keep an appointment.
2243 (That) at this time twelve months ago you took what fell to your
     lot.
2246 Here are no men to part us, let us carry on as we like.
2248 Offer no more resistance than I offered you then.
2250–8 'No,' said Gawain, 'by God who gave me a soul, I shall bear
     you no shred of ill will for any harm that befalls me. Just limit yourself
     to one stroke, and I shall stand still and offer you no resistance to your
     doing as you please, none at all.' He inclined his neck and bowed low,

2255   He lened with the nek and lutte,
            And schewed that schyre al bare,
            And lette as he noght dutte;
            For drede he wolde not dare.

Then the gome in the grene graythed hym   *got ready*
    swythe,   *quickly*
2260 Gederes up hys grymme tole, Gawayn to smyte;   *lifts; tool*
     With alle the bur in his body he ber hit on lofte,
     Munt as maghtyly as marre hym he wolde.
     Hade hit dryven adoun as drey as he atled,
     Ther hade ben ded of his dynt that doghty was ever.
2265 Bot Gawayn on that giserne glyfte hym bysyde
     As hit com glydande adoun on glode hym to schende,
     And schranke a lytel with the schulderes for the scharp yrne.
     That other schalk wyth a schunt the schene wythhaldes,
     And thenne repreved he the prynce with mony   *reproved*
    prowde wordes:
2270 'Thou art not Gawayn,' quoth the gome, 'that is so goud
    halden,   *held to be*
     That never arwed for no here by hylle ne be vale,
     And now thou fles for ferde er thou fele harmes.
     Such cowardise of that knyght cowthe I never here.
     Nawther fyked I ne flaghe, freke, quen thou myntest,
2275 Ne kest no kavelacion in kynges hous Arthor;
     My hede flaw to my fote, and yet flagh I never.   *flew; fled*

---

and showed the white flesh all bare, and behaved as if he feared
nothing; he was determined not to cower for fear.

2261–8 With all the strength in his body he raised it aloft, swung it as
mightily as though he wanted to kill him. Had it come down as fiercely
as he aimed, he who was ever brave (i.e. Gawain) would have been
dead from his blow. But Gawain glanced sideways at that battle-axe as
it came gliding down to destroy him in that (open) place, and he shrank
a little with his shoulders on account of the sharp iron. The other man
holds back the bright blade with a jerk.

2271–5 Who was never frightened of any (group of) armed men by hill
or dale, and now you flee for fear before you suffer hurt. I never heard
of such cowardice on the part of that knight. I neither flinched nor fled,
sir, when you took aim, nor made any quibble in the house of King
Arthur.

And thou, er any harme hent, arwes in   *received; are afraid*
   hert,

Wherfore the better burne me burde be called *man; I ought to*
     therfore.'

2280   Quoth Gawayn: 'I schunt ones,   *flinched*
     And so wyl I no more;
     Bot thagh my hede falle on the stones,   *though*
     I con not hit restore.

'Bot busk, burne, bi thi fayth, and bryng me to the poynt.

2285 Dele to me my destiné and do hit out of honde,   *at once*

For I schal stonde the a strok, and   *stand a stroke from you*
   start no more

Til thyn ax have me hitte – haf here my trawthe.'   *pledge*

'Haf at the thenne,' quoth that other, and heves hit alofte,

And waytes as wrothely as he wode were.

2290 He myntes at hym maghtyly bot not the mon rynes,

Withhelde heterly his honde er hit hurt myght.

Gawayn graythely hit bydes and glent with no membre,

Bot stode stylle as the ston other a   *or*
   stubbe auther   *stump (of a tree); else*

That ratheled is in roché grounde with rotes   *entwined; rocky*
   a hundreth.

2295 Then muryly efte con he mele, the mon in the   *again; spoke*
   grene:

'So now thou has thi hert holle, hitte me bihoves.

Halde the now the hyghe hode that Arthur the raght,

And kepe thy kanel at this kest, yif hit kever may!'

2284 But hurry, man, for your honour's sake, and come to the point
   with me.

2289–92 And glares as fiercely as though he were mad. He swings at him
   mightily but does not touch the man, withheld his hand suddenly
   before it might do injury. Gawain boldly waits for it and did not flinch
   in any limb.

2296–8 So now that you have your heart whole (i.e. you have regained
   your courage), I am obliged to strike. Maintain now the high rank
   which Arthur gave you (i.e. maintain your knightly courage), and keep
   your neck at this blow, if that can be!

Gawayn ful gryndelly with greme thenne   *fiercely; anger*
   sayde:
2300 'Wy, thresch on, thou thro mon, thou thretes   *strike; fierce*
   to longe;   *too*
I hope that thi hert arwe wyth thyn awen selven.'
'For sothe,' quoth that other freke, 'so felly thou   *fiercely*
   spekes,
I wyl no lenger on lyte lette thin ernde
     right nowe.'
2305   Thenne tas he hym strythe to stryke   *he takes stance*
     And frounses bothe lyppe and browe;   *puckers*
     No mervayle thagh hym myslyke
     That hoped of no rescowe.

He lyftes lyghtly his lome and let hit doun fayre,
2310 With the barbe of the bitte bi the bare nek.
Thagh he homered heterly hurt hym no more,
Bot snyrt hym on that on syde, that severed the hyde.
The scharp schrank to the flesche thurgh the schyre grece,
That the schene blod over his schulderes schot   *bright; spurted*
   to the erthe.
2315 And quen the burne sey the blode blenk on   *man; saw; gleam*
   the snawe,
He sprit forth spenne-fote more then a spere lenthe,
Hent heterly his helme and on his hed cast,   *seized quickly*
Schot with his schulderes his fayre schelde under,
Braydes out a bryght sworde, and bremely he   *draws; fiercely*
   spekes.

2301 I think that your heart is frightened of your own self.

2303 I will no longer delay (lit. hinder in delay) your business.

2307–8 No wonder though he was unhappy, the man who expected no
rescue.

2309–13 He lifts his weapon lightly and let it down precisely, with the
edge of the blade beside the bare neck. Though he struck fiercely he did
him no great hurt, but nicked him on the one side, so that the skin was
severed. The sharp blade went down to the flesh through the white fat.

2316 He sprang forward with feet together more than a spear's length.

2318 Jerked his good shield down (in front of him) with his shoulders.

2320 Never syn that he was burne borne of his moder
Was he never in this worlde wyye half so blythe.
'Blynne, burne, of thy bur, bede me no mo!
I haf a stroke in this sted withoute stryf hent,
And if thow reches me any mo, I redyly schal   *give*
    quyte   *repay*
2325 And yelde yederly ayayn – and therto ye tryst –
        and foo.
        Bot on stroke here me falles;
        The covenaunt schop ryght so,   *stated just*
        Festned in Arthures halles,   *made*
2330   And therfore, hende, now hoo!'   *good sir; stop*

The hathel heldet hym fro and on   *man stood back from him*
    his ax rested,
Sette the schaft upon schore and to the scharp lened,
And loked to the leude that on the launde yede,
How that doghty, dredles, dervely ther stondes
2335 Armed, ful awles; in hert hit hym lykes.
Thenn he meles muryly wyth a much steven,
And wyth a rynkande rurde he to the renk   *ringing tone; man*
    sayde:
'Bolde burne, on this bent be not so gryndel.
No mon here unmanerly the mysboden habbes,
2340 Ne kyd bot as covenaunde at kynges kort schaped.
I hyght the a strok and thou hit has,   *promised*
    halde the wel payed;   *consider yourself*

2320–3 Never since he was a man new-born of his mother was he ever
in this world half so happy (a man). 'Stop your blows, sir, offer me no
more! I have taken a stroke in this place without resisting.'
2325–7 And promptly give (your blows) back again – be sure of that –
and without quarter. Only one stroke is due to me here.
2332–6 Set the handle to the ground and leaned on the blade, and
looked towards the man (who was) in the open space, how he stands
there bravely, bold and undaunted, armed, entirely without fear; at
heart he is pleased. Then he speaks cheerfully in a loud voice.
2338–40 Bold knight, do not be so fierce on this (battle-)field. No man
has mistreated you here in an unmannerly way, nor offered (you
anything) except in accordance with the agreement made at the king's
court.

I relece the of the remnaunt of ryghtes alle other.
Iif I deliver had bene, a boffet paraunter
I couthe wrotheloker haf waret, to the haf wrogt anger.
2345 Fyrst I mansed the muryly with a mynt one,
And rove the wyth no rof-sore; with ryght I the profered,
For the forwarde that we fest in the fyrst nyght,
And thou trystyly the trawthe and trwly me haldes –
Al the gayne thow me gef, as god mon schulde.
2350 That other munt for the morne, mon, I the profered;
Thou kyssedes my clere wyf, the cosses me raghtes.
For bothe two here I the bede bot two bare myntes
            boute scathe.
        Trwe mon trwe restore,
2355   Thenne thar mon drede no wathe.
        At the thrid thou fayled thore,
        And therfor – that tappe ta the!

'For hit is my wede that thou weres, that ilke   *garment; same*
    woven girdel;
Myn owen wyf hit the weved, I wot wel for   *gave; know*
    sothe.
2360 Now know I wel thy cosses and thy costes als,
And the wowyng of my wyf; I wrogt hit myselven.
I sende hir to asay the, and sothly me thynkkes   *test; truly*

2342–57 I release you from all the rest of your obligations. If I had
    exerted all my strength (lit. had been at full strength), I could perhaps
    have dealt you a blow more fiercely, to have done you harm. First I
    threatened you in sport with a feinted blow only, and did not tear you
    with a deep wound; I offered (this) to you with justice, because of the
    covenant that we made on the first night, and (because) you loyally and
    truly kept (lit. keep) faith with me – you gave me all your winnings, as
    a good man should. The second feinted blow I offered you for the
    following day, sir; you kissed my lovely wife, and gave the kisses to
    me. For both these two (occasions) I offered you only two mere feints,
    without (doing) injury. A true man must (*mon*) restore truly, then one
    (*mon*) need fear no danger. On the third occasion you failed in this
    respect, and therefore – take that tap!
2360–1 Now I know all about your kisses and your conduct too, and
    my wife's wooing (of you); I brought it about myself.

On the fautlest freke that ever on fote yede.
As perle bi the quite pese is of prys more,
2365 So is Gawayn, in god fayth, bi other gay knyghtes.
Bot here yow lakked a lyttel, sir, and lewté yow wonted;
Bot that was for no wylyde werke, ne wowyng nauther,
Bot for ye lufed your lyf – the lasse I yow blame.'
That other stif mon in study stod a gret whyle,   *brave*
2370 So agreved for greme he gryed withinne.
Alle the blode of his brest blende in his face,   *suffused his*
That al he schrank for schome that the schalk talked.
The forme worde upon folde that the freke meled:
'Corsed worth cowarddyse and covetyse bothe!
2375 In yow is vylany and vyse that vertue disstryes.'   *destroys*
Thenne he kaght to the knot and the kest lawses,
Brayde brothely the belt to the burne selven.
'Lo! ther the falssyng, foule mot hit falle!
For care of thy knokke cowardyse me taght
2380 To acorde me with covetyse, my kynde to forsake
That is larges and lewté that longes to knyghtes.
Now am I fawty and falce, and ferde haf ben ever
Of trecherye and untrawthe – bothe bityde sorwe
                    and care!
2385   I biknowe yow, knyght, here stylle,   *confess; humbly*
              Al fawty is my fare;   *conduct*

2363–7 (That you are) the most truly faultless man who ever lived (lit. went on foot). As the pearl beside the white pea is of greater value, so is Gawain, upon my word, beside other good knights. But in this you fell short a little, sir, and loyalty was lacking in you; but that was not because of any underhand behaviour, or love-making either.

2370 So overcome with mortification he shuddered inwardly.

2372–4 So that he quite shrank back on account of the shameful things that the man talked of. The very first words that the knight spoke (were): 'A curse on both cowardice and covetousness!'

2376–84 Then he caught hold of the knot and undoes the fastening, angrily flung the belt to the man himself. 'Look! so much for the false thing, may bad luck befall it! For fear of your blow cowardice taught me to ally myself with covetousness, (and) to forsake my true nature, which is the generosity and loyalty that belong to knights. Now I am faulty and false, and I have always been afraid of treachery and dishonour – may sorrow and care befall both of them!'

Letes me overtake your wylle,   *know your pleasure*
And efte I schal be ware.'   *henceforth; on guard*

Thenn loghe that other leude and luflyly sayde:
2390 'I halde hit hardily hole, the harme that I hade;
Thou art confessed so clene, beknowen of thy   *cleared of*
    mysses,   *faults*
And has the penaunce apert of the poynt of myn egge.
I halde the polysed of that plyght and pured as clene
As thou hades never forfeted sythen thou was fyrst borne.
2395 And I gif the, sir, the gurdel that is golde-hemmed,
For hit is grene as my goune; Sir Gawayn, ye maye
Thenk upon this ilke threpe ther thou forth thrynges
Among prynces of prys, and this a pure token
Of the chaunce of the grene chapel at chevalrous knyghtes.
2400 And ye schal in this Nwe Yer ayayn to my   *(come) back*
    wones,   *house*
And we schyn revel the remnaunt of this ryche fest
     ful bene.'   *pleasantly*
     Ther lathed hym fast the lorde,   *invited; pressingly*
     And sayde: 'With my wyf, I wene,   *believe*
2405   We schal yow wel acorde,   *reconcile*
     That was your enmy kene.'   *keen*

'Nay, for sothe,' quoth the segge, and sesed hys helme,   *man*
And has hit of hendely, and the hathel thonkkes:
'I haf sojorned sadly; sele yow bytyde,

2389–90 Then that other man laughed and said pleasantly: 'I count it
    entirely put right, the injury that I had.'
2392–4 And you have (accepted) the public penance of the point of my
    blade. I count you cleansed of that offence and purified as completely
    as though you had never transgressed since you were first born.
2397–9 Think of this (same) encounter when you go out amongst noble
    princes, and this (will be) an excellent token of the adventure of the
    green chapel (that took place) between chivalrous knights.
2401 And we shall revel the remainder of this noble festival.
2408–13 And takes it off courteously, and thanks the man: 'I have stayed
    long enough; may good fortune befall you, and may He who bestows

2410 And he yelde hit yow yare that yarkkes al menskes!
And comaundes me to that cortays, your comlych fere,
Bothe that on and that other, myn honoured ladyes,
That thus hor knyght wyth hor kest han koyntly bigyled.
Bot hit is no ferly thagh a fole madde   *wonder; acts foolishly*
2415 And thurgh wyles of wymmen be wonen to sorwe.   *brought*
For so was Adam in erde with one bygyled,
And Salamon with fele sere, and Samson eftsones –
Dalyda dalt hym hys wyrde – and Davyth therafter
Was blended with Barsabe, that much bale tholed.
2420 Now these were wrathed wyth her wyles, hit were a wynne
          huge
To luf hom wel and leve hem not, a leude that couthe.
For thes wer forne the freest, that folwed alle the sele
Exellently of alle thyse other under hevenryche
                    that mused;
2425   And alle thay were biwyled   *beguiled*
               With wymmen that thay used.   *by; had dealings with*
               Thagh I be now bigyled,
               Me think me burde be excused.   *I think I ought to*

'Bot your gordel,' quoth Gawayn, 'God yow
          foryelde!
                                      reward
2430 That wyl I welde wyth guod wylle, not for the   *have*
          wynne golde,   *precious*
Ne the saynt, ne the sylk, ne the syde pendaundes,   *sash; long*

---

all honours repay you fully for it! (i.e. for your hospitality). And
commend me to that courteous lady, your beautiful wife, both the one
and the other, my honoured ladies, who have thus skilfully beguiled
their knight with their trick.
2416–24 For so was Adam in truth beguiled by one, and Solomon by
many different (women), and Samson next – Delilah dealt him his fate
– and then David was deluded by Bathsheba, enduring great misery.
Now as these were brought to disaster by their wiles, it would be a
huge gain to love them well and not believe them, for a man who knew
how to. For these were the noblest men of old, favoured by fortune (lit.
whom all good fortune followed) pre-eminently above all others who
lived under the heavens.

For wele ne for worchyp, ne for the wlonk werkkes.

Bot in syngne of my surfet I schal se hit ofte   *as a sign; fault*

When I ride in renoun, remorde to   *remember with remorse*
    myselven

2435 The faut and the fayntyse of the flesche   *frailty*
    crabbed,   *perverse*

How tender hit is to entyse teches of fylthe.

And thus quen pryde schal me pryk for prowes of armes,   *stir*

The loke to this luf-lace schal lethe my   *looking at; humble*
    hert.

Bot on I wolde yow pray, displeses yow never.

2440 Syn ye be lorde of the yonder londe ther I haf lent inne

Wyth yow wyth worschyp – the wyye hit yow yelde

That uphaldes the heven and on hygh sittes –   *dwells*

How norne ye yowre ryght nome, and thenne no more?'   *say*

'That schal I telle the trwly,' quoth that other thenne,   *you*

2445 'Bercilak de Hautdesert I hat in this londe,   *am called*

Thurgh myght of Morgne la Faye, that in my hous
    lenges,   *lives*

And koyntyse of clergye, bi craftes wel lerned.

The maystrés of Merlyn mony has ho taken,

For ho has dalt drwry ful dere sumtyme

2450 With that conable klerk, that knowes alle your knyghtes
       at hame.

    Morgne the goddes   *goddess*

    Therfore hit is hir name;

2432 (Neither) for the pleasure nor for the honour (of having it), nor for
the beautiful workmanship.

2436 How prone it is to attract spots of sin.

2439–42 But one thing I would ask of you, do not take offence. Since
you are lord of that land where I have stayed with you in honour –
may the Being reward you for it.

2447–51 And (through her) knowledge of magic arts, by skills well
learned. She has acquired many of the powers of Merlin, for she has in
the past had most intimate love-dealings with that accomplished man
of learning, as all your knights at home know.

Weldes non so hyghe hawtesse
2455   That ho ne con make ful tame.

'Ho wayned me upon this wyse to your wynne halle
For to assay the surquidré, yif hit soth were
That rennes of the grete renoun of the Rounde Table.
Ho wayned me this wonder your wyttes to reve,
2460 For to haf greved Gaynour and gart hir to dyye
With glopnyng of that ilke gome that gostlych speked
With his hede in his honde bifore the hyghe table.
That is ho that is at home, the auncian lady;   *aged*
Ho is even thyn aunt, Arthures half-suster,   *indeed*
2465 The duches doghter of Tyntagelle, that dere Vter after
Hade Arthur upon, that athel is nowthe.
Therfore I ethe the, hathel, to com to thyn aunt,   *urge; sir*
Make myry in my hous – my meny the   *household*
    lovies,   *loves*
And I wol the as wel, wyye, bi my faythe,   *wish; sir*
2470 As any gome under God, for thy grete trauthe.'   *integrity*
And he nikked hym naye, he nolde bi no wayes.
Thay acolen and kyssen, bykennen   *embrace; commend*
    ayther other   *each*
To the prynce of paradise, and parten ryght there
            on coolde.   *the cold ground*
2475   Gawayn on blonk ful bene   *horse; fine*
            To the kynges burgh buskes bolde,   *castle; hastens*
            And the knyght in the enker-grene   *bright green*
            Whiderwarde-so-ever he wolde.   *to wherever*

Wylde wayes in the worlde Wowen now rydes   *pathways*

2454–61 No one has such great pride that she cannot make (him) utterly
    tame. She sent me in this guise (i.e. as the Green Knight) to your
    splendid hall in order to test its pride, (to test) whether what is said
    concerning the great renown of the Round Table is true. She sent this
    marvel to deprive you of your senses, (intending) to have frightened
    Guinevere and caused her to die through great fear of that (same) man
    who spoke like a phantom.
2465–6 Daughter of the Duchess of Tintagel, on whom the noble Uther
    afterwards fathered Arthur, who is now famous.
2471 And he (i.e. Gawain) said no to him, he would not on any account
    (accept Bercilak's invitation).

2480 On Gryngolet, that the grace hade geten of his lyve.
Ofte he herbered in house and ofte al   *lodged*
  theroute,   *out of doors*
And mony aventure in vale, and venquyst ofte,
That I ne tyght at this tyme in tale to remene.
The hurt was hole that he hade hent in his   *healed; received*
  nek,
2485 And the blykkande belt he bere theraboute,
Abelef as a bauderyk, bounden bi his syde,
Loken under his lyfte arme, the lace, with a knot,
In tokenyng he was tane in tech of a faute.
And thus he commes to the court, knyght
  al in sounde.   *safety*
2490 Ther wakned wele in that wone when wyst the grete
That gode Gawayn was commen; gayn hit hym thoght.
The kyng kysses the knyght, and the whene alce,   *queen also*
And sythen mony syker knyght that soght   *then; true; came*
  hym to haylce,   *greet*
Of his fare that hym frayned; and ferlyly he telles,
2495 Biknowes alle the costes of care that he hade,
The chaunce of the chapel, the chere of   *adventure; behaviour*
  the knyght,
The luf of the ladi, the lace at the last.   *girdle*
The nirt in the nek he naked hem schewed,   *nick; uncovered*
That he laght for his unleuté at   *received; breaking of faith*
  the leudes hondes   *man's*
2500   for blame.   *as a reproof*

2480 On Gryngolet, (Gawain) who had got a reprieve for his life.

2482-3 And (had) many adventures by the way, and often won victories which I do not intend to recall in story at this time.

2485-8 And he wore the shining belt round it (i.e. his neck), diagonally like a baldric, secured at his side, the girdle fastened with a knot under his left arm, as a sign that he had been caught in the disgrace (lit. stain) of a fault.

2490-1 Joy arose in that house when the nobles knew that good Gawain had come; it seemed an excellent thing to them.

2494-5 Who asked him about his journey; and he tells them of marvellous things, confesses all the tribulations that he had (suffered).

He tened quen he schulde telle,
He groned for gref and grame;   *mortification*
The blod in his face con melle,   *suffused his face*
When he hit schulde schewe, for schame.   *must*

2505 'Lo! lorde,' quoth the leude, and the lace hondeled,   *look!*
'This is the bende of this blame I bere on my nek;
This is the lathe and the losse that I laght have
Of couardise and covetyse that I haf caght thare.
This is the token of untrawthe that I am tan inne,
2510 And I mot nedes hit were wyle I may last.
For mon may hyden his harme bot unhap ne may hit,
For ther hit ones is tachched twynne wil hit never.'
The kyng comfortes the knyght, and alle the court als,   *also*
Laghen loude therat, and luflyly acorden
2515 That lordes and ladis that longed to the Table,
Uche burne of the brotherhede, a bauderyk schulde have,
A bende abelef hym aboute, of a bryght grene,
And that, for sake of that segge, in swete to were.
For that was acorded the renoun of the Rounde Table,
2520 And he honoured that hit hade, evermore after,
As hit is breved in the best boke of romaunce.   *told*

2501 He was troubled when he had to tell (about the nick in his neck).

2506–12 This is the sign (in heraldry a 'bend', as in 'bend sinister', is a
device in an armorial bearing consisting of a band drawn diagonally)
of this reproof which I bear on my neck; this is the injury and the loss
that I have sustained from the cowardice and covetousness which I
caught (i.e. was infected with) there. This is the symbol of the dishonour
which I am taken in, and I must needs wear it as long as I live. For a
man may hide his guilt but may not undo it, for once it is attached it
will never be parted.

2514–20 Laugh loudly at that (i.e. at what Gawain has said) and
graciously agree that the lords and ladies who belonged to the Table,
each member of the brotherhood, should have a baldric, a band (*and*
'bend') diagonally about him, of a bright green, and (they agree) to
wear it in the same fashion (as Gawain), for the sake of that man; for
that (baldric) was accorded the esteem of the Round Table, and he
(was) honoured who had it, ever afterwards.

Thus in Arthurus day this aunter   *adventure*
   bitidde;   *took place*
The Brutus bokes therof beres wyttenesse.
Sythen Brutus, the bolde burne, bowed hider fyrst,
2525 After the segge and the asaute was sesed at   *siege; ended*
   Troye,
                 iwysse,   *indeed*
     Mony aunteres here-biforne
     Haf fallen suche er this.
     Now that bere the croun of thorne,
2530   He bryng uus to his blysse. Amen.

           Hony soyt qui mal pence.

2523–4 The Brutus books (i.e. chronicles of Britain) bear witness to it. Since Brutus, the bold warrior, first came here.

2527–30 Many such adventures have taken place before now in times past. Now may He who wore the crown of thorns bring us to His bliss.

Translation of motto in French: 'Evil be to him who evil thinks.'

MANUSCRIPT EMENDATIONS

The following list indicates where the text of this edition differs significantly from the manuscript. Only the more significant and less certain emendations are noted.

The reading of the edited text is given first, inside the square bracket, followed by the manuscript reading.

Pearl

197 biys] viys
262 nere] here
302, 308 leves] loves
358 fleme] leme
369 kythes] lythes
396 and] in
529 date of day] day of date

616 fere] lere
690 Koyntise] kyntly
    onoure] oure
892 that] thay
997 John *supplied*
1064 refet] reget
1097 enpryse] enpresse

Cleanness

117 soberly] soerly
127 pover] povever *or* povener
318 uponande] upon
385 were] was
427 seventethe] seventhe
577 Thus] that
581 savour] savyour
654 sotyly] sothyly
655 teme] tonne
657 hit] he
659 had bene] byene
839 clater] clatz
840 thys] thyse
935 tayt] tyt
1040 festres] festred

1051 forthered] forferde
1118 ho] hym
1123 ho *supplied*
1164 were *supplied*
1315 gounes] gomes
1406 seves] seved
1460 on] of
1470 amastised] amaffised
1474 bekyr ande bolle]
    bekyrande the bolde
1485 launces *supplied*
1491 ther *supplied*
1618 standes] stande
1696 clawes] clawres
1776 scaled] scathed

Patience

     1   a poynt] apoynt
   104   spynde] spynde *or* sprude
   122   ye] he
   189   hasp-hede] haspede

   313   sayde] say
   344   was] wern
   515   her] his

Sir Gawain and the Green Knight

   144   Both] bot
   210   lenkthe . . . hed] hede . . .
          lenkthe
   531   fage] sage
   591   other] over
   660   I noquere] jquere
   777   gerdes] gederes
   815   yerne and come *supplied*
   835   wone] welde
   884   table] tapit
   958   chalk] mylk
   967   balwe] bay
   971   lent] went
   987   wede] wedes
   992   lord] kyng
  1014   That] and
  1183   dernly] derfly
  1208   gay] fayr
  1265   for *supplied*
  1266   nys ever] nysen
  1283   ho] I
          burne] burde
  1293   not *supplied*
  1334   *first* the] and
  1386   wonnen *supplied*

  1440   fro] for
          soght] wight
  1441   breme *supplied:*
          manuscript illegible
  1580   and *supplied*
  1588   freke] frekes
  1595   yed doun] yedoun
  1623   laghter] laghed
  1639   hent *supplied*
  1700   traveres] trayteres
  1752   dele hym *supplied*
  1755   com *supplied*
  1770   prynces] prynce
  1825   swyfte by] swyftel
  1861   ho *supplied*
  1863   fro] for
  1906   laches him] caches by
  1941   porchas] chepes
  2105   dynges] dynnes
  2187   Here] he
  2329   Festned in *supplied:*
          manuscript illegible
  2448   has *supplied*
  2472   bikennen *supplied*

EXPLANATORY NOTES

Pearl

3 **Oute of oryent:** The best pearls were held to come from the east.

6 This language is used of beautiful women in lyrics and romances.

9 **erbere:** garden. The medieval garden was primarily a place of pleasure, and in courtly literature (notably *The Romance of the Rose*) a place of love. Association with the Garden of Eden may be relevant here, in the light of the poem's themes of mortality/immortality and innocence/loss of innocence.

10 **hit:** The poet has hitherto used the feminine pronoun for the pearl.

11 **luf-daungere:** probably means in context 'power of love'. The word clearly belongs with the vocabulary of courtly love. In *The Romance of the Rose* 'Daunger' is a figure personifying the power of the courtly mistress.

21 The 'many' (*fele*) which came to the Dreamer are probably many songs, bitter ones (so lines 22–4 suggest) to balance the sweet song of line 19. The Dreamer is beginning to express his confusion, which he soon indicates more clearly (cf. lines 55–6).

31–2 The lines reflect John 12:24 (here quoted in the Authorised Version (A.V.)): 'Verily, verily, I say unto you, Except a corn of wheat fall into the ground and die, it abideth alone: but if it die, it bringeth forth much fruit.' Cf. 1 Cor: 15.35–8. These were, and are, texts regularly used in church services for the dead.

39 **hygh seysoun:** The term was applied to a major religious festival. Three August festivals suggest themselves: Lammas (1 August), the Transfiguration (6 August), and the Assumption of the Virgin (15 August). Of these, the Assumption, celebrating the taking up into Heaven of the Virgin Mary on

her death, was by far the most important, and might be thought to have most relevance to the poem. But the poet, as often, avoids specificity.

43–4 The plants are all medieval spice-plants which were thought of as particularly precious and sweetly-scented.

55 kynde of Kryst: 'nature of Christ'. Perhaps the main idea is the dual human/divine nature of Christ, through which He both experienced and overcame death.

61–4 The situation parallels that of St John, who is in Patmos when his spirit experiences the vision of the Heavenly City (Rev.1:9–10), as the Dreamer is in the garden.

68 rych rokkes: The shining rocks and other details establish the dream-landscape as supernatural, as opposed to the 'natural' garden of the first section of the poem. This landscape is the approach to Heaven, from which it is separated by a river (line 107). The details are particularly reminiscent of descriptions of the earthly paradise (sometimes located east of the Caucasus mountains) in the romances of Alexander the Great. The intense colours of the landscape suggest the artifice of tapestry-work (cf. lines 71–2), stained glass, and book illumination.

107 This *water*, which functions in the poem as a dividing line and barrier (see next note), is presumably to be identified with the river of life flowing from beneath the throne of God in the Heavenly City, as described in lines 1055–60; cf. line 974.

137 The Dreamer thinks that the Paradise of Heaven, including the Heavenly City itself (*mote*, 142) must be on the other side of the stream. He sees the stream as an artificial device separating one part of the scene from another, like those in some medieval gardens, and he wants to cross it (line 150). But, as so often later, he is thwarted in his desire (lines 151–2).

161 The first encounter between the Dreamer and the Maiden recalls to some extent Dante and his beloved mentor Beatrice in *The Divine Comedy*.

162–228 The Maiden is described as a beautiful aristocratic woman. Some epithets recall the courtly love tradition, especially the love-lyric, e.g. lines 189–91, which echo the description of the pearl in the opening stanza, and the white as whale's bone comparison in line 212. However, whereas the courtly lady's colouring is traditionally a mixture of white and red, the pearl-maiden has only an intense whiteness set off by the gold of her hair, like a jewel in a gold setting. In lines 197–204, the Maiden's garment of fine linen is from Rev. 19:8. Illustrations at the beginning of the *Pearl* MS clearly show the crowned figure of the Maiden in a white enveloping gown with large hanging sleeves. In the text her gown of *beau biys* is open at the sides, and her *cortel* may therefore be the garment seen underneath the gown; a woman's kirtle was an outer garment which was sometimes worn under a mantle or gown. The principal significance of her crown (lines 205–8) is that it marks her as an inhabitant of Heaven, all of whom are kings and queens (cf. lines 445–8) and wear crowns (cf. line 451). The emphasis on pearls in her dress, while appropriate to fourteenth-century costume, is symbolic of her innocence/virginity, and the whiteness of her costume suggests both baptismal robes and her status as a bride of Christ the Lamb (cf. lines 414, 757–60, 785 (note)). The great pearl in her breast (lines 221–2) is, as the Maiden explains later (lines 733–44) a symbol of the kingdom of Heaven. All the other virgins who follow the Lamb in the heavenly procession at the end of the dream also have this pearl and wear crowns (lines 1101–4).

184 The hawk, kept for hunting, is quiet and still when indoors. Cf. the Dreamer's similar use of a bird metaphor to express his stunned amazement in line 1085.

269 The rose is a well-known image both of feminine beauty and of transience.

273 **wyrde:** The Maiden picks up the Dreamer's use of the word in line 249 to make the point that what he sees as arbitrary and negative she sees as rational and positive; *wyrde* to him is cruel Fortune, to her the benevolence of God.

321–2 The Maiden here alludes to the fall of Adam in the Garden of Eden and the doctrine of original sin which she is to explain more fully later (lines 637–56).

341–60 The Maiden arrives at the argument that to go along with God's will and not to struggle against it is the only sensible course, an argument which is a homiletic commonplace (and here stated with homiletic emphasis), and one which the Dreamer says he unequivocally accepts at the end of the poem (lines 1199–1200). It is the main argument of *Patience*.

383 The three names together bring to mind John 19:26–7,

where Christ on the cross commits his mother to the care of John his beloved disciple.

413–14 The marriage of the Lamb is from Rev. 19:7–8; it was widely understood as an image of Christ's salvation of souls.

417 sesed and herytage: are both legal terms.

430 Chaucer in *The Book of the Duchess*, line 982, similarly calls the lady White *fenyx of Arabye* for her uniqueness. In medieval religious literature the phoenix was usually associated with Christ, though there are a few other instances of association with Mary.

432 quen of cortaysye: This may be a version of a Latin title for Mary, *Regina gratiae* (Queen of grace). The Dreamer's phrase and his word 'cortaysye' are taken up by the Maiden. Courtesy, the virtue of courts, which enables courtiers of differing status to communicate with each other and so in a sense makes them all equal, is said by the Maiden to operate in the court of God's kingdom of heaven (line 445), thereby making possible the co-existence of heavenly equality (where all are queens and kings, line 448) with Mary's pre-eminence (line 454). In the next stanza (lines 457–68) the Maiden identifies this courtesy with the informing spirit which St Paul sees as uniting and making equal the various parts of Christ's body, that is, uniting all Christians in the body of the Church (1 Cor. 12:12–27).

462 Mayster of myste: This title for Christ is appropriate as the Maiden *is* elucidating a spiritual mystery – the relationship of the company of the blessed to Mary, Christ, and each other.

472 A line is missing in the MS; Gollancz in his edition suggests 'Me thynk thou spekes now ful wronge'.

483 This is the first indication that the lost pearl is an infant child. In theology children two years old and under were technically innocent (from Herod's massacre of all male children 'two years old and under', Matt. 2:16).

485 The Paternoster and Apostles' Creed were the first devotions to be learned by children.

501–72 This is a retelling of the parable of the vineyard, Matt. 20:1–16.

581 The usual interpretation of the parable (based on St Augustine) held that the workers who came into the vineyard at different hours were those who took the Christian faith at different times of life, so that those who entered at the

eleventh hour were those who became Christians late in life. The Maiden sees herself as one who entered late because, like those baptised late in life, she had little or no time to work in the vineyard (i.e. to live a Christian life) before she died. There are a few biblical commentaries in which the eleventh hour is taken to refer to all those coming into the church shortly before death, including children.

589–600 The Dreamer attempts scholarly disputation, and his language briefly takes on an inflated legalistic colouring, with weighty technical terms (*determynable, pertermynable*).

595 The line translates Ps. 61:13 (Authorised Version 62:12).

613–744 This, the Maiden's longest speech, is also the longest piece of argumentation in the poem. In justification of her position in Heaven the Maiden turns to the central Christian doctrine of the Fall and Redemption. Her main point is that those who, like herself, die as innocent children are saved as of right: the blood and water of Christ's sacrifice (lines 646–7, see John 19:34), transmitted to them through the sacrament of baptism, have washed them clean of original sin, and they have died too young to commit sin themselves. Because they are entirely free of sin they must in justice be saved. Those who live beyond the age of innocence (i.e. technically those who are more than two years old; see note to line 483) may in theory also merit salvation, through their right living, but that way is difficult (*wayes ful streght* 691) and indeed impossible in practice, for even the most virtuous person sins in one way or another (lines 617–20), thereby forfeiting the right to Heaven; sin is inevitable once one is old enough to make meaningful moral choices. Such sinners may still achieve Heaven, but only by acknowledging their sin through confession and penance (lines 661–4) and so attracting God's mercy (lines 669–70). They then become like innocent children again, and as such they win entry to Heaven (lines 721–8). See also note to lines 701–8.

614 peny: The equation of the penny of the parable with salvation is traditional.

645–56 In the middle ages the outpouring of blood and water which followed the soldier's piercing of the crucified Christ's side with a spear (John 19:34) was understood to signify an outpouring of God's grace. In the apocryphal Gospel of Nicodemus and in medieval literature and drama the soldier is named as Longinus; he is blind, and his blindness is cured by the blood and water flowing into his eyes, the first redemptive consequence of the Crucifixion (as in *Piers Plowman*, B-text, ed. Schmidt (London, 1995), 18.78–86). The water which flowed from Christ's side was traditionally associated with the water of baptism (line 653).

678–9 Cf. Ps. 23:3 (A.V. 24.3)

681–3 Cf. Ps. 23:4 (A.V. 24.4), and, for line 683, Ps. 14:5 (A.V. 15:5).

689–92 The reference is to part of Wisdom 10:10: 'She [Wisdom] conducted the just [i.e. the just man, specifically Jacob fleeing from the wrath of his brother Esau] . . . through the right ways, and showed him the kingdom of God.' The apocryphal Book of Wisdom was written in the person of Solomon. The emendation of MS *oure* to *onoure* in line 690 is supported by a phrase found later on in Wisdom 10:10: 'made him [i.e. the just man] honourable in his labours'. In the Book of Wisdom the personified figure of Wisdom is female, but the poet uses the masculine pronoun in line 691; this suggests the common medieval identification of Wisdom with Christ, found also in *Patience* 39 (note).

699–700 Cf. Ps. 142:2 (A.V. 143:2).

701–8 The meaning is that people like the Dreamer will only be allowed to 'pass' into Heaven on the Day of Judgment if Christ accepts that, as sinners, they have been restored to a state of innocence by penance; in this sense, they are saved *by innocens*. They cannot be saved *by ryghte* (meaning in line 708, which contrasts the states of innocence and righteousness, not 'as of right', which is the meaning of the phrase elsewhere in this section of the poem, but 'by their righteousness'), because, as the Maiden says in the words of the psalm, no one lives a life righteous enough to merit salvation.

711–24 Based mainly on Luke 18:15–17, influenced by Matt. 19:13–15 and Mark 10:13–16.

721 The linking concatenation (see Note on Language and Metre, p. xxv) fails here for the only time in the poem, unless it can be stretched back to *Jesus* in line 717 or forwards to *ryght* in line 723.

729–36 The Maiden alludes to the parable of the pearl of great price (Matt. 13:45–6), in which Christ compares the kingdom of Heaven to a merchant (in line 731 a dealer in woollen and linen goods, a draper) who sells all that he has in order to buy a single pearl.

749–52 Pygmalion, the Greek sculptor, is here referred to as the greatest of all artists, and Aristotle as the greatest of philosophers, as they often are elsewhere. The two names are found together with others in a passage in *The Romance of the Rose* (French text, ed. Lecoy, lines 16135ff., not in Chaucer's version) in which it is argued that men are incapable of imitating Nature successfully. This passage in *The Romance of the Rose* gave rise to a commonplace of courtly literature, the idea that the beauty of Pygmalion's creations could not compete with the natural beauty of the lady who is the object of the writer's praise (see e.g. Chaucer's Physician's Tale, *Canterbury Tales* VI 7–18). The *Pearl*-poet links Aristotle and Pygmalion to another idea found in *The Romance of the Rose* (Chaucerian version, lines 3205–14), namely that the lady is too beautiful to be made by Nature and must be the work of God himself.

763–4 from Song of Songs 4:7–8; the universal Christian understanding of the Song of Songs was that it signified the union of Christ and the Church and/or the union of Christ and the individual soul.

785–92 Cf. Rev. 19:7–8 (lines 785, 791) and Rev. 14:1 (lines 786–9). In Revelation the bride of the Lamb is the heavenly City itself (cf. Rev. 21:2, 9–10); the poet's idea of making the band of virgins into wives of the Lamb is unusual but not entirely unprecedented.

786 One hundred and forty-four thousand is the number in Rev. 14:1; cf. lines 869–70, 1107.

790 St John the apostle was universally held to be the author of Revelation in the middle ages.

797–803 cf. Isaiah 53:7, part of one of the great Messianic prophecies.

806 **boyes bolde**: an apt phrase for those who put Christ to death (as they are characterised for instance in the mystery plays), but it may equally refer to the two thieves who were crucified with Christ on Calvary.

822–8 The words of John the Baptist's prophecy in lines 822–4 are from John 1:29: 'Behold the Lamb of God, which taketh away the sin of the world!' In the following lines the Maiden further 'accords' John's words with Isaiah; the lines reflect phrases in Isaiah 53:6 (line 826), 53:8 (line 827) and 53:9 (line 825).

834–40 Based on Rev. 5:1, 3, 6, 13. The square leaves of the book are not in the Bible; possibly they are intended to mirror the square dimensions of the Heavenly City itself (Rev. 21:16, cf. lines 1023–4). In any event the book appears to be envisaged not as the scroll of Revelation but as a bound book.

835 sayntes: the usual word for the inhabitants of Heaven, here specifically the 'elders' of Rev. 5:6.

848 The emphasis on the harmony of Heaven and the lack of pride, anger and envy amongst its inhabitants, like some other details in the poem, suggests readings from the liturgy for All Saints' Day, which was based on the Book of Revelation. The ninth reading from the Sarum Breviary, a passage of commentary by Augustine on the happiness of the Heavenly City, is especially relevant.

857 It was orthodox doctrine that while the souls of innocent children went straight to Heaven on death, their bodies, like those of the dead generally, remained on earth to await the Day of Judgment.

866–900 Based mainly on Rev. 14:1–5; cf. Rev. 4:4–11.

867–70 The Maiden had already referred to the vision of the company of the Lamb in Rev. 14:1 (lines 786–9), and now she quotes St John's words more exactly. The word may-dennes may mean 'virgins (of either sex)'; Rev. 14:4 has: 'These are they which were not defiled with women; for they are virgins' (the poet uses the word vergynes in line 1099). However, as the Maiden says that she and her companions are all wives of the Lamb (see note to lines 785–92), the poet presumably envisages them as female. The heavenly company of virgins was sometimes understood as the martyred innocents killed by Herod, and it might include other martyred innocents (cf. the martyred boy in Chaucer's Prioress's Tale), or, as in Pearl, those who were not martyrs but who died in infancy untainted by sin. The poet evidently allows the idea of virginity to merge with that of innocence.

879, 882, 894 The 'new song' and 'new fruit' are from Rev. 14:3, 4.

925–36 The Dreamer's tone perhaps takes on a tinge of sarcasm; cf. lines 775–80,

942 **the olde gulte:** Adam's original sin.

952 These are both traditional 'etymological' explanations of the name Jerusalem. The first, 'city of God', is based on scriptural passages in which Jerusalem is so called, e.g. Rev. 3:12: 'the name of the city of my God, which is new Jerusalem'. The second, 'vision of peace', is the more common; cf. Ezekiel 13:16: 'The prophets of Israel which prophesy concerning Jerusalem, and which see visions of peace for her.'

973–1032 Based mainly on Rev. 21:10–21.

976 **to a hyl:** For his sight of the Heavenly City the Dreamer is placed in the same physical position as John in Rev. 21:10: 'And in the Spirit he carried me away to a great, high mountain, and showed me the holy city Jerusalem coming down out of heaven from God.' Cf. lines 979, 981, 988.

999–1016 In his account of the twelve gems the poet draws on medieval lapidary lore to supplement the biblical enumeration; cf. in particular John Trevisa's *On the Properties of Things*, chapter 16.

1007 **rybé:** In Rev. 21:20 the sixth gem is the sardius, i.e. carnelian; but the sardius on the High Priest's breast-plate in Exod. 28:17 was sometimes understood as a ruby, and this may explain the poet's apparent substitution.

1012 **twynne-hew:** In lapidaries and other encyclopedic works the topaz was regularly described as having two colours, gold and clear.

1015 **the gentyleste in uche a plyt:** Perhaps a version of the statement in the London Lapidary, adopted also by the Peterborough Lapidary, that the amethyst is 'comfortable (i.e. gives comfort) in all sorowes'.

1030 **Twelve:** The biblical figure is twelve thousand (Rev. 21:16).

1033–92 Many details are taken from Rev. 21 and Rev. 22.

1039–42 Rev. 21:12 states that the names of the twelve tribes of the sons of Israel were inscribed on the gates. The detail that they were in order of birth-date derives not from Revelation but from the description of the onyx stones on the High Priest's ephod (a sleeveless vestment) in Exod. 28:9–10: 'And you shall take two onyx stones, and engrave on them the names of the sons of Israel, six of their names on the one stone, and the names of the remaining six on the other stone, in the order of their birth.' Because of their similar lists of precious stones, the descriptions of the Heavenly City in Revelation, chapter 21, and of the High Priest's ephod and breastplate in Exodus, chapter 28, (see especially Exod. 28: 17–21) were often associated.

1077–80 The trees which bear twelve fruits every month are, in the Bible, the one tree of life (Rev. 22:2).

1085: Cf. line 184.

1089–92 Both the Dreamer and St John are 'in the spirit' when they see the New Jerusalem; see lines 61–4 (note).

1111 The Lamb has seven horns in Rev. 5:6.

1117–28 Based on details from Rev. 5:8–14.

1152 luf-longyng: This compound is used elsewhere in religious as well as secular writing, but it here recalls the unambiguously secular *luf-daungere* in the poem's first stanza (line 11) and its context of *The Romance of the Rose*.

1158 A line of uncertain meaning. The translation accepts the *Middle English Dictionary*'s reading of *bur* (under *bir(e* n. (1), sense 3b 'strength'; *fecchen, taken bir(e* 'gather strength, get set'). *Halte* is understood as *MED hold* n. (2), sense 2a, 'possession'. Spellings of this word with *t* instead of *d* are unusual, though recorded by *MED*; in this instance the form may be explained by the demands of the rhyme scheme.

1164 Prynces paye: The phrase, which is used several times in the linking of lines in the final section, goes back to the poem's first line. But there is a significant difference: the prince is now specified as 'my prince' or 'that prince', i.e. Christ.

1186 garlande gay: The 'bright garland' is probably a metaphor for the company of the blessed, with the idea also of a circlet or crown of jewels. Cf. Dante's *ghirlande* (*Paradiso* X. 91–3, XII. 19–20), used for the circle of the blessed in Heaven.

1208 This line follows an epistolary formula of blessing used by parents to their children, and so confirms the identification of the Maiden as the Dreamer's daughter. The line gives final expression to the Dreamer's hard-won recognition that she is Christ's as well as his; a phrase often used more or less mechanically here has powerful import.

Cleanness

2 ho: she. The idea is that 'Cleanness' is a lady with an admirer. 'Patience' (*Suffraunce*) is similarly so thought of at the beginning of *Patience*. The idea is not taken beyond the first sentence of *Cleanness*, but in *Patience* the personification of virtues as ladies to be loved is more extensive; see note to *Patience* 30–48.

23–4 The *carp* is the Sermon on the Mount, especially the Beatitudes (Matt. 5:3–10), referred to more extensively in *Patience* 9–28.

27–8 The sixth Beatitude (Matt. 5:8).

51–160 A retelling of the parable of the wedding feast, conflating the two biblical versions, Matt. 22:1–14 and Luke 14:16–24.

211 Satan traditionally had his seat in the north (ultimately from Isaiah 14:13; cf. *Piers Plowman*, C-text, ed. Pearsall (London, 1978), I. 110a–24).

215–16 The poet appears to think that God would have been justified in punishing more than one-tenth of his entourage of angels. Traditionally, God created ten orders of angels, one of which was lost with Satan in the Fall. God intended its place to be taken by mankind (cf. line 240).

224 **forty dayes**: Milton and *Piers Plowman* have the angels falling for nine days; there is no clear authority for a forty day period, though the figure forty is associated with the fall of the angels in the Middle English versified history of the world *Cursor Mundi*, line 510 (ed. Morris, 7 vols, London, 1874–93).

249–540 (and 557–68) The story of Noah is based mainly on Gen. 6:1–9.11.

253–60 These lines span 'the book of the generations of Adam' in Gen. 5:1–32.

260 The poet means the pleasure of sex between men and women; cf. lines 697–708 (note).

265–8 'The wickedness of man' (Gen. 6:5), left vague in the Bible and to some extent also in this passage, is spelt out by other writers as homosexuality, e.g. by Ranulph Higden in *Polychronicon* (ed. Babington and Lumby, 9 vols (London, 1865–86), vol. 2, p. 230): 'men were abused by men, and women by women'.

269 **the fende**: The interpretation of Gen. 6:2 'sons of God' to mean 'devils' goes back to St Augustine's *City of God*, 15.23. The same interpretation is found in *Mandeville's Travels* (ed. Seymour (Oxford, 1967), p. 160).

283-4 In portraying a God with strong emotions, the poet takes his lead from the biblical text; these lines paraphrase part of Gen. 6:6: 'it grieved him to his heart'.

307 strenkle: The verb means primarily 'sprinkle, scatter', often specifically 'sprinkle with holy water' (in church ceremony). The choice of this word to translate the Vulgate's *disperdam* (A.V. 'I will destroy') suggests the power of the Flood to cleanse sin; cf. line 355.

310 cofer: chest, meaning the Ark, reflects the primary meaning of Latin *arca* – chest, box (for valuables, etc.). Cf. *kyst(e)* meaning 'chest', used for the Ark in lines 346, 449, 464, 478, and *whichche* meaning 'chest', used for the Ark in line 362.

368 rayn ryfte: rain-sluice, i.e. floodgate, translating Vulgate *cataractae* in Gen. 7:11. *OED* defines the biblical 'cataract' as 'the "flood-gates" of Heaven, viewed as keeping back the rain'. The word *ryfte* suggests the gaps or sluices in floodgates.

411 Hym aghtsum: him as one of eight, him and seven others. The construction goes back to Old English; cf. *Beowulf* 3123: *ēode eahta sum* 'he went as one of eight'.

447-8 This appears to reflect *Mandeville's Travels* (ed. Seymour, p. 109): 'another hille that men clepen Ararath (but the Iewes clepen it Taneez) where Noes schipp rested'.

459 The detail of the raven finding carrion is not in the Bible, but goes back to early Jewish and Arabic versions of the Flood story. By the later middle ages it had become an accepted part of the story in the West; cf., e.g. the play of Noah from the Towneley cycle, lines 499-504.

554-6 In both transitional passages which link the three main stories, here and more extensively in the second passage (see lines 1068, 1115-40), the beryl and the pearl image the cleanness necessary for salvation. See note to line 1068. The beryl (called 'cler and quyt' in *Pearl* 1011) was thought of as a stone like uncut crystal. The London Lapidary states that the beryl should not be cut to shape, but should be 'plain & polisshed' (*English Medieval Lapidaries*, ed. Evans and Serjeantson (London, 1933), p. 28).

556 maskle other mote: Variants of this phrase are used for the stain of sin also in *Pearl* 726, 843.

581-6 Based on Psalm 93:8-9 (A.V. 94 8-9). The same verses are quoted, in closer translation, in *Patience* 121–4; see note to these lines.

592 **reynyes and hert**: The English version (Wyclif and A.V.) of a phrase common in the Vulgate bible, *renes et corda*, lit. 'kidneys and hearts'.

601–1012 The story of Abraham, Lot, and the destruction of Sodom and Gomorrah is based mainly on Gen 18:1–19.28.

611–12 The poet in these lines, and subsequently, alternates between singular and plural in his references to God, reflecting the variable biblical usage. God as 'three in one' in this scene was understood by commentators as a manifestation of the Trinity. This meaning is made explicit in the treatment of the scene in *Cursor Mundi* 2707–10: 'Toward him com childer thre,/Liknes o god in trinite;/Bot an allan he honired o thaa,/Als anfald godd and in na ma.'

618 **your fette wer waschene**: lit. '(so that) your feet were washed', based on a widely-adopted (e.g. by Wyclif) variant Vulgate text of Gen. 18:4: *et laventur pedes vestri*. The standard text, with the verb in the imperative, is *et lavate pedes vestros* (A.V. 'and wash your feet').

652 **that I haf men yarked**: This refers to the covenant which God made with Abraham and his descendants that they would be his chosen people.

655 **May thow traw for tykle**: A lively rendering of the Vulgate *voluptati operam dabo*? (Gen. 18:12); cf. A.V. 'shall I have pleasure?' In *Piers Plowman* Lady Meed is described as 'tikel of hire tail', i.e. loose with her tail, sexually promiscuous (B-text, ed. Schmidt (London, 1995), 3. 131).

683 **to his corse**: lit. 'to his body'. Cf. *Gawain* 1237 (note).

692 i.e. to see if their behaviour is as bad as it seems to be from the noise they make, which reaches me in Heaven (cf. Gen. 18:21).

697–708 This celebration of the physical pleasure of sex, put into the mouth of God, is unparalleled. In lines 706–7 language which is often found in a derogatory context is here used in a commendatory one. The poet wants to emphasise the excellence of God's gift so as to make man's perversion of it seem all the more intolerable.

769–76 a non-biblical addition, developed from the hint in Gen. 19:29: 'God remembered Abraham, and sent Lot out in the midst of the overthrow.'

786 so was the renkes selven: Lot's wealth is mentioned again in lines 812 and 878. Lot is said to be wealthy in Gen. 13:5–6, before he parts from Abraham and goes to live in Sodom.

799 Lines 1059, 1507 give further examples of speeches begun in mid-line with the introductory verb of saying omitted.

821–8 The detail that Lot's wife deliberately flouts her husband's command to make sure that there is no salt or leaven in her guests' food (because leaven is associated with fermentation and corruption) is invented to give a reason for her being turned into a pillar of salt later (see lines 979–84 and 994–99). The detail is not in the Bible, but there is some precedent for it in Jewish legend.

865–72 Lot's offer of his daughters may seem over-enthusiastic (especially line 869) compared with the biblical version (Gen. 19:8). As in lines 697–708 (note) the poet is concerned to develop a contrast between 'clean' heterosexual relations and 'unclean' homosexual ones.

886 as blynde as Bayard: The phrase is proverbial. Bayard was a horse given by Charlemagne to Renaud and a type of blind self-confidence or blindness, as in *Troilus and Criseyde* I, 218–24. Cf. The Canon's Yeoman's Tale, *Canterbury Tales* VIII 1413–14: 'Ye been as boold as is Bayard the blynde,/That blondreth forth and peril casteth noon', and the quotation from Audelay in *Middle English Dictionary* under blusteren v., sense 2: 'al blustyrne furth unblest as bayard the blynd.'

927 *Mandeville's Travels*, which the poet certainly used for his description of the Dead Sea (see note to lines 1013–51), also in one version (Cotton) puts Zoar on a hill (Seymour edition, p. 74), though other *Mandeville's Travels* manuscripts place it at the foot of a mountain, consonant with its status as one of the five cities of the plain.

961 the houndes of heven: This appears to be the poet's own metaphor for the elements as instruments of God's vengeance.

981–2 Looking over the left shoulder is traditionally a sign of bad omen.

1000 *Cursor Mundi* (lines 2855–60) states that animals lick Lot's wife away every day, and find her restored to a pillar of salt the next morning. The detail originates in Jewish legend.

1007 aparaunt to Paradis: cf. *Cursor Mundi* 2471: '[Gomor] lik to paradis'. The comparison of Sodom and Gomorrah to Paradise comes from the Vulgate text of Gen. 13:10:

Sodomam et Gomorrham, sicut paradisus Domini – 'Sodom and Gomorrah, like the paradise of the Lord' (A.V. 'even as the garden of the Lord').

1013–51 A description of the properties of the Dead Sea came to be associated with the story of the destruction of Sodom and Gomorrah. The poet draws considerably on the description in *Mandeville's Travels* (ed. Seymour, pp. 73–4).

1037–8 Guy de Chauliac in his medical works refers to asphalt as hardened foam or scum.

1057–67 As the poet indicates, lines 1059–64 are based on a passage from the section of *The Romance of the Rose* written by Jean de Meun, also known as Jean Clopinel (ed. F. Lecoy, Paris, 1970, lines 7689–7764). In this passage the Friend advises the Lover to conform to the mood and manner of his mistress if he wants to impress her. The same passage is alluded to in *Patience* 30. Lines 1065–7 transfer the Friend's instruction to love of Christ, maintaining a romantic register of language. 'Confourme the to Kryst' echoes *Romance of the Rose* 7722: 'Confourmez vous a sa maniere'.

1068 The parable of the merchant who sells all that he has in order to buy the pearl of great price (Matt. 13:45–6) identifies the pearl with the kingdom of Heaven, and patristic commentary on the parable often makes the further identification with Christ. These two identifications are present in *Pearl*, where they are of fundamental importance. The emphasis on polishing, however, is more distinctive of *Cleanness*; cf. lines 554 (note), 1085, and 1115–40, especially 1131–2, 1134.

1069–88 The virgin birth is here described as reversing the laws of nature, turning uncleanness into cleanness. The details of the painlessness and purity of the birth are traditional, as are the attendance of the angels and the adoration of the ox and the ass.

1089–1116 The cleanness of Christ, in contrast to Mary's cleanness, was not particularly emphasised in medieval tradition generally. The poet continues the theme of the lines on the virgin birth to show that Christ in his ministry does not merely hate all uncleanness (lines 1090–2) but turns it to cleanness in his healing of the sick, just as he cleans the soul sick of sin through the sacrament of penance (lines 1115–16).

1105–8 These lines refer to a traditional explanation of Luke 24:35, where the two disciples describe to the others how the risen Christ at Emmaus 'was known to them in the breaking of bread'; that is, they recognised Christ because he broke the bread as cleanly as if he had cut it with a knife. The same explanation is found in the mystery plays; cf., e.g., the Towneley *Thomas of India* (ed. Stevens and Cawley), lines 467–8: 'Ther bred he brake as even/As it cutt had beyn.'

1108 **toles of Tolowse:** Toulouse was known as a centre for the manufacture of cutlery from the thirteenth to the eighteenth century.

1127 Washing precious stones in vinegar or wine is a traditional method of restoring their lustre.

1157 **Danyel:** Most of the account of the siege and destruction of Jerusalem comes from Jer. 52: 1–27 (cf. 2 Kings 24:18–25.21) conflated with 2 Chron. 36: 11–20. But the poet also has in mind the reference to Nebuchadnezzar's conquest of Jerusalem at the beginning of the Book of Daniel (see note to lines 1301–2).

1157–8 **dialokes ... profecies:** The terms refer to a recognised distinction between the first six chapters of the Book of Daniel (the 'dialokes' or stories) and the last six (the prophecies).

1190 **brutage of borde:** This was wooden hoarding or bratticing which formed a kind of enclosed platform at the top of the outer face of a wall – a usual feature of castle architecture from the thirteenth century onwards.

1269–80 The lists of Temple furniture here and in lines 1441–88 are based on Jer. 52:17–19, also on the biblical descriptions of the Temple (1 Kings 7: 15–50 and 2 Chron. 3:15–4.22) and of Moses's Tabernacle (Ex. 25:31–9 and Ex. 37:17–38:3).

1272–3 The everlasting light on the lampstand is from Lev. 24:1–4.

1274 **ther selcouth was ofte:** explained in lines 1491–2.

1301–2 The names are from Dan. 1:6, 11, etc.

1326 **samples:** Evidently Daniel's interpretations of Nebuchadnezzar's dreams are meant.

1361–1796 The episode of Belshazzar's feast is based primarily on Dan. 5:1–30.

1384 **overthwart palle:** timbers laid horizontally edge to edge, making up the face and floor of platforms of the kind referred to in line 1190 (note).

1401–16 There are several parallels between this description of the beginning of Belshazzar's feast and the description of Arthur's feast in *Gawain* 116–25.

1407–11 The lines describe a particularly elaborate paper decoration on a dish served at table. Chaucer's Parson castigates such decorations as examples of 'pride of the table' (*Canterbury Tales* X 444): 'bake-metes and dish-metes … peynted and castelled with papir'.

1412 Horses were sometimes found in medieval banqueting halls on grand occasions.

1457–88 The description of the Temple vessels is based ultimately on biblical passages, especially descriptions of the Temple and of the lampstand in the Tabernacle, with its cups, capitals, and flowers (Exod. 37:17 etc.). Some details, notably the list of gems making up the decorative fruit (lines 1468–72) and the richly-wrought birds which appear to have fluttering wings (lines 1482–4) reflect the account of the Great Chan's palace in *Mandeville's Travels* (ed. Seymour, pp. 157–8). In general, the description suggests English decorative art of the first half of the fourteenth century. Cf. the birds and butterflies embroidered on Gawain's clothing (*Gawain* 609–14), and, for the castellated cups especially, the description of the castle towers in *Gawain* 795–802.

1512 i.e. the servants vie with each other to be first to fill their vessels with wine and bring them to their masters.

1520 This line translates Vulgate Dan. 5:1: 'unusquisque secundum suam bibebat aetatem'; cf. Wyclif: 'eche man dranke after his age' (not in A.V., which has 'and [Belshazzar] drank wine in front of the thousand').

1541–5, 1586–90, 1591–2 These line groups are an editorial attempt to correct an apparent displacement of the quatrain pattern.

1608 goddess: The plural is from Dan. 5:11, 14.

1657–1708 The account of Nebuchadnezzar's madness draws on Dan. 4:25–34 as well as Dan. 5:18–21.

1687 The poet exaggerates to emphasise that Nebuchadnezzar is now a monstrous four-legged creature.

1761 The people avoid the descending mist by going home over low-lying ground.

1772 Porus of India is associated with Darius in the romances of Alexander.

1805 upon thrynne wyses: See Introduction, pp. xii–xv.

Patience

3–4 Suffraunce: is evidently here taken as largely equivalent to patience; the feminine pronoun *ho* indicates that Patience/Sufferance is thought of as a lady (cf. lines 30–48, note, and the first sentence of *Cleanness*).

6–8 The language and thought are close to parts of *Pearl*, especially *Pearl* 343–8.

13–28 These lines translate the Vulgate text of the Beatitudes from the Sermon on the Mount (Matt. 5:3–10). Cf. *Cleanness* 23–8, where the Beatitudes are again referred to and the sixth Beatitude is quoted.

27 This amounts to 'blessed are the patient'. The Vulgate text has (Matt. 5:10): 'Beati qui persecutionem patiuntur propter iustitiam'; A.V.: 'Blessed are they which are persecuted for righteousness' sake.' The poet thus goes beyond the biblical verse, seeing the Beatitude as commending the virtue of self-control in all circumstances, not only the capacity to endure misfortune.

30–48 The idea of loving a lady by copying her behaviour comes from *The Romance of the Rose*; see note to *Cleanness* 1057–67. Drawing on a well-established tradition of female virtues the poet chooses to personify the virtues of the Beatitudes as ladies in lines 31–3 and continues to half-personify poverty and patience in the rest of the passage.

39 by quest of her quoyntyse: Perhaps both 'by reason of their wisdom' (i.e. the nature of their virtue) and 'by the judgment of their Lord'. 'Wisdom' was a usual name for Christ in medieval religious writing, supported by biblical identifications such as 1 Cor: 1.24: 'Christ the power of God, and the wisdom of God' (A.V.). It is an appropriate name for Christ in the context of the Beatitudes, and is so used by, amongst others, St Bernard of Clairvaux.

52 to ryde other to renne: is probably no more than a formula for 'to go'. In medieval English writing the journey to Rome as the administrative centre of Christendom is often a stock example of a difficult and unpleasant task.

60 as Holy Wryt telles: The remainder of the poem, except for the last eight lines, re-tells the story of Jonah as it is found in the biblical Book of Jonah.

96 The implied comparison with Christ is contrastive; Jonah's unwillingness to endure crucifixion contrasts with Christ's willingness to do so.

101–8 The poet sees the ship as a medieval ship, specifically a cog (cf. *coge* 152), which was a medium-sized ship, high at prow and stern, with a single mast (which could be lowered), a single square sail, and a stern rudder. Oars were part of the equipment of most cogs, for use when the sail was out of action (lines 106, 217–21). The sailors appear to turn the ship away from the quay by using the oars, on the port side only, until the sail catches the wind. As the ship turns, they at first sail more or less into the wind in a luffing manoeuvre (line 106); as the ship turns further, the wind comes round behind them (line 107).

121–4 A close translation of Psalm 93:8–9 (A.V. 94:8–9). The same verses are quoted, in freer translation, in *Cleanness* 581–6, again supporting the point that it is folly to expect God not to notice misdemeanours.

125 that dotes for elde: There is no obvious source or parallel for the poet's portrayal of Jonah as a foolish old man.

133 Eurus and Aquilon are classical names for a north or north-east wind and an east or south-east wind respectively. The two winds together produce a storm from the north-east (line 137). They are associated in a storm at sea also in Book I of the *Aeneid*, and cf. the Vulgate name of the wind which struck the ship carrying St Paul as a prisoner to Rome in Acts 27:14: 'ventus typhonicus qui vocatur euroaquilo' (Wyclif: 'the wind tifonyk that is clepid northeest').

164–8 These lines expand Jonah 1:5: 'and [the mariners] cried every man unto his god' (A.V.). The point of the names is to suggest a mixture of outlandish faiths. Vernagu is elsewhere a giant in the romances of Charlemagne; Diana and Neptune are classical deities; Mahoun or Mahomet was regarded by many medieval Christians as a pagan god (or a devil); and Mergot (a name probably derived from the biblical Magog in Gen. 10:2 etc.) is a heathen god in the Charlemagne romances.

188 Ragnel: is the name of a devil in medieval English drama, e.g. *Mary Magdalen*, line 1200, and the Chester play of *The Coming of Antichrist*, line 655.

189 hasp-hede: MS *haspede* may be a phonetic spelling for *hasphede*, meaning clasp-head (i.e. the main or protruding part of a clasp fastening two parts of a garment); cf. the

Middle English form *godede* for *godhede* 'godhead'. But a word may be missing in the MS.

194 The sailors evidently cast lots several times.

226-8 The sailors pray that they are not mistaken about Jonah's guilt.

245-304 The second section of the poem (a new section is indicated by a large illuminated initial letter in the MS) expands a single verse in the Bible (Vulgate Jonah 2:1, A.V. Jonah 1:17: 'Now the Lord had prepared a great fish to swallow up Jonah. And Jonah was in the belly of the fish three days and three nights').

258 warlowes: 'the monster's' or 'the Devil's'; *warlow* has both meanings in Middle English, from the primary Old English sense 'oath-breaker'. The description of the inside of the whale, with its stench and darkness, has overtones of Hell which are reinforced by the comparisons in lines 274 and 275. In medieval art and drama the jaws of a monster, often a sea-monster, were the usual symbol for the mouth of Hell; note the whale's *mukel chawles* in line 268.

268 As mote in at a munster dor: *mote* here means 'speck of dust in sunbeam'; also, no doubt, with reference to Jonah's attempt to avoid God's command, 'speck of impurity', as in *Pearl*. The image conveys Jonah's insignificance and connects with lines 247, 251, 252, reminding the reader that the whale is sent by God and that the whole episode is a miracle contrived by God (lines 256-61) for the purpose of bringing Jonah to realise his folly.

305-36 In contrast to the account of the whale, Jonah's prayer from the whale's belly keeps close to the biblical original (Vulgate Jonah 2:2-10, A.V. Jonah 2.1-9), with little expansion.

342 This has figurative as well as literal significance; dirty clothes symbolise the foulness of sin, as in *Cleanness* (see e.g. *Cleanness* 165-8). Cf. Rev. 7:14: 'These are they which came out of great tribulation, and have washed their robes, and made them white in the blood of the Lamb' (A.V.).

472 ho: The feminine pronoun is explained by the feminine gender of Old English *sunne*.

503 materes: the four elements, earth, air, fire and water, which were commonly thought of as constituting the primal matter out of which God created mankind.

513-15: These lines largely repeat the sense of the previous sentence, and they disrupt the sequence of groups of four lines. They may represent a trial version of Jonah 4.11: 'persons that cannot discern between their right hand and their left hand' (A.V.) which the poet cancelled or intended to cancel but which survived in the text, perhaps mistakenly copied by a scribe along with the intended final version (lines 511-12).

514-15 his: refers to *ryght hande*: 'the right hand, and its companion left hand'.

531 The last line of the poem echoes the first, as in *Pearl* and (effectively) *Gawain*.

Sir Gawain and the Green Knight

1-19 The first stanza refers to the legendary history of the founding of Britain by Brutus, great-grandson of Aeneas and ancestor of Arthur and Gawain, thereby giving an epic context to the setting for the events of the poem. The reference to Aeneas as both treacherous and noble is noteworthy; it establishes at the outset the theme of moral ambiguity which is central to the main narrative. Some medieval accounts of the fall of Troy, beginning with that of Guido del Colonna in his *Historia Destructionis Troiae*, couple Aeneas and Antenor together as Trojan traitors who plotted with the Greeks. It is possible however that lines 3-4 simply refer to Antenor.

4 'Truest treachery' appears to be a contradiction. *The trewest on erthe* seems to go most immediately with *tricherie*, which is at first sight contradictory, no doubt an intended effect. By generalising the meaning of *trewest* one may translate 'the most certain on earth', i.e. there is no possible doubt of Aeneas' treachery. At the same time the phrase may be referred back to *The tulk* of line 3, Aeneas, as conventionally appropriate to a great epic hero (with another generalised sense of *trewest*, 'the most excellent man on earth'). The poet perhaps wants to have it both ways.

11 Ticius: Possibly a corrupt form of Tirius, who in some accounts was held to be the founder of Tuscany.

12 Langaberde: the legendary founder of Lombardy.

13 Felix Brutus: The Latin epithet *Felix* 'happy, fortunate' is not used in this way with Brutus's name elsewhere. However

in Latin writing and in inscriptions on coins *felix* is sometimes associated with the names of founders of cities, and in Layamon's *Brut* (written in English c.1200) Brutus is regularly called *sæl* or *sele* ('happy, fortunate, good'), as in the repeated phrase 'Brutus the sele'.

30–6 The precise sense is obscure. The poet promises to tell his tale of Arthur as he himself has heard it and read it. No doubt this is a fiction, at least as far as the detail of his poem is concerned. (Malory, who does work from sources, often refers a detail to 'the boke' as his source, sometimes correctly, sometimes not.) The *Gawain*-poet refers to *the bok(e)* as his source in lines 690, 2521, and he several times uses phrases such as *as I haf herde telle* (1144). In lines 30–2 the poet invites his audience to listen to him tell the story just as he had listened to an earlier recital of it, but lines 33–6 suggest a well-established written text. *With lel letteres loken* (35) may simply develop the sense of line 33, emphasising that the story has an authoritative text, or it may be a reference to the exemplary (*lel*) alliterative technique of the *laye* (i.e. poem) as he supposedly found it. Throughout the poem, the poet uses phrases which suggest that he is constantly aware of his story and himself as the narrator of it; cf. e.g. lines 624, 2483.

37 **Camylot:** Camelot was Arthur's traditional home, evidently thought of by the poet as somewhere in the south of Britain. Malory locates it in Winchester, though Caxton, in the preface to his edition of Malory, states that it was in Wales. A South Wales location such as Caerleon, a place which was traditionally associated with Arthur, would accord well with Gawain's journey into North Wales described in lines 691–701.

upon Krystmasse: The French vulgate *Lancelot* states that Arthur held court five times a year, at the festivals of Easter, Ascension Day, Pentecost, All Saints' Day (cf. line 536), and Christmas.

54 **in her first age:** The Arthurian court is pictured in the poem as young and innocent. There is no sign of the famous complication which will eventually destroy it, the love of Lancelot for Guinevere, Arthur's queen.

66–70 **Bi hand** and **Debated** suggest a game like handy-dandy, in which players had to guess which hand the gift was held in.

Line 69 suggests that those who guessed wrongly paid the forfeit of a kiss.

85, 91–9 This behaviour of Arthur's is traditional to him.

109–13 The poet introduces Gawain unobtrusively together with a sprinkling of well-known Arthurian figures who take no part in the subsequent action; another such list occurs in lines 550–5. Both lists are miscellaneous, with the names selected to give colour and a touch of Arthurian authenticity to the story. In early Arthurian tradition Gawain is often pre-eminent amongst the knights of the Round Table, a mighty warrior and a paragon of courtesy. Chrétien de Troyes in *Erec et Enide* (written c. 1170) states that Gawain is first in eminence amongst the knights, Erec second, and Lancelot third (the *Gawain*-poet mentions Erec and Lancelot in lines 551 and 553 respectively). Another view of him develops in French tradition, however, whereby he becomes something of a womaniser, his prowess diminishes, and he is surpassed by other knights such as Lancelot, as he is in Malory. Chaucer mentions Gawain twice and both times associates him with courtesy. The Squire's reference to him makes him sound remote and old-fashioned: 'Gawain with his olde curteisye / Though he were comen ayeyn out of Fairye' (*Canterbury Tales* V 95–6). Agravayn 'of the hard hand' is Gawain's brother; they are sons of King Lot of Orkney and (line 111) Arthur's half-sister Anna (sometimes named Belisent or, in Malory, Morgawse). Bishop Baldwin, who has the place of honour (*bigines the table*) on the other side of Arthur from Guinevere, is of Celtic origin, Arthur's bishop Bedwini in the Welsh stories of *The Mabinogion*. Ywan (Ywain), son of Uryn (Urien), is the hero of the romance *Yvain* by Chrétien de Troyes.

116–29 A course at a great fourteenth-century banquet would contain many different dishes, and its serving might well be an elaborate performance, with musicians blowing fanfares. Cf. the description of Belshazzar's feast in *Cleanness* 1401–16.

136 aghlich mayster: The visitor is between two worlds, half wild man, half knight, and the first two words used of him already imply this two-sidedness, *aghlich* suggesting something monstrous and beyond the pale, *mayster* the hierarchies of medieval civilisation. His ambiguous status is developed in the next lines, where the poet seems unable to make up his mind as to whether he is half a giant or the largest of men, and in the rest of the description: thus the greenness of his skin is supernatural, that of his clothes is part of their elaborate courtly appearance. His hair and beard are very long, suggesting a wild man of the woods, but they are not unkempt; rather, they are trimmed in such a way as to suggest a royal garment, a *kynges capados* (186), which was a cape fastened round the neck encircling the upper body as far down as the elbows.

160 scholes: shoeless. For a knight to ride in his hose without shoes indicated peacable intentions.

206-7 The branch carried in the hand is a sign of peace (cf. lines 265-6). The holly is a primitive symbol of life in the death of midwinter, but it has Christian connotations too, specifically of Christ and the reconciliation which His birth brought (as in the Christmas carol 'The Holly and the Ivy').

208-20 That the Green Knight carries in the one hand a token of peace and in the other an instrument of war deepens the ambiguity surrounding him. Like its owner the axe has a dual aspect, monstrous but at the same time civilised by its elaborate decorations.

237 This line presumably refers to the servants, who would be standing. Their reaction to the Green Knight is differentiated from that of the sitting courtiers (lines 241-5). In line 302, *the heredmen* [retainers] *in halle* are divided into *the hygh and the lowe*.

252-74 Arthur greets the Green Knight directly but courteously; the Green Knight's speech to Arthur is less courteous. Arthur's use of the second-person singular pronoun (*thou*) in address instead of the more respectful plural form (*ye*) is entirely appropriate to his status, but the Green Knight's use of *thou* in his reply suggests some disrespect.

277 batayl bare: Often translated as 'single combat', but 'battle without armour' is better in that it follows on from the Green Knight's previous speech, and cf. line 290 where *bare* means 'unarmed'.

296 barlay: This is a word of uncertain origin and meaning. It may be the same as the modern dialect word *barley*, signifying a temporary truce in children's games.

298 A twelmonyth and a day: A legal formula meaning '(until) the same day a year later'. Gawain in fact does meet the Green Knight at the green chapel on the next New Year's Day.

Throughout the poem the Green Knight/Bercilak is as obsessed with legal forms, agreements, and rules as Gawain is with courtesy.

304 The red eyes may be a supernatural feature, like the green skin, but according to medieval physiognomy eyes the colour of blood indicated strength, courage, and a violent nature. *Runischly* means 'outlandishly' as well as 'fiercely'.

360 **rych**: Possibly an adjective ('let all this noble court be free of blame'), but the syntax is difficult, with no expression of the verb 'be'. In the light of the following lines the better alternative is to take *rych* as a verb meaning 'counsel, direct', as in line 1223. In this reading 'bout blame' confirms Gawain's courtesy by showing his consideration for the courtiers – by inviting them to decide he does not want to put them in a difficult position.

384 **and wyth no wyy elles**: Gawain wants it to be understood that he will not take the return blow in a year's time from anyone other than the Green Knight (whom he presumably hopes will be unable to deliver it because he will be dead).

412 **slokes**: an obscure word. It may be an exclamation meaning 'stop!' or 'enough! (of this talk)', perhaps the imperative plural of a verb based on Old Norse *slokna* 'go out' (of fire); cf. Middle English and Modern English *slake*.

477 **heng up thyn ax**: The phrase is meant literally but it is also proverbial in the sense 'cease your activity'.

493–4 The usual view is that line 493 refers to the beginning of the feast, with *thay* referring to the courtiers in general and *hym* either to the courtiers or specifically to Arthur. It is simpler however to take *to sete wenten* as referring to Arthur and Gawain's return to the table after the beheading has taken place (cf. line 481), with all the pronouns referring to Arthur and Gawain together. The sentence may allude to a traditional antithesis between 'words' and 'works'.

495–99 The moralising which begins the famous passage on the passing of the seasons draws on proverbial wisdom, for instance lines 495–6 echo Proverbs 14:13 'the end of that mirth is heaviness' (A.V.).

504 **wyth wynter hit threpes**: The passing of the year was commonly represented in medieval literature as a battle between summer and winter.

529 **yisterdayes**: The use of the word here, particularly in

association with the withering grass and other vegetation of the preceding lines, recalls well-known biblical passages on the transitoriness of earthly life, especially Ps. 89:4–6 (A.V. 90:4–6): 'For a thousand years in thy sight are but as yesterday when it is past . . . they are like grass which groweth up. In the morning it flourisheth, and groweth up; in the evening it is cut down, and withereth' (A.V.); the Revised Standard Version has: '. . . in the evening it fades and withers'. Cf. Job 8:9–12.

550–5 This list of well-known Arthurian names recalls the earlier passage (lines 109–13, note) with its similar list. Aywan is the Ywan of the earlier list; the other names occur for the first time. Erec, son of Lac, like Ywan is the subject of a romance by Chrétien de Troyes, *Erec et Enide*. Doddinal de Savage ('Doddinal of the wild places') was so named, according to the French Vulgate *Merlin*, because of his love of hunting in wild forests. The Duke of Clarence is Galeshin, Doddinal's brother or cousin. Lancelot du Lac and Lionel are cousins, and Boos or Bors is brother of Lionel. Lucan and Bydver (or Bedivere, the knight charged with the task of throwing Arthur's sword Excaliber into the lake at the end of Malory's *Le Morte D'Arthur*) are brothers; Lucan, not known elsewhere as 'the good', is Arthur's butler ('Sir Lucan the Butlere' in Malory). Mador de la Port ('Mador the gatekeeper') is regularly so styled, as in Malory.

558 **derne:** The word may be read as *derve*, 'painful'.

566–618: Scenes in which the hero is formally armed are conventional in Arthurian romance. The details suggest armour of the latter part of the fourteenth century.

597 **Gryngolet:** a traditional name for Gawain's horse in French romances.

618 The line probably reflects a distinction made by the lapidaries between clear white diamonds and diamonds of darker colour; see e.g. *English Medieval Lapidaries*, ed. J. Evans and M. S. Serjeantson (London, 1933), p. 30, where it is stated that diamonds from India are called 'males' and are brown of colour, and 'tho that commen oute of arabie be cleped the femmales and ben whitter'.

620 **pentangel:** This is the first instance of the word in English. A pentangle or five-pointed star is not found elsewhere as part of Gawain's arms, or any other knight's. The pentangle was

sometimes identified in the middle ages as Solomon's seal (cf. line 625), with magic properties and occult associations, but as such it was hardly regarded as *bytoknyng ... trawthe* (626). This latter significance suggests rather the learned Pythagorean tradition in which the pentangle was a symbol of perfect physical and spiritual health. The pentangle is used as an ornamental figure in English manuscript illumination and church decoration, but not much is known about its early history in England, though it may have been a symbol with popular appeal. There is little medieval evidence of specific Christian significance, and no parallel for the extended symbolism developed in the poem. In the fifteenth, sixteenth, and seventeenth centuries there are instances of the pentangle signifying the five wounds of Christ (cf. lines 642–3), and the five-lettered names 'Jesus' and 'Maria'.

626 **trawthe:** a medieval form of the word 'truth', which has a wider meaning in the middle ages than the modern word. 'Truth' was thought of as one of the prime chivalric virtues (Chaucer's Knight in The General Prologue loves 'Trouthe and honour, fredom and curteisie'), and the *Gawain*-poet makes it fundamental, the one which underpins all the others. It embraces the concepts of loyalty, honour, fidelity and integrity. The last sense is especially important in the poem in the light of the way in which the poet explains the unity of the pentangle figure. The pentangle only exists as a whole; should any part of it be missing, it ceases to be a pentangle. Likewise the virtue of *trawthe*, as the poet presents it, is made up of all the other virtues, so that if Gawain should fail in any one respect then all his integrity (and therefore all his chivalry) is gone. Thus when he fails later in *lewté* 'loyalty', as the Green Knight explains (line 2366), he sees his pentangle and himself as entirely broken, and accuses himself of every kind of serious moral failing.

629–30 There is no evidence, apart from the poem, that the figure was called 'the endless knot' in popular English usage, alongside the more learned 'pentangle' (cf. lines 662–5).

633 **as golde pured:** A traditional image of moral purity, ultimately from Ecclesiasticus 2:5: 'For gold is tried in the fire, and acceptable men [are tried] in the furnace of humiliation' (A.V.).

636 **nwe:** i.e. (presumably) newly painted/worked.

642-3 The five wounds of Christ (nail-wounds in hands and feet, spear-wound in the side) are a usual medieval devotional subject. They are not specifically mentioned in the Apostles' Creed, though the Crucifixion itself is.

646-7 The five joys of Mary (usually the Annunciation, Nativity, Resurrection, Ascension of Christ, Assumption of the Virgin into Heaven) are another usual medieval devotional subject.

652-4 Though the virtues listed here are not exclusively chivalric, the list has a chivalric colouring. In particular *fraunchyse*, 'liberality, generosity, magnanimity'; *felawschyp*, 'fellowship, sense of community with and respect for others'; and *cortaysye*, 'courtesy, politeness, nobility of disposition and manner', have strong chivalric associations. *Clannes*, particularly in association with *cortaysye*, may be taken to mean not only freedom from sin but freedom from coarseness, and *pité* may be taken to refer both to the knight's duty of piety (the words 'pity' and 'piety' were not clearly differentiated in Middle English), and his duty to show concern for the weak and helpless, especially women.

656-61 Precise translation is tricky. The idea is that all Gawain's virtues connect seamlessly and endlessly with each other like the lines of the figure. Together the virtues constitute *trawthe*, as the lines make up the pentangle.

690 The bok: See note to lines 30–6.

691-743 Gawain appears to journey northwards from Camelot in South Wales (see note to line 37), travelling more or less up the Welsh coast until he turns eastwards at *Alle the iles of Anglesay* (the main ones are Anglesey itself, Holy Island to the west of the main island, and Puffin Island to the east) to travel along the North Wales coast until he finds a place where he can ford the Dee estuary and cross over into the Wirral (a known haunt of outlaws in the fourteenth century). From the fact that he then continues riding for many days, and into high country, it appears that he does not go far up the Wirral peninsula before heading east towards the Pennines. He is of course searching for the green chapel, of which he has no idea of the whereabouts, and so he need not be expected to follow any direct or known route. The poet's geography, when he descends to particulars, is suspect. There is for instance no *Holy Hede* on the Dee estuary; there is a

Holywell one and a half miles from the coast and a Holyhead on Holy Island, on the western tip of Anglesey, a long way from the Dee. One suspects that the place-names are introduced for the same kind of reason as the names of the knights in lines 109–13 and 550–5, i.e. to give a resonance and a flavour of authenticity to the narrative.

691 **Logres:** A traditional name for England or Britain. Geoffrey of Monmouth in his *History of the Kings of Britain* states that it is the name for the middle part of the island, but it was used by others with vaguer reference, as here.

762 **Cros Kryst me spede!:** A phrase from the Primer, the more-or-less standard elementary school textbook from which children in the later middle ages first learned to read, where it is associated with the Paternoster, Ave Maria, and Creed (cf. lines 757–8). Children in school would say the phrase and these three devotions, the first ones to be learned, before reciting the alphabet.

763–4 There is a sense of the miraculous about the sudden appearance of the castle, an indication perhaps that Gawain has indeed received supernatural help in his search for the green chapel, a search which in realistic terms he has little hope of bringing to a successful conclusion unaided.

774 **sayn Gilyan:** St Julian the Hospitaller was the patron saint of travellers.

787–802 The poet describes an idealised version of a castle of his own time (later fourteenth century), when elaborate rooflines were beginning to appear.

802 **pared out of papure:** Cf. the use of the same phrase in *Cleanness* 1408 (note).

813 St Peter, as gatekeeper of Heaven, was the patron saint of porters or gatekeepers.

897–8 The courtiers jokingly allude to the fact that Christmas Eve, the last day of Advent, is a fast day. They have in fact provided Gawain with a sumptuous feast which he has thoroughly enjoyed, but it conforms technically to the rules for fast days because it consists entirely of fish dishes.

943–69 More or less systematic descriptions of beautiful women are common in medieval literature; descriptions of ugly women are far less common, for obvious reasons. The rhetoricians provide model descriptions for authors to refer to and Matthew of Vendôme in his *The Art of Versification* places long model descriptions of the beautiful Helen and the grotesquely ugly Beroe next to each other. But there is no parallel for the *Gawain*-poet's chiastic interlacing of the descriptions of the two ladies.

945 wener then Wenore: The choice of the unusual form in W- (see p. xxiii) makes possible a neat wordplay on the queen's name.

946 He: This is usually emended to *ho*, 'she', because of line 971. But line 946 is perfectly intelligible as it stands in the immediate context, and lines 970–1 may be explained as recapitulating the sense of line 946 after the lengthy description of the ladies.

1066 bot bare thre dayes: The arithmetic is wrong. It is now St John's Day, 27 December (see line 1022), and this leaves four days, not three, before New Year's Day. It is likely that a line or two has been left out in error by the scribe between lines 1022 and 1023, referring to the feasting on Holy Innocents' Day, 28 December; this was a major feast day, like the preceding days, and one would expect the Christmas holiday to include it. The scribe clearly leaves out a line by mistake at *Pearl* 472.

1071–2 The host presumably means that Gawain should take his ease and lie in each morning during his stay, and then leave early on New Year's morning in order to come to the green chapel by mid-morning of that day.

1112 It was common medieval practice to seal a bargain with a drink; cf. lines 1409, 1684.

1124 olde: The adjective in its usual sense hardly fits the vigorous host; 'experienced' is the required connotation.

1133–78 etc. The three hunts which the host undertakes on three successive days, while Gawain remains with his wife in the castle, are described in detail and constitute a major element of the narrative. Particularly striking is the lengthy account of the cutting up of the deer in lines 1325–61. The abundant use of technical language suggests medieval hunting manuals, in French and English, such as *The Master of Game* (written by Edward, second Duke of York, *c.* 1410). More or less detailed descriptions of deer hunts and boar hunts are found in other romances. The fox, though it finds a place in the hunting manuals, did not have the same status as a quarry as the deer and the boar, and there are few other romance descriptions of fox hunts. If the lord's hunting of the animals in the field is taken to parallel the lady's hunting of Gawain in the bedroom then the most obvious parallel is with the fox hunt, where the fox's defensive manoeuvres suggest those of Gawain on all three days.

1154–7 The close season for the male deer (hart and buck), when hunting was forbidden, was from September till June; the female deer (doe and hind) were hunted from September till February.

1237 Ye ar welcum to my cors: sounds like a very explicit sexual invitation, but to take *my cors* as equivalent to 'me' (an accepted Middle English usage) allows a hint of ambiguity to the lady's statement: 'You are welcome to me' in the sense 'I am pleased you are here'. A possible interpretation is that the lady uses the phrase in full knowledge of its ambiguity, deliberately leaving Gawain in uncertainty as to what she means.

1265–6 These lines pose a major textual problem. The MS reads 'fongen hor dedes' in line 1265 and 'for my disert nysen' in line 1266, and it is very difficult to make sense of these readings. The emendations adopted give reasonable if somewhat elliptical sense. The vagueness of Gawain's statement in these two lines, and his rapid switching from *yowre fraunchis* to *other folk* and back to *the worchyp of yourself* in lines 1264–7 may be explained as indicative of his difficulty in finding a suitable answer to the lady, so that he comes out with an extreme example of his characteristically convoluted style of speech.

1283 This line reads in the MS: *thagh I were burde bryghtest the burde in mynde hade* '"though I were the most beautiful of women", the lady thought'. Some editors retain the MS reading, but there are then major difficulties with the following lines. In particular, unless violence is done to the syntax, the awareness of the axe-blow awaiting Gawain must then belong to the lady, but this would make for an unparalleled shift of perspective and there is no hint of such awareness on her part elsewhere. It is possible that the copyist of the MS was confused by the proximity of the similar forms *burde* and *burne*; having mistakenly copied *burne* as *burde* he then tried to make sense of the whole line by changing *ho* to *I*.

1325–61 The undoing or cutting up of deer and other animals

killed in hunting had its own protocol as set out in the hunting manuals and reflected in the poem.

1436 blodhoundes: large hounds used especially in boar-hunting.

1550 what-so scho thoght elles: Deliberately enigmatic, suggesting perhaps a gap between the lady's role as temptress and her private thoughts.

1644 St Giles (Aegidius) was a Provençal saint who was well known in England. The point of the oath here is no doubt that his feast day, 1 September, was a day on which fairs were held (e.g. at Oxford and Winchester), at which buying and selling (*chaffer*, line 1647) took place.

1699 On the fox hunt see note to lines 1133–78 etc.

1788 Again there is an appropriateness about the oath in context; St John the apostle was known for his celibacy.

1876–84 Gawain has gone to mass on the first two days he is with the ladies in Hautdesert, and now makes his private confession to a priest on the third day, evidently desiring to prepare himself spiritually for death the next day by confessing all his sins. The priest hears his confession and gives him full absolution (lines 1883–4), so that his soul should be left in a clean state, ready to face God. The passage has been much discussed by critics on the grounds that it raises the question of whether Gawain's confession is indeed a full one, and whether the absolution granted by the priest can be fully valid for Gawain in the light of the fact that he breaks faith with Bercilak by never returning the lady's girdle to him; had he confessed his intention of keeping the girdle, the priest might have been expected to have asked him not to do so as a condition of the absolution. The narrative works by implication only, but it appears that Gawain's moral and spiritual situation begins to be clouded at this point, becoming progressively more uncertain until his next 'confession' to the Green Knight (see lines 2390–4, note) and the Green Knight's clarifying revelations (lines 2338–68).

2008 Probably an allusion to the popular belief that cocks crow three times during the night, at midnight, three o'clock, and one hour before dawn.

2011–36 This arming scene recalls the one near the beginning of the second fitt, when Gawain sets out from Arthur's court. Despite the fact that his armour is said to be *fresch as upon* *fyrst* (2019), there is a significant difference of emphasis between the two scenes: the first draws attention to the pentangle, the second to the girdle. The *wlonkest wedes* (2025) which Gawain puts on while his horse is being brought are the *cote* of line 2026 and the *lace* of line 2030. The *cote* is the *cote-armure* mentioned in line 586, a surcoat marked with heraldic devices which goes over the armour. In line 637 Gawain is said to have the pentangle on this *cote* as well as on his shield, so the *conysaunce* of line 2026 must be the pentangle figure. The surcoat must be the same as the *ryol red clothe* of line 2036; it is not described elsewhere as red, but the shield with the pentangle on it is red (lines 619, 663). The implication is that in wearing the green girdle over his red surcoat (lines 2035–6), Gawain gives it pride of place over the pentangle (the symbol of his *trawthe*), and possibly that the pentangle is actually hidden by it. It is significant that the pentangle is not explicitly mentioned as such in this second arming scene.

2026 Of the clere werkes: This is ambiguous, meaning both 'fashioned in beautiful embroidery' and 'of the noble deeds', with reference to the meaning of the pentangle.

2027 Jewels were traditionally thought of as having the power to protect against disease, misfortune, etc.; cf. Pearl 1015 (note).

2160–2238 The green chapel is at the bottom of a steep valley in rugged country, with the stream on one side of it and on the other an open space (*launde* 2171, *bent* 2233) where the Green Knight and Gawain confront each other. The chapel itself is a natural feature, evidently a fissure in *an olde cragge* (line 2183) which rises up from the stream; the *bonke* which it is said to be next to in line 2172 is probably the same crag. Across the stream, the Green Knight grinds his axe in another fissure high up in another *bonk* (line 2200), which is called a *clyff* in the next line; the words *bonk*, *cragge*, *hil*, *clyff* in this passage all seem to be used for the same kind of natural feature, a steep rocky slope or escarpment. Attempts have been made to find an actual location which matches the description in the poem; Wetton Mill and Lud's Church (near Danebridge), both in North East Staffordshire, have been suggested, but in neither case are the correspondences fully convincing. In any event the search for actual locations is beside the point as far as the poem is concerned; however realistic its descriptions may be, its landscape is essentially a romance landscape of the imagination.

2226 The mention of the lace reminds the reader of the axe carried by the Green Knight when he came to Arthur's court, which had a lace attached to it (line 217); the suggestion is that the axe as well as the man is *gered as fyrst* (2227).

2374–88 Gawain accuses himself of cowardice because fear for his life led him to accept the girdle from the lady, and covetousness because he kept the girdle instead of giving it to his host. The rather indiscriminate use of heavy moral terms in this speech indicates how seriously Gawain views his lapse and how shocked he is by the Green Knight's revelation of it.

2390–4 The Green Knight picks up Gawain's *I biknowe yow*, 'I confess to you' (2385), and lightly describes his whole encounter with Gawain in terms of a religious confession, with himself in the role of priest and Gawain as the penitent. The language he uses refers to the technical steps of the confession process: Gawain has made verbal confession of his sins (line 2391), and has done the penance for his sins imposed by the Green Knight, i.e. has submitted himself to the axe (line 2392); the Green Knight then absolves him of his sins (*I halde the polysed of that plyght*, 2393), thereby returning him to the state of innocence of a new-born child (lines 2393–4).

2414–19 Gawain's thought takes on an anti-feminist homiletic colouring. The idea that 'woman is man's ruin', mocked by Chaucer in The Nun's Priest's Tale, is a commonplace of medieval sermon literature, as is Gawain's list of Old Testament worthies who fell prey to women's wiles.

2445–6 The name *Bercilak* (so MS) suggests Bachlach in the Irish analogue *The Champion's Bargain*; cf. *Bertolais/Bertolac* in French romance. *Hautdesert*, evidently the name of Bercilak's castle, means 'high solitary place'. The point of the *Thurgh* in line 2446 is presumably that the speaker's very shape and existence is dependent on Morgan; in a sense she creates both Bercilak and his name. He refers to her absolute power over his identity again in line 2456, when he explains that she sent him to Arthur's court *upon this wyse* – 'in this guise' or 'as I am now', i.e. in the shape of the Green Knight.

2446–66 These lines, which allude to well-known personages and episodes, relate the poem to the mainstream of Arthurian tradition. Morgan la Faye is the daughter of Igern, Duchess of Tintagel, who is also the mother of Arthur by Uther Pendragon; hence Morgan is Arthur's half-sister and Gawain's aunt (lines 2464–6). Morgan's hostile attitude is explained by an episode in her life when she had a love affair with Guiomar, one of Arthur's knights, which Guinevere discovered and made public. Consequently Morgan left the court and thenceforward maintained an enmity towards Guinevere (line 2460) and the Round Table (lines 2457–8). She became the lover of Merlin the enchanter (lines 2449–50) and learned his magic arts (line 2448), but when she took to luxurious living and black magic she lost her beauty and became an ugly old woman, as she is described in lines 947–67. In the traditions as in the poem she is a powerful, mysterious, ill-omened figure; in Malory she is one of the three queens who receive the dying Arthur on to their barge to take him to the isle of Avalon at the end of *Le Morte d'Arthur*. The poet appears to draw particularly on the French prose romances for his Arthurian information.

2452 goddes: Morgan is not usually so called, but there is one manuscript of the French vulgate *Lancelot* in which she is named *Morgain la déesse*, 'Morgan the goddess'.

2513–18: There is no real difficulty in understanding that women as well as men 'belonged' to the Round Table and would be entitled to wear the green baldric with the men. In the Order of the Garter (see final note), Edward III's queen and her ladies were made 'Dames of the Fraternity'.

2521 the best boke of romaunce: Presumably another reference to the supposed source of the poem; see note to lines 30–6.

2522–8 The end of the poem returns to the historical context of the beginning, and the last long line (line 2525) repeats the first.

2523 The Brutus bokes: a general term referring to any chronicles, histories, or romances about Britain, not only those which mention Brutus.

Hony soyt qui mal pence: This famous legend in French is written in the space below the poem's last line, in what seems to be a different handwriting. It is the motto of the chivalric Order of the Garter, which was founded by Edward III in 1348. It is not possible to make any convincing connection

between the Order itself and the events of the last stanza;
apart from anything else, the Garter colour is blue, not green.
However, in a general way, the brotherhood of the Garter
was thought of as a real-life version of the brotherhood of the
Round Table. The sense of the motto has some relevance to
the poem's outcome, in which the Green Knight, Gawain, and
Arthur's court all judge Gawain's lapse differently.

SUGGESTIONS FOR FURTHER READING

The following list is confined to books only. More comprehensive specialist bibliographies are R. J. Blanch, *Sir Gawain and the Green Knight: A Reference Guide* (New York, 1983), M. Stainsby, *Sir Gawain and the Green Knight: An Annotated Bibliography, 1978–1989* (New York, 1992), and M. Andrew, *The Gawain-Poet: An Annotated Bibliography 1839–1977* (New York, 1979), and M. Foley, *The Gawain-Poet: An Annotated Bibliography 1978–1985*, *Chaucer Review* 23 (1989), pp. 251–82, supplemented by R. J. Blanch in *Chaucer Review* 25 (1991), pp. 363–86. Also useful are the annual *Year's Work in English Studies*, the *Bibliography of the Modern Humanities Research Association*, and the *PMLA Bibliography* (the latter two available on CD-ROM).

Manuscript

Pearl, Cleanness, Patience and Sir Gawain, reproduced in facsimile from MS. Cotton Nero A.x in the British Library, with Introduction by I. Gollancz (London, 1923).

Editions and translations

The Works of the Gawain-Poet, ed. C. Moorman (Jackson, Miss., 1977).

The Poems of the Pearl Manuscript: Pearl, Cleanness, Patience, Sir Gawain and the Green Knight, ed. M. Andrew and R. A. Waldron (London, 1978).

The Pearl Poems: An Omnibus Edition, ed. W. Vantuono, 2 vols (New York, 1984).

The Complete Works of the Pearl Poet, ed. C. Finch, M. Andrew, R. Waldron, and C. Peterson (Berkeley: California UP, 1993).

The Complete Works of the Gawain-Poet, trans. (verse) J. Gardner (Chicago, 1965).

The Pearl-Poet, trans. (verse) Margaret Williams (New York, 1967).

Pearl, ed. E. V. Gordon (Oxford, 1953).
– trans. (verse) B. Stone, in *Medieval English Verse* (London, 1964).
– trans. (verse) Marie Borroff (New York, 1977).
Purity, ed. R. J. Menner (New Haven, 1920).
Cleanness, ed. I. Gollancz, 2 vols. (London, 1921, 1933); reissued in one vol., with prose trans. by D. S. Brewer, 1974.
– ed. J. J. Anderson (Manchester, 1977).
– trans. (verse) B. Stone, in *The Owl and the Nightingale, Cleanness, St Erkenwald* (London, 1971).
Patience, ed. J. J. Anderson (Manchester, 1969).
– trans. (verse) B. Stone, in *Medieval English Verse* (London, 1964).
Sir Gawain and the Green Knight, ed. J. R. R. Tolkien and E. V. Gordon (Oxford, 1925); 2nd ed., rev. N. Davis, 1967.
– ed. I. Gollancz, with introductory essays by Mabel Day and Mary S. Serjeantson (London, 1940).
– ed. R. A. Waldron (London, 1970).
– ed. J. A. Burrow (London, 1972; New Haven, 1982).
– ed. and trans. (prose) W. R. J. Barron (Manchester, 1974).
– trans. (verse) B. Stone (London, 1959).
– trans. (verse) Marie Borroff (New York, 1967).
– ed. T. Silverstein (Chicago, 1984).
– ed. and trans. (verse) R. H. Osberg (New York, 1990).
– ed. and trans. (verse) W. Vantuono (New York, 1991).

Studies

Borroff, Marie. *Sir Gawain and the Green Knight: A Stylistic and Metrical Study* (New Haven, 1962).

Benson, L. D. *Art and Tradition in Sir Gawain and the Green Knight* (New Brunswick, N.J., 1965).

Burrow, J. A. *A Reading of Sir Gawain and the Green Knight* (London, 1965).

Kean, Patricia M. *The Pearl: An Interpretation* (London, 1967).

Bishop, I. *Pearl in Its Setting* (Oxford, 1968).

Moorman, C. *The Pearl-Poet* (New York, 1968).

Spearing, A. C. *The Gawain-Poet: A Critical Study* (Cambridge, 1970).

Wilson, E. *The Gawain-Poet* (Leiden, 1976).

Davenport, W. A. *The Art of the Gawain-Poet* (London, 1978).

Barron, W. R. J. *'Trawthe' and Treason: the Sin of Gawain Reconsidered* (Manchester, 1980).

Haines, V. Y. *The Fortunate Fall of Sir Gawain: The Typology of 'Sir Gawain and the Green Knight'* (Washington, DC, 1982).

Bogdanos, Theodore. *Pearl: Image of the Ineffable* (University Park, Pa., and London, 1983).

Elliott, R. W. V. *The Gawain Country* (Leeds, 1984).

Johnson, Lynn S. *The Voice of the Gawain Poet* (Wisconsin, 1984).

Shoaf, R. A. *The Poem as Green Girdle: 'Commercium' in Sir Gawain and the Green Knight* (Florida, 1984).

Nicholls, Jonathan. *The Matter of Courtesy: Medieval Courtesy Books and the Gawain-Poet* (Suffolk, 1985).

Arthur, Ross G. *Medieval Sign Theory and Sir Gawain and the Green Knight* (Toronto, 1987).

Morgan, Gerald. *Sir Gawain and the Green Knight and the Idea of Righteousness* (Dublin: Irish Academic Press, 1991).

Stanbury, Sarah. *Seeing the Gawain-Poet* (Philadelphia: Pennsylvania UP, 1991).

Bond, George. *The Pearl Poem: An Introduction and Interpretation* (Lewiston, NY: Mellen Press, 1981).

Marti, Kevin. *Body, Heart, and Text in the Pearl-Poet* (Queenston, Ontario: Mellen Press, 1991).

Phelan, Walter. *The Christmas Hero and Yuletide Tradition in Sir Gawain and the Green Knight* (Queenston, Ontario: Mellen Press, 1993).

Putter, A. *Sir Gawain and the Green Knight and the French Arthurian Romance* (Oxford UP, 1995).

Blanch, R. J. and J. N. Wasserman. *From Pearl to Gawain: Forme to Fynisment* (Florida UP, 1995).

Collections of essays

Sir Gawain and Pearl: Critical Essays, ed. R. J. Blanch (Indiana, 1966).

Critical Studies of Sir Gawain and the Green Knight, ed. D. R. Howard and C. K. Zacher (Notre Dame, 1968).

Twentieth-Century Interpretations of Sir Gawain and the Green Knight, ed. D. Fox (New Jersey, 1968).

The Middle English Pearl: Critical Essays, ed. J. Conley (Notre Dame, 1970).

Text and Matter: New Critical Perspectives on the Pearl Poet, ed. R. J. Blanch, M. Y. Miller, and J. N. Wasserman (Troy, NY, 1991).

MEDIEVAL LITERATURE
IN EVERYMAN

The Canterbury Tales
GEOFFREY CHAUCER
The complete medieval text with translations
£4.99

The Vision of Piers Plowman
WILLIAM LANGLAND
edited by A. V. C. Schmidt
The only complete edition of the B-Text available
£6.99

Sir Gawain and the Green Knight, Pearl, Cleanness, Patience
edited by J. J. Anderson
Four major English medieval poems in one volume
£5.99

Arthurian Romances
CHRÉTIEN DE TROYES
translated by D. D. R. Owen
Classic tales from the father of Arthurian romance
£5.99

Everyman and Medieval Miracle Plays
edited by A. C. Cawley
A fully representative selection from the major play cycles
£4.99

Anglo-Saxon Poetry
edited by S. A. J. Bradley
An anthology of prose translations covering most of the surviving poetry of early medieval literature
£6.99

Six Middle English Romances
edited by Maldwyn Mills
Tales of heroism and piety
£4.99

Ywain and Gawain, Sir Percyvell of Gales, The Anturs of Arther
edited by Maldwyn Mills
Three Middle English romances portraying the adventures of Gawain
£5.99

The Birth of Romance: An Anthology
translated by Judith Weiss
The first-ever English translation of fascinating Anglo-Norman romances
£4.99

The Piers Plowman Tradition
edited by Helen Barr
Four medieval poems of political and religious dissent – available together for the first time
£5.99

All books are available from your local bookshop or direct from:
Littlehampton Book Services Cash Sales, 14 Eldon Way, Lineside Estate,
Littlehampton, West Sussex BN17 7HE *(prices are subject to change)*

To order any of the books, please enclose a cheque (in sterling) made payable to
Littlehampton Book Services, or phone your order through with credit card details (Access,
Visa or Mastercard) on 01903 721596 (24 hour answering service) stating card number
and expiry date. *(Please add £1.25 for package and postage to the total of your order.)*

In the USA, for further information and a complete catalogue call 1-800-526-2778

SAGAS AND OLD ENGLISH LITERATURE
IN EVERYMAN

Egils Saga
translated by Christine Fell
A gripping story of Viking exploits in Iceland, Norway and Britain
£4.99

Edda
SNORRI STURLUSON
The first complete English translation of this important Icelandic text
£5.99

Anglo-Saxon Prose
edited by Michael Swanton
Popular tales of Anglo-Saxon England, written by kings, scribes and saints
£4.99

The Fljotsdale Saga and The Droplaugarsons
translated by Eleanor Howarth *and* Jean Young
A brilliant portrayal of life and times in medieval Iceland
£3.99

Anglo-Saxon Poetry
translated by S. A. J. Bradley
An anthology of prose translations covering most of the surviving poetry of early medieval literature
£6.99

Fergus of Galloway: Knight of King Arthur
GUILLAME LE CLERC
translated by D. D. R. Owen
Essential reading for students of Arthurian romance
£3.99

Three Arthurian Romances from Medieval France
translated and edited by Ross G. Arthur
Caradoc, The Knight with the Sword *and* The Perilous Graveyard – *poems of the Middle Ages for modern readers*
£5.99

All books are available from your local bookshop or direct from:
Littlehampton Book Services Cash Sales, 14 Eldon Way, Lineside Estate,
Littlehampton, West Sussex BN17 7HE (*prices are subject to change*)

To order any of the books, please enclose a cheque (in sterling) made payable to
Littlehampton Book Services, or phone your order through with credit card details (Access,
Visa or Mastercard) on 01903 721596 (24 hour answering service) stating card number
and expiry date. (*Please add £1.25 for package and postage to the total of your order.*)

In the USA, for further information and a complete catalogue call 1-800-526-2778

POETRY
IN EVERYMAN

Amorous Rites: Elizabethan Erotic Verse
edited by Sandra Clark
Erotic and often comic poems dealing with myths of transformation and erotic interaction between humans and gods
£4.99

Selected Poems
JOHN KEATS
An excellent selection of the poetry of one of the principal figures of the Romantic movement
£6.99

Poems and Prose
CHRISTINA ROSSETTI
A new collection of her writings, poetry and prose, marking the centenary of her death
£5.99

Poems and Prose
P. B. SHELLEY
The essential Shelley in one volume
£5.99

Silver Poets of the Sixteenth Century
edited by Douglas Brooks-Davies
An exciting and comprehensive collection
£6.99

Complete English Poems
JOHN DONNE
The father of metaphysical verse in this highly-acclaimed collection
£6.99

Complete English Poems, Of Education, Areopagitica
JOHN MILTON
An excellent introduction to Milton's poetry and prose
£6.99

Women Romantic Poets 1780–1830: An Anthology
edited by Jennifer Breen
Hidden talent from the Romantic era rediscovered
£5.99

Selected Poems
D. H. LAWRENCE
An authoritative selection spanning the whole of Lawrence's literary career
£4.99

The Poems
W. B. YEATS
Ireland's greatest lyric poet surveyed in this ground-breaking edition
£7.99

DRAMA
IN EVERYMAN

The Oresteia
AESCHYLUS
New translation of one of the greatest Greek dramatic trilogies which analyses the plays in performance
£5.99

Everyman and Medieval Miracle Plays
edited by A. C. Cawley
A selection of the most popular medieval plays
£4.99

Complete Plays and Poems
CHRISTOPHER MARLOWE
The complete works of this great Elizabethan in one volume
£5.99

Restoration Plays
edited by Robert Lawrence
Five comedies and two tragedies representing the best of the Restoration stage
£7.99

Female Playwrights of the Restoration: Five Comedies
edited by Paddy Lyons
Rediscovered literary treasures in a unique selection
£5.99

Plays, Prose Writings and Poems
OSCAR WILDE
The full force of Wilde's wit in one volume
£4.99

A Dolls House/The Lady from the Sea/The Wild Duck
HENRIK IBSEN
introduced by Fay Weldon
A popular selection of Ibsen's major plays
£4.99

The Beggar's Opera and Other Eighteenth-Century Plays
JOHN GAY et. al.
Including Goldsmith's She Stoops To Conquer *and Sheridan's* The School for Scandal, *this is a volume which reflects the full scope of the period's theatre*
£6.99

Female Playwrights of the Nineteenth Century
edited by Adrienne Scullion
The full range of female nineteenth-century dramatic development
£6.99

All books are available from your local bookshop or direct from:
Littlehampton Book Services Cash Sales, 14 Eldon Way, Lineside Estate,
Littlehampton, West Sussex BN17 7HE (*prices are subject to change*)

To order any of the books, please enclose a cheque (in sterling) made payable to
Littlehampton Book Services, or phone your order through with credit card details (Access,
Visa or Mastercard) on 01903 721596 (24 hour answering service) stating card number
and expiry date. (*Please add £1.25 for package and postage to the total of your order.*)

In the USA, for further information and a complete catalogue call 1-800-526-2778

ANCIENT CLASSICS
IN EVERYMAN

Legends of Alexander the Great
edited by Richard Stoneman
*The fascinating adventures of
a dominant figure in European,
Jewish and Arabic folklore until
the fifteenth century*
£5.99

**Juvenal's Satires with the
Satires of Persius**
JUVENAL AND PERSIUS
*Unique and acute observations
of contemporary Roman society*
£5.99

The Epicurean Philosophers
edited by John Gaskin
*The surviving works and wise say-
ings of Epicurus, with the account
of his natural science in Lucretius'
On the Nature of the Universe*
£5.99

**History of the
Peloponnesian War**
THUCYDIDES
*The war that brought to an
end a golden age of democracy*
£5.99

The Discourses
EPICTETUS
*The teachings of one of the
greatest Stoic philosophers*
£6.99

The Education of Cyrus
XENOPHON
*An absorbing insight into the
culture and politics of Ancient
Greece*
£6.99

The Oresteia
AESCHYLUS
*New translation and edition
which analyses the plays in
performance*
£5.99

Suppliants and Other Dramas
AESCHYLUS
*New translation of Aeschylus'
first three surviving plays and
the earliest dramas of western
civilisation*
£5.99

The Odyssey
HOMER
*A classic translation of one of
the greatest adventures ever told*
£5.99

The Republic
PLATO
*The most important and
enduring of Plato's works*
£5.99

All books are available from your local bookshop or direct from:
Littlehampton Book Services Cash Sales, 14 Eldon Way, Lineside Estate,
Littlehampton, West Sussex BN17 7HE (*prices are subject to change*)

To order any of the books, please enclose a cheque (in sterling) made payable to
Littlehampton Book Services, or phone your order through with credit card details (Access,
Visa or Mastercard) on 01903 721596 (24 hour answering service) stating card number
and expiry date. (*Please add £1.25 for package and postage to the total of your order.*)

In the USA, for further information and a complete catalogue call 1-800-526-2778

PHILOSOPHY AND RELIGIOUS WRITING
IN EVERYMAN

Modern Philosophy of Mind
edited by William Lyons
This unique anthology of classic readings in philosophy of mind over the last hundred years includes the writings of William James and Ludwig Wittgenstein
£6.99

Selected Writings
WILLIAM JAMES
Taking writings from James's most famous works, this edition is a comprehensive and unique selection
£6.99

The Prince and Other Political Writings
NICCOLÒ MACHIAVELLI
A clinical analysis of the dynamics of power, set in the context of Machiavelli's early political writings
£4.99

Ethics
SPINOZA
Spinoza's famous discourse on the power of understanding
£5.99

The World as Will and Idea
ARTHUR SCHOPENHAUER
New translation of abridged text, Schopenhauer's major work and key text of modern philosophy
£7.99

Utilitarianism, On Liberty, Considerations on Representative Government
J. S. MILL
Three radical works which transformed political science
£5.99

A Discourse on Method, Meditations, and Principles
RENÉ DESCARTES
Takes the theory of mind over matter into a new dimension
£5.99

An Essay Concerning Human Understanding
JOHN LOCKE
A central work in the development of modern philosophy
£5.99

Philosophical Writings
FRANCIS HUTCHESON
Comprehensive selection of Hutcheson's most influential writings
£6.99

Women Philosophers
edited by Mary Warnock
The great subjects of philosophy handled by women spanning four centuries, including Simone de Beauvoir and Iris Murdoch
£6.99

All books are available from your local bookshop or direct from:
Littlehampton Book Services Cash Sales, 14 Eldon Way, Lineside Estate,
Littlehampton, West Sussex BN17 7HE (*prices are subject to change*)

To order any of the books, please enclose a cheque (in sterling) made payable to
Littlehampton Book Services, or phone your order through with credit card details (Access,
Visa or Mastercard) on 01903 721596 (24 hour answering service) stating card number
and expiry date. (*Please add £1.25 for package and postage to the total of your order.*)

In the USA, for further information and a complete catalogue call 1-800-526-2778